THROUGH THE LOOKING GLASS

Also by Anthony Verrier

AN ARMY FOR THE SIXTIES
THE BOMBER OFFENSIVE
INTERNATIONAL PEACEKEEPING

Anthony Verrier

THROUGH THE LOOKING GLASS

British Foreign Policy in an Age of Illusions

W·W·NORTON & COMPANY · *New York · London*

Published simultaneously in Canada by George J. McLeod Limited, Toronto.

Printed in the United States of America.

First Edition

Library of Congress Cataloging in Publication Data

Verrier, Anthony.
Through the looking glass.

Includes index.
1. Great Britain—Foreign relations—1945–
2. Great Britain. Secret Intelligence Service.
I. Title.
DA589.8.V47 1983 327.41 82–24689

ISBN 0-393-01648-X

W. W. Norton & Company, Inc., 500 Fifth Avenue, New York, N.Y. 10110
W. W. Norton & Company Ltd., 37 Great Russell Street, London WC1B 3NU

1 2 3 4 5 6 7 8 9 0

To the British Citizen,
who has some right to know

His stance was that of Everyman, not Insider, airing plain commonsense either on matters of public record in the newspapers or from his own experience.

Bernard Crick, *George Orwell, A Life*

CONTENTS

ACKNOWLEDGMENTS

Collective grateful thanks is given by the author to the many people involved in the events narrated who, over the years illuminated dark corners, and provided confirmation or clarification of his research and occasional experiences: Dean Acheson; Major-General H.T. Alexander; Yigal Allon; Julian Amery; James Angleton; Ray Atherton; Field Marshal Sir Geoffrey Baker; General André Beaufre; the Sherif of Beihan; Robert Belgrave; Lord Blackett; John Bruce Lockhart; The Hon. Alastair Buchan; Lord Bullock; McGeorge Bundy; Michael Burke; Lieutenant-General E.L.M. Burns; Joe Cahill; Lord Chalfont; J.L. Christie; William Clark; Air Chief Marshal The Hon. Sir Ralph Cochrane; William Colby; T.P. Coogan; Liam Cosgrave; Edward Crankshaw; Air Commodore J.F. Davis; Moshe Dayan; Sir Patrick Dean; Sir Geoffrey de Freitas; R.O. Dennys; John de St Jorre; Sir Eric Drake; Major-General Björn Egge; John Ehrman; Nicholas Elliott; Peter Elwes; Marshal of the Royal Air Force Lord Elworthy; Lieutenant-General Vernon Erskine Crum; J.H. Farmer; Brian Faulkner; M.R.D. Foot; Denise Freidin; Raymond Garthoff; Sir Terence Garvey; Roswell Gilpatric; Lord Gorell; Major-General Yakuba Gowon; Lieutenant-Colonel P. Gray; Vice-Admiral Sir Peter Gretton; General Sir John Hackett; Richard Hall; William Hamling; Raymond Hare; General Sir Charles Harington; Lord Harlech; Marshal of the Royal Air Force Sir Arthur Harris; Lord Hatch; Lord Head; Denis Healey; Hassanein Heikal; Richard Helms; Roger Hilsman; Laurence Hobson; Lord Home; Alistair Horne; Sir David Hunt; George Ivan Smith; Colonel Derek Joynes; William Kaufmann; George Kennan; John Fitzgerald Kennedy; Robert Kennedy; John Kimche; Henry Kissinger; Leslie Knight; Admiral Sir Michael Le Fanu; Hugh L'Etang; Walter Levy; Captain E. G. D. Lewin RN; Sir Basil Liddell Hart; Franklin Lindsay; I.D. Lindsay; Major-General D.L. Lloyd Owen; S.H. Longrigg; Richard Luce; Sir William Luce; Major-General J.D. Lunt; Jack Lynch; D.J. McCarthy; Lord MacFadzean; J.M. Mackintosh; Sir Fitzroy

Maclean; Robert McNamara; Sean MacStiofain; Bernard Mallet; John Maury; Golda Meir; Pierre Messmer; Lord Morrison; David Newsom; Paul Nitze; Sir Anthony Nutting Bt; Rory O'Braidaigh; David O'Connell; Hans Ostrum; Henry Owen; Nadim Pachaci; Sir Anthony Parsons; Sir John Peck; the Prior and monks of the Redemptorist Monastery, Balfast; Shridath Ramphal; Robert Rhodes James; Air Chief Marshal Sir Frederick Rosier; Henry Rowen; Helmut Schmidt; Ian Skeet; Marshal of the Royal Air Force Sir John Slessor; Helmut Sonnenfeldt; F.S. Steele; Lord Stewart; Geoffrey Stockwell; General Sir Hugh Stockwell; John Strachey; John Stremlau; Bickham Sweet-Escott; General Maxwell Taylor; Lord Thomas; Sir Robert Thompson; Brigadier W.F.K. Thompson; D. Thomson; Major-General P.T. Tower; Lord Trend; Lord Trevelyan; General Sir Harry Tuzo; Brian Urquhart; Sir Dick White; David Williams; Sir Harold Wilson; The Hon. C.M. Woodehouse; Philip Woodfield; Sir Denis Wright; Adam Yarmolinsky; G.K. Young; Philip Ziegler.

The author also thanks those in Whitehall who read the typescript; Raleigh Trevelyan and Jill Sutcliffe, his good friends at Cape; and Joan Barber, who typed the manuscript.

1982 A.V.

THROUGH THE LOOKING GLASS

INTRODUCTION

With the Falkland Islands in mind the reader is invited to step through the looking glass and view aspects of British foreign policy between the end of the Second World War and the early 1970s. Like Alice, but unlike many of the participants in the events narrated, we can return to a world which is familiar, where what is read in the newspapers or covered by television, although sometimes inaccurate, bears some relation to our own assumptions and experience.

The assumption of British governments from 1945 onwards was that Britain remained a great power, despite losing virtually all the attributes on which power, in international politics, depends: economic resources and military strength. Anthony Eden wrote in November 1942, when the end of the beginning was in sight: 'I assume that the aim of British policy must be, first, that we should continue to exercise the functions and responsibilities of a world Power.'[1] Ernest Bevan in 1949 and Eden himself in 1956 acted on that assumption. But Harold Macmillan in 1961 and 1962 knew that the illusion of power was being dispelled by events. Retaining a strategic presence 'East of Suez' reflected a Whitehall policy concocted by officials on whom Eden had relied for collusion with Israel in 1956. The defence of Kuwait by British troops in 1961 against a threatened Iraqi invasion relied on bluff rather than military strength. By the same token, Macmillan's determination in 1962 to retain the independent nuclear deterrent which Attlee and Bevin had secretly planned in 1947 was based entirely on the premise that the weapons were for prestige, not for deterrence or use.

Cleverly, too cleverly for his successors, Macmillan made some adjustments to reality. Yet Harold Wilson, when he was Prime Minister between 1964 and 1970, behaved as though Britain was still an imperial power. Only with Edward Heath in 1972, and concerning Ireland, was a conscious effort made to live with the realities of power. Ireland breeds tragedies, it does not foster illusions. Nevertheless, illusions persist. The Government plans to spend up to £9 billion on the Trident missile system when over three million British subjects in the United Kingdom are on the dole. To pay for Trident the Royal Navy has been denied surface ships, their logistic support, and even the fuel needed for training and exercises.

The Falklands were invaded by Argentina in April 1982 because the British Government lacked not only the will but the means to defend them, above all by that traditional – but still necessary – element in a maritime nation's strategy, naval power which is relevant to the nature of possible, not merely probable threats. After the Falklands Islands operations were concluded, Government decisions on the virtual closure of dockyards at Portsmouth, Chatham and Gibraltar were followed by a Royal Navy campaign in Whitehall for the production of warships which would be adequately armed; capable of meeting enemy aircraft and missiles on equal terms; and provided with reasonable protection for their crews. These pleas were heeded but nuclear weapons still take priority over the sailor who fights and burns. The imperial sentiments remain in Mrs Thatcher's breast; imperial resources have gone. The task force which was sent to recapture the Falklands seriously weakened NATO's Atlantic defences, and imposed burdens on Britain's armed forces which only a carefully orchestrated Government public relations campaign succeeded in – temporarily – disguising.

Dean Acheson's remark that Britain had lost an empire but had not found a role is as true today as when he made it – and incurred enormous resentment – twenty-one years ago. American governments between 1945 and the early 1970s stepped through the looking glass also, as the narrative will show, but, on balance, they knew how to distinguish between illusion and reality. Above all, this capacity to strike a balance was true of the Middle East, scene of prolonged and often bitter conflict between British and American interests.

Eden also argued to Churchill, in November 1944, that the post-war Foreign Office should control all activities of the Secret Intelligence Service and the Special Operations Executive. (SIS was, to a limited extent, controlled by the Foreign Office, but in 1944 SOE led a maverick existence, with Lord Selborne, the Minister for Economic Warfare, rather dimly responsible for it.) Behind this apparently routine attempt by a Cabinet Minister to expand his empire and check encroachments on it by the Chiefs of Staff and others in Whitehall, lay two factors of great importance for our understanding of the post-war world. Eden believed that SOE, or something similar – in terms of clandestine political activities and irregular warfare – should remain in existence after the war. SIS would become subordinate to this new organisation. The other factor is that between 1942 and 1944 the traditional hostility of British governments towards Russia was revived by Stalin's patent determination to dominate Eastern Europe and exercise influence or exert pressure on the Continent as a whole.

If Eden's 1942 statement and 1944 argument are taken together, the result is a recommendation by one who was then regarded as a major British statesman to sustain great power roles by methods more appropriate to a minor Balkan State or a band of guerrillas. The main requirement laid on the two secret services between 1939 and 1945 was to sustain and extend British interests by methods which ranged from the acquisition of intelligence to the support – or removal – of governments. SIS and SOE concentrated their efforts on Europe and did so because Britain's capacity to affect events there with military forces was limited. Because this capacity remained limited after 1945, Eden's recommendation unwittingly became one basis for the execution of policies designed to contain Russia in Europe and to thwart Stalin when he sought to extend his influence in the Balkans. British governments put less emphasis on clandestine operations after the North Atlantic Treaty Organisation was formed in 1949, but recourse to odd and idiosyncratic attempts to sustain or overthrow governments by no means disappeared from the minds and hearts of British prime ministers and foreign secretaries.

The supposed enmity of Russian governments to Britain and to world-wide British interests remained for a decade and more after 1945 the fundamental conviction of those who advised British governments in matters of foreign policy, defence, and internal security. After Stalin's death in 1953, Khrushchev's determination that Russia should play an active role in the Middle East and Africa – areas of paramount importance to Britain – sustained convictions for a further decade. The roots of these convictions lie deep in Britain's history as an imperial power. The Victorian servants of that power are the progenitors of the twentieth century SIS and SOE.

The inherited and traditional roles of the British secret services are set out in the first four chapters of this book. By the early 1960s, however, much of Whitehall, including the secret services, began to accept that British foreign policy contained large elements of make believe, or illusion. Reliance on clandestine activities or recourse to subversion could not act as substitutes for economic or military strength. The existence of an 'independent nuclear deterrent' – paid for by denying arms and equipment to the three fighting Services – did not make Britain more secure or more respected. Changes in the Middle East and Africa demanded new responses rather than traditional reactions from British governments. This story of Whitehall change in the context of political obstinacy is told in the remaining chapters.

The British secret services do not make recommendations to their political masters, let alone make policy. The services' main task is to acquire and distribute intelligence about Britain's enemies – and friends – on the basis of specific directives from the Prime Minister or Foreign Secretary, and from requirements laid down annually by government departments, principally the Ministry of Defence and, increasingly in recent years, the Foreign Office. These annual requirements are definite and to the point. SIS is provided with a detailed background to them in an internal document known as the Red Book. The title is no longer particularly appropriate, but is, perhaps, a useful reminder of the original purpose for which SIS was established. The objectives to be attained and the methods employed by SIS are far removed from fiction, whether in the hands of a Le Carré or the purveyors of violence on television. It must never be forgotten, however, that, as a result of Eden's 1944 recommendation, SIS became, before all other considerations, a hostile service, actively engaged in counter-intelligence, required to penetrate other intelligence services, even those with which it is in liaison. This requirement has left a residue of assumptions about the value of intelligence gathering and its place in the scheme of things. Britain today is a minor power, a fact consciously accepted in Whitehall, but loss of status is compensated for by a widespread public assumption that the voice of British governments still counts in the international forum.

Le Carré certainly understands this residual assumption. He has said that a secret service is the subconscious of a nation – even of a realistic British governing establishment, that 'permanent Conservative government in countless departments of the state' as a nineteenth century radical, General Sir William Butler, defined it.[2] Allen Dulles, Director of the Central Intelligence Agency in the critical post-war years, believed that, to Americans, intelligence is a profession, to the British a way of life. Dulles stressed also the value to security of reasonable disclosure and public accountability, and the harm done by unnecessary secretiveness. He thus drew a distinction between American and British society. In general, the British secret and security services do continue to see themselves charged with maintaining international status for Britain but by processes which do not concern the citizen. Thus the idea of accountability for monies spent – a cool £400 million annually at the most conservative estimate – and things done is anathema. Realism has not reached the stage where the British public has the right to know. Mrs Thatcher's determination to make even SIS financially accountable and 'cost effective' by methods acceptable to business advisers to the Treasury was not well received.

The prejudice against accountability to the public has nothing to do with security: no sane citizen wants to betray his country or expose its secret servants to danger. The prejudice is almost entirely based on this residual belief, a lingering illusion, that the ethos, the sacred flame, whatever one likes to call it, of a British Empire which, in reality, came to an honourable end decades ago, can be sustained, kept alight by the British public remaining ignorant of matters which are often common knowledge elsewhere.

A complementary assumption, therefore, is that any member of the public who asks questions about intelligence and security is not only ignorant of certain unchanging elements in Britain's international role – whatever that may be – but that he actually and actively damages British interests. If questions are asked about the relationship between foreign policy and intelligence the reaction is likely to be one of extreme vexation. Yet traitors during the Second World War and since eluded or penetrated the secret services because they pretended to share assumptions about British society and Britain's place on the world stage. For decades the secret services were recruited on the basis of Admiral of the Fleet Lord Fisher's dictum: 'Favouritism is the soul of efficiency.' Recruitment by personal recommendation was believed to ensure loyalty and, up to a point, credibility. Even today these services are, as one former member has accurately said, 'self-regulating'. It is not surprising, therefore, that the most searching questions since 1945 about the relationship between British foreign policy and intelligence have been asked by historians and biographers, writers who are concerned to analyse, not to assume. Frequently, historians open Pandora's box, but where the official record and the personal recollection of ministers or their advisers can be compared, the contradictions which result do, indeed, show the survival of foreign policy based on illusions.

Both SIS and the Security Service (MI5 colloquially) have officers with as keen a sense of realities as the most sceptical student of Britain's recent history. A life professionally spent in the shadows does not necessarily distort perspective. One such officer, in Lagos during the Nigerian Civil War, argued for two years that the real requirement was to learn something of the state of Nigerian politics, not the activities of the KGB. There was indirect opposition to Bevin in 1949 and to Eden in 1956. Although SIS in 1961 only succeeded in deeply penetrating the Russian intelligence and security system because of Oleg Penkowsky's repeated overtures, the result did give the Service collectively an idea of strategic and, specifically, nuclear realities which it had hitherto chosen to ignore. The result was salutary. The SIS reaction to the defence of Kuwait in 1961 was that such a damn'd close run thing should not be regarded as establishing a precedent for the maintenance of British prestige in Arabia or the execution of military operations there. In Northern Ireland, from 1971 onwards, SIS officers came to believe that the Provisional Irish Republican Army was a political organisation which could be outwitted, not merely a terrorist organisation which must be destroyed. SIS also provided adequate, and timely, intelligence of Argentinian intentions concerning the Falkland Islands.

The purpose of *Through The Looking Glass* is to adorn a tale, not point a moral. Yet illusions have been fostered by habit. In one sense, what Eden said in 1942 and 1944 echoed sentiments and reflected practices of an Empire where the illusion of power was always more compelling than the necessity for choice.

1 · 'MAY RUSSIA'S WICKED AGGRESSION, AMBITIONS, AND DUPLICITY BE CHECKED!'

Turkestan, Afghanistan, Transcaspia, Persia – to many these words breathe only a sense of utter remoteness, or a memory of strange vicissitudes, and of moribund romance. To me, I confess, they are the pieces on a chess board upon which is being played out a game for the domination of the world.

LORD CURZON, quoted in Firuz Kazemzadeh, *Russia and Britain in Persia, 1864–1914*

When a British Prime Minister or Foreign Secretary decides on a certain course of action which will involve SIS, the word is passed verbally – rarely in writing – to the Cabinet Secretary. He, or more frequently a Deputy Secretary, passes the requirement to the Joint Intelligence Committee, whose Foreign Office Chairman, armed forces, Security Service, and Treasury representatives then discuss it with the Director General of SIS ('C') and his colleagues, including those from the Government Communications Headquarters, the centre for monitoring signals from many foreign governments. 'C' then takes the appropriate action, one which usually, but not invariably, complements the actions of his immediate subordinates, of the Station officers operating under embassy or high commission cover abroad, and of the agents recruited by them, on which the acquisition of raw intelligence, even in the age of electronic marvels, substantially depends.

'C' (from the first Director General of SIS, Sir Mansfield Cumming) normally sees the Prime Minister every Tuesday, being one of the few senior advisers with direct access. Tuesday is normally when the Prime Minister sees the Queen. Before Thursday, invariably a Cabinet day, there is usually a meeting of the JIC 'A' Committee, which deals at Permanent Under Secretary and Chiefs of Staff level with major issues. The 'B' Committee handles the minor variety. These committees, and their complementary 'assessment' sub-committees, decide, as appropriate, what the Cabinet should see, and in what form. One of the Deputy Cabinet Secretaries, usually seconded from the Foreign Office, is responsible for the detailed co-ordination of security and intelligence, and the relationship of the services responsible for them with other departments of state, but it is the JIC which makes the operational recommendations, leaving SIS to execute the tasks as it sees fit. Neither a Foreign Office chairman nor the technical subordination of the JIC to the Cabinet Office implies complete control of SIS; neither does the establishment in recent years of the Cabinet Office's 'Central Assessment System' and the JIC current intelligence groups, whereby the SIS 'CX' and other intelligence reports are given a final review before summaries are sent to the Prime Minister. The SIS is an independent service, deriving from the fact that neither Act of Parliament nor known administrative *fiat* governs its roles and responsibilities. SIS reads Foreign Office telegrams – but that, even today, is a one-way relationship.

By the same token, the Joint Intelligence Committee retains a degree of independence which may be disliked by prime ministers who regard the Cabinet Office as their private domain – which, constitutionally, it is not – but which reflects the relentless determination of Whitehall to resist encroachments on its roles by politicians. But, in the final analysis, the Prime Minister *decides*. 'Suez' was a thing apart. The JIC writes assessments; it does not make recommendations to the Prime Minister which are intended to produce political decisions during a crisis.

The Prime Minister receives a daily box from 'C', the contents of which is distributed to the Cabinet Secretary; selected Cabinet Ministers; and certain senior advisers. The Cabinet Defence and Overseas Policy Committee is not automatically on the distribution list. The Cabinet as a whole, let alone the Government as such, is excluded. The Chief of the Defence Staff and the three Chiefs of Staff are usually included. Parliament remains ignorant of the roles, not merely of the tasks of SIS. But the United States Congress, whose Oversight Committee can order the CIA to produce the President's daily 'Watch Report' – or anything else – knows a great deal. The media in Britain are kept in the dark. Their members, in fact, control themselves by contributing to and supporting a system of voluntary censorship known as the D (Defence) Notice Committee. The Permanent Under Secretary in the Ministry of Defence is Chairman. A comprehensive Notice covers 'British Intelligence Services', advising (there is no mandatory authority) against identifying or publishing the names of the Directors General and serving officers of the secret services. Meetings are private, and there is no public accountability for the Committee's actions. Security, secretiveness, and unaccountability are thus a seamless web. The Permanent Government orders it so. An inhibition against identification of serving officers is, in most cases, reasonable. A blanket inhibition on all but the most obvious facts may be defensible regarding current issue but cannot be defended in historical terms. We must ask ourselves why secrecy is so all-enveloping.

One answer, or part of it, has been given in the Introduction:

secrecy as the preservative of illusions, not for ensuring that the national interest is safeguarded. Another part of the answer reflects not only the delegation of executive authority from the political to the permanent government, but the latter's historic concentration on strategic rather than economic issues in the formulation of foreign policy. Moreover, British foreign policy was imperial policy in the years of splendid isolation. When that isolation became dangerous in the decade before the First World War, *ententes* and treaties continued to reflect imperial priorities. Between the world wars, the permanent government was more likely to concentrate on the defence of India than on the rise of Hitler or the economic consequences of the peace made at Versailles. Nearly four decades after the Second World War ended, Whitehall's foreign policy is almost entirely a matter of survival in an Economic Community where Britain is the sick man of Europe. Yet the Joint Intelligence Committee still sits – and there are still residual tasks to perform which call for the use of intelligence in more than the technical sense.

Another part of the answer can be found in a letter written by Disraeli to the Queen on 27 March 1878. The Russians were at the gates of Constantinople, watched by capital ships of the Royal Navy's Mediterranean Fleet. Admiral Hornby knew, and Sir Henry Layard, Ambassador to the Sublime Porte, knew that 'six washing tubs with flags', in Lord Salisbury's sarcastic phrase, could not deter a Russian Army of twenty corps. Disraeli had pledged the Sultan that Britain would defend Constantinople. Privately, Disraeli doubted this prospect. His letter says it all: 'The only military preparations are in the hands of His Royal Highness the Field Marshal Commanding in Chief. They seemed to Lord Beaconsfield meager.'[1] The preparations were meagre. India, the colonies, and home defence – a euphemism for providing drafts for India, the colonies, and Ireland – absorbed Britain's military strength which, in relation to Russia, stood at 1 : 20. Disraeli was forced to ask Bismarck to warn the Russians off, an acknowledgment of the facts of power which was duly noted in all the courts of Europe.

Fifty-six years later the facts were still being ignored in Whitehall. 'Until 1934 the Royal Navy and the Army had been preoccupied with the possible attack by Russia on India.' This statement by General Playfair, an official historian of the Second World War, is based on a 1928 War Office appreciation which said: 'The most probable war of the near future in which the British

Empire might be engaged is against Russia in Central Asia.'[2] In 1939, despite the Berlin-Tokyo axis being firmly established, the British Army in India and the Indian Army were still concentrated in the north-west, to meet a Russian threat, not in the east, to meet a Japanese one.

Russia was seen as a permanent enemy of Britain, of the British Empire, of national security. Neither Britain nor the British Empire was able to counter that enmity on the field of battle: neither the *pax Britannica* nor its instrument, the Royal Navy, was relevant to a permanent strategic threat – once the Russophobias took hold of British governments – posed by a power operating on interior lines. The Empire's exterior lines were world-wide, drawn by the Royal Navy's cruisers and marked along their way by the garrisons and the gunboats. But this appearance of power, and the real, if limited and temporary peace it brought, depended in truth on Russia. Nicholas II, writing to his sister in November 1899, at the beginning of the South African, or 'Boer' War, emphasised the fact that the *pax Britannica* did not extend to Eurasia, or apply to the Eastern Question – the survival or collapse of the Ottoman Empire and the European balance of power. 'I do like knowing it lies with me to change the course of the war in Africa. Telegraph an order for the whole Turkestan army to mobilise and march to the frontier. The strongest fleet in the world can't prevent us from settling our scores with England precisely at her most vulnerable point.'[3]

Russia was thus more than a threat to British prestige; the Power with twenty army corps menaced the empire with two – only one of which could be considered as a formation capable of active operations. Russia became more than a phobia to British imperialists. A strategic obsession developed throughout the last decades of a century which saw the evolution of a united Germany and an industrial Japan, both ruled by autocrats or dictators seeking territory even at the risk of world war.

The obsession – and the lack of resources – led British governments and their men on the spot to rely to an exceptional degree on intelligence, buffer states, attacks on an enemy's flank (in the widest geographical sense) and special operations. These expedients were what Lloyd George was to call sideshows. He was alone in that opinion. Secrecy and secretiveness became habitual, not because of security but in order to hide the truth that discovering the enemy's hostile intentions and defeating them by ingenuity was an exercise in wish-fulfilment, a tacit but undisclosed admission by the ruling few that real resources were, indeed, meagre. There were illusions in Whitehall about other substitutes for twenty army corps: the Empire provided cheap military manpower; the battleship, or the bomber, could deter wars or win them quickly; America would come to Britain's aid in a European conflict into which we might be dragged by the French. But, excepting the last, other 'powers' shared comparable illusions. Other governments operated intelligence services, more highly organised in fact than the British variety. These services, however, were adjuncts to policy, not substitutes for it.

Sir Henry Layard had neither an intelligence officer, nor a clerk to encode and decode for him. British diplomatic missions were also meagrely provided in 1878, and thereafter. Lady Layard was in effect the embassy 'Diplomatic Wireless Service' officer. She dealt with the signals and the codes: few ciphers were used in those days. In 1887, when the Directorate of Military Intelligence was established – administratively part of, but physically separate from, the War Office – an attempt was belatedly made to put the acquisition and distribution of political and military intelligence on a systematic basis. But no consideration was given to the possibility that embassies and legations might have anything to contribute to these processes, and no attempt was made to relate intelligence operations to diplomacy. Intelligence was an imperial affair; diplomacy a European one.

Imperial interests were spread wide. Maintaining the lines of communication with India, and 'the Empire of the East' as the Victorians called the area between Cairo and Calcutta, justified the seizure of Cyprus in 1878; the occupation of Egypt in 1882; subsequent penetration of the Sudan and much of the Horn of Africa; attempts to establish British India's frontier on the Pamirs in the 1890s; the invasion of Tibet in 1904; and the virtual partition of Persia in 1907. Ironically – or appropriately – the partition, marking an armistice in the struggle between Britain and Russia for mastery in Asia, took place at the conclusion of a three-year study by the newly-formed Committee of Imperial Defence. Subject: the invasion of Russia. Method: a pre-emptive attack (not that the phrase had been coined in 1907) mounted from Quetta, and directed at Transcaspia and Turkestan through Afghanistan and Persia. The plan assumed that British resources were sufficient for this surprise attack on the enemy's open flank, but not for a concentrated offensive directed at his centre.

The CID was the creation of that consummate Conservative

Party politician Arthur Balfour. His purpose in establishing a committee whose deliberations would justify past and define future imperial policy had little to do with strategy in the technical, military sense. Balfour, a philosopher rather than a servant of Empire, needed an establishment group which would continue to urge the case for splendid imperial isolation. Treaties and *ententes* would take care of Britain's limited commitment to European security. Balfour, like the Liberal Party imperialists Rosebery and Grey, believed the Empire could best be preserved by 'sitting loose' – as they would have said – to European commitments. The British Army, after its humiliations in the South African War between 1899 and 1902, was ready to talk to politicians and officials, provided the imperial priorities were reaffirmed despite lack of resources to sustain them. Between 1904 and 1914 the CID concentrated its collective energies on maintaining the lines of communication with India, and the preservation of a positively Victorian belief in dangers to Britain's interests at every point along or adjoining them. These were the years when Germany armed to conquer Europe and built a battle fleet to fight the Royal Navy in the North Sea.

Whilst a Liberal Secretary of State for War (Richard Haldane) fought against time and inertia to prepare Britain for the coming European conflict, the CID went its isolationist way. Men in distant places felt that the right ideas were still held at home. Not only Viceroys in India and proconsuls in Arabia but their shadowy subordinates knew they could go straight to the CID and find the right answers. Haldane struggled on, not entirely in vain, but without encouragement from his political colleagues. In the meantime, the defence of India remained the overriding strategic preoccupation; hence the defence of British interests in Arabia assumed a growing importance, because these touched the lines of communication at every sensitive point. Intelligence operations in and beyond India were reasonably well defined: in Arabia the shadowy figure of the archaeologist D.G. Hogarth not only reflected assumptions about executing imperial strategy by way of bluff and bribes but a belief that the amateur intelligence officer was an adequate substitute for the professional. In the First World War, Gilbert Clayton's Cairo-based Arab Bureau was not only responsible for organising a revolt against Turkish rule by the Sherif of Mecca and the sheikhs of the Hejaz, but produced thereafter a version of events in the Middle East which was distinctly at variance with the facts. The Bureau was the ideal place for T.E. Lawrence to employ his unusual talents for deceiving himself, his colleagues, and the Arabs. The Arab Bureau cast a long shadow. Lesser Lawrences, dreaming his dream of Empire, could be found in Arabia until the 1970s.[4]

Long before the extinction of British power in the Middle East, T.E. Lawrence and the Liberal MP and traveller Aubrey Herbert (John Buchan's Sandy Arbuthnot) asserted that Russia was a far graver threat there than Germany. But long before Hogarth, Clayton and the Arab Bureau, General Gordon (of Khartoum) and others seconded for intelligence duties argued that a Russian presence adjoining Britain's lines of communication to India posed a threat to the Empire of the East which could only be met by unorthodox strategies. For decades before Disraeli's admission to the Queen that real strategic assets for confounding Russia were inadequate or unavailable, intelligence officers in and out of uniform had played 'the great game' of defending India by recourse to bribes, bluff, and subterfuge. The Amir of Afghanistan and tribal chiefs on his borders based loyalty to the British Raj and resistance to Russian blandishments on the amount of gold which British intelligence officers put into their hands. Behind the glass in which imperial Britain appeared strong and resolute was a world of make-believe.

British governments and viceroys rarely defined the Russian threat with any precision, and failed to accept, or even understand, that British rule in India, relatively just and reasonably humane, was a more effective deterrent to the Tsar's ambitions than frontier operations and the pre-emptive strategy. Nevertheless, the pervasive influence of the great game, extending throughout Victoria's reign – and, a mirror for ministers, alternately supported and questioned by her – explains much of what happened long after her death. Belief in a Russian threat to India's internal security remained strong throughout the 1920s and 1930s. The Indian Police and the Intelligence Bureau of the Indian Government's Home Department were admirably professional in their methods, but collective assumptions about Russian subversion distorted their outlook on nationalist political activities. When officers from the Police and the Intelligence Bureau joined the Security Service in Britain on retirement or secondment they did much to strengthen convictions about the Russian menace to Britain's internal security.

Salisbury, who, as Foreign Secretary and Prime Minister, dominated British politics for the last twenty years of Victoria's reign, disliked the unvaryingly alarmist tone of intelligence officers' reports, whether from those in Anatolia operating under consular cover, from Persia (run from the Intelligence Centre in Peshawar and much disliked by the British Legation in Teheran), or those 'Indian Politicals' whose Gilgit Agency, stuck in a cleft of the Pamirs, epitomised the lone hand and resort to bluff. Salisbury scoffed at alarms. He told Lytton, the Viceroy, in 1887: 'You listen too much to the soldiers . . . You should never trust experts. If you believe the doctors, nothing is wholesome; if you believe the soldiers, nothing is safe.'[5] Salisbury disliked the evidence of maps, the words of men who insisted – accurately enough – that, by short marches from Gilgit 'you step in a day from India into Asia'.[6] Salisbury did not like people who stepped through that particular looking glass. He did not believe that in a day, or ever, the Russians would step from Asia into India.

Yet even Salisbury, as he said, could only put out a few boat-hooks whilst the stream of Victorian sentiment carried Britain into imperial adventures of seemingly limitless extent. Even the 'opening up of Africa' – for which, in truth, Salisbury when both Prime Minister and Foreign Secretary was largely responsible, as it was he who bargained over the disposal of territories with successive French and German governments – was seen by late Victorian strategists as completing the imperial pattern. Russia would be checked on the Pamirs; thwarted in Persia; denied access to the Empire's lines of communication running through the Ottoman Empire; and shut out of those African markets which ensured Britain a place in the economic sun.

General Sir Henry Brackenbury was one of those late-Victorian strategists, and it is wholly appropriate that he became the first Director of Military Intelligence – and hence one of the godfathers of SIS – on 1 January 1887. In a sense, Brackenbury was more at home in the gaslit world of Victorian London, where Salisbury's private hansom could be glimpsed of an evening dashing along Whitehall to Euston Station and the refinement of Hatfield, and where the dinner party was the diplomatic battlefield, than in those outposts of empire where 'the great game for mastery in Asia' was played with gold and petty rulers for counters. Brackenbury spoke French and German, had witnessed the Franco-Prussian war, had even written for the newspapers. He was singular in the British Army in virtually lacking Indian experience.

But Brackenbury's heart, politically and emotionally, was in the right place. He inherited an intelligence department whose annual reports – *The Progress of Russia in Central Asia*, handsome volumes, bound in calf, illustrated with brightly coloured maps, and generously provided with painstaking orders of battle – reflected an earlier, more confident age. In the 1850s, when the Crimean War and the Indian Mutiny seemed to have settled some issues for good, Russia's conquest of the Steppe and the crumbling Khanates of Bokhara and Samarkand was regarded by Viceroys and in the Cabinet room as inevitable, if not particularly welcome. By the time that Brackenbury set up shop, adopted a distinctive style, established a definite aim, Russia was seen as a power which menaced the British Empire, not only India. The Penjdeh incident in 1885, when two British officers surveying territory near the Oxus were forced out by Russian troops, led the Queen to attack Gladstone for leaving them 'wretchedly in the lurch'. Russophobia and imperial sentiment were mirror images.

Brackenbury got to work. One of his first acts as DMI was to abandon his journalism and cease analysis of continental strategic issues. He ordered his staff to do the same and 'to sign a declaration that during their tenure of office . . . [they] would not hold any communication, direct or indirect with the press.'[7] 'At a time when Britain's economic position and strategic strength began to give way decisively to Germany, Brackenbury – '*the* cleverest man in the British Army'[8] – could write to Roberts: 'To my mind the best thing that could happen would be war with Russia in Europe – Austria, Turkey, the Balkan States, and England allied against her – we could beat her so – Germany and Italy free meanwhile to give France her quietus for another twenty years – you could come in for your share of the fighting in Afghanistan. But what I should dread is Russia's advance in Asia, where no European power would help us – and then Germany crushed between France and Russia. Where should we be then?'[9]

By the 1890s the DMI at 6 Queen Anne's Gate had become the secret arbiter of British imperial policy. Brackenbury's reports enjoyed a restricted distribution: the Queen; the Prime Minister; the Secretaries of State for Foreign Affairs, India, and War; the Viceroy; the Commander-in-Chief at home; selected permanent officials.

In those years, Francis Younghusband, the boldest and most foolhardy player of the game, capped his efforts in China and on the Karakoram when he was captured by a Russian party on the Pamirs. Younghusband, whose aims were nothing if not imperial, had moved – on the map – the Afghan frontier east and the Chinese frontier west in order to prevent Russia establishing a frontier with India on the roof of the world. Colonel Ianov and his Cossacks courteously moved Younghusband off – on 17 August 1891. Ianov was also map-making. He secured the Pamirs for the Tsar. Playing the lone hand, Younghusband had no choice but to decamp. As he rode dejectedly away he was wrung with a sudden desire to be out of his mess and with his family in the English countryside, and not 'stuck up here alone in these desert Pamirs'.[10]

Younghusband was depressed and tired – 'I am horribly sick of myself' – but the whole business had only strengthened his conviction that a showdown between Britain and Russia was inevitable. He saw himself as the catalyst: 'This will be a big business & I don't [know] when Govt. will be able to spare me & I only hope I may at least have the satisfaction of being of some use.' Younghusband fervently hoped there would be no Boundary Commission – a favourite device of Salisbury's to settle disputed frontiers: 'Let all the talkee talkee be done in London & on the spot let us have nothing but fighting. The mistake we made on the frontier of Afghanistan was that we sent gentlemen to talk with the Russians – expecting that they would also send gentlemen on their side. But they in fact do not possess any gentlemen in their political service, & if we are wise we will not let ourselves in for being insulted again but answer to their system of using force by using force ourselves & my belief is that they will cave in if they see we are in earnest.'[11]

But, on this occasion, Salisbury was not to be moved. Apart from asking Sir Robert Morier, the British Ambassador in St Petersburg to lodge a formal protest, Salisbury turned his mind to more pressing matters. He could well have reflected that a hostile operation like Younghusband's – sanctioned by the Viceroy, Lord Lansdowne – requires either that the enemy's intelligence system is penetrated or a client, whether individual or state, is found to thwart him in some other way. Younghusband had failed to do either of these things. He had played the game for its own sake. It never occurred to Younghusband – and his masters never told him – that Ianov and his colleague Colonel Gromchevsky (on whom Younghusband had played a singularly dirty trick shortly before his capture) took their orders from the 'Special Committee' under the Tsar's direct control.[12] If Younghusband had grasped that the 'hostiles' in 1891, like the KGB today, did as they were told, he might have cultivated them. Some raw intelligence would then have been acquired: Russia's limited capacity to threaten India, not merely the Tsar's supposed intention of doing so could then have been appreciated.

Brackenbury's successor was Edward Chapman, an 'Indian' soldier, indeed an intelligence officer for much of his service. Chapman had played the great game with more skill than Younghusband, but his views about Russia were exactly the same: the pre-emptive plan put to the CID was largely based on his appreciations that India was threatened by an expansionist and aggressive Russia. But despite the arguments of the Directorate of Military Intelligence and the Committee of Imperial Defence, the Kaiser's Germany, aggressive and threatening, could not be entirely ignored. By the time that Younghusband was finally rejected as an imperial agent by his patron Curzon – after a mission to Lhasa in 1904 of which only King Edward VII approved – Lord Fisher at the Admiralty had begun to interfere in the intelligence business. Fisher had his illusions also, but he knew an enemy when he saw one. Between the early years of this century and 1914, intelligence as a piece of the Whitehall machinery increasingly came under the Admiralty's aegis. Fisher insisted that Germany was the threat and should be the intelligence target. A third claimant for the control of British Intelligence, competing with the Foreign Office and Queen Anne's Gate, came on to the scene.

The critical date is 1909. In that year the Secret Service Bureau was established, in an internal, Whitehall, administrative effort to define and rationalise intelligence acquisition, assessment, and distribution; to relate these activities to internal security; to curtail the roles of the War Office; and to extend those of the Directorate of Naval Intelligence (also dating from 1887) by bringing the whole apparatus within the ambit, if not under the control of the CID. Men like Chapman were powerful figures, not only influential behind the political scenes but capable in Whitehall of getting their own way concerning policies.

The DMI during the 1890s, for example, was also responsible for mobilisation and home defence. When Chapman argued that the pre-emptive strategy demanded the despatch of both army corps from Home Forces – thus effectively stripping the country of all its reserves and denying Britain any role in European affairs – there was no individual or system available to counter either his plans or the methods of implementing them. Despite objections throughout Whitehall to Chapman's arguments, no alternative 'grand strategy' emerged. Although the DMI's functions were somewhat changed after 1904 – on paper, the post was briefly abolished – the War Office waged an unrelenting campaign to keep India as the first strategic priority.

By 1909, however, with the naval arms race between Britain and Germany accelerating – HMS *Dreadnought*, a battleship whose weapons, speed, and armour rendered all others obsolete, was launched in 1906 – both the Foreign Office and the Admiralty were determined to reduce the War Office's power. The Foreign Office at last consciously accepted the fact that although the DMI and his counterparts in India operated officers and agents, both overt and covert, throughout the Empire of the East, there were no agents in Europe. Foreign Office officials who inherited Salisbury's outlook were not amused when the War Office commented in 1907: 'Every foreign government implicitly believes that we already have a thoroughly organised and efficient European Secret Service.'[13] In reality, foreign governments – as distinct from public opinion – knew in 1909 we had nothing of the kind: they knew it in 1939.

Despite criticisms of the DMI, the Secret Service Bureau was initially placed under the War Office, mainly because the latter co-operated with the Home Office, as the Ministry of Defence does today, in establishing the requirements and tasks of what was to become the Security Service. In 1910, however, Fisher, as part of his draconian reforms – which swept away the washing tubs and produced an oil-burning battle fleet equal in firepower to any two enemies combined – achieved nominal control of that part of the SSB which was responsible for intelligence overseas. Captain Mansfield Cumming was appointed Director. In practice, the War Office retained control of an imperial intelligence system, but Fisher's men could, from 1910 onwards, begin to supply the Admiralty and the Foreign Office with raw intelligence about German naval capacities.

This descent into the Whitehall labyrinth has been necessary in order to show that the 1909 reforms were important because valid distinctions were drawn at last between what an enemy might do, what his foreign policy suggested he would do in certain circumstances, and what he was capable of doing in terms of overall resources. Russophobia was – and is – largely based on supposition and assumption, hardly at all on inference and evidence. Fisher was almost unique in the Royal Navy of his time in understanding the importance of technical change; he knew that unless intelligence concentrated on capability and demoted intention to the realm of speculation – where one man's guess about the enemy's war plans might be as good as another's – the Britain he loved would fight a losing battle.

In any case, intelligence which is confined to intentions has always led, by a paradox more apparent than real, to bad security. The players of the great game were notoriously insecure: their reports could be read in the Russian press. Younghusband's disclosures to his family broke every rule in the book. Maurice Hankey, for nearly fifty years *the* grey eminence of British intelligence, had no hesitation in writing to his mother on April Fool's Day 1900: 'I get information of the most secret nature. I knew of the Russian war preparations some weeks ago. You mustn't mention that though.'[14] An insider never seems to realise that there may be outsiders – somewhere.

In the event, the young naval officers who were despatched to spy in Germany discovered little of value. Intelligence acquisition in the field is not a craft which is learned in five minutes. A belief in the superiority of one's national attributes is no substitute. *The Riddle of the Sands* was not a training manual. Several officers landed in German gaols; between 1914 and 1918 the Royal Navy continued to be unpleasantly surprised at German technical superiority in such matters as range finders and armour. There was indeed, as Beatty remarked during Jutland's opening salvoes, something wrong with our bloody ships. There was more wrong with the organisation and operation of intelligence, and so it remained. *Bismarck* blew HMS *Hood* out of the water in a matter of minutes on 24 May 1941; it took the combined resources of the Home Fleet, and other units besides, to despatch the pride of the Nazi fleet a week later. We did not know, because we did not know where to ask, that there wasn't much wrong with the German ships.

Nevertheless, Fisher's legacy is scientific intelligence, which eventually achieved so much in the Second World War. By sharp contrast, the First World War agents of imperial intelligence were given, or seized, new and expanded means to play the game, ensuring that SIS, at birth, would emerge as a hybrid, nominally concerned with the capabilities of the industrial powers, in practice committed to an operational role in support of strategies devoted above all to the defence of India and of British interests in the Middle East. The huge apparent increase in imperial power throughout Arabia which resulted from the defeat of Turkish armies and the final extinction of the Ottoman Empire in 1918 was largely due to the Arab Bureau in Cairo and members of the Indian

Political Service who were attached to the Expeditionary Force 'D' which sailed from Bombay in 1914 to occupy Mesopotamia. It has been well said that the realisation of the schemes wrought by such men – and that designing woman Gertrude Bell – 'proceeded by improvisation, often completely outside the control of London'.[15]

Yes, indeed. Lawrence was only one amongst many, as he said, 'labouring stoutly for the cause'. What that cause was might be hard to say. The Indian Political Service backed the Emir of Nejd, Ibn Saud. The Arab Bureau and their masters in Cairo supported Ibn Saud's closest enemy, Sherif Hussein of Mecca. But in the sands of Arabia imperial ambitions concentrated on new found wealth from oil. That in the event overall British support for Hussein – as a suitable tool – led Ibn Saud to seek his own, genuinely independent path, is a quirk of history. Lawrence also said, 'All men dream: but not equally.' His dream, presumably, was that false claims would become credible. The Arab Revolt 'was an Arab war waged and led by Arabs for an Arab aim in Arabia.' This was, and is, nonsense, whether Lawrence consciously knew it to be so or not. Lawrence certainly knew British aims to be concerned with imperial objectives.[16] There was no Arab revolt, in the sense of a planned, or widespread or spontaneous national uprising against Ottoman rule, even although an 'Arab Awakening' – as the Arabs called it – undoubtedly existed. Arab Sheikhs who rose (once bribed) and took the field against the Turks asserted that kingdoms would be their reward. Hussein believed this would happen. It is doubtful if his sons Abdullah and Feisal (later to be Emir of Transjordan and King of Iraq) did so. Both rulers kept their thrones exclusively and entirely on the understanding that they would support British aims, not Arab aspirations. The British aim was client states, protecting the lines of communication – and the oil of Persia and Mesopotamia. Behind the aim lay an enduring belief in the buffer and the bribe. Bribery was employed even in defeat. In April 1916 Lawrence and Herbert, at night and conveyed by stealth, offered a million pounds in gold to Khalil Pasha, the Turkish Commander besieging General Townshend's forces in Kut. He refused. 'It is not by these means that England fights', he said. Two million pounds were then offered, with the same result.[17]

Alas for illusions, it was by such means that Britain played the game as the stakes were raised. In the 1870s one British agent operating against Russian reconnaissance parties in Persia – and known to his colleagues as 'The Aga' – could note in his diary, 'weather hot and atmosphere thievish'. By 1917, with Tsarist Russia disintegrating but with the new and more frightful spectre of international socialist, anti-imperialist revolution menacing the Empire of the East at all points, British officers sent to bolster the Whites were living in a grimmer world. Two years later these officers were told explicitly: 'The purpose of His Majesty's Government is to assist the Armed Forces of South Russia to such an extent as may be possible, in order that the Bolsheviks may be defeated.'[18] This directive to Major-General H.G. Holman, Commander of the British Military Mission to South Russia is the only known written evidence that the specific aim of 'intervention' – so enthusiastically espoused by Winston Churchill and Lord Curzon, so sardonically derided by Lloyd George – was to destroy a revolution, not keep Russia in the war. Churchill, as Secretary of State for War and Air, gave further support to the Holman Mission by despatching to the Crimea Number 47 Squadron Royal Air Force for bombing operations against the Bolsheviks. 'Winston has backed Denikin [the White Russian Commander] magnificently', noted a member of Holman's Staff.[19]

The Holman Mission, like that to Archangel, was, in any case, only one piece on the board, one pawn in Churchill's strategy of 'closing the ring' round Russia. South of the Caspian, in northern Persia, and in Turkestan, smaller missions were given virtually the same directives – verbally – as General Holman, and encouraged not merely to oppose bolshevism where it might infect buffer states, but to extend British influence in its place. A few scrambling battles were fought by Red Army units with British and Indian troops. But elsewhere along a vast, fluid front Denikin's forces were supported by adventurers like Hugh Boustead, wearing the kilt and Balmoral of his regiment, 'young and idealistic and ready for anything'.[20] Military operations of the guerrilla variety were complemented by acceptance of political murder. The death of the twenty-six Baku Commissars on 20 September 1918 is a gory signpost to certain techniques, widely practised in the Second World War.[21] In retrospect the adventures of Dunsterville at Baku, of Malleson around Merv, and of Bailey at Tashkent seem mere footnotes to history. Nevertheless, not only some of the methods employed in pursuit of hopeless causes but the overall aim provide other signposts to the later, ideological war.

Intelligence operations in connection with the defence of the Empire of the East became a substitute for policy. From small beginnings at the level of straight-forward reconnaissance and agent running, fears for India's security plus the entirely new factor of Middle East oil led to financed revolt and counter-revolutionary campaigns. Even orthodox military operations were subordinated to these aims.

For once Lawrence got it right: 'I went up the Tigris with one hundred Devon Territorials, young, clean, delightful fellows, full of the power of happiness and of making women and children glad. By them one saw vividly how great it was to be their kin, and English. And we were casting them by thousands into the fire to the worst of deaths, not to win the war but that the corn and rice and oil of Mesopotamia might be ours.'[22] In similar vein Herbert wrote of Gallipoli, where he had fought and suffered: 'The despair of generals, the grave and oblivion of soldiers.' Gallipoli, Churchill's imperial sideshow, was not designed merely to threaten a German flank: it was conceived as a means of Britain establishing and extending a new Eastern Empire.

The Chief of the Imperial General Staff, Sir William Robertson, dismissed introspection by men like Lawrence and Herbert which, if allowed to spread, might have stopped the game altogether. Referring to the campaigns against bolshevism, Robertson said: 'What was needed in Persia and Transcaspia was to despatch to the centres of intrigue and disaffection a few Englishmen of the right type to give our version of affairs, furnish them with money to pay handsomely for intelligence, and other services rendered, and provide them with just sufficient escort to ensure their personal safety.'[23] In pursuit of this War Office policy, Britain fought a third Afghan War in 1919, crushed a nationalist revolt in Iraq during 1921, and contained Egyptian nationalism in the 1920s by punitive means. Through the useful device of the League of Nations' Mandate for Palestine, additional clients, Jews and Arabs, were secured on the basis of ambiguous, indeed conflicting, pledges.

Robertson's words could well have been applied to the Special Operations Executive when, in 1940, Churchill ordered it to 'Set Europe ablaze'. SOE, as we shall see, was lineally the successor to the Transcaspian and Turkestan missions, and bore little resemblance to an organisation which remains associated in popular imagination with the liberation of Western Europe from Nazi occupation. Churchill's Europe was a reflection of his interpretation of history and his ideas about strategy. Western Europe, France above all, was an area to be defended on the basis of certain roles history gave to States. The French role was to preserve a

European balance of power, thus freeing Britain for the prosecution of imperial strategies, above all in the Middle East. Despite Churchill's professed love for France, the role was not merely subordinate to British imperial policies but could only be executed by governments of the right. During the Second World War there was no disposition by Churchill to use SOE for supporting resistance movements in France and the Low Countries if *résistants* were followers of de Gaulle or men of the left. The SOE effort in Western Europe, although sustained and heroic, was subordinate to its tasks in the Mediterranean and the Balkans. The area, this other Churchillian Europe, reflected not only his convictions about the Middle East and the need to defend its flanks and lines of communication, but his belief that guerrilla campaigns were both a viable substitute for divisions of troops and a peculiarly British method of waging war. The Churchill of the Second World War was, in most respects, the Churchill of the campaigns against bolshevism which he waged after 1918. SOE was an imperial secret army.

Churchill's belief in intelligence operations was thus strictly confined to the robust variety. He virtually ignored the role of SIS until it provided him with what he called 'pure gold' – the Enigma machine. Churchill, however, was not singular in ignoring SIS. From the outset, roles were neither clearly defined nor articulated. The Foreign Office disliked the establishment of a department for which, in the final analysis, it was responsible but regarding whose activities it could neither claim credit nor impose control. Diplomats disliked SIS for its independence. They contested 'C's' argument that intelligence covertly acquired was intrinsically more valuable than information collected on the basis of overt contact, mutual exchange of confidence with other diplomats, and long experience of foreign governments, bureaucracies, and chancelleries. Hence the real problem for SIS in the twenty years between world wars was that successive 'Cs' were unwilling or unable to state what their much disliked organisation was for.

Between 1919 – when SIS, by name, was established under nominal Foreign Office supervision – and 1939 Cumming and his successor, Admiral Hugh Sinclair, failed to reassert the priority of raw intelligence in terms of a potential enemy's strategic capacities and intentions. In the meantime, the Committee of Imperial Defence and successive Directors of Military Intelligence not only continued to regard the defence of India as the first strategic priority, but supported plans for fighting any future war by guerrilla and other irregular means. In 1919 the Government Code and Cypher School was also established; in 1921, the Cabinet's Secret Service Committee recommended that SIS should add the Home, India and Colonial Offices as customers to the existing arrangements with the Admiralty and War Office. In theory, SIS supported the DMI outside Europe and the Foreign Office within it. In practice, SIS was an asset neither to imperial strategy nor to British diplomacy.

Not only was scientific intelligence neglected; the capacity of Germany to prepare almost secretly for war was ignored both at the political and technical levels. Yet Russophobia increased, to the point, indeed, where anyone in Britain who professed sympathy with Russia – not necessarily with communism – was likely to come under surveillance. SIS co-operated with MI5 – and the Foreign Office – in producing intelligence of Soviet subversion. Moreover, these operations were carried out in a spirit of domestic political partiality which endured at least until 1945. Allegations of subversion were made in order to discredit the Labour Party – and, specifically, the Labour Government of 1924 – not to expose the machinations of the Russian Government. In 1924 SIS penetrated the Sovnarkom (The Soviet Council of Commissars), but failed to report that German troops were being trained in Russia. SIS authenticated the letter from Zinoviev, President of the Communist International, authorising British communists to undermine the Labour Government, but failed to report on Hitler's rise to power and the methods by which he intended to retain – and increase – it.[24]

Sinclair's long period as 'C', from 1923 to 1939, was thus characterised by a steady determination to follow the imperial path at all costs. His single good eye – the black eyeglass, like Cumming's wooden leg, suggests a buccaneering approach which the records belie – looked steadily to the Empire of the East. The Whitehall reorganisations of 1936, when the Joint Intelligence Committee was formed by Hankey's guiding hand, did something for the co-ordination of Whitehall activities as rearmament began; little effort was made to task SIS so that intelligence could be acquired about a rapidly rearming Germany. On the eve of war, by which time the nucleus of SOE had been formed in the War Office, the unpaid officers of SIS in Germany still had nothing to report about the dispersal of key sections of a war industry – prefabricated U-boats, radar, ball bearings – because they were untrained for the task. Private enterprise prevailed. Ironically, in view of the fact that SIS failed to locate Hitler's war industry, Sinclair authorised clandestine flights over Germany by a private individual, Sydney Cotton, using a converted Lockheed 12A aircraft. The 'Aeronautical Research and Sales Corporation' – cover provided by SIS – proceeded to photograph the German Fleet and the Italian empire of the Mediterranean. Embassy Passport Control Offices provided some additional cover for SIS and its agents on the ground, but Foreign Office control and Cabinet knowledge of intelligence activities remained derisory. When war broke out, SIS in Germany was rolled up by the SS. Himmler, Chief of the SS, named all the senior ranks of SIS in a public speech, beginning with 'C'.

A staff of no more than thirty at SIS headquarters, 55 Broadway, a building of singular gloom, whose only interesting feature was the passage to 'C's' flat in Queen Anne's Gate, administered a budget which had hardly increased from the purely nominal sums of the 1920s. Recruitment was governed by the Fisher dictum, producing in Broadway not the heroes of fiction, but a mixture of ex-Indian policemen and those from middle-class professional backgrounds: Anglican clergymen, schoolmasters, solicitors. Kim Philby was recruited in the late 1930s, fitting easily into a milieu where extreme right wing views were regarded as normal. Philby was not the only member of SIS actively to support Franco. Men of great ability did join SIS, some possessed of that 'dog-like sixth sense' which is the mark of a good intelligence officer. Their abilities availed them nothing. Sinclair told them they would be of service to the State; this virtue would have to be its own reward. The Foreign Office remained critical of SIS and most of its works.

On the eve of war, however, one great piece of good luck came the way of SIS, which was to sustain its fortunes throughout six years of conflict characterised by new attacks from Whitehall enemies. The Enigma machine, a cyphering device, brilliantly simple in concept but capable of almost infinite permutation, came, literally, into the hands of Colonel Stewart Menzies, Sinclair's Deputy. The machine, looking like a typewriter, was the key element in a system consisting of a series of drums – or 'bombes' as the wartime cypher breakers called them – which enabled cyphers to be changed frequently, and to be composed in groups which defied analysis by mathematical probability or intellectual brilliance. The machine, which was patented in the 1920s, was acquired by the German High Command for ulterior purposes. He who read signals cyphered by Enigma, or Ultra, as the British called it in the Second World War, read the intentions of Hitler and his generals. But he read more than mere intention. Ultra, after enormous, devoted effort, came to provide so much in terms of intention that the overall capabilities of Hitler's war machine, its weaknesses and its strengths, became plain to Churchill in his War Room and Britain's commanders in the field. Hitler's ambition for empire in Europe was revealed, interpreted, and shattered by Ultra.

Arguably, the war was won by Ultra, in which case we should thank the Polish, French and German intelligence officers (the latter being defectors) who offered the machine to Britain. SIS in Poland was 'primarily interested in Russia'.[25] The Poles, nevertheless, told SIS. The intelligence was lodged in Menzies's politically agile mind. When on 31 March 1939, Neville Chamberlain announced support for Poland, a temporary alliance of Polish, French, and British intelligence officers was formed. The alliance survived war years in which loyalties amongst allies were more strained than cordial. Yet Menzies kept his Polish and French lines of communication open, knowing that Ultra was the key to his survival – and to that of SIS.

In 1939 Menzies had the wit to do two things. He contacted a former member of the Director of Naval Intelligence's cryptological section, Commander Alastair Denniston. Denniston was Head of the Code and Cypher School, not then, strictly speaking, subject to 'C's' directives. Denniston had already heard of Enigma, and had met the Poles. Menzies provided himself with the cover of an academic visiting Poland – a certain rather distinguished and ascetic air enabling this to be done without much difficulty. In July 1939, Menzies and Denniston arrived in Warsaw, together with one of Denniston's former colleagues, Dillwyn Knox, a genuine academic. By 16 August, two Enigmas had arrived in London, via the British Embassy in Paris. Menzies met the train at Victoria, in a dinner jacket but – a courteous touch – the Legion of Honour rosette in his buttonhole. Thereafter, Ultra and the huge organisation which was established between 1939 and 1945 to operate it came securely within 'C's' domain. The Code and Cypher School did so also. SIS, 'that generally lax organisation', was not ready for the war in the field; its Whitehall strategy had certainly been strengthened.[26]

2 · BLOWING UP TRAINS IN THE RESISTANCE

We must admit to a feeling for the appropriateness of Flaubert's recipe for the perfect realistic novel: *pas de monstres, et pas de héros*. The performance of the war-time intelligence community, its shortcomings no less than its successes, rested not only on the activities of a large number of organisations but also, within each organisation, on the work of many individuals.

F.H. HINSLEY,
British Intelligence in the Second World War

Neville Chamberlain's Britain embarked on war in 1939 not only lacking conviction about the issues but certainty regarding the aims. Until the last moment the Foreign Office collectively, if not unanimously, hoped for a deal with Hitler. An alliance against him was 'not possible'. Despite the Anglo-Russian talks in Moscow during June 1939, bolshevism was seen as a greater threat in Whitehall than Nazism.[1] There were those who would have approved the assassination of Hitler – an idea half-seriously entertained by the British Military Attaché in Berlin, Colonel Noel Mason-Macfarlane – but they were not found in high British places. Sinclair, 'a terrific anti-Bolshevik', had made absolutely no effort to undertake hostile operations against the Nazi regime.[2] Section D of SIS and MI(R) in the War Office, whose offspring SOE grew to be such a handful, did not start planning guerrilla war throughout the Balkans in order to promote social revolution.[3] When Russia attacked Finland in November 1939 plans were made in the War Office for raising a unit, the 5th (Ski) battalion Scots Guards, to fight with the Finnish Army.

Winston Churchill's British Empire survived after 1945 for far longer and in much better shape than critics at home and abroad, above all in the United States, thought possible. Churchill said at intervals during the war that he had not been appointed the King's First Minister to preside over the liquidation of the British Empire. For all practical purposes Churchill's boast held good until 1974, when British forces were, officially, withdrawn from the Persian Gulf. For nearly thirty years after the end of a war which had reduced Britain to the economic and strategic level of a minor power, the lines of communication to an Eastern Empire were kept open.

In 1945, America left Europe, as it had done in 1918, and not until 1949 did Bevin succeed in bringing the GIs back again. France rebuilt its colonial empire in Indochina after 1945, with the overt assistance of the Indian Army and the covert involvement of SOE. Comparable help was given to the Netherlands in the East

Indies. By the 1950s, all this expenditure of blood and toil was dust and ashes. By the early 1960s, when Russia, at last, began to realise Peter the Great's dream of access to the open seas, France and Belgium had also lost their African empires. Britain alone, despite India's independence in 1947 – after a stubborn rearguard action by Bevin – could still be called an imperial power. Not until Aden was evacuated in 1967, in circumstances both humiliating and farcical, did the Empire of the East finally collapse. Arab and Persian oil would, thereafter, be bought, not owned. Britain's imperial century ended; the search for a foreign policy began.

Between August 1939 and September 1945 the combined assault on British interests – from friends and enemies – was defeated. The price, in 1945, did not seem high. The bills had not yet come in. Victory – and today's sceptical reader should never forget its magnitude – had owed much to British arms, to men well led and trained, fit, adequately equipped. The Royal Navy and Royal Air Force won the Battle of the Atlantic; the Royal Air Force won the Battle of Britain. Although the issues of the Second World War were decided at Stalingrad and Kursk, in the Pacific and over Hiroshima, Britain's victories when standing alone made those decisive defeats possible.

On the ground, however, British arms fared badly. Montgomery and Slim have their place in history – for their command of intelligent and thinking soldiers rather than for strategic grasp or tactical flair – but even in 1944 British formations came off second best in a direct, relatively equal encounter with German armour. Deficiences in arms and equipment is a partial explanation, but the real answer lies in the fact that even the conscript British Army of the Second World War remained imperial in outlook and, above all, in role. Between Gibraltar and Calcutta lay an area in which, during the darkest days, with the fires from burnt Baghdad and Cairo Embassy secret files signalling danger and defeat, the British Army and its imperial cohorts remained in garrison roles. The war in the desert was the sideshow: the imperial role was maintained in Egypt, Sudan, East Africa, Palestine, Transjordan, the Levant, Iraq, and Persia. In 1942, with the Japanese menacing India's eastern gate, sixty British and Indian battalions remained committed to internal security and the North West frontier. The figures speak for themselves.

This imperial role was more bitterly opposed by Roosevelt and his Cabinet than by Hitler, who had hopes for a place in Arab affairs, or by Stalin with ambitions in Persia. Churchill spent more time fending off American attacks than defending the imperial record. American aims in the Middle East, disguised in high-minded phrases, were to remove Britain and gain the oil. The State Department called Britain in Arabia a 'foreign power' and treated it as a hostile one. Roosevelt and Ibn Saud, in February 1945, agreed to call Britain false and greedy, anxious only to preserve its place in the sun. The President of the United States and the Ruler of Saudi Arabia met in the Gulf of Suez on board USS *Quincy*. Roosevelt told Ibn Saud: 'We like the English, but we also know the English and the way they insist on doing good [to] themselves. You and I want freedom and prosperity for our people and their neighbours after the war. How and by whose hand freedom and prosperity arrive concerns us but little. The English also work and sacrifice to bring freedom and prosperity to the world, but on the condition that it be brought by them and marked "made in Britain" '. To this adroit and damaging attack on an ally Ibn Saud replied, 'Never have I heard the English so accurately described.' Roosevelt then moved out into the open: Churchill was devious; Britain would always seek to order Saudi Arabia and its neighbours about, declaring, moreover, that a British Government's concern was enduring, the American interest transitory.[4]

Churchill knew about these exchanges. They were the consummation of earlier attacks on British imperialism. From 1941 onwards Churchill resisted these attacks by arguing that the British Empire, if not an arsenal of democracy, was the source of military strength and strategic opportunity for the defeat of Hitler. Yet Churchill could not indefinitely resist the President's argument that Britain must shoulder much of the European burden whilst America fought its Pacific war. Churchill, nevertheless, was determined to keep a place in the sun. He was equally determined to extend British interests wherever possible. He knew that the British Army could not retain an exclusively imperial role; thus his objective was to sustain it by conciliating Roosevelt wherever and whenever possible, opposing him on matters of ultimate necessity. A 'second front', wherever opened and by whatever means, meant the commitment of British troops and hence the inevitable dilution of imperial garrisons.

Churchill thought that he had found at least a compromise solution to this problem when he urged his Mediterranean strategy on Roosevelt. A second front there would be less costly than one in Flanders and the Low Countries. Troops could be despatched from, and returned to, the garrisons. Even here Churchill was disingenuous. His real objective was not the Mediterranean – a theatre of war ultimately dominated by the Royal Navy and one of obvious strategic importance – but the Balkans, a flank from which to thwart or threaten Russia. Roosevelt was strongly and consistently opposed to Balkan operations; he wished to appease Stalin, not confront him. On 18 March 1942 Roosevelt told Churchill: 'I know you will not mind my being brutally frank when I tell you that I think I can personally handle Stalin better than your Foreign office or my State Department. Stalin hates the guts of all your top people.'[5]

Churchill not only ignored Roosevelt's objections to the Balkan strategy on political grounds; he did so because he prosecuted the strategy by methods which rarely called on American logistic resources, elsewhere indispensable for any major military effort under British command. Churchill's case, in all essentials and as he communicated it to the British Chiefs of Staff, was that operations on the southern flank of Hitler's Europe would enable several imperial objectives to be attained. The area, with its challenging terrain and diverse societies, would also offer the chance to practise those skills in irregular warfare and political persuasion which Churchill, above all, regarded as the hallmark of the British soldier and the agents of Empire. Churchill was the man who had failed at the Dardanelles in 1915 and throughout Russia after the 1917 Revolution. His belief in a strategy of the indirect approach was not destroyed by those failures.

Churchill's dislike of the Commander-in-Chief Middle East, Sir Archibald Wavell, did not extend to the latter's strategic notions. Wavell had also participated in sideshows against the Turks. As a result, Wavell believed the British soldier should be 'part bandit, part cat burglar'. In the Middle East and Burma Wavell always backed the irregular soldier against the orthodox. That latter-day Lawrence, Orde Wingate, owes his fame to the withdrawn, taciturn commander of imperial armies. Wavell's successors in the Middle East, Auchinleck and Alexander, were more concerned with fighting in the desert than with what they saw as sideshows. But Wavell provided a legacy for Churchill to spend. By the time he left Cairo in June 1941 he had fathered or fostered enough irregular units, special forces, and secret organisations for Churchill's plans to be given shadowy form.

Churchill, in a sense, lost his second front battle with Roosevelt. Yet, in a context which it is necessary to grasp for an understanding of post-war events, he also won it. British troops crossed the Channel on 6 June 1944; but it was Alexander's capture of Rome at the same moment which enabled Churchill to argue that German forces should be driven from South East Europe. Events in Greece concerned Churchill not only from loyalty to its king but from a determination to establish a British presence. During Christmas 1944 Churchill was in Athens, personally conducting operations against communist guerrillas, putting further touches to a policy which he had fashioned at least a year before. By early 1945 a strong force of British and Indian troops was maintaining a precarious lodgement against open communist revolt.

By 1945, the imperial frontiers had reached the Balkans. Churchill's own second front, the Italian campaign, and even his support for Tito, were imperial in a context which defined a revived threat to British interests from Stalin's move into Eastern and South Eastern Europe once Hitler retreated from Stalingrad in February 1943. Allen Dulles, who shared Churchill's attitude to Russia, reckoned that America's temporary alliance with Russia ended after Stalingrad, 'when the cold war really began'. To Churchill, not at Fulton in 1946, but in the War Room during his finest hour, there had merely been an armistice with Russia once Hitler invaded on 22 June 1941. The real war, not so much against 'the foul baboonery of bolshevism' but more against a Russia historically expansionist and aggressive – in Churchill's view – was renewed after Stalingrad.

In fighting to defend imperial interests Churchill, from the time he became Prime Minister in May 1940, drew on personal resources of courage and imagination; a deep, romantic sense of history in the making; and a perspective shared with the Chiefs of Staff that Russia would again become an enemy once the enforced alliance brought about by world war had collapsed from its internal contradictions. Churchill and his generals argued, disagreed, and sometimes quarrelled. But they were united on imperial fundamentals. Once Germany's defeat seemed assured, the Chiefs, through their various sub-committees (and the Joint Intelligence Committee), began to make outline plans for the post-war years on the basis of Russia as a potential enemy. Such plans went well beyond the usual practice of preparing for all eventualities. The Chiefs argued that the Russian threat, not only to British interests but to European security, was so real that it might be necessary to rearm Germany. Russia's intention to dominate Europe would be thwarted at the Elbe if not the Oder.

Both politically and geographically, however, the Chiefs' ideas owed more to events following Hitler's invasion of the Balkans in 1941 than to a possible Russian thrust across the North German plain.

Thinking along these lines met with Foreign Office objections on detail rather than principle. Two members of the Foreign Office, Victor Cavendish-Bentinck and Gladwyn Jebb, were chairmen respectively of the JIC and the Post-Hostilities Planning Sub-Committee. This robust pair enabled a diplomatic gloss to be put on strategic assumptions. Foreign Office officials in general hoped that a post-war Russia would be 'accommodating'. But the Foreign Office maintained a 'reserved' attitude to Russia, and feared a return of American isolationism once the war ended. The Foreign Office also strongly resisted the American and Russian belief that 'Britain was now a secondary power'. This belief was 'a misconception to be opposed'. But how? Anthony Eden, as Foreign Secretary, tried to mould strategic assumptions and diplomatic warnings into a policy which he could put to Stalin and discuss with Cordell Hull. This was a mistake. Churchill, learning of Eden's manoeuvres, 'emitted a series of most vicious screams of rage'. Eden retired hurt, accepting but resenting that British foreign policy would be made by others.[6]

The basic identity of outlook between Churchill and the men responsible for the business of war was cemented by Ultra. Churchill plus Ultra was the centre of the Whitehall web, of war waged by a combination of democratically invested – but autocratically executed – prime ministerial responsibility, the Chiefs in committee, and a handful of key officials and favoured advisers. Ultra, the unique weapon, not only gave Churchill the intelligence advantage over Roosevelt and Stalin; it gave him what he needed for the prosecution of his imperial strategy. If Churchill had not known Hitler's intentions for the Balkans in 1941 even the Chiefs of Staff would have been hard to convince that this area offered long-term possibilities for independent British action. If Ultra had not provided the German order of battle and intelligence of resistance to Hitler in the Balkans from 1941 onwards, few in Whitehall would have been convinced that a new imperial frontier could be established and maintained.

Those responsible for the Ultra distribution were the servants of imperial strategy. But they also ensured that the war in Whitehall would be fought at two levels: that of strategic priority, operational decision, and, above all, disposition of always limited resources; and the determination, by arbitrary personal choice, of who kept close to Churchill and who, whatever their responsibilities, remained at the web's outer circle. Ultra convinced Churchill that operations in the Balkans were feasible, and could be conducted by seeking and securing the support of national leaders, communists or kings. Yet there is irony in the fact that not until 1943 was Churchill able to find an effective ally in the Balkans: Tito. When Churchill backed Tito he met with sustained hostility, above all from SOE. The explanation for this situation lies in SOE itself, and Menzies's place in the Whitehall war of who should know what, above all concerning secret intelligence and special operations.

Much has been written about SOE in recent years, a good deal of it critical, some of it abusive. Fitzroy Maclean, Churchill's personal liaison officer with Tito, regarded SOE as riff-raff; others have used harsher words. The Chiefs of Staff were never happy about an organisation over which they had little direct control. Eden and the Foreign Office disliked an independent organisation for the execution of foreign policy by irregular means. The arguments about SOE's origins and roles hint at, but do not reveal the essential truth: ambitious soldiers and the War Office were determined to establish an organisation which could sabotage Britain's enemies *and* support, in Europe above all, governments, regimes, and societies whose belief in 'law and order' precisely matched Whitehall's fear of Russia. It is no accident that SOE, under its prototype names, began operations in the Balkans before war broke out.[7] Events there took strange courses, but 64 Baker Street (SOE Headquarters in London) always preferred kings to communists. Desmond Morton, a greyer eminence than Menzies, was not only very close to Churchill – and SIS. He arbitrated many SOE issues. Morton 'was certainly no friend of the left; he was deeply concerned with the spectre of post-war European communism'.[8]

Nor was it an accident, or the fortunes of war, that SOE was originally regarded by Churchill as an instrument for the execution of his policies. When Hugh Dalton, as first Minister of Economic Warfare, took Churchill's prescription for setting Europe ablaze as a call for social revolution he was promptly sacked. Dalton was a moderate socialist. His successor, Lord Selborne, was somewhat to the right of Churchill himself. The story of the part played by SOE in the restoration of essentially conservative governments in the Low Countries after the liberation has still to be written, but some comment here is essential. In late 1944, and after British forces had cleared Belgium of the German Army, many young *résistants*, in various groups, were thought to be dominated by 'communist elements whose aim was to spread confusion with a view to revolution'. SOE had operated with these groups. With Desmond Morton on Churchill's orders playing his usual background role, 30,000 Belgians were rounded up and sent to Northern Ireland for training as soldiers. No revolution – assuming one to have been intended – occurred.[9]

De Gaulle was altogether a more formidable proposition than rampaging young Belgians. De Gaulle detested SIS – which penetrated the Free French from the moment they arrived in Britain – but SOE was seen, correctly, by him as Churchill's device for restoring 'legitimacy' to a France whose *résistants* were as likely to be communist as Catholic – or conservative. Churchill also had 'a certain idea of France', and it was not de Gaulle's. Churchill recognised the Vichy Government; SOE maintained official liaison with the Free French on a basis which was always equivocal and, in practice, hostile. SOE ran two French 'country' sections, one in liaison with de Gaulle, the other concerned with resistance groups who were, supposedly, free of his influence or could be weaned from it. De Gaulle's biographer, although a man of the right (and hazy on dates and details), makes a telling point: 'SOE was an independent Secret Service, formed in July 1940 – a month after de Gaulle's arrival in London – and disbanded, by an arresting coincidence, about the time when he resigned as Prime Minister of France in January 1946.'[10]

Menzies, who became 'C' on 28 November 1939, was to retain extremely ambivalent views about SOE throughout the war. Menzies knew, and quite liked, SOE's real godfather, Colin Gubbins, but the Lowland Scot's attitude to war in the shadows was a touch too robust for the Life Guardsman. Gubbins, like his eccentric colleague Laurence Grand, accurately perceived and predicted that modern war was revolutionary war. Gubbins had learned something from his service in North Russia during 'intervention'. Strong-arm methods were needed in such warfare. All enemies of the realm – informers, spies, traitors and, by extension, revolutionaries – should not be treated, if captured, as prisoners of war. They should be killed, quickly. Several of Gubbins's War Office colleagues had served in Ireland during the 'Troubles' following the end of the First World War. This violent experience had taught them a short way with dissenters.

Gubbins, who became 'CD', or Executive Director of SOE in 1943 – after a series of internal convulsions which threw out the bankers and other businessmen originally recruited – rarely descended to Whitehall intrigue. This detachment reflected Gubbins's conviction that special operations were assured of Churchill's automatic support. Gubbins had commanded the 'independent companies' – forerunners of the Commandos – in the 1940 Norwegian campaign, and had emerged with credit from that disaster. He had his own line of communication to Desmond Morton. But until 1943, SOE was excluded by Menzies from the regular Ultra distribution. Moreover, much of Gubbins's time in SOE's early years was wasted by a political chief whose nominal role was economic warfare – one neither defined nor executed – and in fighting criticism from the Foreign Office. Collectively, the latter not only disliked SOE but wrangled with it over who should conduct propaganda warfare in occupied and neutral countries. The Foreign Office had an offshoot called the Political Warfare Executive; SOE ran a section committed to the same task. Gubbins, a regular soldier dedicated to irregular warfare, spent his first three years in SOE fighting and losing Whitehall battles.[11]

Menzies, by contrast, was known for 'his shrewd management of a network of powerful contacts'. He has been described as 'a rather elegant and inoffensive spider'.[12] Not so: he preferred to trap his enemies, for later consumption. The enemies, however, were in Whitehall, and Menzies sought to defeat them by spinning his own web, at a careful distance from Churchill and the Chiefs, but strong and complex enough to trap the unwary and importunate competitors for roles and favours. MI5 was largely responsible for a counter-intelligence operation, *Double X*, which went well beyond the confines of the United Kingdom but extended to SIS territory in Europe. Success with *Double X* – run through turned agents who penetrated the Abwehr and other German intelligence services – led to plans, vague yet disquieting to Menzies, for the establishment of a single intelligence and security service, combining MI5, SIS, and SOE. Menzies's opposite number in MI5, David Petrie, was credited with this idea. Beyond Whitehall lay innumerable wartime secret headquarters and safe houses, where as much time was spent in bureaucratic feuds as in fighting the enemy. Certain restaurants, like Wilton's in St James, and many clubs, were the resort of tired, patriotic men whose addiction to intrigue was, perhaps, a necessary antidote to the business of war. On the fringes hovered literary or sub-literary figures – Evelyn Waugh, Goronwy Rees, Guy Burgess – whose loyalty whether unquestioned or debatable, was of a kind to give an exotic flavour to a war of files and frustrations.[13]

In the short run, Menzies defeated all attempts to weaken his position because the Ultra distribution under his direct control reflected unique entrée: the Prime Minister; the Chiefs of Staff Committee – including General Ismay, member because of his talents and as Secretary to the Committee of Imperial Defence; the Services Directorates of Plans, Operations, and Intelligence; the Secretary to the Cabinet; Morton, and other particular cronies and confidants surrounding Churchill. Members of the War Cabinet like Attlee and Bevin were outside this circle. For much of the war Eden was outside it also. MI5 read Ultra material when Menzies thought fit. Those who were on the Ultra distribution or privy to this secret weapon came to understand the business – and cost – of war for Britain so well that their subsequent careers and convictions were defined as a result. Amongst this ruling few were Norman Brook, Deputy to Sir Edward Bridges as Cabinet Secretary, and Antony Head, a regular soldier who, after the fall of France, served in the Cabinet Secretariat and with the Joint Planning Staff.

Menzies's privileged role, plus the fact that SIS, by the war's fourth year, had recruited a motley collection of amateurs who seemed to be neither intelligent nor secure, aroused the most intense hostility in Whitehall. Here, said the critics, are the armed forces, fighting, if not very brilliantly; there, they said, is SOE, at least trying something new – or reverting to something very basic in the British way of war. But what on earth, said the critics, is SIS doing except sit on a lot of crucial intelligence and employ some very peculiar people? The criticisms gained in force from the undoubted fact that Menzies consistently failed to produce intelligence from Germany on matters which lay beyond the scope of Ultra, but which was vital for the conduct of major operations. The strategic air offensive, to take the most important case, was based on the assumption that if Germans were slaughtered and 'dehoused' in sufficient numbers the survivors' morale would crack. In consequence, Hitler's troops would also be demoralised by fears for their families. SIS was repeatedly asked to acquire intelligence about German morale. None of any consequence was produced.

Menzies could well have answered, and did so obliquely, that SIS was not concerned with blood and thunder but with 'continuities', with reporting on an Empire which had to be kept in business and a Europe which had not entirely disappeared under Hitler's yoke. Although the claim regarding Europe was hard to sustain in 1939 and 1940 as Stations in Austria, Czechoslovakia and The Netherlands were also put out of business by the SS – Foreign Office criticisms of Menzies's failings fell on receptive War Office ears – it is a fact of some historical importance that once France, the Low Countries, Norway, and Denmark were occupied by Hitler and the Gestapo turned the screws, brave men and women volunteered to become SIS agents.

Menzies argued that intelligence from these volunteers should be taken seriously, and plans laid for a post-war Europe governed by responsible people, not bandits of the left – or the right. In this regard Menzies certainly had the support of all Europe's governments-in-exile, gathered in London, and hoping for better days. Menzies made sure that MI9, which was responsible for prisoner of war escape lines and much else besides, looked on SIS as the senior service, and provided intelligence from prisoners on the run who could keep their wits about them. MI9's staff were close by old Army associations to SOE, but Menzies prevailed. SIS got its way over priority for its agents when requests were made for aircraft to drop them in occupied Europe. SOE had to wait. Until 1942 SIS virtually controlled SOE communications with missions to resistance groups, because all receivers and transmitters were issued to Broadway.

Menzies's case was powerfully supported by SOE's enemies in Whitehall – a matter of personalities as much as policies – and key SIS successes in the Middle East and in neutral Europe. In Spain and Portugal SIS also ran effective counter-intelligence operations against the Abwehr, although basic political intelligence, as before the war, was more likely to come from overt Embassy sources. Turkey and Sweden were a different story, but in the Middle East SIS retained a reputation for good political intelligence. The 1941 'Golden Square' coup in Iraq, intended to put a pro-Nazi regime in power, was forecast – and thwarted; Farouk's Egypt, in truth the fief of Miles Lampson, the British Ambassador, was provided with a succession of client, and pliant governments. SIS in Persia virtually ran the elections. The British Minister, Sir Reader Bullard, complained. The process continued. A good many of SIS's post-war officers, and one future 'C', spent their apprenticeship in a Middle East where the presence of troops and the operations of assorted odd and irregular units seemed merely to reinforce the fact that the game was still afoot. SOE as an operator in Arab countries was relatively unimportant, despite inheriting the Arab Bureau's approach and methods, and notwithstanding the employment during the war's early years of Jews from Palestine who were skilled in unorthodox activities, whether penetrating Arab organisations or blowing people to bits. SOE's presence in Lebanon and Syria merely added to de Gaulle's obsession about Churchill. Menzies noted these conflicts, and waited for SOE to destroy itself.

By late 1942, however, the end of the beginning signalled the beginning of the end for 'continuities' on the Menzies model. Whilst the Whitehall battles had been raging, Churchill's Balkan strategy had developed to the stage of new designs and the revival of old ambitions. SOE could claim a role in the Balkans which went back to 1939, and it was one which met Churchill's objectives in terms which he expressed to Roosevelt on 7 October 1943: 'I have never wished to send an army into the Balkans, but only by agents, supplies and commandos to stimulate the intense guerrilla [activity] prevailing there.'[14] Churchill intended to stimulate more than guerrilla war, but his need for agents pointed directly to SOE. There had been no comparable SIS activity in the Balkans; MI5 had been active, extending counter-intelligence operations far and wide. Menzies had been a mere spectator of these events.

Thus SOE, whether riff-raff or not, had become Churchill's instrument for the execution of a Balkan strategy which appeared to meet all the imperial requirements and the views about Russia which he (and an increasingly acquiescent Eden) shared with the Chiefs of Staff. More to the point, by mid-1943 SOE in Cairo forced its way on to the Ultra distribution by reading what was clearly intended for others. Rough stuff had become the order of the day, above all in relations between SIS and SOE. Menzies, preoccupied with power struggles within SIS and Kim Philby's seemingly effortless rise through the hierarchy, accepted defeat. He turned to other matters, cultivating *inter alia* a friendship with Bevin, 'the one indispensable man in the Cabinet', and ensuring, by a visit to Algiers in late 1942, that relations with the ex-Vichy French remained close. Menzies, who had his eccentricities, used to write the SIS budget, under its country sections, on a blackboard, adding or subtracting as occasion served. As the war progressed, the budget for Europe was dusted out and reduced. SOE was bribing the right people, not SIS.

Ironically, it was Tito, the hard-line Stalinist – on the surface – who provided the catalyst for SOE's Balkans victory over SIS, and it was a left-wing journalist serving under Gubbins who forced his masters in Cairo to cut their losses with Draja Mihailovic, the Royalist Yugoslav general, and turn, reluctantly, to guerrilla forces who were actually fighting the German Army. By a further irony, James Klugman, one of the few undisputed, known, paid up members of the Communist Party loyally serving in SOE's Cairo headquarters, failed to grasp what the Conservative MP Fitzroy Maclean and the Socialist Staff Officer Basil Davidson knew from personal experience, grasp of political realities, and a careful study of Ultra material: Tito was his own man, a nationalist, not a Stalinist, who would not only kill Germans but eject Russians. Yet neither Maclean nor SOE succeeded in establishing a secure Balkan flank for Churchill in the terms which he sought. Nor did the American wartime equivalent of SOE, the Office of Strategic Services, succeed in establishing such a flank. In the reason for this failure during 1943 lies much of the explanation for Churchill's division of the Greek and Balkan spoils with Stalin in 1944 and 1945.

Post-war events throughout the area as a whole and, indeed, elsewhere, reflected three factors, whose existence between 1939 and 1945 – and particularly from 1942 onwards – was ignored or distorted by Churchill and those about him who shared his strategic obsessions. The first factor has been described: intelligence acquisition and distribution was a highly individual affair, reflecting an intensely personal conduct of the war by Churchill. There was no obvious or immediate case for SOE to be included on the Ultra distribution except in areas where German forces were heavily committed against guerrillas and *résistants*; yet exclusion not only bred bitterness in Whitehall (and Cairo), but exaggerated SOE's problems during years when a clear aim for it was hard to define. Moreover, Menzies's use of Ultra for the preservation of his own roles did nothing but harm to SIS, an organisation which needed professional leadership and the establishment of equally clear aims. If SOE and SIS had been able to achieve a common aim it is arguable that they would have succeeded in backing and sustaining social democratic movements in the Balkans, capable of thwarting Stalin's determination to establish a monolithic communist system.

The second factor was lack of military resources, for which neither SOE nor OSS could be a substitute. At the precise moment when Churchill accepted Maclean's recommendation that Tito deserved maximum support – a case which Ultra for months had shown to be valid – an operation, revealingly codenamed *Hardihood* was mounted to capture islands in the Aegean. The operation was essentially a reflection of Churchill's Balkan strategy and his theories about flanking movements and the indirect approach. Roosevelt point blank refused to support Churchill – his response to the latter's letter of 7 October was as chilly as anything in their protracted and one-sided exchanges – and *Hardihood* was doomed to failure on a scale which would have been a cause for censure in an earlier stage of the war. Elements of an overstretched Royal Navy and several thousand troops were committed to an enterprise which presumed scant opposition from German and Italian forces. This appreciation turned out to be wrong. Churchill broke the inexorable strategic law that the scale of complex operations must be measured by the overall resources available, not by the numbers of men or the fighting qualities which they may display. Churchill was forced to admit that, as a result of *Hardihood*, 'there was no question of the British intervening in Greece, but only in Greek affairs'.[15]

Churchill lacked the resources for *Hardihood*; by extension, he lacked them for the Balkans. Thus the SOE role grew in importance. Yet SOE was not a strategic instrument but a substitute. Bulgaria, Rumania, and Hungary were too far from any base for concerted operations to be mounted or sustained unless major resources, above all at the level of co-ordinated intelligence, were committed. Operations in Greece and Albania were governed predominantly by Churchill's political views, not his strategic theories. With the singular exception of Yugoslavia, British agents failed to find a guerrilla leader who could be regarded as a national figure. The essence of guerrilla war – and of resistance movements in general – is political motive. Wellington understood this truth in Spain. Lawrence and his superiors distorted the truth in order to meet British aims. Churchill did the same; he equated guerrilla war and resistance movements with British interests. SOE, individually and collectively, shared most of Churchill's outlook. To see how this third factor affected events in the Balkans we must briefly step back in time, and penetrate still further the looking glass world.

'Typically Balkan' had for long been a Foreign Office phrase to indicate the general hopelessness of those relics of the Ottoman

Empire, and the virtual impossibility of doing much with their mistress-ridden rulers and sullen populations except a little gentle bribery and hopes for continued neutrality. In the 1930s, however, Balkan alliances with either Hitler or Stalin would have caused concern in London. The fear reflected the belief that an aggressive Hitler would seek further conquests to the east, even into Arabia, rather than attack a supposedly strong France. But the greater fear lay in the rooted conviction that Stalin believed in a pan-Slav policy as much as his Tsarist predecessors. The existence of strong, well-organised communist parties in the Balkans, ruthlessly suppressed but never extirpated, coloured these fears. By 1939, SIS, then quite well placed in the Balkans for the acquisition of purely political intelligence, found that Colin Gubbins and Section D had begun to move in. Hitler's occupation of Austria was the pretext. The brief was beautifully simple: economic sabotage and political penetration. At much the same time, and as Whitehall collectively accepted that Hitler was the immediate enemy, Section D began to think about Czechoslovakia and Poland. 'The *Anschluss* had prompted the creation of Section D and the other clandestine organisations.'[16]

Given that Gubbins had the revealing if irrational conviction that right-wing views were what every member of society should hold, it is to his credit that he saw at once the impossibility of effective action in the Balkans on the basis of merely supporting existing regimes. King Carol's Rumania was primarily a sabotage target, given its oil and outlets to the Black Sea; Hungary, with Admiral Horthy determined to keep the helm, presented few opportunities. Yugoslavia was a different proposition. The Regent was flirting with the Axis; proximity to Greece and the Eastern Mediterranean was an inherently important strategic consideration.

Nothing was achieved in Rumania or Hungary. Some harebrained schemes were concocted for plugging the Rumanian wells and blowing up the Iron Gates. Removing the axle boxes from railway trains had a vogue. Security was not so much breached as ignored; the *boulevardiers* of Bucharest could have written the operation orders themselves. The British Legation protested: the thing was typically Balkan. George Taylor, Gubbins's representative, was, however, a man not easily deterred. These were early days. His opportunity came in March 1941 when Hitler, at last, moved into Yugoslavia. SOE, on 27 March, deposed the Regent of Yugoslavia and installed the young King Peter. Behind the façade of a positively Ruritanian escapade lay a reasonably intelligent attempt at installing a ruler to whom all Yugoslavs, left and right, would rally.

Taylor was an Australian and in no sense an Establishment figure. His politics were, nevertheless, imperial. Would a united Yugoslavia resist Hitler and bar his way to the East? Events overtook these hopes. By the end of May Hitler's commanders were sitting in Athens; Yugoslavia was also in his grip. The young king was removed; he left behind a divided nation where Serbs and Croats, not merely communists and monarchists, were soon to engage in open conflict. Thereafter the Croat Mihailovic appeared, in Cairo's collective assumptions and those of SOE on the ground, to be the man for Britain's money: he was fighting Hitler; he was staunchly anti-communist. Not for another two years, and after Maclean had discovered the truth for himself, did Cairo accept that Mihailovic was killing Serbs, not Germans.

'Accept' meant different things to different people. Cairo by 1943 had not merely become the citadel of British power in a new Mediterranean empire; in and out of its myriad offices swarmed as many eccentrics and fanatics as could be found in the wartime London of Baker Street and Broadway. SOE in Cairo, annually purged, perpetually riven with intrigue and dissent, clung to the conviction that Mihailovic was both resolutely anti-communist and anti-German. Taylor's approach was replaced by a weird combination of ultra conservative politics and belief in special operations for their own sake. Cairo housed – and intermittently removed – commanders of and front men for every known and untried variety of irregular warfare. The Special Air Service; Popski's Private Army; the Special Boat Service; the Levant Schooner Flotilla – these were but some of the irregular units which flourished in that corrupting air. Orthodox military units committed to deep or shallow penetration – the Parachute Regiment, the Commandos; units raised for classic military intelligence or reconnaissance tasks – Force A, the Long Range Desert Group – ignored or suffered the freebooters on their flanks with more, or less, patience. SOE loomed over all, a pyramid of competing aims and conflicting methods.

A decision to abandon Mihailovic and support Tito might have been taken earlier, and without Churchill's direct intervention, if it had not been for the Greek factor. SOE teams which had been dropped in Greece during August and November 1942 (on the second occasion to blow, as something more than a gesture, the

Gorgopotamus viaduct, thus effectively sabotaging German troop movements and the reinforcement of Yugoslav garrisons) reported that communist guerrillas must be taken seriously, and that all resistance groups opposed King George's return. Those who took part in Operation *Harling* were in no sense men of the left – a decade later one of them had much to do with restoring the Shah of Persia to his throne – but all of them grasped that Greek resistance to the German occupation required a cause and a leader more potent than an absentee monarch. Brigadier Myers, the senior British officer in Greece, duly wrote an appreciation of this political factor and sent it to higher authority. After a year of wrangling, Myers was sacked and ordered not to return to Greece. The decision was made personally by Churchill who had decided, on grounds inimitably individual, to support King George at all costs – and, in default of operations against German forces to wage war, sooner or later, on Greek communists. *Ergo*, said Lord Glenconner, SOE Head of Mission in Cairo, support for Mihailovic, a good monarchist, must continue.

Glenconner did not reckon on the inimitable individualities. When Maclean reported to Churchill in September 1943 that Tito was the man to back, the latter decided that Mihailovic must be abandoned. Churchill had reached similar conclusions regarding SOE support for resistance movements in Czechoslovakia and Poland – in the latter case conceding to Stalin a European role which simply reflected the realities of power. Churchill shortened his front, preparing a Balkan flank against Stalin by a combination of political compromise and buffer state. Few of Churchill's moves in the last two years of the war are more revealing of his essential pragmatism, devotion to imperial interests – and blind spots – than his assiduous cultivation of Tito and his equally ardent support for a rejected King George. The culmination of this policy were the Conferences in Moscow during November 1944 and at Yalta in February 1945, where the Balkan interests were shared between Churchill and Stalin on percentage bases. Yugoslavia was split 50 : 50; Greece, 90 : 10. Stalin collected the remainder of the Balkans.

Maclean was not, and never became, a member of SOE. That fact would hardly rate a mention but for the sustained attempts made by SOE in Baker Street to prevent his return to the field. When that ploy failed, SOE in Cairo ran a campaign against Maclean ranging from allegations of homosexuality and cowardice to the provision of a, possibly, faulty parachute. Maclean survived this curious example of professional jealousy: the late 1943 purge of SOE in Cairo was more drastic than usual; Glenconner departed. SOE came increasingly under the control of the Chiefs of Staff. The Chiefs supported Churchill's imperial strategy; they supported special operations – up to a point. During the last eighteen months of the war operations in Yugoslavia achieved the status of a minor front. But SOE had failed to secure the Balkan flank. Whitehall collectively accepted the need for a post-war SOE, of sorts. But of what sort remained undecided. A memorandum of 22 November 1945, the work of Gubbins *incognito*, argued for stay-behind parties in a Europe occupied by Russia. From 'the earliest stages of conflict with Russia' SOE and SIS would operate as one.

In preparing for the next war, Gubbins made his peace with SIS. The Chiefs of Staff and the new Labour Government had other preoccupations: India, Palestine, a starving Germany occupied by troops hungry for demobilisation. What kind of post-war world awaited the thousands who had found their vocation under SOE's spreading rafters? What kind of world would SIS be left to tackle? Would 'the part-time stockbrokers and retired Indian policemen, the agreeable epicureans from the bars of White's and Boodles, the jolly, conventional ex-naval officers and the robust adventurers from the bucket-shop'[17] fit easily into a world which their hated rivals had made peculiarly their own? Would this post-war world be one of 'continuities', in which the Foreign Office and SIS, all ambition spent, could restore the fabric of Europe and Empire, or would rough stuff be the order of the day?

3 · A CONSEQUENCE OF PEACE: ALBANIA, 1949

In the course of eight months from January 1945 every possible source of trouble, from Azerbaijan to the Pillars of Hercules, became active. At each point a traditional British interest met an intangible Soviet pressure.

BARRY RUBIN,
The Great Powers in the Middle East, 1941–1947

Menzies's hope that SIS could return to the straightforward acquisition of raw intelligence when Germany surrendered in May 1945 was destroyed by circumstance, not by his rivals in Whitehall. Eden's assertion that 'in war diplomacy is strategy's twin' implied that in peace the men at arms deferred to those who made foreign policy. The assertion was not only belied by Eden's plans for a post-war SIS on SOE lines, but by Orwell's state of perpetual war, which began between the democratic West and a totalitarian Russia well before the bombs stopped falling on Hitler's Reich. Once the war ended even the diplomatic conventions were abandoned. Bevin, attending the Lancaster House four-power foreign ministers' meeting, and listening to Molotov's description of Stalin's new order for Rumania, Bulgaria, and Hungary declared: 'Now I know 'ow 'itler must have sounded.' The war in Europe had been over for four months. Bevin would continue to top and tail his letters to Molotov with 'Dear Comrade' and 'Yours fraternally', but between these faintly comic salutations lay plenty of venom.

Attlee's choice of Bevin as Foreign Secretary rather than Dalton – who badly wanted, and had been half promised it – was the one consolation Eden drew from the Labour Party's landslide victory in the July 1945 general election. The red flag flying over the cookhouse of the headquarters of a Royal Marine Commando on election day – a tease by Will Hamling, a troop commander who was later to become an impeccably orthodox Labour MP – would doubtless have convinced Churchill and Eden that the enemy was already within the gates. Churchill said as much during the election, and although many of the 259 new Labour MPs had been front line soldiers and airmen, MI5 at once proceeded to probe and pry. Chuter Ede, the Home Secretary, did not find this investigation acceptable. He was an old-fashioned English radical, and disliked MI5's conspiracy-ridden world. Ede had a word with Herbert Morrison who, having been Home Secretary during most of the War, knew the Whitehall ropes. The new intake – and the new Ministers – saw more of their files than MI5 realised.[1]

Bevin would not have found Ede's riposte to MI5 acceptable either. The new Foreign Secretary's stature in Churchill's War Cabinet had been based not only on his unique capacity, as Minister of Labour, to mobilise Britain for war but on his knowledge of the Russian communist movement abroad and at home. Bevin's loathing of Stalin and all his works was not based on insular and chauvinistic prejudice; it had grown from experience as a trades union official who had fought communists for twenty years, and had done so in alliance with socialists and social democrats throughout Europe. If Bevin had not become Foreign Secretary in 1945, the post-war years might have been those when Stalin entrenched himself in Berlin, and elsewhere. Bevin consolidated his comparison of Stalin with Hitler when he told Molotov in December 1947: 'You are playing with fire: one day you will get badly burnt.'[2]

By the time of this warning, SIS's Special Operations Branch and Political Action Group had been established for over a year. These revamped SOE units, supported by the Royal Navy and RAF, conducted operations in the Baltic States and the Ukraine. Bevin liked Menzies and respected Bridges, who remained as Cabinet Secretary until 1947.[3] But Bevin did not believe that the Foreign Office should leave everything to SIS. Much of Bevin's propaganda effort was directed by Bevin's Parliamentary Under-Secretary from September 1946, Christopher Mayhew, whose war-time intelligence experience made him an obvious choice. He was made responsible for a new Foreign Office Department, 'Information Research'.

This was the war-time Political Warfare Executive writ small, but Bevin made sure that IRD owed allegiance to the Foreign Office, exclusively. Ironically, one result of this move was to involve the Foreign Office in some of the more dubious intelligence operations which characterised the early days of the cold war. In the recollection of a former SIS officer who witnessed several of these operations, 'imperial sentiments were re-invested in the cold war' – but produced few bonuses. IRD also imposed on a reluctant BBC new tasks of propaganda and disinformation, directed at Russia and Eastern Europe. A Foreign Office 'Grant-in-Aid' for these tasks relieved the BBC of the financial burden, sweetening a pill which some journalists found hard to swallow.

Despite the fact that some Foreign Office officials were keen to assert a comparable control over SIS and the remnants of SOE – mainly by arguing for Embassy and Consular cover as routine, not occasional – the Permanent Under Secretary, Sir Alexander Cadogan, viewed the prospects of taking 'these fantastic things' under his wing with distaste. 'We aren't a department store.' Cadogan's successor in 1948, Sir Orme Sargent, took a more robust view, and the things, fantastic or otherwise, continued to operate ambiguously: they executed government policy; they retained their independence. Bevin approved: a cold war had to be fought by all available means.[4]

From the first Bevin not only took a line, used language, and adopted a policy towards Stalin which was hostile. He also split his own party. Bevin saw the threat as worldwide: he believed passionately in Britain as a world power – and was, in consequence, fervent in advocating a nuclear weapons system independent of the United States. Bevin was determined to resist Stalin at every point along the line. Yet Bevin laid down his priorities, and did so to Molotov in words which Salisbury – one of his few heroes – would have supported: 'You can't 'ave Austria, Turkey or the Straits. You stay be'ind your iron curtain.'[5] Bevin's Palestine policy – the cause of the real detestation felt for him in many parts of the Labour Party – was due entirely to his conviction that an independent Zionist State would become a Russian satellite. The lines of communication would be menaced. If they were cut, the Russian road to Britain's oil Empire of the East would be open.

For nearly three years Attlee and Bevin fought their battle with Stalin virtually alone. This was a far longer period of British isolation than that between the fall of France in June 1940 and Hitler's attack on Russia exactly a year later. Churchill and Eden gave their successors all the help they could behind the Parliamentary scenes, but Attlee's and Bevin's isolation was not from their Cabinet colleagues or Party critics but from the United States. Truman and two of his three Secretaries of State, George Marshall and Dean Acheson, respected the Labour Prime Minister and his outspoken Foreign Secretary, but it was only the latter who fully accepted Bevin's policy regarding Stalin. Truman's first Secretary, James Byrnes, neither liked nor understood Bevin, and made no effort at co-operation. Bevin saw Byrnes 'as another cocky and unreliable Irishman'. He was incensed and alarmed when, at Potsdam, Byrnes made it clear that he preferred to communicate with Molotov directly, not only over Europe, but about nuclear matters also.

The conflict of interest between Britain and America during the years of isolation was a direct legacy of world war. Churchill and

Roosevelt achieved a marriage of convenience, no more, despite the former's 'visceral admiration' for the President. Even if Roosevelt had lived and Churchill had won the 1945 election, it is doubtful if Britain would have been treated generously by its prosperous partner in victory. As it was, an impoverished Britain found 'Lend-lease' (Roosevelt's war-time economic aid programme) cut off once the Potsdam Conference was over – and Bevin's defiance of Stalin had been made plain. In 1946, partly because of treachery amongst Britain's atomic scientists, but primarily because of strained relationships, effective nuclear co-operation at the level of classified scientific information stopped also. The American McMahon Act virtually precluded scientific co-operation. The 1947 Truman Declaration and the Marshall Plan in no sense restored the balance or the special relationship. Despite Truman's words on providing security for Greece, British conscript troops – another sore point with Bevin's critics – continued to garrison the country. The Marshall Plan was intended to speed Europe's economic recovery from the ravages of war but, as a 1951 Congressional Report disclosed, primarily enriched the American oil industry, whose major companies shipped cheap Middle East crude to Europe and sold it at arbitrarily fixed prices.

Truman and his two later Secretaries did not privately dissent from Bevin's assessment of the Russian threat in Europe. The State Department privately accepted that Stalin must be 'contained' in Europe, by some means or other. In February 1946, George Kennan, from the United States Embassy in Moscow, sent an 8,000 word despatch – the so-called 'long telegram' – which said in measured prose what Bevin put in the vernacular. But when, in the June 1947 issue of *Foreign Affairs* an edited version of Kennan's despatch was given to the public – signed by 'Mr X', and advocating containment wherever possible – the Administration's response was a swift, and total rejection of substance and proposals. Truman was simply not prepared, until the Czech coup in February 1948, to do anything, overtly, to co-operate with the British Government concerning Palestine, or Persia, or anywhere else outside Germany and Austria. Byrnes opposed Bevin over Palestine, and although verbal support was given to British protests about Russian policy in Azerbaijan, the real American effort in Persia was directed at undercutting the position of the Anglo-Iranian Oil Company. Bevin knew what was toward, and resented it. He said in the House of Commons in May 1947: 'So far as foreign policy is concerned, we have not altered our commitments in the slightest. His Majesty's Government do not accept the view that we have ceased to be a great Power, or the contention that we have ceased to play that role. We regard ourselves as one of the Powers most vital to the peace of the world, and we still have an historic part to play.'

To the Americans, this was simply rhetoric. Britain did not have the bomb, and would not have it. Bevin's tendency to remind Byrnes that if it had not been for British scientists America might not have had the bomb either only reflected his determination to ignore isolation and press ahead with containment of Russia none the less. 1947 was the year of the Cominform and continued tension over Berlin. In August, India and Pakistan became independent and, in the words of Lord Alanbrooke, Churchill's Chief of the Imperial General Staff, 'the keystone of the arch was lost and our Imperial Defence crashed'.[6] No longer was the Indian Army available to fight imperial wars. But in 1947, with secrecy comparable to that in wartime, Attlee and Bevin accepted a Whitehall committee's recommendation that a British nuclear deterrent must be built.

The Report was a classic example of the Permanent Government in action. Indeed, the committee's Chairman was Sir John Anderson, a pillar of Whitehall in the 1920s, a potent member of the Viceroy of India's Council thereafter, a war-time Ministerial colleague of Churchill's. In becoming Chairman of the Committee on Britain's nuclear deterrent Anderson thus reverted to his bureaucratic career despite remaining a Conservative MP.[7] There is little doubt that Attlee and Bevin, as leaders of a Labour Government, wanted the bomb. Bevin brushed aside criticisms from right and left, from scientists unavoidably privy to the secret. Sir Henry Tizard, an Englishman of Englishmen, had played a vital role in the late 1930s preparing the Royal Air Force for war. In 1949 Tizard declared: 'We persist in regarding ourselves as a Great Power, capable of everything and only temporarily handicapped by economic difficulties. We are *not* a Great Power and never will be again. We are a great nation but if we continue to behave like a Great Power we shall cease to be a great nation.'[8] Tizard was excluded from the Whitehall corridors of power. Patrick Blackett was a former naval officer, a lapsed communist, a physicist with an international reputation – and an acknowledged expert in operational research for support of the Royal Navy and RAF. Blackett argued against nuclear independence for Britain and analysed why the attempt to achieve it would bring no strategic gain. Bevin was unmoved. 'He ought to stick to science.'[9]

Bevin's attitude to Russia was essentially robust; he saw no point in merely defending the British Empire – above all, the Empire of the East – against attack or subversion. At some point Stalin had to be stopped, not merely contained. For three years, however, Bevin was forced to play for time, fighting and losing a series of holding actions, not only 'stabbed in the back' by the left of his Party – or so he declared – but isolated from an America which had the overall strength to contain Stalin but lacked the political will to do so. Britain's economy had been virtually destroyed by the war. Bevin had few cards with which to play great power politics. He remarked as Britain froze in the cruel winter of 1947: 'If only I had another million tons of coal a year it would make all the difference to these negotiations of mine.'[10] In June 1946, before this winter of denial, Britain was forced to ration bread, the first occasion in its peacetime history. Supplies of wheat from America and Canada were tardy; Britain sent wheat to India – and Germany.

The accidents of history trapped Bevin in dilemmas which would have defeated an ordinary man, a routine politician. Bevin supported the idea of a united Western Europe – inevitable corollary to that divided Germany on which he did find agreement with Marshall. The tunnel which SIS – and the Royal Engineers – dug beneath Berlin in order to monitor Russian signals was, probably, the best if most covert indication of enmity between war-time allies, of a Germany divided into two armed camps. Another tunnel was dug beneath Vienna's streets, indicative of the city's role at the crossroads of the intelligence war.

Bevin also sought to consolidate Britain's hold on the Levant, Iraq, and Persia. The Portsmouth Treaty of January 1948 between Britain and Iraq, whereby RAF Squadrons could be stationed there, as they had been before and during the war, was an insurance policy against the loss of garrisons in Palestine and, prospectively, in Egypt.[11] Inheriting the legacy not only of imperial commitments but threats to lines of communications, the Cabinet Defence Committee (initially ignorant of nuclear plans and their £100 million budget) sought for new or expanded bases in Kenya and Cyprus. After India and Pakistan became independent the Government succeeded in retaining docking and repair facilities, over-flying rights and, secretly, agreement for the despatch of British forces in unspecified emergencies.

These Arabian and Asian manoeuvres meant nothing in

Washington. In February 1948, however, democracy was extinguished for a generation in Czechoslovakia. Within weeks Tito finally broke with Stalin. By the summer Berlin was blockaded. These events marked the end of isolation. Bevin was no longer alone. There was no American interest in or understanding of Malaya, where British troops were about to fight an 'Emergency' caused by the Malayan Communist Party organising armed rebellion against colonial rule. The rebellion was described by British soldiers and intelligence officers on the spot as 'part of a wider scheme aimed at establishing communism throughout the world by armed insurrection'.[12] To the collective American mind the subject peoples of Malaya had a right to independence from the British imperial yoke. To Americans who had backed the State of Israel the British invoked 'communist' in their empire as a bogey word.

The counter-attack on communism in Europe was another matter. The point chosen was the Balkans. The immediate objective was the removal of a communist ruler. The chosen instruments were SIS and the Central Intelligence Agency. The longer term objective was the establishment of a Western strategic presence on the Balkan flank. The year of preparation was 1948; 1949 the year of action. The Balkans was chosen because, in strategic terms, the need for a counter-attack reflected the appalling weakness of the Western position on the central European front. Throughout 1948 the British Chiefs of Staff continued to impress on Attlee the difficulties of defending Berlin and the Western zones of Germany against an outright Russian attack. Adequate conventional forces did not exist. Relieving the Berlin blockade by air was simply a means of buying time. SOE-type stay-behind parties, for sabotage and counter-intelligence, might be all very well in the Balkans, the Baltic, even in Austria. They made no kind of sense in Germany.[13]

The matter was not only one of capability but of intention. The Chiefs of Staff disliked the American intention to withdraw troops from Germany and rely on the atom bomb to deter or defeat a Russian attack. If the Chiefs had known that the stock of usable nuclear bombs was in single figures, their belief in capability would have wavered also. Bevin reacted to these factors by selecting the Balkans for counter-attack. The area offered, or appeared to offer, both political and strategic advantages. Tito's rift with Stalin was an open secret well before it widened into a final breach. In Greece, British troops and American cash had contained the communists; by late 1948, the Greek Army was about to take the offensive in a civil war which, in the British view, had already lasted for five years.

Stalin's acceptance of a 10 per cent interest in Greece when he bartered the Balkans with Churchill in no sense inhibited the Albanian, Bulgarian and Yugoslav Communist parties from providing sanctuaries for their comrades to the south. By the end of 1946, Stalin had subjugated the remnants of 'social democracy' in Bulgaria, as he had in Hungary and Rumania. Bulgarian support for Greek communists followed as a matter of course. Yugoslav and Albanian support reflected different aims – territorial ambitions and defence against Greek designs respectively. The total effect of this combined support was, nevertheless, to provide the Greek communists with the means to carry on the struggle. For three years after the end of the war in Europe it was touch and go whether Stalin's 10 per cent would not turn out to be 100. A communist government in Greece would have forced Bevin to rephrase his warnings to Molotov, to seek some dramatic means of redressing the balance of power. By 1948 Churchill's Balkan flank had become a potential Russian bridgehead, which could threaten Britain's lines of communication at their most vulnerable point, the Eastern Mediterranean.

The British role in the Greek civil war ensured that a succession of weak governments retained enough willpower to enact draconian laws, parade the king as a symbol of unity, and accept that an effective Greek Army must fight in the mountains, not loiter in the plains. Hector McNeil, Bevin's Minister of State, was several times sent to Athens to see for himself. During an early visit, in September 1945, McNeil said to the SIS Station Officer that Greece was 'an Egypt without Cromer'. McNeil, like his master, saw Greece as a British satellite. 'Up to 1947 the British Government appointed and dismissed Greek Prime Ministers with the barest attention to constitutional formalities. British experts dictated economic and financial policy, defence and foreign policy, security and legal policy, trade union and employment policy. But on the whole Britain's illusory power was used benevolently, if not always wisely.'[14]

On 12 March 1947, two months after Marshall became Secretary of State, the Truman Doctrine was announced. The conventional version of history states that the Doctrine, one of American involvement in the security of Greece and Turkey, was an unavoidable response to the British Government's statement of

21 February that it could no longer shoulder these burdens. The fact is that neither Attlee nor Bevin had the slightest intention of dropping the load but were determined that their rich war-time ally must eventually share it. Guy Burgess (McNeil's Personal Assistant), Kim Philby, and Donald Maclean had other views. Maclean (who, throughout much of 1947, was acting Counsellor at the British Embassy in Washington) shared with his fellow traitors Philby and Burgess a conviction that Britain was 'finished' as a nation, let alone as an imperial power. The treachery of these three men – or, on another interpretation, their loyalty to Russia – differed in motive and method, but they all failed to see that Bevin's hostility to Stalin was supported at the critical moment by Truman and Marshall. Philby's and Maclean's treachery was severe and damaging, given their responsibilities and senior rank in SIS and the Foreign Office, but failure to understand Bevin's achievement in ending American isolationism is what history will remember.[15] The treason of these three clerks was intellectual, not only political because, in common with many other traitors and 'fellow travellers' they measured national strength in purely material terms.

Superficially, such men took a realistic, 'objective' view of current events, but they also failed to appreciate Attlee's role in establishing a new front against Stalin. Attlee, although keen for Truman to shoulder some of the Greek burden, was determined that Britain's relationship with Turkey should not suffer. Attlee had respected 'Johnny Turk' since he had fought him at Gallipoli. The Labour Prime Minister shared with his Conservative predecessor a conviction that support for Turkey would protect Britain's lines of communication even more effectively than a campaign against communism in Greece. Unfortunately, this support in the late 1940s was, perforce, confined to intelligence operations. Much SIS counter-intelligence was based on Turkey. Philby had been sent from Broadway in 1946 to assist the Station Officer. Philby served his Russian masters with his usual obtrusive skill. The RAF lost at least one aircraft on the Turkish-Russian border in consequence. Nevertheless, the British Government, the Foreign Office, and SIS continued to regard Turkey as a potential bridgehead from which to threaten Russia across the Black Sea. The culmination of this policy was Turkey's membership of NATO in the 1950s and the emplacement of American missiles at Black Sea sites.

A comparably robust approach governed British policy in

Greece. It was not until early 1948 that the American Cromer, General Van Fleet, arrived in Greece as Commander of the Military Mission, and another year before the CIA, in various guises, took a real hand in the campaign. Initially the new, untried Agency's role was confined to providing cash for the right people. To that extent the Truman Doctrine was put into effect. On 22 January 1949 the CIA lost their first man killed in action against the communists, an unmarked aircraft being shot down near Karpenesi, in the Pindus mountains. Britain's power had lain in choosing the right moment to adjust the burdens of empire. Van Fleet was 'a vigorous and fearless soldier who spoke his mind'.[16] He later made his name in the Korean War, where he came to admire the qualities of British troops serving under him in the United Nations force. This was a pro-consular, a diplomatic touch which was much appreciated. But, in Greece, Van Fleet was not yet a Cromer: he saw the Greek Civil War through a soldier's eyes. Van Fleet was supported by an equally vigorous American Ambassador, Lincoln Macveagh, who knew Greece better than most foreigners. Yet the Western counter-attack in Greece was an affair of Bevin's hostility to Stalin, one based on defence of Britain's traditional imperial interests. In 1948 America was the junior partner in a new Atlantic Alliance, providing the cash but not the strategy. Rooted American dislike of British imperialism was temporarily modified by the existence of the iron curtain and the cold war.

On 5 September 1949, at the first meeting, in Washington, of the Council of the North Atlantic Treaty Organisation, Bevin proposed to institute counter-revolution in Albania. He was well aware that Acheson, the new Secretary of State, shared his views. Bevin also knew that American Chiefs of Staff had their eye on Valona, a natural harbour just north of the Greek frontier, as a potential forward base for their fleet in the Mediterranean. The Chiefs had already urged Greece as an advanced nuclear bomber base. The Royal Navy, reduced to a handful of cruisers and destroyers, had surrendered its *mare nostrum* to the United States. The Royal Air Force had no atom bombs to drop.

Bevin had reasons for urging counter-attack, and doing so whilst Acheson was by his side. Six days before the Council meeting, four years before the officially predicted date, Russia exploded an atom bomb. Bevin knew that it would be three years before Britain could do likewise. British and American scientists had calculated that Russia could well explode a device three years after the end of the war. Western intelligence services had provided nothing by way of accurate forecast. An urgent need existed not only for America and Britain to act as one in opposing Stalin, but for their intelligence services to do so also. A joint operation in the Balkans would enable both objectives to be attained. Bevin's argument can be criticised on strategic grounds: recourse to clandestine operations was not an effective substitute for military forces. But Bevin's case for co-operation between SIS and CIA begged the question of how this was to be achieved, given the great differences in outlook and approach between the two services.

In 1946 and 1947 Attlee and Truman established a liaison system on intelligence. SIS and the Central Intelligence Group, the post-war successor to the Office of Strategic Services, exchanged liaison officers. But co-operation on scientific intelligence was low on the agenda. The McMahon Act was partial explanation; the FBI (and the Royal Canadian Mounted Police) interrogation in September 1945 of Igor Gouzenko, a defector from the Russian Embassy in Ottawa, also increased American suspicions that security procedures in Britain might need examination. MI5's seeming indifference to Gouzenko and a palpable unwillingness to put its own house in order were hardly a prescription for Anglo-American co-operation on intelligence and security issues. Gouzenko's defection not only revealed treachery by British atomic scientists but, to American eyes, a British Security Service whose members, like those of the wartime SIS, were neither intelligent nor secure. American suspicions were well founded; over thirty years later, the scale of treachery and insecurity in the war-time and immediate post-war MI5 continues to be revealed. *Double-X* has been forgotten; the memory of treachery endures.

From the closing days of the war some fundamental differences of approach had developed between British and American intelligence and special operations services. Collectively, and aside from frequently close personal relations, the British thought the Americans politically inept, and bureaucratic in their determination to separate clearly intelligence acquisition, counter-intelligence, and special operations. Almost without exception, and despite much admiration for British achievements and many attempts by the 'Knights Templars' of OSS to emulate the 'we'll do it, what is it?' style of SOE, the Americans were critical of Whitehall ways and, above all, ineradicably convinced that the three roles Menzies and Gubbins appeared to have jumbled together were distinctively different, and should be kept so. Behind these disagreements and contradictions lay the deep shadow of treachery from which, in those days of American innocents abroad, their society was almost immune.

Illusions about power in Whitehall were such that little detailed thought was given to SIS as an instrument of policy, despite Eden's 1944 Paper, and the presumed need for greater reliance on covert activities in place of demonstrable military strength. SIS made a few trifling administrative changes; the personnel pack was shuffled in order to promote the ambitious (Philby above all) and remove critics. No root and branch reorganisation was considered or attempted. The 'robber barons' – directors under 'C', whose responsibilities were territorial, not functional – remained in place. A kind of institutional, and national, conceit was a more telling indication of decline than the treachery which ate into SIS and MI5, and of which perceptive and antagonistic intelligence officers in Washington became unhappily aware. Bevin's resolute determination to stop Stalin in his tracks cleared no decks or desks, physical or figurative, in 55 Broadway. Only Menzies had access, not just to Attlee but to Bevin also. Menzies alone, as he rode up and down alone in the creaking Broadway lifts, had the wider picture. That a Foreign Secretary should oppose communism was to be expected. That meeting the requirement to oppose by robust methods also demanded careful thought about men never crossed Menzies's mind. The robber barons, safeguarding their territorial perquisites and responsible for all tasks within them, were certainly immune from introspection about organisation and methods.

It has been well said by a former member of the CIA that counter-intelligence is 'the hard core and essential resource of any intelligence service, for its primary purpose is to assist in guarding the nation's diplomatic and military secrets, including its own intelligence operations'. Yet this definition, admirable on the blackboard, is capable of different interpretations. In Broadway, between 1945 and 1949 – and for long afterwards – the requirements of earlier times in general and the Second World War in particular held good. Counter-intelligence was still regarded primarily a hostile operation in support of acquisition, not as an adjunct to the post-war SOE which lurked within SIS. Broadway's counter-intelligence sections were, in practice, subordinate to the regional directors, whose requirement to produce material dominated all other considerations. *Penetration* of an enemy – or any other foreign – intelligence organisation was a secondary requirement, a factor which enabled Philby to be a traitor secure from detection for many years. That Philby was for a time responsible for Communist bloc counter-intelligence operations in SIS merely adds irony to treachery and the British establishment's rooted belief that 'everyone knew everyone else, everyone knew where everything was, and everything and everyone not so known was not worth knowing'.[17]

Ultra and wartime deception organisations compounded the problem inside SIS of clearly defining and efficiently co-ordinating different intelligence tasks. Ultra appeared to diminish the value of raw intelligence acquired from agents, a trend which developed still further when interception of signals traffic by electronic means became a major requirement for all Western and communist intelligence services. Menzies, whatever his other preoccupations, made sure that SIS took 'Sigint' (signals intelligence) firmly within its grasp, and did so by consolidating control of Government Communications Headquarters. Deception organisation and operations, however, raised questions about which British Service was best fitted to conduct counter-intelligence. The Special Political Action Group and Operations Branch were SOE's legacy to SIS. Menzies was overlord of this 'department store'; he was unable to reorganise SIS so that it became an intelligence supermarket. Above all, SOE's continued grip in Balkan and Greek affairs in the last two years of the war meant that the post-war SIS emphasis in this area concentrated on 'counter-revolutionary' activities, where something is planned to happen at a given time. By contrast, counter-intelligence is an acid, eating into the enemy's vitals, causing collapse – sometimes – at a moment not always easy to predict.

Reflective men in Broadway saw dangers in working for a department store; so did some in the embryonic CIA. Post-war entrants to SIS – largely from SOE – found themselves being trained, rather haphazardly, for tasks ranging from agent running on classic intelligence lines to planning 'an opposed river crossing' as so many had done in the war. The club life in London was refreshed by visits to Fort Blockhouse, near Portsmouth, to practise these para-military arts. The war years left their mark. We see not so much the men from the bucket shop as, in Cyril Connolly's mocking and knowledgeable words: 'Brigadier Brilliant, DSO, FRS, the famous historian, with boyish grin and cold blue eyes, seconded now for special duties. With long stride and hunched shoulders, untidy, chain-smoking, he talks – walks and talks – while the whole devilish simplicity of his plan unfolds and the men from MI This and MI That, SIS and SOE listen dumbfounded. "My God, Brilliant, I believe you're right – it could be done", said the quiet-voiced man with greying hair. The Brigadier looked at his watch and a chilled blue eye fixed the Chief of the Secret Service. "At this moment, Sir," and there was pack-ice in his voice, "my chaps are doing it".'[18] Guerrilla war found its justification in so-called peace; its gallant practitioners, bred by John Buchan out of William Henty, were considered absurd by the longer heads in SIS. The times were against the professionals.

The post-war SIS enabled Philby to get away with murder. He moved easily about the department store, a senior manager who had reached the top. By contrast, the post-war organisation of American intelligence was not only based on the separation of powers, but on a conviction, more cultural than political, that professionals should operate within clearly defined structures. Acquiring intelligence was legitimate; assessing such intelligence – a task which SIS was not, and is not, required to perform – was essential. Counter-intelligence was an extension of foreign policy, particularly in the strengthening of a friendly government or the weakening of a hostile one. By contrast, special operations – or what came to be called by its critics inside and beyond CIA 'dirty tricks' – was something so essentially un-American that it should either be foresworn or given direct Presidential authority. In July 1947, when the CIA and the National Security Council were established, these various roles were formally separated within the Agency. In June 1948 the 'Office of Policy Co-ordination' – a euphemism worthy of Whitehall – was given responsibility for special operations. Ex-members of the OSS who had fought an irregular war on the ground, men like William Colby, Frank Wisner, Richard Bissell, and Frank Lindsay, were natural candidates for service in OPC.

OSS was officially disbanded in 1946. But, from 1945 onwards, and ostensibly under War Department control and cover, counter-intelligence operations were mounted by OSS personnel which ranked in importance with support for the right kind of resistance movements. The Director of OSS, General William Donovan, was an Irish-American of genuine and pronounced liberal sympathies. Nevertheless, OSS collectively grasped that post-war governments in Western Europe might cause as much trouble to America as those in Stalin's empire. By methods far simpler and cruder than

SOE in Western Europe had attempted, OSS's counter-intelligence section (the Office of Special Operations) in which James Angleton and Richard Helms soon achieved distinction, set to work bribing parties and politicians to toe the line. Italy received the most careful attention, acquiring 'centre-right' governments for decades as a result. By 1947, the CIA was looking further afield, in Eastern Europe and Russia. Refugees from Stalin who had fled to the West but were willing to return clandestinely were placed at possible points of future uprising. These operations were seen in terms of military rather than political counter-intelligence. But these agents, these assets, were in place. Their job was to sit tight, listen, and report, not stir things up.

On paper, the distinctions between special operations and counter-intelligence were clear enough. Clashes of personality and strong differences of opinion ensured that, in practice, the new American intelligence agency had problems akin to SIS. One result of these clashes was that the acquisition of raw intelligence from human sources – not necessarily from agents – became a matter of dispute between CIA and the State Department. The latter, which had unwillingly acquired the Research and Analysis Unit (responsible for acquisition and assessment) from OSS, took a sombre view of CIA's future role and a far from cordial one about the advent of the National Security Council. The real point at issue in 1947, when the CIA was established to fight a cold war which the Administration publicly refused to recognise, was that the NSC knew far more about this un-American organisation than the State Department. The constitutional relationship between the NSC and the CIA virtually ensured that whoever ran the CIA would have direct access to the President. The CIA 'was an openly acknowledged arm of the executive branch of the government, although, of course, it had many duties of a secret nature. President Truman saw to it that the new agency was equipped to support our government's effort to meet communist tactics of "coercion, subterfuge, and political infiltration".'[19]

This statement by Allen Dulles, the coldest warrior of them all, conceals the more important fact that in June 1948 the Office of Policy Co-ordination was given a direct line to the President via the NSC and, specifically by a directive which said: 'Operations must be so planned and conducted that any United States Government responsibility for them is not evident to unauthorised persons, and if uncovered the United States Government can plausibly disclaim responsibility for them.' The directive further said that such covert operations should extend to 'sabotage, subversion, and assistance to underground resistance groups'. The 1947 National Security Act, in putting the CIA in direct and continuous contact with the NSC, and the June 1948 directive, by giving the OPC virtual *carte blanche*, had ensured that separation of powers did not preclude dirty tricks. Un-American activities were, specifically and secretly, approved. Intentions and methods were complemented by a specific objective for the OPC to defeat: 'the vicious and covert activities of the USSR, its satellite countries and communist groups.'[20]

The Albanian operation was, therefore, not merely Bevin's and Acheson's resort to SIS and CIA as instruments for the execution of a major foreign policy decision; the operation reflected the conviction, at various levels, that the cold war would be fought in the shadows, by men with guns in their hands. When the NATO Council gathered round the State Department table on 5 September 1949 Bevin and Acheson knew that their arguments about ridding Albania of Enver Hoxha reflected decisions which had been taken several months earlier. The statements which Bevin and Acheson made are nevertheless important. A military alliance committed to the defence of Western Europe was about to approve an operation on the flanks, not the central front. The operation would be outside the NATO area. Churchill's strategic arguments were to receive a belated vindication. Acheson, however, although in agreement with Bevin on the overall objective, was already beginning to have doubts about method.

The outcome of the Greek civil war was still uncertain. This factor was not decisive, least of all to Acheson. Bevin stated bluntly that it was Albania's communist government as such which was the target. He said that a decision must be taken by the Council 'to weaken the position of the present Soviet dominated regime in Albania and, in connection with a possible revolt seek, as an immediate priority objective, to eliminate Soviet control'. The Council, perhaps alarmed at intelligence of the Soviet presence in Albania – 1,500 'advisers' and 4,000 'technicians' to train an army of 25,000; plans to develop Valona as a submarine base – and reassured by the top secret classification given to its deliberations, agreed. What the Canadian, French, Belgian, Dutch, and Danish delegates did not know was that, as Bevin said in subsequent restricted meetings, 'Britain had followed a policy of unrelenting hostility to the Hoxha Government'. Bevin made it quite clear that he intended to do more than merely warn Stalin not to go too far. Bevin asked: 'Are there any kings around that could be put in?'[21] There was such a king of Albania, Zog. Julian Amery, a former member of SOE who had fought in Albania had already contacted Zog in Alexandria.

The Albanian operation had been described in various quarters as SIS and CIA playing games. In truth, SOE – and the Great Game – were responsible. Colin Gubbins, whose 'unusually clear perception of communism' only reinforced his opposition to it, certainly took a hand, although retired. He did so at Menzies's behest, who in early 1949 received his orders from Bevin and Brook. Ostensibly, the NATO Council had agreed to a counter-revolutionary operation. In fact, Bevin had virtually imposed the decision on minor allies who were ignorant of the details and on a major ally who acquiesced in the principle. SIS was thus left to start planning an operation for which it was unsuited. Despite the survival of SOE methods and personnel in SIS, there were political factors in the Balkans' situation and in Anglo-American relations which Menzies was unfitted to handle. Ironically, the key political factor was again Tito. In 1949 Bevin said of Tito: 'He's a bastard, but he's our bastard'.

Bevin was nevertheless loth to involve Tito in the Albanian operation, and there were good grounds for this attitude. Bevin's overtures to Tito were always cautious. Acheson, by contrast, and ignoring in 1949 earlier American phobias about Tito, was anxious to build him up as a Western ally in all but name. Comparable discord about operational objectives and methods bred misunderstandings between Washington and London. But behind the policy decision about Albania lay a more fundamental disagreement. Bevin – who confined knowledge of both decision and execution to Attlee, Hugh Dalton and the select few in Whitehall – wanted above all to bring Stalin to the negotiating table, to say to him what, two years earlier, he had said to Molotov. Bevin, for all his opposition to Stalin, wanted to reduce tension in Europe, not perpetuate it. Acheson had decided that Orwell's state of perpetual war demanded a great deal more than a policy of mere containment. By 1949 America was fighting the cold war in earnest.

Acheson's policy was based on the visible expression of American military strength. Negotiation with Stalin could only be from a position of strength. Bevin hoped that counter-revolution in Albania would not only bring Stalin to the negotiating table but also provide an economical way of preserving Britain's role as a major power. Acheson agreed with the Chiefs of Staff in Washington, who argued that any place or country which came within the American sway should be a base for ships and aircraft. Sea and air power combined was more formidable in its mobility and destructive capacity than garrisons of troops. The latter, in any case, were a political liability, not a strategic asset. Garrisons aroused local hostility rather than support. Such, at all events, was the American belief. In 1949 the atomic bomb already dominated American strategic thought; Russia's explosion strengthened America's determination to keep one jump ahead. A hydrogen bomb was to be the answer. The star of airmen like Curtis Le May – who had burned Japan's cities to the ground and who advocated breaking the Berlin blockade by bombing Russian forces in East Germany – was rising. 'Massive retaliation' was on the way. Greece and Albania offered the prospect of bases for naval and air forces which could directly threaten Russia's cities.

Greece was the focal point of the Albanian operation in both political and tactical terms. Despite Bevin's hopes for Albania, the Foreign Office and the British Chiefs of Staff knew that Greece remained a difficult proposition politically and militarily. Van Fleet's belief that cash would buy victory was not shared in London. Even assuming such a victory, the Foreign Office did not believe that a Greek Government which triumphed in the Civil War would necessarily remain subservient to British political designs and American strategic requirements. Greece consumed most of Julian Amery's time in 1949 when he set off to promote Albanian revolt. Airfields in Greece provided the forward positions in the attempt to get rid of Hoxha. Withdrawal of Hoxha's support for Greek communists in 1950 – after his Minister of the Interior, General Mehmet Sheha, had captured and killed the last of the brave men parachuted in – gave some comfort to those who planned the operation and believed, irrationally, in its feasibility.

Amery was not chosen by Menzies and Gubbins mainly because of his wartime record and connections. There were plenty of men who had fought in Albania, who had either returned to civilian life or were serving as regular soldiers. The most professionally competent of them, however, former members of the disbanded reconnaissance unit, the Long Range Desert Group, were either indifferent or sceptical about counter-revolution. Amery was available, and he was committed. An early speech in the House of Commons summarised his enduring convictions: 'It must be the task of statesmanship, while American atomic supremacy persists, to obtain from Russia a settlement which will ensure its retreat behind the Curzon line, and the breaking of the monopoly of power by the Communist parties in the countries of Eastern Europe.'[22]

These sentiments, expressed by the son of Leo Amery (a former Conservative Cabinet Minister, a Zionist – and ardent imperialist) cloaked a strong, occasional passionate belief that the retreat in question would only take place if right wing government in Eastern Europe replaced communist regimes. Amery was the obvious choice – to Gubbins and Menzies. When Amery set off in the spring of 1949 for a reconnaissance, of which Yanina, near the Greek-Albanian border, was the operational objective, he was convinced that he knew where to find the men who would raise the flag of revolt. SIS ensured that enough funds were available to strengthen Amery's hand.

Amery and another ex-SOE member with Albanian experience, Billy McLean, later to become Conservative MP for Inverness, were pretty sure that Zog would not do. Amery and McLean shared with Aubrey Herbert a belief in the Rob Roy virtues of tribal leaders; they already had their eye on Abas Kupi, with whom they had served. Amery's reasoning was that Zog, who had won his crown in the 1920s by dividing before ruling the tribes, was no longer acceptable to men who had fought Italians, Germans, and communists of their own race. Zog had fled from Albania during the 1939 Italian invasion. In 1949 he was living comfortably in exile, appropriately enough in Alexandria, that Levantine home of lost causes. Amery, for all that he saw large issues in terms of right and left, was well aware that the counter-revolution must have a leader who gave lip-service to social democracy.

Amery's notion about Zog was right. He was approached, as a matter of form. He gave the counter-revolution his blessing; continued to regard himself as king – over the water; but declined to raise his standard in the Albanian heather. The Foreign Office during the war had regarded Zog as 'a valuable pawn'; Bevin appeared to think so also. But when Churchill had asked Eden 'which side are we on?', the latter had plumped for Kupi. He was, on paper, SOE's man. Others, above all the Long Range Desert Group – who did more fighting in Albania than SOE, in gorier circumstances of ambush and bitter German reprisal – had a poor view of Kupi. David Lloyd Owen, LRDG's Commander, believed 'Kupi's day was nearly over'. He was 'an inveterate royalist', but he was playing his own, tribal, game. His preference for fighting communists rather than Germans at the precise moment in 1944 when a major deception scheme against the former was being hatched had resulted in SOE eventually denying him arms.

Amery was not repelled by these factors. He believed that Kupi had the necessary qualifications for counter-revolution: political adroitness; tribal backing; royalist sentiments – which might come in useful at a later stage; some military skills, derived from his days in Zog's army. Kupi had defeated the Italians at Durazzo in 1939. He had at least earned the right to raise the flag. Amery found Kupi in Istanbul – SOE had initially run him from this Cairo outstation – and put the proposition direct. Kupi, accompanied by Midhat Frasheri, Nuci Kotta, Zef Pali, and Said Kryeziv, responded with a counter-proposal as temporising as Zog's. Yes, they would come to London, by way of Paris. Yes, they would think it over there. No, they would not go further until they saw how the land lay. With the exception of Kryeziv, Kupi's compatriots were politicians, not fighting men. Frasheri, indeed, had been Zog's Prime Minister before the war and President of the Council of Regency when the king fled.

Before returning to London with this quintet of quasi counter-revolutionaries, Amery had other work to do. He had to square the Greek Government; on the premise that something more than a reconnaissance in force was intended when the Free Albanians – as by August, they started to call themselves – returned to their homeland, locations were needed for recruiting and operational planning. Amery chose Rome, where SIS operated a large and active station, for the latter, Malta for the former. The immediate problem, however, was embedded in Athenian politics. Papagos, the Commander-in-Chief, and the most important man in the country after Van Fleet, ran the war from Athens. Subject to what Van Fleet might say, Papagos insisted that the frontiers with Albania and Yugoslavia and the areas behind them were closed to visitors. Athenian politics, eternally divisive, united over territorial demands on Southern Albania and Macedonian Yugoslavia. An unnamed, unknown pseudo-military mission fossicking about in the north would, to much Athenian opinion, increase rather than diminish the degree of Albanian and Yugoslav support for communist guerrillas and their 'Greek Democratic Army'. Clearing the frontier and, subsequently, arguing about territorial claims were Papagos's priorities and, in his view, perquisites.

Acheson was wrong when he minuted on 15 August: 'the Greek Government views very favourably the planned establishment of the Albanian National Committee in exile.'

Yet Amery had no choice but to get at least the tacit support of the Greek Government. The reason lay in the Yugoslav factor, or one aspect of it. Amery believed that clandestine operations directed at Hoxha would lead to a major uprising. The success of this uprising would depend on the million odd Albanians living in the Yugoslav Kosovo region. At the right time they would cross the frontier to take Hoxha in the rear. Amery nevertheless accepted the French intelligence appreciation from its Embassy in Tirana (the solitary example of Western diplomatic relations with Hoxha's government) that although 'the Albanian population as a whole was largely hostile to the regime and increasingly anti-Russian, they are under complete control and no dissident or resistance movements exist except potentially'. Success therefore depended on a first phase reconnaissance – largely in order to acquire operational intelligence; and a second phase uprising, with the main effort coming from Yugoslavia.

Amery knew that Tito would be violently opposed to such a move if it was planned by Western clandestine agencies, above all if they started organising dissident Albanians on Yugoslav soil. All sources, including the British and American embassies in Belgrade, stressed that Tito's moves towards the West would be damaged if he suspected that what he regarded as a prize for a clean break with Moscow, the reversion of a non-Stalinist Albania, was taken from his grasp. Fitzroy Maclean, Bevin's go-between with Tito, was emphatic on these points. These pros and cons were not lost on Amery. Tito's Yugoslavia – Kupi's manpower reservoir – would have to wait. The initial concentration of effort must be on Greece. A successful first phase would increase the chances of a positive reaction from Albanians in Yugoslavia. If Amery had known that Bevin, by the time of the NATO Council meeting, was prepared to quarrel with Tito if necessary over the Albanian issue, he might have paid less attention to Greece. As it was, he took soundings there. The British Embassy in Athens and, at this stage, the Station Officer, were kept in the dark. Amery went about his business, cultivating opposition politicians, engaging in just the kind of activities – totally serious in purpose, yet marked by a Balkan touch of fantasy – for which his wartime experiences had fitted him all too well. Eventually Amery's main contact told him that both opposition and government had been sounded. If, when Amery returned to his hotel room he found twelve bottles of brandy, all was well. Papagos would also have seen that whatever was in the wind indicated bigger things than he could control. But if Amery found only one bottle – he had better go home and stick to British politics.

On the night in question Amery returned with hope – and doubt. But there were the twelve bottles. If not ready for action this day, Amery could leave Athens, make arrangements in Rome – which presented no problems – and return to London. His Albanian charges had meanwhile formalised their 'Free Albanian Committee', in Paris. Realising that these were hardly the men to go on to the mountain with, Menzies and Amery made the best of a bad job. Kupi and his colleagues were encouraged to hold a press conference in London to match that in Paris. Acheson's minute, read between the lines, meant that Papagos had decided to look the other way. Behind the cover of almost legitimate political protest, Kupi was installed in the Berkeley hotel – the manager, a former member of SOE, thus providing something rather luxurious by way of a safe house – shortly afterwards being sent to Amery's house in the country. There, SIS started to question him about what he proposed to do. The answers were not encouraging. He would return to Albania, but on the heels, not in the van of the liberators.

At this point, several people sat down to plan and to argue. Amery and McLean had done their work. Planners and operational people were needed now, not missionaries and politicians. Menzies told nobody in Broadway that Bevin had ordered Hoxha's destruction, few that Amery was playing that hero of Edwardian, Ruritanian romance, Rudolph Rassendyll. Menzies had no choice, however, but to discuss operational details with the Directors. The Vienna regional station and others to south and east were put in the picture, such as it was. Even if Kupi had been ready and willing to risk his neck again, the whole plan depended on requests to the Admiralty and War Office for equipment and support, and on liaison with the CIA for the recruitment of Albanians who were willing to take a night journey to their homeland.

Once the Whitehall system started to creak into action eyebrows were raised and lips were pursed. SIS was *not* SOE. The Foreign Office Adviser in SIS (a middle rank official who does a tour there, sees even most secret files and acts as a kind of bellwether for what seems feasible or not in terms of 'wider policy considerations') was strongly opposed. Menzies's recruitment of

Amery and McLean, plus Gubbins's backstairs role, aroused strong protest once identities were disclosed. All to no avail. A serving soldier, David Smiley, another old Albanian hand with entrenched views on politics, was given command of the planning staff. A brigadier from the War Office was despatched to Washington and then to Malta to organise training. The Chiefs of Staff muttered, but were told that wider considerations did prevail.

Recruitment of Albanians concentrated not only on the area around Boston, where many exiles lived, but on displaced persons camps in West Germany. Proposals were made for raising a parachute battalion from this flotsam. The Rome and Athens SIS Stations began to find additional safe houses. Both Station Commanders had served with Amery in Albania. Pilots and navigators to crew unmarked DC3s were found from former Polish Air Force personnel living in Britain. The Royal Navy at Malta was given responsibility for landings from the sea. The Mediterranean Fleet had not forgotten 22 October 1946 when HMS *Saumerez* and HMS *Volage* had been mined in the Corfu Channel. Forty-four men had been killed. The British Government alleged that the mines had been laid by Albanian vessels. The International Court of Justice agreed. Hoxha ignored the judgment. No compensation was paid. By the time of the NATO Council meeting several hundred people were involved in planning and training for the operation.

Clandestine and irregular operations can be harder to cancel or amend than the orthodox and overt kind. The aim, rarely defined with military precision and frequently given verbally, becomes confused, merging into the assertion that bandits and cat burglars are more suitable for toppling totalitarian regimes than patient diplomacy and the maintenance of spheres of interest by economic or military strength. The methods rely on those whose talent for deception is not necessarily confined to the task in hand. Security is harder to maintain when secrets matter. In Washington, after the 5 September NATO meeting, State Department, CIA, and British Embassy officials attempted to keep a strange venture within the bounds of feasibility. Lord Jellicoe and Philby represented the Embassy. Jellicoe had served with the Special Boat Service in the Aegean during the war. Philby, as a senior SIS officer with particular responsibilities for liaison with the CIA, was there as a matter of course. Jellicoe, one of nature's adventurers, raised no eyebrows. Philby had more important matters on his mind. His published account is substantially inaccurate on details. His treachery compounded, it did not cause failure.

The American side was more varied and interesting. The State Department man, Robert Joyce, said little. His OSS career had been at headquarters rather than in the field. He knew the Balkan scene; disliked what he saw. The CIA's Frank Lindsay had much to say and the authority to say it. He had been OSS's Senior Staff Officer at Tito's headquarters; service in the field had led to the rare award of a British Military Cross. Lindsay knew and respected Fitzroy Maclean. The sentiment was mutual. Lindsay had worked with Byrnes, and attended the first post-war four-power meetings. As Chief Political Adviser to General Sir Terence Airey in Trieste thereafter Lindsay had grasped that Tito was the man for the West to back. Before Tito openly broke with Stalin, he sent his foreign minister, Prima Bebler, to Washington. The Yugoslav Ambassador to the United Nations was a war-time comrade of Lindsay. In Lindsay's Georgetown house, plans were made to run arms to a Yugoslavia which, arguably, was threatened by Russian invasion. By the time Lindsay got to work on the Albanian operation, five shiploads of arms had been sent covertly by the American Government to a dictator whose chances of survival from Stalin looked slim.

Lindsay was unhappy about the aims and methods of raising the Social Democrat flag in Albania. His views were shared by Fitzroy Maclean, Menzies's Directors, and two colleagues who were beginning to argue a case for counter-intelligence as the CIA's central task. Within the Agency Dick Helms, committed to the acquisition of intelligence, disliked 'all this scampering about'. James Angleton, a man of the extreme right, regarded Tito as the reason for the 'unforgivable' desertion of Mihailovic, and saw no point in backing him, indirectly or otherwise. But Angleton's strongest objection to the Albanian operation was that it put at risk CIA's agents in place. Helms and Angleton realised, however, that the CIA had not been established for its members to fight each other. The period of serious dispute and rivalry lay in the next decade. In any case, the Balkan operation's momentum, its labyrinth of political manoeuvres by Kupi and its planning complexities throughout the Mediterranean would have required an order to stop from Acheson – and Bevin. If Truman and Congress had known, if the Press had got the story, it is probable that men's lives would have been saved. In 1949 even the American fourth estate ignored dirty tricks.

Concerted opposition by Lindsay, Helms, and Angleton might have succeeded. Their colleague Frank Wisner, as OPC's Director, ensured that the operation ramified; a check might be imposed here and there, but Wisner was both ambitious and devious. Many then saw Wisner as the CIA's white hope. 'A Southerner with money; with a facile intelligence and a broad interest in world affairs. He wanted to do things; he even fancied he would have something of a role in the very formation of American foreign policy.'[23] Angleton, 'tall, thin, unapproachable',[24] shared Wisner's ultra right-wing views; where they split was on method. Wisner believed blowing up Hoxha would be as effective as blowing up trains; Angleton, whose innate gifts as an intelligence officer were weakened by an almost morbid suspicion of those different from him in temperament and background, hoped to see the entire communist system weakened by internal contradictions and sapped by counter-intelligence.

Wisner had served with OSS in Rumania. There, in 1945, he had seen that 'a broad popular feeling of support for the monarchy had developed spontaneously. As evidence of this loyalty, people wore badges with the royal coat of arms. Communist thugs began systematically beating up people wearing the monarchist symbol whom they were able to catch alone in back streets after dark. There was no reaction from the population other than to stop wearing these pins when they were alone at night. Thus emboldened, the communists became more aggressive until they beat up, in broad daylight and in the open streets, those who still wore the monarchist pins. Finally the pins were driven completely from the streets; the will of the people had been broken and the first step in the communist takeover had been accomplished.'[25]

Wisner did not forget his experience. By 1949 he wanted counter-revolution, not containment. Recruitment of ex-OSS types who had a comparably robust approach took place as antidote to the doubts and hesitations now seeping down from the higher levels. On 21 September the State Department summarised objectives and indicated methods. 'The short range United States objectives in Albania are the weakening and eventual elimination of the Soviet dominated Hoxha regime; and the denial to the Soviets of military rights and bases. Action to attain these foregoing objectives should be primarily concerned with pressure on Yugoslavia and Greece to ignore Albania.'[26] The Chiefs of Staff, expressing renewed interest and increased concern about Valona, agreed with this summary. At the higher American levels the theory was developing that if Tito was brought to the Western negotiating table by pledges of support he could be told to take the necessary hint over Albania. Hoxha should be left on the vine for others to pluck.

It was too late for such subtleties. The men on the ground were training brave but simple Albanians to parachute. Wisner's particular OPC colleagues Kim Roosevelt and Richard Bissell had earlier approved Lindsay's choice of Michael Burke to work with David Smiley in Malta. Burke had served with OSS in France and the Balkans, adapting to parachuting, reverting to small boat operations with ease. He liked doing things. Lindsay, however, had also picked Burke because, behind his taste for danger was a reflective outlook on men and events. Lindsay, half aware that failure was stalking the operation, wanted a man who could save something from the wreckage. Lindsay asked Burke to accept a short term assignment, and write a detailed report when the operation was over. Moonless nights at the end of November would define the time for the first phase to start. By March 1950 it was hoped that all would be in train for a national uprising. Burke, in his own words, 'divided between curiosity, loyalty, and scepticism', agreed to serve.

The five months' period suggests that, by mid-October, a compromise had been worked out between State Department doubts and OPC convictions. The State Department, looking down the road, saw endless trouble. Wisner assured Joyce that the operation was 'a clinical experiment to see whether larger rollback operations would be feasible elsewhere'. Such a compromise, however, had little bearing on the situation confronting Burke. Using his cover as a film executive – Warner Brothers had agreed to release him – for investigating Italian and Greek locations, Burke found the SIS Station Officers in Rome and Athens cheerfully disposed to help. Unlike Acheson, Bevin had delegated. That, for the moment, was the end of the affair. A former OSS officer, Howard Fuller, was loaned to Burke once he established himself in Athens. Burke had few doubts about Malta; the operation might be cock-eyed, but it would be executed professionally. Parachuting Albanian exiles blind was another matter.

The root of the trouble was shortage of time, compounded by lack of trained Albanians. Even if these problems could have been overcome, inadequate equipment signalled disaster. The first phase required the use of Greek airfields so that the three-man parties could be flown in with the objective of recruiting agents and acquiring operational intelligence. Given that the parties were then to make their way to Yanina on foot, communications might seem relatively unimportant. The key factor was that Burke and Smiley had to know what kind of reception awaited the parties. If poor, wait and see; if good, increase the drops and advance the date of phase two.

Endless discussions took place on communications. Vienna was asked to help; a dreary search took place for sets still in working order after four years in store. Finally, sheer necessity produced an expedient almost guaranteed to fail. Communication would be ground to air. The parties would call up the DC3 navigators and summarise their reception. The crews of the DC3s were willing to take the risk of hanging about in Albania's hostile sky. Late in November the first of some sixty Albanians went in. Not a single message came back, even although Radowsky's DC3s 'bloody nearly flew down the main streets of Tirana' hoping to pick one up. A few men from the Malta parties got through to Yanina some weeks later, enough of them, with encouraging reports, to send others to their death. In March 1950, the first phase being marked by increasing casualties, SIS and CIA cried quits. Not only Angleton and Helms had lost their assets. Aided by Philby's treachery – to SIS rather than Britain – Menzies had suffered a loss comparable to Sinclair in 1939. Bevin's attempt at power by proxy had failed.

The aftermath is curious in its variety of reactions. Amery claimed that Hoxha had been given a shock. Certainly Albanian support for the Greek communists had ended by mid-1950. Bevin kept his own counsel, as did Menzies. Albania's ten million odd pounds in gold, seized at the end of the war, remained in the Bank of England. It is there today. Hoxha remains as Albania's dictator. Mehmet Shehu committed suicide in December 1981. He had a lot of blood on his hands. Smiley went back to proper – and irregular – soldiering. Burke's harsh report stressed that the political requirement could only have been met by a major military operation. Lindsay agreed. Others in CIA did not. Wisner apologised to Philby: 'We'll get it right next time.' Allen Dulles said: 'At least we're getting the kind of experience we need for the next war.' Agents continued to be sent into Albania in ones and twos. Not until the 1956 Hungarian uprising was crushed by Russian tanks did CIA and SIS accept that clandestine operations in the Balkans were counter-productive. But in 1956 another British Foreign Secretary – turned Prime Minister – tried his hand at the game.

4 · THE LAST TEMPTATION: SUEZ 1956

I · *Eden as Foreign Secretary 1951–5*

'. . . We assume that our future will be one of a piece with our past and that we shall continue as a Great Power. What is noteworthy is the way we take this for granted. It is not a belief arrived at after reflection by a conscious decision. It is part of the habit and furniture of our minds: a principle so much one with our outlook and character that it determines the way we act without emerging itself into clear consciousness.'

SIR OLIVER FRANKS,
British Ambassador to Washington,
1948 to 1952 – speaking
in November 1954

'My world began in war. It has been spent in war, its preparation and its aftermath.'[1] Anthony Eden invoked Mars in these words two years after his career had been ended by the total collapse of his imperial policy as a result of the Suez operation in November 1956. Invocation can be dangerous. Eden's is misleading, although unwittingly it gives us a clue to his proud and solitary character. Certainly Eden's youth was marred and marked by his gallant service in the Flanders trenches – an experience from which he never recovered – but he played no part in preparing Britain for the Second World War, nor did he turn his energies into constructive fields after 1945.

Eden's resignation as Foreign Secretary in February 1938 strengthened parliamentary opposition to Neville Chamberlain as Prime Minister, which culminated in his virtual dismissal by the House of Commons in May 1940. Winston Churchill's belated achievement of the prize which he had always sought owed something to Eden's resignation two years earlier. But Eden was careful not to oppose Chamberlain in the House. The rearmament programme, begun in 1936 and well into its stride by 1939, owed more to Whitehall than Westminster. Airmen forgotten today, and scientists like Tizard, were the architects of rearmament; the critics of appeasement, Churchill excepted, rarely bothered to discuss Britain's defences against Hitler. In 1945 Eden went into Opposition with, as he admits in his memoirs, a sense of frustration, indeed of deprivation. Eden nowhere said so, but it is possible that a Conservative victory in 1945 could have enabled him to become Prime Minister within a few years. If Churchill had continued in office, his exhausted body might well have forced him to retire.

Eden had to wait a full decade before succeeding Churchill. Although only fifty-eight in 1955, Eden was seriously ill and quite unsuited on several counts to be Prime Minister. A constitution from childhood of dangerous frailty periodically caused collapses from physical exhaustion. In the early 1950s, whilst Foreign

Secretary and Deputy Prime Minister, Eden had three serious operations, to remove his gall bladder and cure blockages in his bile duct. All the operations failed. Temporary bouts of apparent good health were followed by prostrating sickness. Eden's temperament, one of dangerous sensitivity to criticism or opposition, produced crises of nerves. Officials would be abused verbally or in writing in terms which suggested that the debonair good looks and charm were a façade. Behind was a man who feared to be called, or thought a failure. 'Eden simply had no skin', said one who saw him daily throughout the Suez crisis.

Eden's tragedy, his succumbing to the temptation of the illusion of power, thus had its origins in personal characteristics. He lacked Churchill's magnanimity and resilience, his sense that personal failure, depression, even rejection could be subsumed in work, in an earthy vision of life lived at many levels in an English society of long descent. Apart from worrying about the state of the world, Eden was forced to concentrate on domestic issues between 1945 and 1951. He disliked the House of Commons, except when at the despatch box and had few real friends there. Churchill, despite repeated strokes and the sudden arrival of old age, wrote a masterful, subjective history of his finest years. After October 1951, when Churchill 'crawled back into No. 10 Downing Street', Eden had to endure four more years as Churchill's heir, knowing that the old man feared to retire and see the country led by one who had never learned the rough and tumble of English politics. 'Anthony wants it so much', said Churchill on the eve of his resignation in April 1955.[2] But he had denied the prize to his heir. It is probable that by the time Eden became Prime Minister he no longer did want it, particularly. One of his first acts as Prime Minister was to throw into a corner of the Cabinet Room a notice Churchill had put on the table in 1940. 'We are not interested in the possibilities of defeat: they do not exist.' Queen Victoria's characteristic reaction to 'Black Week' in the South African War, which had so heartened Churchill, made no appeal to Eden.

The relationship between Churchill and Eden has usually been presented in terms of elder statesman and protégé. This view requires amendment. It should be remembered that Eden became Foreign Secretary in 1935, aged thirty-eight, at a time when Churchill, at sixty-one and with unique political experience, was seen by many as a brilliant failure. Eden was on the way up; Churchill, it seemed, on the way out. When they joined forces on the outbreak of war, no basis for mutual understanding had been established. Throughout the war Eden's relationship with Churchill was made more ambiguous and complex by the roles imposed on them. Churchill knew that to preserve the illusion of power ultimate dependence on America must form the cornerstone of all his policies. From the Anglo-American invasion of French North Africa in November 1942 until the defeat of Japan in August 1945, Roosevelt made the basic decisions for the conduct of grand strategy. Churchill concentrated on preserving the British Empire from real or imagined threats. Churchill knew that a major threat came from the United States.[3] Churchill, in reality, was Prime Minister and Foreign Secretary. The one issue where, to a limited extent, Eden's views prevailed over Churchill's was relations with de Gaulle. Eden was recognised by another proud and solitary man as a true friend of France.

Eden had little knowledge of domestic issues, although his relative liberalism on class and education was refreshing. In any case, Attlee, Bevin, Morrison, and Sir John Anderson[4] dealt with the home front, to Churchill's satisfaction and admiration. Eden was forced to walk in Churchill's shadow. This unsatisfactory role, sustained for five years of strain and challenge, produced two consequences for Eden. Both of them bear directly on what happened in 1956. Eden was never able to define, in his own mind or as the basis for policy, where he stood in relation to Roosevelt and his Secretaries of State. Eden knew as clearly as Churchill that an independent strategy or foreign policy for Britain depended on America confining rather than expanding its spheres of influence. Eden feared the morbid interest which Roosevelt and Cordell Hull took in dismembering the Empire. Where possible and when not otherwise preoccupied, Eden tried to fend his allies off. This was an unsatisfactory business, and Eden never mastered it. Eden lacked 'the instinct for the jugular', a fatal weakness in dealing with Americans, who fight to win.

Eden therefore failed to define, except in words which were both vague and misleading, how Britain could play a role in the post-war world. He simply remained convinced that there was such a role and that he would have a major part in executing it. Above all, Eden failed to realise that Britain's strength in the Middle East was illusory, depending, as always, on buffer states and bribes, rather than military forces which could operate at will throughout the area. Eden practised his diplomatic gifts in a context where Britain lacked real imperial authority and in which the presence of British troops was as likely to be resented as accepted.

Eden promoted The Arab League (formed in March 1945) as a means of ensuring that Egypt and its neighbours would remain client states – and that an independent Arab Palestinian State would keep the Jews in their place, even if they achieved their aim of a 'National Home'. In February 1920 Churchill wrote: 'If, as may well happen, there should be created in our own lifetime by the banks of the Jordan a Jewish State under the protection of the British Crown which might comprise three or four million Jews, an event will have occurred in the history of the world which would from every point of view be beneficial, and would be especially in harmony with the truest interests of the British Empire.'[5] Eden had no share in this sentiment, no sympathy for the Jews. His Middle East comprised Arab clients, not citizens, or victims of persecution. Seeking genuine independence, the Jews of Palestine forfeited British protection. By 1944, Eden and the Jews were locked in conflict.

The League never functioned as Eden desired. No Arab leader was prepared to remain a client indefinitely; too many broken pledges – or what Arabs called promises – frustrated Eden's schemes. No solution devised for Palestine by British governments stood any chance of acceptance in Arab eyes so long as the Jews gained a separate State. Churchill's Zionism, although it remained with him to the end, was thwarted by Eden and Whitehall. Bribes became a competitive business. Post-war British governments discovered that American oil money was the one kind of bribe which Arab and Persian leaders understood. When French and Russian weapons began to replace British in the 1950s, reality should have dispelled illusion. It did not. But the most dangerous illusion was Eden's belief that he could engage in collusion with his former enemies the Jews of Palestine without forfeiting Arab support. In 1956 Britain reached the nadir of its fortunes in the Middle East, not because of the culpability of the acts, but because of the absurdity of the premises on which they were based.

In Opposition, Eden's dislike of American motives and methods increased. Churchill's affection for Eden also increased; but belief in his suitability as Prime Minister faltered. Eden, in limbo, did think about the realities of power and come to sensible conclusions about some of them. He saw that the Britain of his youth had gone. His views on Western European unity were enlightened, compared with those of most of his colleagues. If Eden had become Prime Minister in 1945 or 1951 it is doubtful if he would have embarked on the Suez operation. His insistence in 1954, despite

Churchill's opposition, that British troops must leave Egypt showed a partial acceptance of change.

Eden's period as statesman ended in 1954. The burden of being Prime Minister and the need to be thought a leader was such that he was unable to think clearly about the consequences of his acts. Nor did he have confidants who could sustain or warn him. Churchill said to Antony Head (a member of Eden's Cabinet) after the Suez operation had failed: 'I might not have started it; I certainly would not have stopped it.' Eden started without rationally considering what would happen when President Eisenhower and his Secretary of State, Foster Dulles, made it plain to him that in no circumstances would they support a military operation designed to destroy Gamal Abdel Nasser. Churchill would have heeded the warning. He would not have started on a path leading to his own destruction. Eisenhower, who knew all about Eden's collusion with Israel, allowed Eden to invade Egypt – then destroyed him.

American policy during Suez was more damaging to British interests than Nasser's revolutionary and nationalist rhetoric. But Eden should have known better than to look for American support in any Middle East venture. Eden called Dulles 'that terrible man'; the terror really lay in Dulles not merely deserting Eden but actively opposing him. Churchill shared many of Eden's antipathies to American foreign policy. Years earlier, a guest at Chartwell noted in his diary: 'Winston thinks the United States arrogant and fundamentally hostile to us. They wish to dominate world politics.'[6] But Churchill's ambitions quickened his instinctive understanding of the sources of power. He learned to live with American power. Eden did not. He was not an ambitious man in the instinctive sense. He allowed his antipathies to affect his judgment. Churchill said that 'politics must be inclusive, not exclusive. There must be room for everybody'. Eden was able to follow this precept as a diplomat; he rejected it as Prime Minister, with disastrous results, not only in terms of Anglo-American relations but concerning his political and parliamentary colleagues.

Churchill, despite his Zionism, would not have made collusion with Israel the basis of an imperial strategy designed to destroy Nasser's Egypt with the minimum loss of British lives and the maximum acclaim for upholding the legality of an international convention which dealt with the right of passage through the Suez Canal. The Israelis, temperamentally attracted to plots and often forced to execute them, became puzzled by Eden's tortuous approach about what, to them, was a straightforward trial of strength. To the Israelis, nationalisation of the Anglo-French Suez Canal Company by Nasser was a minor affair. To Eden it was an affront, not to international law and practice, but to his esteem. Eden ignored the fact that the Canal functioned normally after Nasser nationalised the Company. Even David Ben-Gurion, who 'loved England' and knew a good deal about it, failed to realise that Eden was pulled all ways at once. Eden understood what was happening in the world; he knew Britain could no longer arbitrate issues alone; he hated submission to American dictates; he needed to prove his critics wrong; he succumbed to temptation.

Eden stepped through the looking glass. He did so well before Nasser nationalised the Suez Canal Company in July 1956. Once in the looking-glass world, all events were distorted and magnified, above all Nasser's attacks on Britain's Middle East role and his appeal to Moscow for weapons. Nationalisation of the Canal Company was not the cause of 'Suez', merely the culmination of events, inflamed to monstrous size by Eden's imagination and fears. Most of Eden's views and fears were shared by Whitehall; his prescription for destroying Nasser was not. Eden was a very sick man indeed in 1956; he did some very strange things. He was a confidant adviser, with a deserved diplomatic reputation; but he could never take a positive and rational decision alone.

So much ink has been spilled over the Suez operation that these reflections on the measure of Eden's problems are an essential preliminary to a further look at the available material and the hitherto publicly unknown events. The official material on Suez has been destroyed; when historians come to look for it in 1986 they will open another Pandora's box. Eden has given us his version, one which reflects a psychological need to posture. But, in a self-sufficient age, where illusions were seen as such, Eden would have been denied the chance. Britain, in the 1950s, needed to posture also. Nothing surprised Hugh Gaitskell and his colleagues of the Parliamentary Labour Party more than the discovery that the British working man was, for a brief period of manufactured chauvinism, solidly behind Eden. Julian Amery, who also wanted to destroy Nasser, recalls standing in the House of Commons when it was all over: 'I felt a hand on my shoulder. I turned. It was Nye Bevan. "You were right all along", he said.' Bevan was a former Labour Cabinet Minister and an undoubted tribune of the people. Yet he failed to understand the emotions of a Britain which was losing an empire but failing to find a role.

The Permanent Government and the Chiefs of Staff were united in opposition to Eden, knowing that the means to restore Britain's position in the Middle East simply did not exist. Yet one of Eden's Private Secretaries, close to his Master through wartime service, said as the troops went in: 'I suppose we must have a war now and then.' President Bulganin's threats to Eden on 11 September and 6 November that Russia could support Nasser by a nuclear attack on Britain united the country in derision rather than fear. But the country wanted only a little war, not a major national effort, entailing sacrifice. Eden shared a widespread assumption that Egyptians could be knocked about with impunity. There were precedents. In May 1882, Lord Granville, then Foreign Secretary, wrote to Gladstone who, as Prime Minister, was, covertly, also planning to overthrow an Egyptian leader: 'A bombardment is a horrible thing, but it will clear the air and accelerate a solution of some sort or other.'[7] Much the same kind of emotion explained Eden's actions and Britain's reactions to them.

The Britain of the early 1950s, Eden's Britain, can seem as distant in time as Gladstone and Granville's world. The difference is that Gladstone, more devious than Eden but with the Mediterranean Fleet at his back, could 'accelerate a solution' and Eden could not. The bombardment of Alexandria on 11 July 1882 was carried out by a fleet whose gunnery was appallingly bad. Arabi Pasha[8] was destroyed none the less in the almost bloodless campaign which followed. Thereafter, Britain ruled Egypt more imperially than India or any African colony. Whether Britain ruled through Cromer, a Consul-General who was nominally there at the behest of a Khedive – in turn the vassal of an Ottoman Emperor – or gave the country 'independence', made absolutely no difference to the reality of the situation or the illusion that it would continue indefinitely. Egyptian governments were formed and dismissed by Cromer and his successors in order to sustain imperial interests. These were the Suez Canal Company and, in Egypt and the Sudan, the cotton industry. By 1914, the Canal and Persian oil were links in an imperial chain. British governments owned minority but critical shares in the Canal Company and controlled the Anglo-Persian Oil Company,[9] not merely by a majority shareholding but by acts of policy. British shipping dominated traffic through the Canal, and continued to do so until well after the end of the Second World War.[10]

King Farouk's Egypt of 1950, a country of pashas and

corruption, of acquired riches and inherited poverty, of venal politicians and conscientious administrators, was familiar to Eden and his peers. Their predecessors in office and their pro-consular relations had made this land in their own image. Cromer wrote in 1907, at the end of his twenty-year reign: 'The method of Parliamentary institutions is thoroughly uncongenial to Oriental habits of thought. Our primary duty is not to introduce a system which, under the specious cloak of free institutions, will enable a small minority of natives to misgovern their countrymen, but to establish one which will enable the mass of the population to be governed according to the code of Christian morality.'[11]

There was not much morality about imperial rule in Egypt. The people were nominally governed by their own politicians, but in practice Egypt was ruled by Britain, and for imperial reasons alone. The Canal was the Empire's main artery: no further justification was sought, or given. After the First World War, Churchill, as Colonial Secretary, established the strategic principle that Britain's hold on the Middle East must be maintained economically. Garrisons were reduced. Reliance was placed on air power, coercive, not merely deterrent. In December 1924 Churchill minuted for the Cabinet: 'Our position in Egypt has always rested on a fiction supported by force.'[12] Churchill did not change these views in thirty years. T.E. Lawrence declared, 'Bombing tribes is ineffective.'[13] But it did not prove to be so in Iraq where, between 1919 and 1921, a national revolt was crushed by British air power. Egyptians, who were not tribesmen, not fighting men at all, were assumed to be legitimate – and easy – targets.

Power was inherited; it was exercised by agents, military and civil. Unlike India, where imperial service became a way of life for generations, Egypt bred emotions ranging from affection for individuals to loathing of Levantine habits. English men and women eulogised the Arab of the desert. To the Egyptian of the Delta was reserved a particular contempt from which even the best and most committed administrator was rarely immune. Whereas in India the English made a second home, the Englishman in Egypt felt himself to be an exile. The soldiers had nothing to do and little to do it with. On the eve of the Second World War the Mobile Force, which was to be committed to the Western Desert if the Italian Army in Cyrenaica invaded Egypt, was known by its junior officers as the 'immobile farce'. The civilians, working long hours in a demanding climate, spared enough bile from criticisms of Egyptian politicians to expend on their colleagues.

Throughout the Second World War Egypt reflected the fortunes of a Britain which was fighting to preserve an Empire. Cairo also had its black week in June 1942, when Rommel was reckoned to be at the gates of Alexandria. Burning Embassy files sent columns of black smoke drifting across the Cairo skyline. Egyptian governments were always ready to change sides. On 4 February 1942, the British Ambassador, Sir Miles Lampson, had driven to Farouk's Abdin Palace, escorted by armoured cars, and accompanied by a group of officers 'armed to the teeth'. Lampson, six foot five inches and eighteen stone of imperial assurance, told Farouk to abdicate or concoct a government amenable to British interests. Farouk – 'a rotter' in Lampson's opinion, widely shared – promptly did as he was told. Lord Moyne (Minister of State Resident in the Middle East) was assassinated in Cairo on 6 November 1944 by two members of the Jewish Stern Gang. On 18 January 1945 the assassins were hanged, Churchill insisting to Lampson beforehand that 'unless the sentences duly passed are executed it will cause a marked breach between Great Britain and Egypt'.[14] The Prime Minister, Ahmed Mahir, was abjectly willing to agree. But he was assassinated for his pains before Moyne's killers were hanged, arguably a sign of the nationalist times which Lampson and his colleagues should have heeded and reported. They did neither. By 1945, Wavell, as Viceroy of India, was preparing the country for independence. His Journal reflects the struggle to achieve justice and security. Lampson's Diary does not even record Ahmed Mahir's death. Egyptian Prime Ministers were expendable and trivial in pro-consular eyes.

As the tide of war turned, Lampson's diaries mirrored the belief that in the wheedling world of Egyptian politics, the Pashas would always know who was master. Eden, following in Churchill's wake between Moscow, Teheran and Yalta, tying up the loose ends of policies fashioned with Stalin and Roosevelt, was a frequent guest at Lampson's dinner table. Cairo, as an imperial headquarters, brought diverse talents together, united by assumptions which neither visitor nor exile was able to question. Whilst SOE and its rivals fought their backstairs battles, Lampson discussed with Eden such matters as Ibn Saud's 'devotion to His Britannic Majesty's Government, second only to his devotion to Allah'. Such fatuities were possible in a world from which all sense of reality had departed.

Beyond the Embassy was an Egypt unknown to the pro-consuls and their imperial guests. Nasser and his fellow conspirators in the

Free Officers Organisation committed to Farouk's downfall were active by 1945; they risked discovery from treachery, not penetration. SIS in Egypt, although effective in the business of squaring politicians, relied on agents for intelligence of internal unrest. The agents' usual qualification for recruitment was relationship to one already recruited. Members of the large, long-established expatriate community, British by nationality, mixed in blood, more loyal than the exiles, were also recruited as unofficial assistants. The Station Officer in the Embassy and his subordinates at Alexandria, Suez, Port Said and Ismailia relied on literally hundreds of low-grade agents, many producing glowing reports of peace, prosperity, and an undying devotion to that Britannic Majesty whom none had ever seen.

Egyptians do not like being the bearers of bad news. Unlike their colleagues in Persia, Iraq and, indeed, the Arab world in general, SIS in Egypt shared the assumptions of their masters. The Free Officers was a secret and subversive organisation unknown to SIS. The requirement laid on SIS to produce operational military intelligence for British forces in Egypt absorbed much time and energy. Beneath the apparently smooth surface of Egyptian political life and beyond the garrisons and the military townships of the Canal Zone was a society in ferment. SIS had neither the inclination nor the qualifications to investigate this society and report on its activities.

By the end of the war the British High Commission in Cairo had become the British Embassy. This apparent concession to Egyptian susceptibilities made no real difference to how things were done, or who did them. A huge staff led an existence not only imperial but free from co-ordination of responsibility. Few of the Chancery or commercial staff spoke Arabic; the Oriental Counsellor, for many years the enigmatic John Hamilton, possessed and hugged this supposedly arcane gift. The SIS Station was a law unto itself, and remained so until after Suez. During these wartime and post-war years, heads of Chancery who ventured to question this law retired hurt. One such, recalling Suez more in anger than in sorrow, remarked that it was impossible ever to know what the Station was for. 'If', he said reflectively, 'you look across a field and see three trees and a scarecrow you can distinguish one from the others. If you look across a field and see a dense wood, there may be dozens of scarecrows but they will all be hidden. SIS in Egypt was in that position. We never knew where the scarecrows were, or what they were for.'

Nothing which happened between 1945 and 1951 shook the complacency of men who had found in wartime Cairo all the imperial bits and pieces still firmly tacked into place. Harold Macmillan, who had served as Minister Resident in North Africa, and thereafter in Italy and Greece, could have told a different tale. In Algeria Macmillan had seen nationalism at first hand, recognised, and identified it. Macmillan had worked closely with Eisenhower and other Americans. Cairo had remained a British outpost, with the Americans all but excluded until, in February 1945, Roosevelt passed through it on the way to see Ibn Saud and undermine Britain's standing in the latter's kingdom. Algiers was an American headquarters, and Macmillan learned there a lesson which he never forgot. Eisenhower and his political adviser, Robert Murphy, respected Macmillan who, unlike Eden, knew how to be agreeable to men more powerful than he was.

In Algiers Macmillan remarked: 'These Americans represent the new Roman Empire and we Britons, like the Greeks of old, must teach them how to make it go.'[15] Macmillan could make remarks like that without giving offence. If Eden had reflected aloud in these terms, he would have emphasised 'teach' – and caused resentment. Macmillan was clear in his own mind that Britain depended on America. By 1945 Eden was prematurely set in his ways, lacking political flexibility and intellectual penetration. Even Eden's tolerant view of British society reflected nostalgia for the past rather than perception of the present. He became obsessed with the delusion that Britain was a great power because of its independence from America. Therein lay one of the prime causes of Suez and, for Eden, its tragic effect.

Macmillan was made Minister of Housing in Churchill's 1951 Cabinet. He was a success, but hankered for the telegrams and the boxes, for the excitements of Algiers, Rome, and Athens. Yet Macmillan's domestic tasks gave him the chance to observe a Britain which was still governed by illusions, at home and abroad. Churchill's Cabinet inherited problems which had been not so much unsolved as ignored. Attlee and Bevin were exhausted by six years of struggle and achievement. Bevin by 1950 was a dying man; on 14 March 1951 he was dead. Other Ministers – Stafford Cripps, Dalton, Morrison – had shared with Attlee and Bevin six years of war. Cripps also died, in April 1952, from devotion to duty. Despite great success in restoring Britain to economic activity and providing a social basis for peaceful change – from an Empire ruled by the few to a nation governed by consensus – Attlee and his ministers had not dispelled imperial illusions, had failed to tackle four problems which were directly relevant to the tasks which faced their successors. Britain's progressive loss of power had been ignored; no satisfactory relationship had been established with America; the strategic purpose of a nuclear weapons programme had not been defined; the crucial role of intelligence in a nation still aspiring to an international role had been overlooked. In consequence, the deficiencies in SIS and MI5 were ignored; when they were revealed, no genuine effort was made to cure them or reorganise two services on which so much of Britain's security depended.

The cold war shifted its focus and emphasis with the final victories of Chinese communism in 1949 and the invasion of South Korea by the North in June 1950. Western governments assumed, justifiably, that Russian and Chinese communist governments would unite in their attacks on capitalist and imperialist systems. The Korean War appeared to open a new front in a struggle already being waged in Europe and Asia. Attlee and Bevin had no hesitation in backing President Truman and in committing forces to this front. Attlee was lukewarm, not to say hostile, about closer relationships with Western Europe. He supported Bevin over NATO but was opposed to a 'European Community' in which Britain would be but one amongst many. Bevin welcomed any relief from confrontation in Central Europe. Although the Korean War was fought by the West under American leadership, Attlee was the one allied leader whom Truman consulted and heeded. Attlee dissuaded Truman from using the atom bomb in December 1950. This was the last time an American President took the advice of a British Prime Minister. Truman decided not to use the bomb against Chinese forces committed to the support of North Korea because he respected Attlee's experience and judgment. Britain's international roles did not influence the President's decision.

The Attlee Government's willing participation in the war and strong support for America in fighting it strained Britain's economic resources when recovery from years of austerity seemed to be on the way. The strain was hidden behind illusions of power. The war, together with the 'Emergency' in Malaya and a huge colonial Empire in Africa untouched by change, projected an image of Britain continuing to play a major, and essentially independent international role. Yet the military and economic resources to assert independence were decreasing throughout these post-war years, and were doing so in relation to situations of increasing complexity. In 1951, for example, 80,000 troops were stationed in the Suez Canal Zone, a legacy of world war which had been neither wound up nor re-invested. The troops sat in camp, enduring dust, flies and, from nationalists, abuse, unable to play any part defending Britain's Middle East empire. This immobile force lacked the logistic resources which America had provided for amphibious and airborne operations in the Second World War. In 1951 a Persian demagogue, Mohammed Mossadeq, closed Anglo-Iranian's refinery at Abadan by the simple process of mobilising street violence. In 1932, Reza Shah had arbitrarily terminated the Company's concession, only to make a new one when his treasury became bankrupt. Until 1947 the Indian Army was available to keep Persia quiet. By 1951 neither financial nor military strength sufficed for Britain to coerce its enemies – unless this was done with American support.

Britain's international role was welcome enough to American governments provided it did not interfere with their own priorities. These were the maintenance of a nuclear weapons' programme which would deter Russia in Europe and the use of the United Nations as an instrument of a policy whereby a bloc of minor states supported America. Bevin backed this use of the UN over Korea, but saw dangers in it elsewhere, above all in the Middle East. The area had never been one of Anglo-American accord. A third American priority – domination of the international oil business – was, indeed, the basis for discord. In 1954 and 1956 the area was marked by two bitter disagreements between America and England, of which only 'Suez' has passed into history. The aftermath of 'Abadan' has not done so.

The nuclear weapons programme which Churchill began and Attlee developed was quickly overtaken by America and Russia in terms of explosive power, the means of delivering it, the accuracy of guidance systems for manned aircraft, and hence the evolution of strategic theories based on mutual deterrence. The first British atomic explosion took place in October 1952; a month later the first American *hydrogen* bomb exploded. The first British hydrogen bomb was not exploded until October 1957, shortly before Russia launched the sputnik research satellite into orbit. By then both America and Russia were developing missile systems designed to carry hydrogen bombs. Thus, both superpowers were developing relatively invulnerable retaliatory systems. In 1957 the Royal Air Force had just completed delivery of *aircraft* designed to carry hydrogen bombs. This British nuclear force, in terms of presenting the enemy with a threat, could only be used in a 'first strike' role; American and Russian forces were capable of retaliation. Britain's forces were designed to provide a 'strategic' deterrent of long range aircraft (Vulcan, Victor, Valiant; the 'V bombers'), primarily but not exclusively targeted on Moscow and other major Russian cities.

For short and medium range 'tactical' use the Buccaneer aircraft was developed from a wartime design. In its first operational version, the Buccaneer was flown from aircraft carriers, carrying a twenty kiloton bomb. The Canberra medium bomber was adapted for a similar purpose by the late 1950s. The Canberra was committed to what became known as LABS, the low altitude bombing system. This was a version of nuclear first strike which not only put a very high premium on the skill and courage of Canberra crews but on the inadequacy of an enemy's ground-to-air defences. Proponents of LABS hoped the defences would be manned by the forces of minor powers, hence, presumably, inadequate. All these aircraft and their weapons represented a genuinely independent nuclear force which, so far as a specific role was assigned to it, extended to any part of the world where British interests might be threatened. But such a force could only be used in retaliation against an enemy which lacked nuclear weapons. The vulnerability of the force in relation to Russia, the only potential enemy likely to possess nuclear weapons, lay in the directly related fact that Britain's small size and concentrated population provided targets easy to find and destroy. Theoretical retaliation against Russian cities offered little compensation for this fact; the relatively slow manned British bombers had an extremely limited capacity to escape destruction from Russian defences before reaching their targets, even in a surprise 'first strike'.

These rather elementary facts are given in order to emphasise that American governments were prepared to share neither nuclear nor related scientific and technological secrets with their faithful ally except on terms which suited the White House – and the Congress. Even when the rigours of the McMahon Act were relaxed by the 1954 Atomic Energy Act, the decision to give some nuclear secrets to Britain was based on one simple American priority, combining commercial shrewdness, political convenience, and strategic belief. Britain would get secrets and thus retain a nuclear deterrent force if its governments bought American weapons, or the vital parts for them. Buying American would mean White House control of a supposedly independent deterrent. Such a deterrent would also be promoted to the retaliatory level.

Long before American strategists argued that nations which were not super powers should not have nuclear weapons, Truman's and Eisenhower's advisers were clear that there was no point in Britain independently having them. Indeed, there was danger to America in Britain developing an 'independent' nuclear force. Which powers was it supposed to deter? Against which would it be used? If used – in a first strike – where would retaliation fall? Would Britain or America be the target? Foster Dulles's 'agonising reappraisal' of America's commitment to European security masked an agonising question: why should America take risks for Britain's sake? These were questions which no British government was able, then – or has been able since – to answer to anything but its own satisfaction. Churchill's return in October 1951 did not fundamentally change Britain's nuclear dependence on America, as the Chiefs of Staff pointed out the following year in the 'Global Strategy' Paper.

The Chiefs declared: 'One unfortunate but inevitable result of British withdrawal of forces (from India and, to a considerable extent from Germany) is the predominantly decisive influence of America.' The Chiefs then engaged in a *tour d'horizon*, concluding with the observation that to prevent America, 'Whose experience, judgement, and internal political system are ill-adapted to her enormous responsibilities', making mistakes in Europe or Asia, Britain must develop a nuclear deterrent system for the exercise of 'British influence on United States policy'. The Global Strategy Paper, although nominally reflecting agreed views, was written, in his own distinctive hand, by Sir John Slessor, Chief of the Air Staff. 'Jack' Slessor liked, admired, and knew Americans; he was totally sceptical of America's readiness to make sacrifices for Britain's sake unless a coercive or persuasive means was devised. Slessor believed that a British nuclear force – in reality, so long as it remained genuinely independent, a vulnerable first strike affair – would enable influence to be exercised. The vulnerability in question would force America to support Britain in a crisis in order to pre-empt the risk of American cities being the target of a retaliatory strike. This was nothing more nor less than a blackmail argument, one with some attractions for Churchill, and a very strong appeal to Eden, being based on the superficially reasonable premise that American nuclear strength would deter Russia. Much of Whitehall outside the Service Departments disliked the argument because officials knew there was no way in which Britain could play either an independent or a blackmail role in any issue which involved American interests. These interests were the yardstick of what Britain could, and could not do, alone. Independence resided only in the maintenance of a limited imperial role. By 1956, the Chiefs of Staff had grasped and accepted these facts. Their opposition to Eden was based on hard thought about strategic realities.

These three problems, of sustaining commitments, maintaining relations with America, and relying on nuclear weapons to preserve international status, were also directly related to the role of intelligence and the means of executing it. SIS had ended the war in poor shape, lacking both a clearly defined aim and officers who believed they knew how to achieve one. Neither was achieved in the decade which followed. As a result, illusions persisted because the means of dispelling them were not found. Nothing which had happened since 1945 suggested that the kind of intelligence would be provided which was needed to convince governments that times had changed. The requirements laid on SIS by Whitehall reflected the political and strategic assumptions of governments which were so enmeshed in attempts to preserve Britain's international roles and status that conscious 'forward planning' by the middle ranks of Whitehall was not translated into policy.

Nevertheless, Menzies and others who had lived through the years of Churchill's special relationships with Roosevelt were committed to the necessity of preserving one with American governments whatever the circumstances and whoever sat in the White House. Such men believed in the sheer necessity for the relationship because, up to a point, they also shared a delusion: that America would not desert Britain *in extremis* – provided the status of dependence was accepted in No. 10. Menzies, who had, on Churchill's orders, added OSS to the Ultra distribution, was particularly sensitive to the political, not merely the intelligence aspects of this unequal relationship. Menzies, like his officers, was indifferent to economic realities and, for a soldier, rather hazy about strategic requirements. But Menzies knew where power lay. He had no particular affection for Americans. He knew they were essential to the survival of SIS.

The Albanian operation was disliked by many in Broadway – and discreetly opposed by some – because of the 'SOE' approach to removing Hoxha, not the declared objective of doing so. Menzies carried out Bevin's orders; he showed no enthusiasm for them. Menzies was interested in – not just professionally committed to – the acquisition of intelligence. That process required liaison – exchange of intelligence – as much as, and probably more than, it relied on counter-intelligence, let alone special operations or dirty tricks. Menzies retained his ambivalent attitude to SOE methods during the cold war years. He accepted the necessity for robust action, but preferred to believe in the possibilities of the classic intelligence approach. Hence 'continuities' were maintained where possible.

The critical instance of 'continuities' was Israel. Eden had opposed an independent Jewish state because he totally lacked sympathy for Jewish aspirations in Palestine. Bevin had opposed an independent Israel because he feared a Russian bridgehead in the Middle East. But when the State of Israel was proclaimed on 14 May 1948, after the Union Flag had been lowered over the Citadel in Jerusalem, Bevin recognised the fact – and instructed Menzies to open a station once diplomatic relations had been established. Bevin accepted that Israel was the one democratic and stable state in the Middle East. Mossad Letafkidim Meyouchadim (the Israeli Intelligence Services), owed much to SIS; liaison was soon established. There was precedent. Although Hogarth and many in the Arab Bureau had disliked working with Jews who volunteered their services to Britain, the achievements and sacrifices of intelligence officers and agents like Aaron and Sarah Aaronsohn were not forgotten. The Balfour Declaration, promising Jews, worldwide, a 'National Home', was, after all, a device for providing Britain with a secure strategic outpost in an Arab world which was habitually insecure and never wholly loyal to British interests. From 1948 onwards the SIS Station in Tel Aviv, its incumbent usually one of the few women officers, ensured a two-way flow of intelligence during years when overt relations between the governments varied from cool to frigid.[16]

Throughout the years between 1945 and 1951, Menzies and his directors strove to re-establish SIS on such foundations. Circumstance was against SIS, although more success attended Menzies's efforts than could be appreciated at the time or has been recognised since. 'Continuities' implied relative international stability; a relatively prosperous, strategically strong, and hence internationally respected Britain, a society, recognisable by the Menzies of the intelligence world as one where everyone did know everyone else. That world had come to an end long before 1939, and the Cambridge undergraduates who betrayed their country were amongst the first to recognise the fact. From 1946 onwards an assortment of traitors, inside and beyond Whitehall, reflected the weaknesses of an establishment which operated on inherited assumptions instead of subjecting situations and developments to objective analysis.

The flight from London of Guy Burgess and Donald Maclean on 25 May 1951 was, strictly speaking, a matter for MI5 and the Metropolitan Police Special Branch. But SIS was involved in many ways. By 1951 SIS was deeply troubled with doubts about its own collective loyalties, but this problem for Menzies and his Deputy, John Sinclair, was seen as trivial compared with the effect of the episode on relations with the CIA and, by extension, with American governments. The agreement which Attlee and Truman made in 1946 governing relations between SIS and American intelligence services was intended to go beyond routine liaison, despite issues posed by the McMahon Act. Menzies knew that in order to preserve the privileged position in Whitehall which control of the Ultra distribution had given SIS during the war it was essential to have access to signals intelligence from American sources. By 1945 American technological skills had begun to affect the entire business of acquiring intelligence and, indeed, the requirements laid on intelligence officers. Despite the inhibition on disclosure of nuclear information, the CIA co-operated with SIS on the terms which Menzies sought. In the late 1940s, SIS was ahead in the signals intelligence business, a fact which the embryonic CIA acknowledged. Both services knew that it would not be long before the CIA was in the lead.

In return for access to American signals intelligence, Menzies hoped to provide intelligence acquired from agents which would imbue Washington with the belief that SIS knew its way about the world. Curiously enough, many in Washington were convinced that the British Empire which, as good Americans they were sworn to dismember, was alive and well. SIS said so. The quality of SIS intelligence varied greatly, but it was invariably presented in the kind of dry, detached style which both the State Department and other official agencies so admired. In those early post-war years SIS, in a specifically American sense, quite unconnected with social origins, had class. Neither strong disagreements on objectives and methods nor the Albanian fiasco destroyed this belief.

Until Burgess and Maclean disappeared, American suspicions about security lapses in the English official establishment were concentrated on MI5. Thereafter, much of it focussed on SIS. Philby, and others, had fixed the escape of Burgess and Maclean. Despite circumstantial evidence, CIA could not prove Philby's guilt; lacking proof, some in CIA resorted to condemnation of SIS. To Philby alone was reserved the full venom for a traitor, but SIS as a whole was never to be the same in American eyes.

An intelligence service has problems when the men at the top have to spend more of their time reassuring friends than co-operating with them and penetrating enemies. The problems lay deep in SIS, in a society whose permanently governing class proceeded by assumptions about loyalty, not only about imperial destiny. Between 1951 and 1956 SIS was in grave trouble – the period became known as 'the horrors' to survivors. Menzies and Sinclair – who became 'C' in 1953 – spent much of their time trying to reassure an increasingly critical Allan Dulles that SIS and the Whitehall intelligence system as a whole was basically sound.[17] Some officers were retired; others chose to leave. Yet extraordinary attempts were made to protect Philby, investigated and interrogated by both MI5 and SIS; suspended thereafter; but officially cleared in November 1955 by Macmillan (as Foreign Secretary), and then sent as a newspaper correspondent to Beirut. In that city of doubtful reputations Philby was no longer an SIS officer, but he was the occasional recipient of its funds and, for good measure, the KGB's (the Soviet Committee for State Security).

George Blake joined SIS in 1948; by 1952 he was a KGB agent. In related fields – of naval intelligence – the small fry Harry Houghton and John Vassall were sent to the British Embassies in Warsaw and Moscow in 1951 and 1953, and were left thereafter to go their traitorous ways. It was indeed a time of 'horrors' whose effects were to last for many years. At intervals during his service in Moscow Vassall nearly admitted to the Station Officer that he had been blackmailed into working for the KGB, and dropped enough hints to alert anyone with his wits about him. The Station Officer, like so many others at the time, preferred not to ask questions or uncover further horrors.

Not until Dick Goldsmith White, a product of Bishop's Stortford College and Christ Church, became 'C' in 1956 did SIS adapt to the post-war world. White was a civilian; he had spent virtually his entire adult life in MI5, of which he had become Director-

General in 1953 before moving across St James's Park to Broadway. White neither had an imperial background nor did he dream of empire. He was an office man, who would have reorganised MI5 if his energies had not, perforce, been given to catching traitors, Philby included – or trying to do so. White was an immensely suitable choice for SIS in 1956, when Whitehall, almost to a man, decided that Britain could not afford a Prime Minister who was determined to live in a looking-glass world. Menzies saw reality, but was not the man to stand against headstrong characters. Sinclair, rather aptly nicknamed 'Sinbad', was a colourless sailor-turned-soldier, who wanted peace at any price. White, slim, blue-eyed, prematurely white-haired, calm at all times, elegant and cultivated, with an almost aesthetic appreciation of what took place in Whitehall corridors, was a tougher proposition altogether. His sense of reality had matured in a hard school. From his first day as 'C' White made it plain to his masters, not merely to his colleagues, that SIS must begin to have ideas and arguments about the post-imperial world, not merely develop the capacity to know more about it. Such ideas and arguments would be kept in reserve: SIS would not start writing appreciations. But if the masters asked SIS to do something absurd, the 'Office' collectively must be able to say that it was no part of its tasks to foster illusions.

When Eden returned to the Foreign Office in 1951, however, the looking-glass could show a world which did not seem so vastly different from when he left it in 1945. Eden's troubles lay in the future. The glass showed an unchanged picture: Britain was still a major power; nuclear weapons would maintain that position. American governments would treat Britain as an equal. Little evidence was produced by the permanent government to indicate that Britain could no longer afford an independent foreign policy. Even within NATO, and in the protracted but eventually abortive discussions about a European Defence Community, Eden – rather than Churchill – assumed that his would be the determining voice. NATO appeared to re-create the wartime special relationship. 'Pug' Ismay, NATO's first Secretary-General, seemed a comforting reminder of shared wartime crises and triumphs.

Eisenhower and Foster Dulles, when they set about reshaping American foreign policy in 1953, had other ideas. To Dulles, Britain was merely 'the weak sister' in a shaky Atlantic Alliance. Dulles was also convinced that even an independent imperial policy was impossible where this conflicted with American political and commercial interests. This particular truth was neither understood nor accepted by Eden until November 1956, when he – and the pound sterling – collapsed under pressure exerted by Eisenhower and Dulles. If America became involved in shoring up the Middle East, the decision would be on American terms, not those dictated by a British Government which assumed that help *in extremis* would be available.

If these comments seem odd, given that Churchill had established the special relationship and Eden, however reluctantly, had maintained it, the aftermath of the 1951 Abadan crisis provides the first concrete evidence for the truth of them. In May 1951 Anglo-Iranian was expropriated, 'the greatest blow ever inflicted on the British economic empire in the Middle East'.[18] In October 1954 an agreement was signed with Mossadeq's successor which gave American oil companies a 40 per cent interest in Persian oil. After fifty years of successful attempts by the Permanent Government to exclude major American oil companies from Persia, the entrée had been gained. What happened in Persia between 1951 and 1954 – in fact, as compared with versions by Eden, and others – can only be understood by a brief account regarding some aspects of Britain's oil empire. What happened in the Middle East between 1954 and 1956 was directly affected by these Persian events.

Between 1951 and 1954 America had gained a position in the area as a whole which was marked by two characteristics: it filled a vacuum left by the loss of Britain's power to direct events; no political burdens or strategic commitments were laid on American governments. America's gain was Britain's loss: the gain at Britain's expense was above all in terms of that prestige by which British governments measured their role in the Middle East. The cost to America was a mere $700 million in economic aid to Persia. Despite Eden's bland account of the aftermath to 'Abadan', there is no doubt that American tactics rankled, and Dulles's insistence that a new deal in Persia depended on a place for American oil companies there was not only resented but increased friction between two men who made no secret of their strong dislike for each other. Selwyn Lloyd, Eden's Minister of State at the Foreign Office, is more candid in his recollections of Abadan's aftermath, referring to the steady undermining of our position by Oklahoma oil millionaires[19] – and, by implication, the big business government in Washington.

One of the myths of modern history is that the major British and American oil companies have achieved multi-national status and enormous economic influence by their own efforts, with their respective governments merely playing a benevolent background role. This myth is strongest concerning the Middle East, and continues to be fostered by oil companies and governments to hide the fact that from the time of the 1901 D'Arcy Concession in Persia until at least the early 1970s, practically no oil event of any importance in the area occurred without instigation by or the direct intervention of the Foreign Office and the State Department, usually in outright competition with each other. When Churchill, as First Lord of the Admiralty in 1914 bought for the State a majority shareholding in William Knox D'Arcy's Anglo-Persian Oil Company, a Treasury official minuted: 'This means that HMG controls the company.' In pencil a cautious hand added: 'This minute had better not be circulated too widely.'[20] American companies remained in private hands, but their security overseas and financial stability at home was ensured by governments whose members believed in big oil business and supported a price structure designed to enrich it. But American governments never backed these policies overseas with military forces. In Iraq the companies – which included American corporate shareholders – were protected by a British military presence. Thus American companies avoided criticism from nationalists yet achieved protection from them, a prescription for survival never ignored by Secretaries of State.

The one notable exception to the controlling hand of British and American governments is the Concession which Ibn Saud granted in 1933 to Standard Oil of California. This concession was gained by Harold Philby, Kim's father, double-crossing Stephen Longrigg, the representative of the British managed Iraq Petroleum Company. Philby, an Arabist and occasional confidant of Ibn Saud, was the perfect go-between for an oil deal. In 1933 America had no diplomatic relations with Ibn Saud. Andrew Ryan, the British Minister in Jeddah, when not scoffing at the pretensions of American 'prospectors', assumed that Philby, despite his rancorous criticism of imperial ways, would sew up the deal in Britain's interest. Philby, as complex a character as his son, had in fact offered to negotiate a concession some years earlier on behalf of APOC. The offer declined, Philby had no compunction in giving Longrigg's asking price – in 'rupees, where gold was demanded' – to his American paymasters.[21] They raised the price, offered gold, and gained the concession. As a result America won what, in 1938, a State Department official accurately called 'the richest material prize in history'. The prize was some compensation for the fact that, despite benefits in 1928 from the so-called 'Red Line' Agreement (which covered the area in Arabia of the former Ottoman Empire, and provided that the seven major British, Anglo-Dutch, and American oil companies would not bid against each other for concessions) the American majors were excluded from Persia.

By 1950 Anglo-Iranian was the target of the concentrated criticisms of all nationalists from the Shah on the right to the communist Tudeh Party on the left. The Company remained the sole concessionaire; it had prospered in the 1920s; with British forces available from Iraq or India, occasional riots in Abadan were taken calmly. Reza Shah's termination of the concession in 1932 served to convince Eden, as Parliamentary Under-Secretary in the Foreign Office, that adroit diplomacy could divert nationalism into co-operative paths. When the British Government disputed Reza Shah's actions before the International Court of Justice, an inconclusive judgment resulted. APOC withheld payments, thus forcing surrender. A new concession was made, which strengthened APOC's position.

In 1937, the Company's Chairman, Sir John Cadman, a wise and farsighted imperial industrialist, suggested to Eden that not only his Company's but Britain's relationship with Persia should be put on the footing of at least nominal equals. Why not elevate the Legations to Embassies? Would it not be both courteous and prudent to remove those twenty-foot high walls surrounding the British legation compound? They made the place look like Government House in a colony. Eden, as Foreign Secretary, curtly rebutted both these good ideas. It was essential to convince the Shah that he remained on his throne by virtue of British goodwill. Gestures were futile. The British and the Persians were not equals. There was some force in Acheson's jibe many years later that Eden saw Mossadeq 'as little more than a rug merchant'.[22]

Throughout the 1930s, the State Department, its representatives in Persia, and the American oil industry noted the prevailing attitudes of Britain towards Persia with a mixture of expectation and disdain. The Russian interest in Persia, once dominant and ever present, caused little concern in the State Department, although the men on the spot did occasionally take a more realistic view of strategic issues. This Russian interest had been stimulated by Reza Shah's expropriation. When the Royal Navy appeared in the Shatt Al'Arab (a 'Palmerstonian stroke' said *The Economist* critically which, in fact, was not required) *Izvestia* had commented that the whole episode would 'widen the cracks in the ruined structure of the British Empire'. American interests were also unaware of the tacit admissions of the Committee of Imperial Defence that propping up the Empire of oil might put an unacceptable strain on strategic resources. If these interests had been aware, they would also have been indifferent. Britain's problems were of its own making.

During the war, Persia's occupation by British and Russian troops silenced, but did not stifle, American interest in 'vast crude oil reserves at strategically located points in friendly countries'.[23] The fundamental American attitude was well expressed by their Joint Chiefs of Staff who said in August 1941: 'The Middle East is a liability from which Britain should withdraw.'[24] Their opposite numbers in Whitehall, preoccupied with actually fighting the war in the Middle East, were slow to respond to this warning but, by the spring of 1944, and with the area reconquered, stated boldly: 'We must resist any concessions to the Americans which are likely to result in the introduction into the area of a foreign power to rival our influence.'[25] In January 1947 the British Chiefs of Staff warned Attlee: 'The Middle East is the base from which British forces can attack the Soviet flank. Its significance as a focal point of imperial communications has been vindicated by the war and is still of great value as a half-way house between the United Kingdom and the Far East. Oil from the Persian Gulf area is rendered secure by control of the Suez Canal. The Middle East also protects Africa from Soviet penetration.'[26] The Chiefs did not say how these objectives were to be attained, except by the retention of garrisons, nor did they refer to the fact that, between 1941 and 1943, much consideration had been given to the defence of Iraq and Persia, and no satisfactory plan had emerged – except to plug the oil wells and otherwise conduct a scorched earth campaign. Attlee accepted the 1947 recommendations none the less. In terms of assumption rather than policy it may be said that neither Truman nor Acheson did so. Nor did their successors. 'Containment' did not extend to the Middle East, particularly if this meant supporting a weak sister. Thirty years ago, America produced its own oil; Britain depended on oil from Persia and Iraq for survival. America could afford a selective containment policy.

The State Department argued that survival demanded concessions. If AIOC would only concede to demands for more cash and a greater say in the Company's affairs, the siren voices of the Tudeh Party would be stilled by a general murmur of consensus.

This argument was openly opposed by successive British Ambassadors (Cadman's suggestion of promoting legations to embassies was accepted in 1944), who knew perfectly well that in seeking to deflect communist agitation for the absolute expropriation of AIOC their American colleagues were establishing a basis for the long delayed entrée of Standard New Jersey and other companies. Moreover, on 30 December 1950, the American companies operating in Saudi Arabia made a deal with Ibn Saud which gave him 50 per cent of the gross production revenues; the ground was cut completely from under the feet of AIOC. Such a deal, long demanded by the Shah, had been 'examined and considered' by AIOC in 1948 and 1949 – only to be rejected as a surrender to blackmail. The Company cannot be blamed for rejecting demands which reflected nationalist sentiment and economic justice. Britain needed all the cheap oil it could get; this requirement was emphasised by Ibn Saud's agreement with Roosevelt that Britain must be kept out of Saudi Arabian oil developments (and much else besides), and by the artificially high price which American oil companies charged in Europe for products refined from low cost Arabian oil. Thirty years ago, with oil a thirtieth of its present price, American companies dominated the European products markets, Britain included.

Thus matters stood when in June 1950, General Ali Razmara became Persia's Prime Minister. Although not the British stooge Mossadeq – a veteran politician of ancient family, great wealth, demagogic powers, and opportunist nationalism – dubbed him, Razmara was near enough one to reject a February 1951 Majlis resolution calling for AIOC's nationalisation. Sir Francis Shepheard, the British Ambassador, believed in Razmara on the old yet rarely helpful precept that soldiers carry out orders. The SIS Station Officer, who had agents amongst Majlis members, was not so sure. On 7 March the question was resolved. Razmara was assassinated by members of the Fida'yan-i-Islam (Devotees of Islam). Kissing the British flag had been the least of the crimes attributed to him. Eight days later the Majlis passed a Bill, of one short article, nationalising AIOC. The Shah approved the Bill on 2 May. Mossadeq was by then Prime Minister; he had done the deed – in the streets of Teheran and within the industrial city of Abadan.

During the next four months Attlee and AIOC sent teams from London to Teheran in hopes of a compromise. On 15 July President Truman sent Averell Harriman there. Harriman was another of those American diplomats at large whose wartime admiration for Britain cooled rapidly once business as usual again became the prescription for the conduct of American foreign policy. All efforts failed. Violence in Abadan increased. On 4 October the last AIOC expatriates, in charge of the imperturbable but extremely angry General Manager Eric Drake, were evacuated from the jetties. HMS *Mauritius* took them away. This was tactless. Mauritius had been the wartime exile of the Shah's father who, in 1941, refused to accept the presence of British troops. Eden, on Churchill's order, had him removed from the Peacock Throne.

Herbert Morrison, Bevin's successor as Foreign Secretary, has always been blamed for the humiliation of Abadan. He had nothing to do with it, either its cause, course, or consequences. In June and July the Chiefs of Staff considered whether it would be possible to commit an airborne force in Eastern Persia. Doing so might divert attention from an amphibious operation, intended to provide internal security in Abadan. Such a combined operation would enable the future of AIOC to be negotiated with some prospects of success. The Government of Pakistan was willing to co-operate in providing facilities for the airborne formation. The Government of Iraq was not actively hostile, indeed co-operative rather than otherwise, but only a 'show of force' could be found for Abadan. The RAF flew over the area; Marines from *Mauritius* provided the shadow rather than the substance of security. No troops were available from Egypt – by 1951 the garrison there was enduring a trial prescribed by Nasser in suitably chilling words: 'Grenades will be thrown in the night. British soldiers will be stabbed stealthily.'[27] The huge military townships of the Canal Zone were defending themselves.

No troops were available from Britain, or other overseas bases and garrisons. Ships and aircraft were fully committed. Korea, Malaya, and Germany soaked up the military manpower. The Chiefs reluctantly told Attlee that military operations in Persia were not possible. The Prime Minister knew what he meant when he said: 'This is the destruction of British prestige in the Middle East.'[28] Freezing Persia's sterling assets in retaliation for AIOC's nationalisation was no way to re-establish a strategy of prestige. Attlee grimly accepted that what the Chiefs of Staff said reflected the facts of Britain's imperial decline. The Chiefs' 'global strategy' bore little relation to the facts of strategic life.

There is no doubt, however, that a force would have been

scraped together if Truman had not warned Attlee, in the clearest possible terms, that his Administration would not support intervention.[29] Harriman may have had something to do with his hard line. Truman may have disliked the thought of support for AIOC. On meeting AIOC's Chairman Sir William Fraser, Truman recorded that 'he looked like a typical nineteenth century colonial exploiter'.[30] Differences between Attlee and Truman were, however, more fundamental. Attlee believed that containment required a stiff line over Persia; Truman believed that the country would be less, not more exposed to Russian machinations if nationalism was given its head. Truman's advisers, more cynically, and whether Anglophobe or not, could also point out that the temporary loss of Persian oil would maintain price stability in a world oil market in which Middle East crude, cheap to produce and increasing rapidly in production, was coming to be the deciding factor.

In any event, once Truman had personally invited Mossadeq to visit him in Washington – a visit eagerly paid at the end of October when AIOC had finally been bundled out of Persia – American diplomats and oil men decided how things would be arranged. Churchill's government and AIOC's directors were mere spectators. They were forced to watch a process whereby American oil companies, although refusing to produce, buy, transport, or refine Persian crude, sent representatives to Teheran to negotiate a new deal. Churchill and Eden took what comfort they could from the fact that production from Kuwait filled the gap left by the shutdown in Persia. Yet both Prime Minister and Foreign Secretary were determined to recover prestige for Britain in Persia to compensate for the loss of absolute power to decide oil issues there. Diplomatic relations between Britain and Persia were broken off in October 1952, and only SIS, on the spot and at long range, was able to maintain connection with Mossadeq's rivals, amongst whom the Shah, well aware that he might be next in line for summary treatment, was chief.

Whilst Harriman and his confederates George McGhee and Walter Levy in Teheran laid the foundations for an oil deal, SIS was required to save something for Britain's future. For two years, SIS planned an operation, subsequently codenamed *Boot*, whereby Mossadeq was to be removed from the scene, and the Shah encouraged, rather than directly supported, to resume his autocratic sway. The influence of SOE and its collective penchant for political theory was still strong in SIS. Those responsible for *Boot* argued that Mossedeq's downfall would hamstring Russia's Persian breed of communism, the Tudeh Party.

The SIS opportunity came when the Shah, nervous for his life, fled from his palace at Ramsar (by the Caspian) on 18 August 1953. He returned in triumph to Teheran a week later. The CIA has been given credit for the Shah's return and Mossadeq's subsequent downfall. One former member of the CIA, Kermit Roosevelt, has even claimed as much in an idiosyncratic version of these events.[31] The truth is that the CIA took little part in the business, except in the final phase and after Washington had decided that a policy of working with Britain to restore the Shah's powers and against Britain to increase America's stake in Middle East oil was, indeed, a sound combination of diplomacy and commerce. The Shah was restored by the Army, the Court, and unofficial assistants of SIS known collectively as 'The Brothers', aided by former AIOC employees who saw themselves as the Shah's men. The CIA was new to playing games with kings, whereas SIS was well aware that Mossadeq, having overreached himself and further impoverished the people, had created a situation from which a chastened Shah, suitably supported, could only benefit. Sinclair left the details of the operation to the Director Middle East, who had the wit to realise that the mobs who cheered for Mossadeq could be induced to shout for his Monarch.

The difficult part of the operation was persuading the Shah to return. But by December 1953 Mossadeq was in prison; the Shah had been provided with new powers; and diplomatic relations with Britain had been resumed. Denis Wright, a diplomat without illusions, took over where Shepheard left off. Mohammed Reza Shah Pahlevi knew to whom he owed his fresh lease of life. It is a fact of some slight historical interest that from the time of his return until his fall in 1978 the one member of any diplomatic mission in Teheran who had a regular audience with the Shah and virtually automatic access to him was the SIS Station Officer. That the advice occasionally and informally offered was increasingly rejected is another matter.

In 1954 SIS could do nothing about negotiations between the Shah's advisers and the American oil companies when they got down to details of a new concession. Eighteen years were to pass before sheer necessity and a Whitehall requirement forced SIS to consider whether the American oil industry could be penetrated. In 1954, SIS, like Eden, Lloyd and the rest of Churchill's government could only watch a process whereby American interests, having by 1953 acquired 60 per cent of Middle East oil (compared with 45 per cent in 1951), were ready to achieve a dominating position through shareholding in a new company, or 'consortium', successor to AIOC. Eden was reduced to observing in April 1954 that renewed access to Persian crude was more important to Britain than even the Suez Canal.[32] Commercial domination also met America's political and strategic objectives. An utterly intransigent – or wholly conciliatory – policy by Attlee's Government towards Mossadeq might have forced Truman and his advisers to take sides openly. But fumbling in London – or what was seen as such in Washington – solved Truman's dilemma. America was absolved from the need to consider its ally's interests; it could pose – and it was not wholly a pose – as a neutral, rather hesitant third party, anxious for a sensible, a compromise settlement.

American interests, drawn into the arbitration of Persian issues by circumstance rather than by conscious design, were able to deal, by 1954, a kind of political royal flush: assertion of commercial priorities; repudiation of British ways, intransigent in principle, out-of-date, and out of touch. A British riposte was inevitable. The year of America's triumph in Persia was also the year when Eden coaxed and cajoled several Middle East governments (Persia's eventually, amongst them) into a treaty of mutual defence known as the Baghdad Pact. When the Pact was formally established under the British Government's leadership on 4 April 1955, the day before Eden became Prime Minister, America – and Egypt – were conspicuous absentees. The October 1954 oil deal in Persia was an aspect of Middle East realities. The Baghdad Pact was an event in the looking-glass world. 'The British Cabinet decided that, in spite of recent experiences in Egypt, there were places in the Arab world where military requirements outweighed the drawback of alienating nationalists.'[33]

4 · THE LAST TEMPTATION: SUEZ, 1956

II · *Eden as Prime Minister 1955–6*

The history of the English is full of alternations between an indifference which makes people think them decadent and a rage which baffles their foes. They are seen turning from peace at any price to war to the death.

ALBERT SOREL,
quoted by Lord Strang in his contribution to *Retreat from Power; Studies in Britain's Foreign Policy of the Twentieth Century*

Eden admitted in his memoirs that what happened in Persia during 1951 influenced nationalist sentiment in Egypt. Yet during the following four years Eden failed to relate Abadan and its sequel to a pattern of events and policies which were being shaped in places as far apart as Washington and Cairo. Sadly, for a statesman who prided himself on a world view – and not without some justification – Eden failed at the time to see either the overall pattern or the connecting strands within it. Even Eden's deserved triumph in arbitrating the Trieste dispute between Italy and Yugoslavia, his major role in the Austrian Peace Treaty, and his efforts to make something of a European Defence Community were, in a cruel but compelling sense, the acts of a statesman who did not draw the distinction between diplomacy and power.

Resolution of all these issues finally depended on what America was, or was not, prepared to do for the maintenance of European security. Resolution of imperial issues depended on America also. Eden's memoirs are, understandably, selective and, given the circumstances, much more so than those of other public men. But it is essential to realise, in looking at Eden's twenty-one months as Prime Minister, that his picture of the world differed above all from that of the Arab – and other – nationalists whose right to genuine independence from Britain he and many of his colleagues so tenaciously resisted. Such independence lay in the power to establish and execute foreign policies which reflected national, not imperial interests.

It is equally, perhaps more important, to realise that Eden's picture differed fundamentally from the one seen by President Eisenhower and John Foster Dulles. Eden thought that his old friend Ike and that terrible Secretary of State had a different perspective, namely the wrong one. Above all, Eden saw a persistent, an historic Russian threat to the Middle East – his Middle East. Eisenhower and Dulles saw no Russian threat to American interests that could not be contained by the American nuclear deterrent. Their Middle East was totally different from Eden's *imperium*, not only in the perception of threats and the means of deterring them, but in attitudes and responses to nationalism. Thus it was Eden who was wrong in failing to realise that his erstwhile and ostensible ally was looking at a different picture altogether. Above all, Eden quite failed to answer the key question: would the American nuclear deterrent really be invoked in defence of British interests? These differences were fundamental, not incidental. Much comment on Suez has assumed that Dulles and Eden fell out because of caprice or temperament, because Eden told lies, or the operation itself was ill-conceived, or 'immoral'. All these factors are relevant – except that Dulles was quite cynical about using for purely American ends that supposed cure for international immorality, the United Nations – but none bears on these fundamentally different views of the world.

Eden, in short, misused his four and a half years as post-war Foreign Secretary, and a comparison of what struck him as important with what was actually happening and how others reacted to events illustrates this fatal element in Suez clearly enough. Allowance must be made for acute illness and nervous depression. One Cabinet colleague caustically remarked: 'It is not surprising that Anthony's operations failed. So many people crowded round the surgeons to see what wonders were going to be performed in putting in a plastic bile duct that there was no room to wield the knife properly.' Although this example of the House of Commons smoking room humour which Eden so much detested suggests scorn rather than compassion, his colleagues did look at him with sorrow and understanding. Churchill, a stooping and sometimes stumbling figure in the corridors of the House, would seize one of Eden's few friends by the arm and ask: 'How is he?' A temporising answer would be given. The old giant would move sombrely away. Between May and October 1953 Eden was under the knife, completely out of action. Thereafter, increasing doses of benzedrine disguised the realities of his condition. The plastic duct was corroded by bile, which began to seep into the blood stream. Eden, in consequence, began to suffer what the layman would call brain fever.

That said, Eden's preoccupation as Foreign Secretary with the international statesman role has to be compared with a world in which the power of independent action began to be acquired and developed by Britain's former imperial subjects. This power was also asserted at all times by an America whose President was determined to fight the cold war with policies of containment and massive nuclear retaliation – in situations deemed critical by the National Security Council. Eisenhower was convinced that outside Europe and the American strongholds of Latin America, Japan, South Korea, and Taiwan, Roosevelt's policy of encouraging nationalism should be re-adopted and reconfirmed. In the years of Eisenhower's first Presidency the final collapse of the British Empire remained a basic assumption of American foreign policy. The assumption lay deep in American attitudes to Britain; was not confined to Dulles, or to isolationists; was not deflected by CIA reactions to SIS reports; and could often be found in Anglophiles. The full dimension of Suez cannot be appreciated unless the strength of American assumptions about the end of Empire is appreciated.

In the years when Eden was declining in vigour and vision – as, indeed, was Britain – Dulles created an American foreign policy which was independent and bi-polar in two senses. There was one given enemy: Russian and, by extension, Chinese communism. Nuclear weapons would deter that enemy, above all in Europe; the policy, by the nature of the strategic instrument adopted, would lead eventually to a kind of tacit understanding with the men in Moscow, if not in Peking. Should Russia reach approximate nuclear parity with America, a deterrent balance would be created. Recourse to war would become pointless. But the balance could only be maintained if America's nuclear weapons were constantly improved in their retaliatory capacity. Thus the weapons must be widely dispersed throughout European NATO rather than confined to continental America. Outside European NATO, and beyond the strongholds, American ideas and American money would establish new relationships with leaders and peoples who were opposed to colonialism and communism alike. The American presence in this rapidly changing, this new world, would consist of the political missionary and the commercial bagman. Both would be accompanied by the CIA, whose function would be covertly to undermine the colonial systems of Britain and France. French governments of the Fourth Republic, left, right, and centre, never suffered from any illusions on this point.

Stalin's concentration on Europe and his refusal to experiment with Arabia or Africa explains the perspective of the National Security Council's all embracing yet elementary prescription of 7 April 1950, given in a policy paper, formally adopted by the Truman and Eisenhower Administrations thereafter, and known in its classified form as NSC 68. The language of the Paper suggests an America menaced by Russia, but a careful reading provides a more subtle interpretation. NSC 68 summarises a doctrine of strategic independence, one which masks the search for accommodation with a Russia potentially America's equal as a nuclear super power. 'Recent technological developments have greatly intensified the Soviet threat to the United States. In particular, the United States now faces the contingency that within the next four or five years the Soviet Union will possess the military capability of delivering a surprise attack of such weight that the United States must have substantially increased air, ground, and sea strength, atomic capabilities and air and civilian defences to deter war, and to provide reasonable assurance, in the event of war, that it could survive the initial blow and go on to the eventual attainment of its objectives.'

The danger of Russian nuclear supremacy (not necessarily the probability of its being used coercively or destructively) was assumed in NSC 68; 'objectives' were not defined. There was a simple assertion that: 'The Kremlin's policy towards the United States is animated by a peculiarly virulent blend of hatred and fear; the Kremlin is inescapably militant.' There was, however, no assumption that the Kremlin sought world dominion in classic Marxist-Leninist terms. Indeed, NSC 68 ignored this aspect of affairs entirely. The paper was concerned with American security. There was, therefore, no necessity to station American troops in sensitive areas. Friendly countries would be encouraged to lease bases instead, enabling America's long range bomber force to operate at will as an instrument of deterrence or when massively retaliating after a Russian first strike. The authors of NSC 68 were not, collectively, as experienced in international affairs as their opposite numbers in Whitehall, but they expressed one truth about politics and strategy which applied with particular force to the 1950s: garrisons of foreign troops provoked nationalist, indeed revolutionary outbreaks; aircraft arriving and departing did not. Dulles's interest in a 'Northern Tier' of States against Russian encroachments (Turkey, Persia, Pakistan) has been confused with Eden's Baghdad Pact aspirations. Dulles was only interested in points on the map from which the B-29 could operate or its missile successor could be emplaced. Eden wanted the support of actively anti-Russian governments, backed by large armies, as the outer-works of a defensive position in the Middle East, behind which Egypt would remain a client state and the Suez Canal would be secure.

America's allies were conveniently ignored in NSC 68 because by 1954 – 'the year of maximum danger' in terms of Russia's presumed nuclear capacities – it was hoped that the doctrine of massive retaliation would have impressed even an inescapably militant Kremlin with the risk of picking a quarrel with any one of them. But the corollary to this doctrine was that the allies should do as they were told, should not be the cause of quarrels. Weak allies, weak sisters, should be particularly careful not to get America into trouble. Massive retaliation against an unspecified threat was only credible if nothing was allowed to provoke Russian hostility. 'The negotiation from strength' and the promised 'roll back' of Russian forces from Eastern Europe, which Dulles linked to massive retaliation, were nothing more than a smokescreen for horse trading with the Kremlin. Between 1953 and 1956 America and Russia reached more of an accommodation about Europe than was realised – or admitted – at the time. This was a super-power accommodation based on the mutual possession of constantly improved nuclear weapons systems: no others were involved. Britain's search for a crude first strike system did more than provoke American unease; Britain was excluded from the nuclear top table.

The Geneva Summit of July 1955 was a smokescreen hiding the realities of international life. The reality was that America and Russia accepted a divided Germany in a Europe where the war remained cold and did not become hot because deterrent strategies were perceived by these super powers as mutually acceptable. There was, however, one qualification to this bi-polar approach, tacitly accepted by Eden in 1954, forgotten by him, in terms of its strategic implication, in 1956. During 1954, and following the breakdown of negotiations for a European Defence Community, Eden accepted Dulles's case for German membership of NATO. Eden went further; he reaffirmed the EDC pledge to maintain four British divisions on the continent of Europe. When the Federal German Republic joined NATO in 1955, the four divisions were committed, to 'A.D. 2000', as an overt British contribution to European security, a covert insurance against a revival of German militarism. But Eden's reaffirmation of a commitment to European security was extracted at a time when strains on the British Army were growing; rebellion in Kenya and discontent in Cyprus were contained by troops, in large numbers. Yet an American Secretary of State was determined to meet the Kremlin half-way, to ensure that America's allies were kept in their place on the super power chess board. As Dulles himself said at the time: 'Treaties of alliance mean little except as they spell out what the people concerned would do anyway.'[1] Western Europe in general and Britain in particular did what Dulles wanted. One consequence of doing so was that Dulles locked up most of the British Army on German soil.

Moreover, American military strength, which had grown during the rearmament programme of the Korean War, was deliberately tailored in the Eisenhower years to an economy which was encouraged to put business before defence. When Charles Wilson, Eisenhower's Defence Secretary, declared, 'What's good for America is good for General Motors, he was both reflecting a policy and echoing a sentiment which had a direct bearing on the fate of any American ally which might cause trouble with Russia – *or* get into trouble on its own account. Despite the warnings and exhortations in NSC 68, its substance as a policy offered no indication that General Eisenhower intended to contain Russia by forceful means. In his 1952 election campaign Eisenhower promised to bring the boys out of Korea. He kept his word. Whatever Allan Dulles might say, there wasn't going to be a next war whilst Eisenhower was President. American military strength throughout the 1950s increased only in terms of nuclear weapons and the means of delivering them. Fear of Russian potential remained, but it was a fear tempered by facts. The first Russian intercontinental bomber, the TU 95 or Bear, did not appear until 1955. By then, the American Air Force had nearly two thousand bombers capable of reaching Russian targets, most expeditiously from bases in European NATO. By contrast, the American military capacity to intervene quickly with conventional forces if an ally called for help remained extremely limited.

There is no mention of American strategic priorities, as reflected by NSC 68, in any accounts of the years in question by Eden and his colleagues. They appeared equally blind to the realities of events outside the American containment area. These experienced politicians, these outwardly self-assured and confident late-imperialists narrate events between 1951 and 1956, above all in the Middle East, as if someone, somewhere was not playing the game. The Labour Party, in opposition, was divided between supporters of an imperial system and a minority who favoured independence at any price for satellites and colonies. As a result, the Party in the House of Commons was divided, and offered no constructive criticism. Attlee's retirement from leadership of the

Party in December 1955 robbed Britain of a national figure, an international statesman. Attlee's successor, the thin-skinned and ineffectual Hugh Gaitskell, was interested in foreign affairs; he knew little about them. Eden, known to dislike parliamentary debate on equal terms, had an easy time in projecting a picture of Britain beset by unscrupulous opportunists. Eden's comfortable victory in the May 1955 General Election convinced him he would not have much explaining to do in the House. Here was another illusion which only the humiliations of Suez dispelled.

From the time in that foreboding October 1951 when Nahas Pasha, Prime Minister of Egypt, unilaterally abrogated the 1936 Treaty of Alliance with Britain to the final stages of the Suez operation, Eden, Lloyd, and many in the Cabinet consistently failed to accept that there were two sides to the issue of who was to be master. If, during these years the inheritors of power had stopped to consider what Eisenhower and Dulles really intended for America as a super power the issues might well have been resolved by compromise. Even Nasser, that 'malicious swine' as Churchill, rather uncharacteristically – and quite inaccurately – called him, was in 1954 loth to eject Britain from Egypt if doing so opened the doors to the super powers. This was a factor in the situation which both Eden and Dulles failed to grasp – at the time. They shared little else, then or later. Eden turned to thoughts of replacing Nasser by what a sceptical colleague called a stooge; Dulles worked out the means whereby Nasser could be propitiated.

Dulles's public comments on the events following Nahas Pasha's démarche, Farouk's overthrow by Neguib and Nasser in July 1952, and subsequent plans for the withdrawal of British troops from Egypt were so non-committal as to suggest he had no active policy regarding the Middle East, but was merely waiting to see how events developed. This was not so. Eden, not Dulles, let events master him. Dulles was determined to remove Britain from the Middle East – as were the American Joint Chiefs of Staff in the Second World War – not only by conciliating nationalists but by overtly and covertly opposing everything which Eden believed in. Because Eden's attitude towards Egypt was founded on assumptions, his policies lacked substance. They were also ambiguous.

Eden genuinely wanted to withdraw troops from Egypt. One reason for doing so was that the Conservative Government was planning by October 1954, when a withdrawal agreement was signed with Nasser, to abolish conscription, and run down the

Army to pay for the remorselessly accelerating cost of the nuclear weapons programme. In 1955 one of Eden's first acts as Prime Minister was to order a reduction in the size of the reserve forces. Field Marshal Alexander, Churchill's Minister of Defence, Antony Head (Secretary of State for War), and the Chiefs of Staff supported the decision to withdraw from Egypt, but did so believing it marked the end of an imperial chapter. The troops should be made available to defend Britain's real interests in the Middle East. The continued flow of oil from Persia, Iraq, and Kuwait was seen as the overriding strategic priority, one which had been underlined by Abadan – and the American response. Indeed the Persian Gulf area as a whole was a priority, given the potential value of oilfields in the Sheikhdoms of Abu Dhabi and Qatar. The logistic problems associated with an area remote from outright British control forced the Chiefs to argue in more realistic terms than appeared in their warnings to Attlee. They said throughout the early 1950s that Britain must improve relations with governments in the Middle East as a whole, conceding something to nationalism and more to the demand for treatment as equals. If these concessions were not made, airfields and other facilities would be lacking when required to support new doctrines of rapid deployment and improved mobility. Early in 1954 a Strategic Reserve was established (on paper) with such objectives in view.

Eden paid little attention to these arguments. He had none of Churchill's absorbed interest in strategy as an element in imperial policy. Eden was, however, determined to send troops back to Egypt on the slightest pretext. Eden had negotiated the 1936 Treaty which stipulated that not more than 10,000 British troops should be stationed in Egypt in peace-time. Attlee and Churchill had ignored this provision. Eden went one better. He made an agreement with Nasser which provided for the return of British troops 'in certain circumstances', specifically, an attack on Egypt, another Arab State, or Turkey, by 'an outside power'. Nasser did not take the conditions seriously, and Eden did not lack for advisers who pointed this out to him. He chose to ignore the advice of Sir Ralph Stevenson, the British Ambassador, as he later rejected the warnings of his successor Sir Humphrey Trevelyan. Eden also ignored what Anthony Nutting said. The views of the Chiefs of Staff were derided. When Eden became Prime Minister he gave Macmillan the Foreign Office but, by the following December, had moved him, protests ignored and mutual antipathies intensified, to the Treasury. Selwyn Lloyd, merely remarking, 'Eden and Macmillan had not found it easy to work with each other', became Foreign Secretary.[2] Nutting and Antony Head had negotiated much of the Canal Base Agreement. Nutting then spent weeks during 1955 in Cairo as Minister of State, working out withdrawal details, and making plans with Nasser for mothballing the Base facilities against circumstances which were never defined in terms of probable threats and possible contingencies.

Nutting came to know, like, and trust Nasser. Here was a big man, to be reckoned with, who could use phrases like 'dignity for my people' and not sound absurd in doing so. The trust was mutual. Nutting became convinced that there could be no circumstances except world war – a contingency so remote for Nasser as to be irrelevant – in which British troops could return to Egypt. Nasser had thrice nearly been assassinated by the Moslem Brotherhood for signing the Agreement. He was unlikely to court downfall by implementing provisions which would enable British troops to return. Nasser had more than a conspirator's suspicion that Eden intended to invoke the 'return' clauses in the Agreement in order to get rid of him. Kneeling on the floor in Nasser's study looking at maps, amiably enduring his rather simple jokes about turning the imperialists out, Nutting became convinced that, to Nasser, getting rid of the British was not a diplomatic manoeuvre but a stage in revolution. Nasser had no objection to uniformed British technicians remaining in the Base. Indeed, he welcomed this compromise as some compensation for the economic aid which he sought but which Eden did not give. Nasser hoped that the Base would gradually be transformed into a centre for Egyptian industry. But the imperial presence must go.

Nutting gave his appreciation to Eden. Lloyd was told officially but, in 1955, Nutting and Eden communicated directly, as friends. Eden took no notice. He also conspicuously ignored Nutting's warning that any attempt by the British Government to enlarge the Baghdad Pact would be construed by Nasser as a direct threat to him and the Egyptian revolution. By the time Eden became Prime Minister dislike of comment which might reflect on his handling of affairs had become more than an irritant to his colleagues; they were saddled with the liability of a Chief who refused to listen. Eden had not forgiven Churchill and Attlee for jointly criticising the Base Agreement when it had been debated in the House on 29 July 1954. Churchill's tone was valedictory, both for himself and for Empire, but Attlee, his usual astringent self, was not slow to accuse Eden of 'scuttle', of shirking his imperial responsibilities.

Perhaps Eden did believe, up to a point, in the 'new era of friendship and mutual understanding', the phrase by which the Agreement was announced. Initially at least Eden would not have shared the sardonic remarks in the Cairo Embassy about 'The great God Nefmu'. The Embassy was not slow to tell Eden that Nefmu and the Baghdad Pact were virtually irreconcilable. Nasser made his opposition to the Pact clear from the start. The Embassy, with the notable exception of the SIS Station, believed Nasser to be not just a new figure on the Arab scene, but likely to be an enduring one, with whom British governments must learn to live. Eden rejected this appreciation. He intended the new era to be one of friendship and understanding on his terms, with Nasser playing a role not fundamentally different from that of the pliant men he had met at Lampson's Embassy a decade ago. Such men kept their jobs strictly by virtue of respect for Britain's imperial obligations. Eden hoped to play on Nasser's dislike of foreign interference by warning him that a Russian friendship would be as dangerous for him as it would be for Britain. Nasser listened politely to these messages, as he did to those from Selwyn Lloyd, who privately noted: 'In the other areas in the Middle East where we had control – Kuwait, Bahrain and other shaikhdoms in the Gulf – we should seek to create politically viable entities buttressed by a comparatively scanty military presence on our part . . . Along these lines I believed that we could reduce our commitments in an orderly fashion but retain our influence and capacity to intervene in an emergency'. Whilst Lloyd indulged in these strategic pipe dreams – sufficiently cloudy for Eden to assume he shared his belief that a return to *Egypt* was militarily feasible – Nasser proceeded on his deliberate revolutionary path.[3]

Nasser promised to abide by the 1888 Suez Canal Convention, and thus keep that waterway free to international shipping at all times. But Nasser agreed to comply with international practice in terms which were not defined with much regard for international lawyers' language. Nasser was promised arms by Eden – none had been supplied since the 1951 abrogation – but showed no obvious impatience for them. Nasser hoped to get arms and economic aid from Russia. Dulles was unwilling to supply American weapons because of pressure from the Zionist lobby. Nasser, a born conspirator, hedged his bets – but with the American Embassy in Cairo, not the cautious diplomats from Moscow. Nasser was told by the Embassy what he had already guessed: Dulles saw him as a better deterrent than the Baghdad Pact to communism in the Middle East. A relationship was established between American Secretaries of State and Nasser, via successive astute American Ambassadors in Cairo, which was to have its stormy moments – above all in 1967, when diplomatic relations were broken – but which endured for all practical purposes throughout the sixteen years when Nasser was leader of the Egyptian people.

The American Ambassador in Cairo, Jefferson Caffery, had been 'malevolently anti-British'.[4] Trevelyan had to contend with the more sophisticated Henry Byroade, whose task was to convince Nasser that the Base Agreement was a bogus prospectus peddled by a bankrupt sharepusher. Byroade had the distressing habit of calling Nasser 'Gamal' to his face, but he and his Chancery established relationships with the Revolutionary Command Council which were closer than anything which Trevelyan and his experienced colleagues could manage. The State Department sent roving ambassadors alternately to tempt Nasser with aid and to harangue him for lapses from the path of pro-Western revolution. Byroade fielded these visitors and kept Nasser, if not exactly happy, then in the state of pleasing expectation for a revolutionary conspirator that something substantial could be expected from a power which was so resolutely opposed to imperial pretensions.

But more was needed than American bonhomie. Byroade's staff gave to Hakim Amer, Nasser's Army Commander, the British contingency plan for return to Egypt in the one circumstance which had been mooted in the Ministry of Defence: nationalisation of the Canal Company, coupled with threats by Nasser to shipping and personnel. The plan was given to the American Embassy in the belief that the State Department would emphasise to Dulles that seizure of the Company's assets and threats to British personnel would damage international commerce as a whole, justifying retaliation by forceful means. This diplomatic manoeuvre failed: very few ships flying the Stars and Stripes passed through the Suez Canal. American indifference on this score is understandable; providing Hakim Amer with the contingency plan can only be explained by Dulles's insistence on thwarting Britain by any means which came to hand.

Failure of communication between Cairo and London was of more immediate consequence than lack of American response to British warnings. SIS did not tell Eden that the plan was in American hands. This lapse reflected states of confusion in a

Broadway where anything went and little worked. Sinclair had other things on his mind. Although Nasser's final seizure of power from his rival Neguib in November 1954 had led to an SIS effort in the Middle East which used more resources than those concentrated on Russia and Eastern Europe, Sinclair was too weak a 'C' to decide whether SIS in the former area should meet the requirements laid on it by acquiring intelligence about Nasser's intentions or by conducting operations to ensure they were not put into effect. In the event, SIS did neither to any purpose.

The SIS position in Egypt had in no sense improved since wartime days. Political intelligence – on which, in any case, the Embassy claimed a prior right – was either inadequate or misleading, or both. Operational intelligence, both for SIS as such and, in military terms, for the Joint Intelligence Bureau in the Ministry of Defence, was characterised by the kind of mistakes which, in a properly regulated service, get those responsible into trouble. Maps for the JIB, for example, marked roads that no longer existed; urban sprawl had obliterated them. One map even gave the site of an imaginary city – Thalata. This word is a transliteration of the Arabic for 'three'. When the map was marked up for use by the JIB – and for issue to Army units – the word, noting, in fact, the Third Signal Station on the Canal south from Port Said, was elevated into a place of some pretensions. Commanders of units and formations, briefed for an attack on the basis of such intelligence, would have found themselves with axes of advance that had become built-up areas leading to an objective which did not exist. SIS did not draw maps; SIS officers and agents were given the requirement to ensure their accuracy. In this case, the Cairo Station failed to do its job properly.

As withdrawal of British troops from Egypt accelerated, military intelligence staffs were run down. The SIS responsibility for operational intelligence increased. In the Ministry of Defence doubts began to be privately expressed about whether SIS in Egypt was simply incompetent or had, at the Station Commander level, a vested interest in confusing the issue. The officer in question was a friend of Philby; they had worked together intermittently since 1944. He planned his own operations without Broadway's final determination on whether they were feasible or not – as, indeed, did all Stations in those days of local enterprise. One very necessary operation was to penetrate the Egyptian Intelligence Service, whose quality had markedly improved once Nasser's leadership became accepted and acceptable to the armed forces and police, and whose activities throughout Arabia became a major SIS target in consequence. In Egypt itself, moreover, the intelligence services came to occupy much of the middle ground between discredited politicians and revolutionary soldiers. Penetration of the EIS reflected the Whitehall requirement to distinguish between Nasser's friends and enemies. Such an operation needed more verve than the Cairo Station provided. The SIS regional headquarters in Cyprus was tasked. In the meantime Cairo continued to send back reports which only Eden wanted to read. But he needed more than rumours to remove Nasser.

Fundamental differences of policy between Eden and Dulles regarding Egypt's future became acute when Nasser accepted Russian arms in September 1955. Dulles offered Nasser more economic aid; Eden planned retaliation, convinced he had been right all along in not trusting Nasser, in disliking him when they met in March. Eden decided to destroy Nasser – his own word – Dulles to regard him as the best hope for the Arab future. Immediately after the signing of the Base Agreement, Dulles had offered Nasser $40 million in aid. Considerable undercover payments were also made, reflecting Dulles's belief that Nasser would remain a pro-Western revolutionary if he was subsidised. The probability that Nasser would use these funds to extend the coverage of Cairo Radio – since its start up in May 1953 the most potent threat to Britain's position in Arabia – never crossed Dulles's mind. If it had, he would have lost no sleep. Britain's wider Middle Eastern interests – above all the Suez Canal as, in Eden's words 'the swing door' protecting Persian Gulf oil – were genuinely beyond comprehension by a Secretary of State whose mind worked in grooves. Although some of Dulles's motives and antagonisms concerning Britain remain obscure and although he occasionally threatened Nasser, the basic thrust of his policy was that the latter was a man to do business with.

Dulles was not averse from devious policies. Moreover, he not only liked to win: he had to. 'The exterior of ruthlessness which Dulles presented to the world did not altogether belie what lay within. He scarcely knew the meaning of compromise, and in so far as he understood it he despised it, an attitude of mind which has much too readily been overlooked when considering his relations with Britain; the British so-called "genius for compromise" led Dulles to misunderstand and suspect the behaviour of many other people in London besides the unfortunate Anthony Eden. Dulles could be unswerving, hard, dogmatic, opinionated and even cruel, if he believed, as he often did, that the end justified the means. In the exceedingly tough school of American corporation law where Dulles grew up, it is not enough as it is in England merely to defeat your opponent; he must be crushed and pulverized so that he can never be a threat again.'[5] Britain, the weak sister, was a threat to Dulles if its leaders started playing games again in the Middle East. Indeed, Russia's entrée, however limited and hesitant, accentuated the threat. Dulles did not change his views about how to deal with Russia; his convictions were strengthened on how to dispose of British pretensions. Eden saw none of this. In late 1955 he started on the road to Suez believing that a common perception of the same threat would see Dulles marching, however reluctantly and resentfully, beside him.

Eden's first deliberate move was to send General Sir Gerald Templer, Chief of the Imperial General Staff, to see King Hussein in Jordan. But this visit did not take place until January 1956 – when Eden and Selwyn Lloyd also went to see Dulles in Washington. Much of 1955 had found Eden preoccupied with summitry in Geneva and problems at home. Geneva, although affording relief from a whispering campaign amongst Conservative MPs that 'the deft diplomat was no leader; he had no control over his Ministers', was not only an escape from domestic realities into a world where he could display his virtuoso gifts: it was a refuge from the situation which had been inexorably developing since the Egyptian revolution of July 1952.[6] Eden lost precious months, during which nemesis, hobbling after him slow but sure, prepared his doom.

Eden's reactions to what Nasser represented operated at so many levels, from calculation to fear, that it is essential to appreciate that his motives in sending Templer to Amman in the hopes of Hussein joining the Baghdad Pact were in stark contrast to Whitehall opinion about British interests in the Middle East. Doubts about the Pact deterring a Russian entrée had been expressed by more than one Ambassador, and there was no enthusiasm for it in the Foreign Office. The Chiefs of Staff believed that good Anglo-Jordanian relations were essential if Britain's strategic commitments in the Persian Gulf were to be sustained. The Chiefs did not believe that urging Hussein to join the Baghdad Pact would improve relations with him. Hussein had to walk a tight-rope between a moderately pro-British attitude and respect for Arab nationalism. Caution, not demands to join the Pact, was the only way to keep Hussein on the tight-rope.

Eden's determination after September 1955 to widen the Pact's membership as a deterrent to Nasser's influence in the area produced further critical comments from the men on the spot. But none was able to deny that Nasser's revolutionary rhetoric needed a riposte of some kind. Nor were Eden and Selwyn Lloyd given any evidence that Dulles's policy of encouraging Nasser to concentrate on Egypt's economic needs would deter him from continuing a propaganda campaign through Cairo Radio. 'The Voice of the Arabs' was potent in Arabia because its message was so simple: 'We have rid ourselves of the British. Do you likewise.' Nasser believed that this message would be particularly well received in the Persian Gulf, where Britain's ambiguously exercised authority over nominally independent sheikhs, emirs, and sultans was thought by many Arab nationalists to be less acceptable than outright imperial control. By 1956 Cairo Radio was heard from the Shatt 'Al Arab to the Straits of Hormuz.

Templer, a soldier, went reluctantly to Amman knowing he was the symbol of Eden's belief that a British 'presence' in Arabia was as essential in 1956 as in 1882. Templer agreed, but his belief was based on strategic arguments, not imperial emotions. Nasser's intention – conveyed by nods and winks to Trevelyan and others – to intensify his propaganda once the last British soldier left Egypt in June 1956 only served to harden Eden's prejudice. The Embassy and SIS in Cairo reported that the Suez Canal Company might well be nationalised immediately after the final withdrawal. Such rare unanimity alerted some officials in Whitehall. The reports were supported by Antony Head's independent assessment. Eden made no positive response. He compensated for his personal ailments and political frustrations by dreaming of his enemy's destruction.

As Templer prepared for his journey it would have taken a rare Whitehall radical to point out he was wasting his time. The only effective deterrent to Nasser was a policy designed to safeguard Britain's vital interests in the Middle East by a strategy which concentrated on the Gulf, plus a political programme similar to that of the American Government: meeting nationalists half-way and taking some notice of economic stagnation and the frustrations and animosities which it bred. By 1955 Britain's economic situation was superficially much better than in 1951. No fundamental industrial reconstruction had been made despite post-war efforts by Attlee's Governments, but austerity had been left behind. Eden referred, rather revealingly, to 'the plagues of prosperity'. He could have afforded both political and economic generosity in dealing with Nasser.

If the British Army had possessed, in real terms, either a strategic reserve or the aircraft to fly it, imperial convictions would have been weakened about the prime importance of the Suez Canal as a line of communication for the Royal Navy, and for troopships to Singapore and Hong Kong. Lord Mountbatten (First Sea Lord) and Sir Dermot Boyle (Chief of the Air Staff) agreed with Templer. Oil and the Suez Canal no longer belonged to the same set of strategic priorities. The Chiefs of Staff in short, never very happy about any plan to 'retake' the Canal, were hoping the need to do so would not arise. There was decreasing need to do so on economic grounds. The oil companies in the mid-1950s had begun to point out that they would soon be sending their new, very large tankers round the Cape of Good Hope. The Suez Canal Company had refused to widen and deepen the Canal sufficiently for these tankers to use it; the Company preferred revenue to investment. By 1955 the Canal, in real strategic and economic terms, was ceasing to be a swing door; it was important, but not vital. Yet the Canal was 'ours'. Most of the Canal pilots were British master mariners. The thought of 'losing' it was only a shade less painful than the dread of having to 'retake' it.

Whitehall in general, moreover, accepted Eden's argument that further Russian moves in the Middle East must be resisted. Yet Eden's case that Nasser, in taking Russian arms, had become an agent for communist penetration, did not receive the kind of critical political analysis which it required. In the mid-1950s Russian policy for and in the Middle East was characterised by extreme caution. Instability in Syria and Jordan, which led to major political crises in 1957, and family quarrels between the Hashemite rulers of Jordan and Iraq reflected the legacies of British imperialism, a struggle for power between the legatees and their radical nationalist rivals. These factors were ignored in the No. 10 Cabinet Room. British policy for the Middle East was still governed by imperial emotions or strategic appreciations based on military rather than economic factors, and indifferent alike to local ambitions and Russian hesitation. Eden could well have said to himself, in the words of Lord Lytton, who as Viceroy of India fought an unnecessary war in 1878 to deter a supposed Russian threat to Afghanistan, bamboozling the home government in the process: 'Whilst we have been sleeping sound the Russians, more wakeful and alert, have stolen away our clothes; and we now have to get ourselves new political garments before we can appear, without cutting a sorry figure, on the stage of Asian politics.'[7]

This was the kind of sentiment which also appealed to Nuri Said Pasha, Iraq's dictator – under the guise of being the young King Feisal's Prime Minister. Nuri, a politician of fortune once he deserted his Ottoman masters in 1915, was one of those friends of Britain in Arabia on whom Eden relied for assurance. Nuri had served imperial interests faithfully. As Prime Minister of Iraq in 1951 he had hoped Britain would crush Mossadeq. National sentiments were robustly repressed in Baghdad. Yet Eden might have remembered that the Voice of the Arabs was heard there also, that Nuri was willing to hob-nob with Nasser, to hear him attack the Baghdad Pact (of which Iraq had been a founder member) without doing more than shake his head. Even Nuri urged the Iraq Petroleum Company to emulate the Americans in Saudi Arabia – and Persia. Nuri said that the Company should pay higher oil revenues, and do so before a revolution took place in Iraq which would damage Britain far more seriously than anything which Nasser could do in Egypt. Nuri's warning went virtually unheeded. The Company educated and employed promising Iraqis, and kept the Iraq Government financially afloat. Surely that was enough?[8]

The power of a British prime minister to believe what he – or she – chooses without effective, rational, argued opposition, was never better expressed than in the Templer mission. The CIGS had made his post-war reputation by beating communists in Malaya at their own game. As High Commissioner in the early 1950s he had strongly backed the policy of eventual independence from colonial rule. Templer had fought communists intelligently, but ruthlessly. He was, to Eden's way of looking at issues, the man to warn Hussein of the perils of friendship with Nasser. In consequence the rebuff Templer received had a greater effect on Eden than if some military mediocrity had been sent to express the permanence of British prestige in Arabia. Templer was sent away with a flea in his ear; Hussein point blank refused to join the Baghdad Pact; Nasser intensified his campaign against it; on 1 March as Selwyn Lloyd was dining with Nasser and Trevelyan during the course of a Middle East tour which should have, but did not, bring realities home to all those who went on it, news came through that Hussein had sacked the British Commander of his Praetorian Guard. Lieutenant-General Sir John Bagot Glubb Pasha and the Arab Legion had become post-war, post-imperial symbols of the kind of 'continuities' sought by Eden and his like. Young Hussein, the Harrovian, the Sandhurst boy, king of a country invented for his grandfather Abdullah, could hardly have delivered a more calculated snub if he had publicly announced support for Nasser and all his works. Hussein's great grandfather, the Sherif of Mecca, had, reluctantly, done what the British told him to do; the boy king bent to the nationalist wind.

The blow came at a bad moment in Anglo-American relations. Eden and Lloyd had returned from their American visit tired and depressed. Neither Eisenhower nor Dulles showed interest in or knowledge about an Egypt which, in Eden's eyes, was fast becoming a Russian satellite. Eisenhower was intent on his forthcoming election campaign, determined to become a peace-making President for a second term. Dulles, the corporation lawyer, was weighing the pros and cons of a World Bank loan to Nasser for the building of a dam at Aswan on the Upper Nile. Eisenhower had become a consummate politician, and every warning of Eden's was judged by the effect on his campaign. Eisenhower did not need the Zionist Lobby to remind him that 'hasten slowly' was a good motto in election year. In deference to the far more powerful oil lobby, Eisenhower hastened with extreme slowness in supplying Israel with weapons: he supplied none.

Dulles, convinced that Nasser was America's best Arabian bet, nevertheless disliked putting down good money, mostly American money on the Aswan Dam, a project whose purpose and scale went far beyond the kind of aid which would buttress Egypt economically and keep it firmly in the Western camp. For all his talk, Dulles was no keener than Eden to see nationalists get to the point where Western aid would enable them to have independent, or even 'neutralist' foreign policies. Who was not with Dulles was very much against him. Yet this outlook did not enable Dulles to support Eden. The British Prime Minister was not a good bet. Two international statesmen, both sick men, were left to nourish a morbid dislike and distrust for each other.[9]

By early March, with the final departure of British troops but three months away and with even SIS in Egypt unable to produce convincing evidence of effective local opposition to Nasser, Eden's determination to destroy him had reached the stage in his increasingly fevered mind where only the means to do so were wanting. No further search for a reason, or justification, would be made. Publicly, in a deluded House of Commons above all, justifications for action would take the form of lies. These lies, however, would reflect the unavoidable processes of political hypocrisy, imposed on Eden and his colleagues by collusion and their fear of its consequences. Men said of R.A. Butler (Lord Privy Seal and Leader of the House of Commons), Eden's most troubled, disloyal, and discreet colleague: 'He is full of accurate information which he is too cautious to divulge.'[10] Eden's collusions imposed the same caution on the Cabinet as a whole. The full extent of Eden's illness was also hidden from the public by Cabinet collusion.

The means of destroying Nasser came from the one quarter which Eden suspected of aggravating rather than easing his obsessions about the Middle East. In late March, David Ben-Gurion made an indirect proposal to Eden for a joint military operation against Nasser. Ben-Gurion, after meeting Selwyn Lloyd in Tel Aviv, made the first move, initiated the critical collusion, the one most carefully concealed, the act of deception which made Eden's later involvement with France – and the latter's with Israel – almost trivial by comparison, and he did so knowing Eden's indifference to the issue of Israel's survival. Eden's memoirs contain *one* reference to this issue in the context of specific threats in 1956: the raids from Gaza by Egyptian commandos (Fedayeen), intended as a prelude to full-scale Egyptian attack. At the annual Guildhall banquet, on 9 November 1955, Eden had said a new effort should be made for Middle East peace. When Ben-Gurion read the speech he could see nothing in it for Israel. But the covert approach was made; the deal was done; the consequences were fatal to Eden for a reason which has also lain concealed for twenty years. Eden planned to destroy Nasser because he also determined to reoccupy Egypt, with British troops, and to install a successor, a Nuri if he could be found, a stooge if he could not. Eden's initial reaction to Ben-Gurion's temptation was 'over my dead body'. As the possibilities of collusion sank in, the desire for Nasser's destruction was transmogrified into a major operation of war.

Ben-Gurion approached Eden because he had been rebuffed by the French Government concerning the sale of bombers. Throughout the years when Nasser had been establishing himself as the one undisputed voice of the Arabs, Israeli governments had been waiting for the moment when it would be heard in Moscow. Whether the Russian Government sought out Nasser or vice versa – there is a good deal of circumstantial evidence that, in 1955, the Russian Government was in no hurry to supply him with arms – the strategic fact remained that once Egyptian forces were re-equipped, Israel would be in peril. Nasser, in his last years, came to regret his attempts to destroy Israel. He thought and behaved very differently in 1956. Destruction of Israel would cement his leadership of the Arab world. That this prize, gained by such a method, would destroy his relations with America did not worry Nasser – in 1956. He was more of a gambler then than in later years.

Apart from France and Canada, no government was prepared to sell modern weapons to Israel. In 1956 the Israeli armed forces were distinguished mainly by morale; their weapons were worn out or obsolescent, even for operations against Arab armies. The one strategy available to an Israeli government which believed that raids from Egyptian soil were the prelude to invasion was pre-emptive. But to strike first required weapons sufficient in numbers and calibre not only to destroy the Egyptian Air Force on the ground but to halt armour before it reached the Israeli frontier. The French Government of Guy Mollet refused to meet that basic Israeli requirement, arguing that Ben-Gurion should concentrate on a defensive strategy. Mollet was prepared to sell twenty-four Mystère fighters – for cash, in advance – so that Tel Aviv could be defended from Egyptian bombers. More were promised, with French crews to fly them if necessary.

The Canadian Government pledged twenty-four (American) F86 fighters to Ben-Gurion. None was delivered in 1956. Mollet's advisers knew that Ben-Gurion, most lionhearted but most emotional of leaders, feared the effect of bombing on a civilian population, increasingly of Jews from Algeria, Morocco, Tunisia, Libya, Egypt, Iraq and Yemen who, in his jaundiced view, lacked the stoic virtues of their settler brethren from Europe. By early March, Ben-Gurion had most of his Mystères, but no bombers. Mollet and his colleagues were antagonistic to Nasser because he supported, by propaganda if little else, the liberation war in Algeria. But Mollet was not prepared to mount an offensive against Nasser.

Ben-Gurion's advisers discounted the Egyptian bombing threat, but were insistent that pre-emptive and interdiction weapons were essential, to be supplied – or made available – before the Egyptians re-trained, more or less effectively, with Russian aircraft and armour. Specifically, Yehoshafat Harkabi, the Director of Military Intelligence, argued that a combined attack must be made at the critical moment not only on the Egyptian Air Force in the Delta but against the two armoured divisions at El Arish which would form the spearhead of any offensive. These formations should be attacked; their supply columns must be destroyed. Yes, said Moshe Dayan, Chief of Staff, and Shimon Peres, Director-General of the Defence Ministry, but these operations can only be carried out by experienced crews in modern medium bombers, capable of attacks at various heights on both static and mobile targets. There were such bombers – in the Royal Air Force Canberra Squadrons based in Britain, and Cyprus. Ben-Gurion and his Foreign Minister, Golda Meir, knew that Eden sought a pretext to destroy Nasser.

The Israeli Government did not lack for Zionists in the British Conservative Party. The British Government's Balfour Declaration of 2 November 1917, Leo Amery's promised National Home, had been transformed during forty years of frustration and persecution into a passionate commitment by Zionists, gentile and Jew, that Israel would be born, would live, and prosper. Despite the equivocation of British governments in the 1930s and 1940s, British Zionists had supported Israel as a reality, not an aspiration. The strongest rhetorical support was from the Labour Party; effective support was centred on the Conservative Party, where the inner circle, all imperialists and some of them Zionists, were Eden's strongest critics, scathing about his vacillations over Egypt, convinced that his opposition to Nasser needed an ally for a pretext to be translated into a policy. Withdrawal of British forces from Egypt had been strongly opposed by this Conservative Zionist lobby, whose members stressed that Nasser intended to destroy Israel with Russian weapons. As withdrawal accelerated, the lobby redoubled its efforts to provide Israel with new guarantees of security. The lobby was not responsible for the collusion, but its influence should not be underestimated.

Until Ben-Gurion was assured that Canberras from Cyprus would bomb targets selected by his advisers he refused to approve operational planning for what became known later in Israel as the Sinai Campaign. Patrick Dean, until 29 August the Foreign Office Adviser in SIS (thereafter chairman of the Joint Intelligence Committee, and by an arresting coincidence, Eden's go-between in the subsequent detailed collusion), refused to commit his master to a date. Eden, planning to destroy Nasser and not, as with Ben-Gurion, merely seeking the defeat of his armed forces, needed time to assemble an invasion force. Ideally, Eden also needed a pretext for such a force. A threat by Nasser to control the Canal would be one pretext. An attack by Israel on Egypt would provide an even more acceptable excuse; after an 'ultimatum' British forces would land in Egypt, 'To bring about a cessation of hostilities between Israel and Egyptian forces'.[11] In either case, Eden would not be rushed by Ben-Gurion into any move which would benefit Israel but leave Nasser in place. The Canberras were Eden's secret weapon, but they were only part of a larger design. There was the additional factor that the final stages of withdrawal from Egypt were being completed in April and May. Whilst Ben-Gurion and his colleagues continued to plan the broad outlines of their pre-emptive strategy, Eden waited for his moment. Hitherto Nasser, with Dulles behind him, had made the running. Now it was Eden's turn.

Selwyn Lloyd was perfectly correct in saying that between Glubb's sacking and Nasser's nationalisation of the Suez Canal Company on 26 July 'a kind of interregnum' occurred.[12] So it did – on the surface. Of the many curious elements in Suez none was more puzzling to commentators at the time than the alternations in Eden between rage at what Nasser did – or, more usually, said – and his moods of lethargy when he appeared to let events take their course. Selwyn Lloyd, however, was not fully in Eden's confidence. Between April and July Eden preoccupied himself with collusion. He also, on the surface, played the world statesman role. As a result, three crucial months passed, during which Dulles uncharacteristically hesitated over the Aswan Dam loan; the Voice of the Arabs was turned up to full pitch; Britain became increasingly isolated from Arab friends and American critics. Selwyn Lloyd had been stoned in Bahrein during his Middle East tour; in Kuwait, the British Political Agent's house was attacked. Neither affair was particularly serious, but Cairo Radio was automatically, and rightly, blamed in London for these attacks on the British presence in the Middle East.

If Eden and Dulles had been able to communicate during these months, even on a basis of enlightened self-interest, a common policy for the area might yet have been possible. Despite the oil lobby's influence on Eisenhower, Israel's vulnerability to an Egypt armed with Russian weapons could have provided a basis for understanding. But Eden saw Israel as an element in his own strategy for destroying Nasser; Dulles regarded the beleaguered country as a pawn on the American political chess board. In April Dulles backed a Security Council resolution which, in effect, encouraged rather than deterred Fedayeen raids. A concerted Anglo-American policy for the Middle East would have depended on Eisenhower rather than Dulles. The May 1950 tripartite 'doctrine' for the Middle East (America, Britain, France) was 'a proclaimed guarantee of the Arab-Israeli *status quo* as laid down in the [1948] Armistice Agreements'.[13] Unlike Dulles, Eisenhower had some respect for doctrines. He also had much admiration for Eden. But the latter sought co-operation from Dulles. This was a major error of judgment.

Inconclusive talks with Dulles in January about the Aswan Dam had hardened Eden's conviction that he stood almost alone against Nasser's intrigues. Was Nuri really an ally? Eden asked him to send Iraqi armed police to stamp on rioters in Kuwait and Bahrain. Nuri wisely declined, knowing in any case that the local police could wield batons. Seeking to prove himself, and on more familiar territory, Eden, on 9 March, had ordered the expulsion from Cyprus of the nationalist leader, Archbishop Makarios. Civil disturbances immediately worsened, forcing the Governor, Field Marshal Sir John Harding, to commit to local operations battalions of the parachute brigade earmarked for the Strategic Reserve – and the seizure of the Canal by a *coup de main*. Whitehall began to despair of Eden. The Conservative Party had already done so: 'weak and vacillating, and in fact hopeless'.[14] The day before deporting Makarios to the Seychelles Eden endured the rare experience of a full dress censure debate in the House of Commons, concentrating on the Middle East. There was tacit agreement in all parts of the House that Eden was his own Foreign Secretary, and that Lloyd merely did as he was told. More to the point, Eden was barracked by the Opposition and heard in a morose silence by his own Party. Thereafter, Eden made his plans, and turned to the stage management of an international role.

In mid-April President Bulganin and First Secretary Khrushchev paid the equivalent of a State visit to Britain, one nominally designed to restore Eden's prestige. 'It seemed to me that we had invited the Soviet leaders to Britain not because it suited them to come, but because it suited us to receive them, and I thought, on balance, that the visit would be to our advantage.'[15] Such presumption was almost bound to produce absurdities, and did; the visit was a kind of farcical preliminary to the melodramas and black comedy of the ensuing summer. Whilst the Russian leaders exchanged boasts with Eden – he told them 'we would fight for Middle Eastern oil'[16] – or traded insults with the more robust members of the Labour Party, SIS tried to penetrate the secrets of anti-submarine and mine detection equipment on, and in, the cruiser *Ordjonikidze*.

Lying in Portsmouth harbour, the cruiser, which had brought Bulganin and Khrushchev to Britain, was the same class as *Sverdlov*, also the target of frogmen in October 1955 when she was anchored by Spithead. The first operation was successful; the second, undertaken by a frogman, heroic yet incapacitated by age and ill health, was a total failure. The story, carefully peddled, that 'Buster' Crabbe's mysterious death was the result of a kind of free enterprise, SOE-type lark can be discounted. The operations were directed by a senior member of SIS and approved by Sinclair after higher authority had passed the word. Crabbe's capture by the cruiser's underwater sentries on 19 April led to a public apology by Eden in the House of Commons on 4 May, and Sinclair's departure as 'C' immediately afterwards. Eden denied responsibility for the operation, an unconstitutional cover-up which fooled nobody. The incident rankled with people in Broadway. What next, and where, might SIS be expected to do something for a Prime Minister who was rapidly losing all sense of perspective and proportion?

On 13 June the last British troops left Port Said, 'with their tails between their legs' in Cairo Radio's version, 'quietly and with dignity' according to the British Army spokesman. 'Egypt has ended her sufferings' declared *Al Ahram*. Nasser made a speech two days later at Port Said, during which he promised 'liberation to all Arabs, from Morocco to Baghdad'. Celebrations in Cairo, at which the guest of honour was Dmitri Shepilov, Russian Foreign Minister, saw Russian aircraft and tanks handled with more enthusiasm than skill. Shepilov was preoccupied by unrest against Russian rule in Eastern Europe but turned up to see that, in Trevelyan's sardonic words: 'Our Centurions performed better than the Russian tanks'.[17] The party over, there was a pause. Only the Fedayeen were active.

On 19 July, and on the Wall Street principle that unsecured loans are bad business, Dulles cancelled the American offer to build the Aswan Dam. On 26 July, in Alexandria, Nasser announced the nationalisation of the Suez Canal Company, during a speech described by his critics in Europe as combining hysteria and bombast but which was, in fact, relaxed, calm, and, being by an Arab, lengthy. Nasser reserved his bitter remarks for Dulles, an ironic touch which Eden, if in a normal frame of mind, would have appreciated. These two events have an obvious, but not a causal connection. They furnished Eden with a pretext and the Israelis with a timetable. Ben-Gurion intended to defeat Nasser in the field and Eden was determined to reoccupy Egypt. Cancellation of the loan and nationalisation of the Company were the stage props.

There was melodrama in the House of Commons. The Labour Party, under Hugh Gaitskell's leadership and Attlee's residual influence, was unwilling to ask awkward questions, so made noises instead. The Conservative Party, with a few courageous exceptions, gave Eden chauvinistic support. The Canal continued to operate normally. The Egyptian people remained calm and relaxed; they took their cue from Nasser. Foreigners were allowed to go about their business. Several SIS agents were arrested, two British subjects amongst them. Nasser expected some reaction to nationalisation, and saboteurs were better out of the way. The American Embassy in Cairo, together with roving ambassadors and CIA officers, reported to Washington all was quiet but that Nasser was prepared for guerrilla war if Eden overreacted.

The relatively trivial events of cancellation and nationalisation have passed into history as the reasons why Eden attacked Egypt. They certainly have enabled Eden's apologists and critics to write accounts which stress either the intense provocation which he suffered or the risks to Britain's international reputation which he incurred. Much has been written about Dulles's ambiguous behaviour, backing the idea of a Suez Canal Users' Association, rejecting the use of force after Nasser hedged concerning any kind of international arbitration on the Canal's future. Eden's collusion was soon revealed, in the context of the French Government's relations with Israel, but only in recent years has a valuable study been published about the quite extraordinary problems which faced the unfortunate commanders and staff officers who were ordered to direct and plan that singular enterprise, operation *Musketeer*.[18] The effect of the whole affair – called the 'Seven Day War' in more than one dismissive account – on Britain's strategic roles and responsbilities has been discussed, by academic strategists. But virtually nothing has appeared on the two central issues: Eden's collusion with Israel in pursuit of his long-term objectives; and how these objectives were, at the eleventh hour, frustrated. No more than a hint has been given publicly that Eisenhower and Dulles knew what was happening between July and December.

From the moment Nasser nationalised the Suez Canal Company, Eden was locked in a struggle with the Chiefs of Staff and Whitehall. The permanent government became determined to show the Prime Minister who really ran the country in a crisis. Eden had two initial advantages. He was Prime Minister, politically vulnerable only to Cabinet revolt or an adverse vote in the House of Commons. Eden dramatised and exploited the apparent infamy of Nasser's acts – although it was Hugh Gaitskell who compared him with Hitler – and won thereby a sufficient respite from Cabinet and Parliamentary opposition. Eden also succeeded in keeping collusion with Israel and the reason for it secret from likely critics during the initial period when all the latter were united in opposing his obsessive belief that something must be done 'to knock Nasser off his perch', in short, to destroy him.[19] Members of Eden's Cabinet told their parliamentary friends that *Musketeer* was a purely precautionary measure. Eden's opponents had nothing initially with which to counter prime ministerial power, Cabinet deceit, and the necessity for some action. Once the collusion was known and its purpose understood, a combination of factors, grasped and exploited by men who were determined to frustrate a lunatic adventure, eventually established the conditions in which Dulles was able to destroy Eden. On 6 November, Dulles did so.

The conflict, which continued for those thirteen weeks, began when Eden summoned the Chiefs of Staff to a meeting at No. 10 on the night of the 26th. Rather appropriately, Eden was dining with Nuri when details of Nasser's speech were delivered. Dinner over, and Nuri having departed – with the admonition 'hit him hard' – Eden summoned Mountbatten and Templer. The Chief of the Air Staff, Dermot Boyle, coincidentally, or not, was already present. Eden demanded an answer as to how quickly, and by what forceful means, the Canal Company could be restored to its Anglo-French owners. From conflicting accounts of the meeting – witnessed rather than attended by two others who had been present at the dinner, the French Ambassador and the American Chargé d'Affaires, and to the consternation of Eden's Secretaries, who fruitlessly, *sotto voce*, reminded him there were 'strangers present' – one crucial statement survives.[20]

In answer to a question from Eden, Templer said: 'Prime Minister, we can take Cairo; we cannot hold it.' The preliminary talk had concerned an airborne operation directed at Port Said, Ismailia and Suez. Although a contingency plan existed for this operation, the Chiefs, by July 1956, were averse from recommending it. The one regular parachute brigade had become committed in Cyprus. There was no other suitable formation available, and the Chiefs had no intention of relying on Territorial Army parachute units. An airborne attack would mean substantial planning and operational changes, so that troops could be released from Cyprus, re-trained, and re-formed. To do this would take between six and eight weeks. Providing air and sea lift would take up to three months.

These factors strengthened Service convictions which had grown since defeat at Arnhem twelve years before. Then airborne forces had landed 'a bridge too far'. The British Army decided that airborne operations which were not supported by a ground offensive were likely to fail. Eden was asked to consider the implications of attempting to seize key points with inadequate airborne forces which might not get timely and strong support from troops landed over the beaches at Port Said. The discussion inevitably broadened to a consideration of what kind of resistance the Egyptians might offer. Templer stressed the need to control the Delta in order to dominate the Canal. He did so to emphasise that these elements in any plan presumed the availability of troops which were, in fact, committed around the world. Whether Templer guessed at Eden's long-term objectives or not is irrelevant. Nor can his recent experience with Hussein be considered as relevant, except in broad political terms. Templer was a shrewd, unusually outspoken soldier. He was determined to prevent British troops being committed to a hopeless venture. Templer's threat of resignation must be seen in this context.

Templer, strongly supported by Mountbatten, therefore gave Eden advance notice that the re-occupation of Egypt was not an option; if an operation was mounted to seize the Canal, troops landed from the sea would be needed in close support of airborne forces; they could not be committed to the absurd idea of taking and then attempting to occupy Nasser's capital. This requirement of close support would be insisted on by the British Chiefs of Staff whether or not the operation also involved France. The French Ambassador's presence at the meeting virtually ensured some form of French participation, but Templer wanted to make his position clear from the start. Eden did not pay much attention to Templer. All others who were present at the meeting listened carefully – and reported, where appropriate, to higher authority.

Two days later Eden set off for his country retreat, his 'haven in the fields at the lane's end', leaving in London a group of men who had two major campaigns to plan: to seize the Canal if sufficient force could be assembled; to deter Eden from turning a crisis into a disaster. An early recruit was Macmillan's old friend from Algiers, Robert Murphy, sent post-haste by Eisenhower to open a line of communication with Whitehall. Whilst Eden cultivated his garden, Murphy took soundings, above all from Macmillan. Murphy found the Chancellor of the Exchequer breathing fire about Nasser and, apparently, the strongest advocate in Eden's Cabinet for military operations. But Murphy, the self-styled diplomat among the warriors, knew his Macmillan and was quite aware that when he waved the Union Jack most belligerently he was considering the effect on the Romans in Washington. Murphy began to mark his card for those in Eden's Cabinet and the Establishment who would be seriously aware of the folly of Britain going anywhere alone. Already, as Eden enjoyed 'the Gainsborough scenery in the Ebble Valley', a Washington-Whitehall alliance was being formed, of which Macmillan was to be the eventual beneficiary.

On 2 August a Royal Proclamation was published, enabling reservists to be called out. Even a limited operation would require, in Templer's estimate, approximately 100,000 troops, of whom nearly a third would, perforce, come from various categories of reserve. Templer expected the Egyptians to fight, and had no intention of the parachute brigade being surrounded and destroyed piecemeal. There was no possibility of committing the British garrison in Libya; King Idris made his position clear from the outset. The following weekend, August Bank Holiday, planning for *Musketeer* began in a war-time secret headquarters deep beneath Charing Cross Station. French officers shortly appeared, expressed horror at their cavernous surroundings, haunted by past victories and defeats, whose corridors of seemingly endless length eventually surfaced in Trafalgar Square, and settled down to work – if work it can be called. The French might well have echoed Alice when she followed the White Rabbit: 'Down, down, down, would the journey never end?'

Memories of Churchill's uneasy relationship with de Gaulle were strong in French minds: the *Entente* was not particularly cordial. On 29 July the French Government had been invited by Eden 'to discuss the military resources which might be available for joint action'.[21] Neither Mollet nor his Foreign Minister, Christian Pineau, committed themselves to a combined operation. Cool relations with Britain aside, the French Government by July had revived a degree of bilateral collusion with Ben-Gurion, specifically relating to naval and air support in defence of Israel if Egypt attacked. Mystères in a ground attack role were promised – and provided. But Mollet had again refused to commit France in support of an Israeli attack. No French bombers were provided, or assigned targets. Yet French equivocations over Israel did not produce straightforward relations with Britain. Mollet and Pineau were former *résistants*, Socialists who had accepted de Gaulle as leader of the true France. Neither trusted British governments. Eden's relations with de Gaulle were remembered with occasional gratitude, but in French minds during the months of July to November 1956 Albion was still *perfide*.

The known and outspoken opposition by Sir Ivone Kirkpatrick (Permanent Under Secretary at the Foreign Office) to close Anglo-French relations further soured the atmosphere. The French Government certainly wanted to deflect Nasser's attention from Algeria, and the French directors and shareholders of the Suez Canal Company made all the right noises when their property – as they saw it – was seized on 26 July. But the French Government as a whole accepted Nasser as a new force in Arab affairs. The presence of French officers in the Charing Cross bunker reflected Eden's need to preserve the fiction of concerted action for restoring the Canal Company to its rightful owners and maintaining the Canal as an international maritime highway. The presence of French officers also reflected the more fundamental need for an overstretched British Army to be supported by trained regulars from a NATO ally. Of this second fact the politically conscious French officers were sharply aware.

Thus there were few natural associations between French and British officers when they descended to the bunker's gloomy depths. Moreover, the French found their British colleagues in a strange mood. All British survivors of *Musketeer* and its attendant activities – Commanders, Staff Officers, officials – have a particular reaction when questioned, a kind of amazed grimace at the absurdities, 'the madness' of what, for three months, they were forced to endure. The code name for the planning stages was *Terrapin*. The obscure joke was rarely appreciated, least of all by Major-General André Beaufre, the senior French Commander, a man monumentally *sérieux* – and with unhappy memories of French subjection to British dictates in North Africa during the Second World War. Beaufre found his opposite number, Lieutenant-General Hugh Stockwell, almost 'unBritish' in his outspoken criticisms of a crazy enterprise. Stockwell relieved his feelings by expressing them about politicians, another unBritish trait to which Beaufre reacted with marked disapproval. Beaufre, something of a military intellectual, lived in an uneasy world during *Terrapin*, one both subterranean and absurd. Stockwell was no intellectual; he was the fighting man's general. Beaufre's government had reservations about *Musketeer*; his British counterparts had few hopes of success.

Whilst Eden consulted with the 'Egypt' Committee of the Cabinet – Lloyd, Macmillan, Monckton, Lennox Boyd, and Salisbury (Minister of Defence, Colonial Secretary, and Lord President of the Council respectively) – froze Egypt's sterling balances, and fired off exhortations in all directions, Norman Brook, as Cabinet Secretary, re-activated the Transition to War Committee, consisting of himself and the Permanent Secretaries of the Foreign Office, Treasury, Home Office, and Defence Ministry. All these moves towards undeclared war had to be concerted by Brook because, by 1956, the Cabinet Secretary had become the single most powerful individual in the permanent government of Britain. Fortunately for Britain, Brook had a very clear idea of what was, and was not, possible, and had no hesitation in confronting his Prime Minister with evidence of the difference between the two. Brook, a grammar school boy with views comparable to Dick White's, had been at the centre of things since 1940. He knew everyone who mattered in both the permanent government and the political one, and did so literally, not figuratively. Brook was severe and unusually restrained, the very model of a modern bureaucrat; he had seen war and illusory peace at the Chiefs of Staff level for sixteen years. As a result of this experience, Brook was determined that the armed forces should not be expected, from political whim, to do the impossible, above all when fully committed in many ways and places to maintaining for Britain a valid, if no longer potent, international role.

Brook had watched Eden with concern and dismay for years, noting his sheer unfitness for the highest office, his outbursts, his relapses. As with others, compassion mingled with doubt, but Eden's vanity, his lack of skin, his decline from physical frailty to seemingly endemic illness had been observed by Brook, not merely accepted as the wear and tear of politics. The incident of Queen Victoria's 'Black Week' notice, petty in itself, was nevertheless regarded by Brook as a symptom of bad nerves, not bad temper. Brook did not particularly like Macmillan – although 'he foresaw him as a possible Prime Minister'. Brook appreciated that Butler's feline comment about Eden – 'He's the best Prime Minister we've got' – differed from Macmillan's assessment of their Chief only in the characteristic ambiguity of the phrase. Brook reflected on Macmillan's estimate, also made by Murphy, that Eden might have lost his nerve from the time Glubb Pasha was dismissed and he shouted for the world to hear: 'I want Nasser destroyed, not removed, destroyed, and I don't care how much chaos in Egypt this causes.'[22] At the time, this was taken as an hysterical outburst. Later, it was pondered. But Brook did not know in the summer of 1956 that collusion with Israel was seen by Eden as the means of translating that outburst into an act of deliberate policy. Indeed, Brook did not then know about the collusion.

One thing, however, Brook did know in August – for sure. Whatever the Cabinet as a whole, or its Egypt Committee did, or did not, know or guess about Eden's temptations and craving to satisfy them by any means, the whole business of *Musketeer* would fall on Whitehall's shoulders. The Prime Minister could still seek to enlist Eisenhower's support and the Foreign Secretary could try and present a case at the United Nations. The Lord Chancellor and the Attorney General could debate whether or not Nasser's nationalisation was a breach of international law. (Opinion was evenly divided, to Eden's palpable disgust.) The illusion of power could be enjoyed by the Cabinet – or the Commons. The Egypt Committee could order, and it did, that the export of TNT to Egypt be stopped. But the realities, the nuts and bolts, would be left to Brook and his peers. Amongst those nuts and bolts was SIS, for which, leaving details to his Deputy, Brook had co-ordinating responsibility, and amongst which moved and had his being 'the fair haired Dean', the Foreign Office Adviser. Dean 'had long worked in intelligence, and knew a good deal about it'. More to the point, Dean shared Eden's conviction that Nasser so menaced Britain's Middle East interests that he had to be removed from the scene, and by any method which came to hand.

In the early stages of *Terrapin*, Brook made one move whose sequel strengthened his conviction that if Eden would not respond to official advice he would have to be replaced by a Prime Minister who did. By mid-August, *Terrapin*'s planners had concluded that a landing at Port Said presented almost unsurmountable difficulties for a force whose amphibious ships were old and unseaworthy. To lie off Port Said with that winter Mediterranean hazard, a 'Levanter', blowing, would mean the expedition risking humiliation by the elements rather than the enemy. Alexandria, a modern port, could accommodate an armada whose doubtful capacity to survive the passage from Britain indicated the difference between the Royal Navy's Second World War reliance on American logistic support and its own limited resources.

These considerations focussed attention on shipping. This was the responsibility of the Minister of Transport, Harold Watkinson. Not a member of the Cabinet, not one of the Egypt Committee, merely one of Eden's ministers, Watkinson was none the less a key man. When approached by a member of Boyle's staff, armed with *Terrapin* and *Musketeer* as passwords to open Ministerial cupboards and search for ships, Watkinson expressed total ignorance of either the operation or the plans for it. The ignorance was not feigned, was not a welcome display of a concern for security not universally to be found in politicians. Watkinson simply did not know. It was not his fault; nobody had told him.

Armed with these and other, unpalatable, facts – of which the British Army's inferiority to the Egyptian in terms of infantry and anti-tank weapons inexorably became chief – Brook sought, and won, agreement from his colleagues of the Transition to War Committee for a reasoned submission to Eden that *Musketeer*, however limited its aim, was simply not a feasible operation of war. The meeting was held, the submission was made. Brook's predecessor as Secretary to the Cabinet was Edward Bridges. By 1956 Bridges had become Permanent Under Secretary to the Treasury, and the most senior figure in Whitehall. Brook had good reason to believe that Eden would pay some attention not only to his views but to the ripe experience of the permanent government's most distinguished mandarin. Eden listened – Brook had that rare privilege – then dismissed the Committee to its tasks. *Musketeer* would go forward. Remarking, 'he's for the high-jump some day', Brook returned to his office and sat down to think. By late September, and with the futile conference in London of the Suez Canal Users' Association out of the way – attended by a Dulles whose relish for snide remarks annoyed even those who agreed with him – Brook had accepted that Eden was not going to be deterred by Whitehall opposition or Presidential dismay.

Eisenhower had written to Eden on 31 July, 2 and 8 September, long, rambling letters, full of affection and reproof, appeals for restraint, reminders that 'there are many areas of endeavour which are not fully explored because exploration takes time'. The letters were as futile as the September London Conference; they were more than futile, they were a goad. When Eisenhower wrote, 'It seems to Foster and to me that the result that you and I both want can best be assured by slower and less dramatic processes than military force',[23] Eden's reaction was to declare that there was no 'both' about it. He had come to accept that Dulles would oppose, not support him in Egypt, whatever the issue. What Eden did not – could not – grasp was the reality that without American backing even a confidently planned *Musketeer* provided with adequate forces and first-class logistic support, was doomed to fail.

Although Brook knew that Eisenhower had written, and could accurately guess the contents, he did not see these letters; he observed, however, a deterioration in Eden after the SCUA Conference. The reasons for this deterioration are clear enough today. Eden's plans were bogged down because British resources were lacking and France, the reluctant ally, was critical of his intentions. Two months after Nasser had nationalised the Canal Company, *Musketeer*, in its different versions and several 'revises', was still an affair of British doubt and French hesitation. Although planning of operational details had reached an advanced stage, and the French appeared reluctantly committed to a joint operation under British command, Mollet and Pineau were concentrating on collusion with Israel which had moved from the defensive to the offensive. The French Government knew nothing of Anglo-Israeli collusion; their version was based on concerted, limited ground operations, reflecting growing suspicion that *Musketeer* would fail from strategic inadequacies and collapse under the pressure of American disapproval. Following a Paris meeting between French and Israeli planners in early September, Mollet and Ben-Gurion had agreed to act together in an attack on Egypt if British nerve should falter as American attitudes changed, from disapproval, through hostility, to total opposition. French attitudes to Nasser had hardened by the time of the SCUA Conference, but the change from defensive to offensive collusion indicates that, in Paris, suspicion of being abandoned by Britain and opposed by America was a more compelling reason for taking risks than the desire to thwart an Arab revolutionary.

Yet in September Ben-Gurion was still loth to embark on Operation *Kadesh* until the Royal Air Force Canberras had the El Arish armoured divisions and the interdiction targets in their bomb sights. These aircraft were regarded as the critical element in any Israeli attack on Egypt; Eden's plan to destroy Nasser also depended on the effect of bombs falling on Egyptian targets. Yet Eden was also determined to cloak his aggression with an operation to preserve the sanctity of international law. By late September Ben-Gurion and Mollet were ready to go; Eden had agreed to a full dress debate in the Security Council on all aspects of the Suez Canal issue. To men anxious for a *coup de main* which would preserve

Israel's security and improve French prospects in Algeria, recourse to legal arguments in a hostile forum thousands of miles away was a waste of precious time and opportunity.

The Security Council met on 26 September. Dulles was not at all co-operative. He had his own plans for using the Security Council or General Assembly to settle the whole Egyptian business, but they differed rather fundamentally from Eden's ambitions. Dulles had no intention of talking frankly. Selwyn Lloyd did not arrive to represent Britain at the Security Council until 2 October. Britain's UN Ambassador, Pierson Dixon, was comprehensively in the dark about both Eden's collusion and Dulles's riposte. Dulles knew that another round in the Arab-Israeli war was likely. CIA aircraft and reports from the United Nations Truce Supervisory Organisation provided reliable intelligence of Egyptian and Israeli preparations for armoured offensives. UNTSO was an excellent intelligence source: the military observers moved with relative freedom through areas of likely conflict; their reports were coded and classified; predominantly American membership of the UN Secretariat's upper echelons guaranteed that the reports were on Dulles's desk before Secretary-General Dag Hammarskjöld saw them. Hammarskjöld wanted the UN to arbitrate Arab-Israeli issues. Dulles intended to use the UN as an instrument for ousting Britain from the Middle East and entrenching America, cheaply and profitably.

Armed with good intelligence, and determined to oppose an Anglo-French invasion of Egypt, Dulles in early October ordered a total close-down on *all* overt communication from the State Department and the American Embassy in London to the Foreign Office. Whatever Dulles was planning to do by way of thwarting Eden he did not intend that his victim should know. Eden attempted to tighten his grip on conspiracy. The orders he gave for a propaganda war were meant to be severely restricted in their distribution; propaganda was to be black, and it was to be part of his long-term objective. Related orders were drafted for bombing operations, to be carried out by over 150 aircraft, from Cyprus – and Turkey. Lloyd, a routine politician completely out of his depth, added unwittingly to conspiracy by reporting to the Foreign Office from the UN during an otherwise pointless three weeks' visit that Nasser might be prepared to discuss a compromise arrangement for ownership and operation of the Canal.

It is impossible to say at precisely what point Brook and those about him at last consciously realised the implications of advising a Prime Minister who was planning to re-occupy, not merely invade, an Egypt which had been terrified by propaganda and bombs into submission and the acceptance of military forces ostensibly committed to protection of the Canal. There is no single date and there was no one episode which illuminated the dark corners of Eden's mind. Discussion about Nasser's contrived death and the installation of a successor took place in an atmosphere which, by early October, had become too frenetic even for the strong-nerved Brook to endure without showing his feelings. On one occasion during these weeks he arrived at a friend's house for drinks. His host expressed surprise that he had found the time to come – well aware what was going on beneath Charing Cross Station – provoking Brook to say: 'There is such a cock-up there that if I don't get away for an hour or two I shall burst.' Eden attended a meeting of a Chiefs of Staff Committee where Nasser's death was discussed – hypothetically. One present recalls Eden's 'toothy grin' as the SIS representative remarked that 'thuggery' was not on the agenda. White had made it clear that SIS was a hostile service, but not a collection of hit men. Brook has taken his secrets with him; the survivors will not write their memoirs candidly or, in the crucial cases, at all; the destruction of official files was a wholesale affair.

What can be said is that once Eden's real aim became known his end was ordained. On 5 October he was admitted to University College Hospital with a temperature of 106°, 'intoxicated with drugs' in the words of one Cabinet colleague; 'clinically incapable' according to Israelis in London; 'Quite simply mad' to more than one official. In retrospect, none of these remarks is surprising. Collusion had become a conspiracy whose members neither trusted each other nor agreed on when to strike. Israeli pressure on Eden to commit the Canberras had become intense. Eden, at the end of his tether, continued to deceive everyone, including himself. He therefore took refuge in paranoic secrecy. A superintending Under Secretary in the Foreign Office was indirectly responsible for Egypt, a country with which, in October, Britain still maintained diplomatic relations. This official had been excluded on Eden's orders from all most secret communications. But he knew; he ventured to ask a question or two. He found himself on the receiving end of Lady Eden's wrath. In something like despair he consulted a Minister. 'Wait', he was told, 'it can't last much longer.'

Perhaps even more relevant to this looking-glass world is the remark of one who had been close to Eden until the full dimension of his temptation became clear: 'After he left that hospital, he never lost his temper again.' Eden was a burned-out case. The final stage could be set in train by the mandarins whose warnings he had scorned. Eden was left to confuse the issues more thoroughly than a man in his right mind would have done: on 12 October he warned Israel that any further attacks on *Jordan* border posts would bring in Britain on the latter's side. This cover for continued collusion with Israel was developed on the 14th. Eden, at Chequers, saw Mollet's emissaries Albert Grazier and General Challe. On the 16th Eden spent a day in Paris with Mollet. On the 21st a further meeting at Chequers agreed to tripartite collusion. The Canberras had proved to be Eden's trump card, or so it seemed to men who had gone too far to turn back. Revised directives were issued to the weary planners in their bunker. These men in uniform had no choice but to obey. Defiance, however, was found in other places.

The first, and most effective step took place in Cyprus, involving SIS only indirectly in one sense, but sufficiently so for Brook to warn Washington what was really at stake. Cyprus became, in September 1956 – when the complications of collusion and planned military operations were creating a nightmare atmosphere in Whitehall – the focal point of Eden's campaign against Nasser. Cyprus was crucial to Eden not only because it was a permanent aircraft carrier anchored thirty minutes' flying time from Cairo, but also due to the fact that it contained the regional headquarters of the Foreign Office and SIS, grouped together in the 'Middle East Office'. Although there were relatively few airfields in Cyprus, they all but sufficed for Eden's bombing strategy, devised, as Ben-Gurion supposed in March, to support his pre-emptive campaign by attacks on the Egyptian Air Force and the divisions at El Arish. Eden had other ideas and needed additional airfields to develop them fully, but Cyprus was essential to his basic approach and his belief that a campaign of frightfulness against the Egyptian people would, indeed, destroy Nasser.

Activity by the Middle East Office was intended, in Eden's mind, to complement, in fact to precede the bombing strategy, and to do so by recourse to black propaganda. Since the early days of the Second World War, when a Forces' broadcasting station had been established within Wavell's Middle East Command, British officials had been alert to the value of radio for propaganda in the area. Progressively during and after the war, radio was used to inform Arab populations, from Libya to the Gulf, of the work of

British governments and the benefits of the British presence. The broadcasts were relatively straightforward; the impression conveyed was of imperial benevolence, above all in terms of economic aid; the propaganda was off-white. Nothing was distorted, even though much was slanted. Economic aid, on closer examination, was more likely to be promised than provided. But there was a marked, a deliberate absence in these broadcasts of attacks on nationalists in Arabia who were opposed to the British presence. Nasser's Cairo Radio was as much a riposte to this propaganda as it was a means of preaching the revolutionary, nationalist, anti-imperialist message.

By the early 1950s and with the end of British rule in Egypt not merely accepted but welcomed in the Foreign Office, a Near East Arab Broadcasting Service had been established in Cyprus. A plate on a modest office in Oxford Street, not far from the BBC, bore the legend 'Near East Arab Broadcasting Company'. The Company was real; it had directors; it made money, because one popular feature of Neabs, as it was colloquially known – or, in its Arabic title, Sharkh el Adna – was advertising. A larger audience than Cairo Radio not only listened to news, feature programmes, and light entertainment, but to advertisements extolling the merits of detergents and shaving cream.

The revenue thus earned was, however, a headache for the accountants – of SIS in Broadway. The Near East Arab Broadcasting Company was an SIS operation, and Sharkh el Adna, undoubtedly a service which provided legitimate news, was part of an approach to maintaining the British Middle East presence which ranged from propaganda at one end of the scale to hostile, to robust operations at the other. The bureaucratic complexities of the Foreign Office's Information Research Department and SIS's Special Political Action Group were absorbed in the comparative simplicities of the Middle East office and Neabs. It was the latter which Eden proposed to pervert in order to destroy Nasser, encouraged by the belief that SIS would support a distinctively hostile operation. Despite protests from the BBC's Director-General (Sir Ian Jacob) Eden succeeded in dissuading the overseas service from transmitting the views of those who opposed his policies towards Egypt. Eden had no doubt that SIS and IRD would go one better. Jacob, who had been Military Assistant Secretary of the War Cabinet, and who had remained after 1945 at Whitehall's secretive centre, made his protest in form, and then left matters to his subordinates. Eden was determined that no such latitude would be allowed to official propagandists.

Neabs was run from day to day by a Director and staff whose main interest was in good broadcasting. The Director was British; the staff was Palestinian. The Director, Ralph Poston, knew his real paymaster, but was otherwise ignorant of SIS activities. By early September, however, ignorance had been replaced by knowledge, of a kind, and growing indignation, for 'In late August Brigadier Bernard Fergusson was pulled off the night train from Perth and told he had been appointed Director of Psychological Warfare' – for the Suez campaign.[24] 'This unfortunate appointment'[25] meant that Fergusson, a regular serving soldier of unconventional views and good connections, whose career had nevertheless become marooned in low-grade posts, was put in charge of Eden's black propaganda. Fergusson, an honourable and outspoken man, had allowed himself to be persuaded into executing a task against which all his instincts rebelled.

Well before Fergusson arrived in Cyprus, Neabs's Director began receiving guidance telegrams via SIS making sufficiently clear that his broadcasts, as one participant in these events has put it, 'were to be shaded from white through grey to black'. Despite Eden's coercion, the BBC's domestic services were still broadcasting all points of view in the Canal dispute. Eden ordered this even-handed policy to stop. The Neabs Director, and SIS, began to smell something more than a large sized rat: men of very different attributes, temperaments and convictions – the Director was given to emotional outbursts; the SIS regional officer was a former member of SOE not easily moved by examples of political, or any other, human folly – saw with dismayed clarity that their Prime Minister expected them to launch a campaign against Nasser which could well have been conceived by Dr Goebbels.

By mid-October Brook in London had all that he needed to know. The picture had become both clear and detailed. In addition to the impending propaganda campaign, hopes had been entertained by Eden that the Turkish Government would provide airfields for additional RAF Canberra and Valiant bombers. Eden expected to use Turkey's recent membership of NATO as a means of exerting pressure, and instructed subordinates accordingly. The Turkish Government refused. A member of the *Terrapin* staff was then picked to bell the cat. Eden was at Chequers when the officer, an Air Commodore, arrived. Eden was busy, or otherwise unavailable. One of his Private Office Secretaries was told. He shrugged his shoulders. 'It won't make any difference. He'll just cram more aircraft into Cyprus.' Eden did so.

A month before *Musketeer*'s D-Day, 31 October, Cyprus resembled a human anthill. Preparations for nearly forty squadrons of aircraft; the staffs of innumerable formations, including those of two French divisions – whose members, guests of a British mess, were amazed to see their British opposite numbers in dinner jackets; the headquarters of forces engaged in fighting the island's liberation army Eoka; the Middle East office and its offshoots, still struggling to carry out a policy which Eden had effectively destroyed. In Cairo Trevelyan, quite ignorant of Eden's real aims patiently continued to advise his Government towards an acceptance of moderate revolution. Trevelyan also reported Nasser's willingness to negotiate a compromise solution to the Canal issue. But even Trevelyan, like others of goodwill and commonsense, was not immune from the influence of signs and portents. 'For weeks Mars presented a warlike face, blood red and looming large in the Eastern sky. Surely, we thought, this must be a good omen; for the Heavens would not foretell war in such an obvious way.'[26] The omen should have been heeded.

Dulles's close-down of all overt communication with the Foreign Office was a scheme designed to hide his intentions from Eden. Initially, these were confined to selecting Hammarskjöld and the Security Council as the instruments for condemning Eden's planned campaign – at a time of Dulles's choosing – but the close-down as such imposed on Brook the necessity for using SIS to tell Washington what he believed Eisenhower must know. Brook knew that the President had been told by the CIA of revived Franco-Israeli collusion; such knowledge only emphasised the necessity of telling him that Eden's interest in this collusion was concentrated on the destruction of Nasser and bore little or no relation to the Franco-Israeli determination to defeat him in the field. Brook therefore used SIS liaison with CIA as a means of telling the President what was really at stake. An uncovenanted bonus resulted. Intelligence from reconnaissance of Egypt and Israel by CIA aircraft was distributed to SIS. But Foster Dulles was the real beneficiary of this unusual form of liaison between SIS and his brother's CIA. Dulles knew that any 'ultimatum' which the British Government might issue as Egypt and Israel went to war would merely be a smokescreen behind which Eden could use *Musketeer* for his own ends.

White had been 'C' for six months when these developments occurred, too short a time for his headmaster's cane to be used with much effect in an organisation where directors were almost a law unto themselves, acting like prefects in an expensive but unruly private school. Attitudes to the real purpose of *Musketeer* differed quite sharply in Broadway. 'Thuggery' was repudiated but some were for robust action; others agreed with Brook and the Foreign Office. An SIS party, in uniform, was included in the first group planned to land over the beaches. The group's tasks were to interrogate prisoners – 'vigorously'; and to assess Nasser's support in the Army. These tasks formed one element in a major requirement: the search for Nasser's successor, one who would prove amenable to another British occupation. This element in *Musketeer*, all other factors apart, was enough to convince doubters in Whitehall that something more than restoring the Canal to its rightful owners was in Eden's mind. Not everyone in Broadway believed re-occupation to be a lunatic idea or an impossible operation, although the thought of Arab governments' reactions when they discovered the extent of Eden's collusion with Israel caused unbounded dismay.

But whatever White thought he kept to himself. Matters by mid-October had gone beyond the relative simplicities of intelligence operations and the search for an Egyptian stooge. White was part of a small group of mandarins whose duty, as they saw it, was to tell Washington what they knew. Doing so might not stop *Musketeer* from being launched but would ensure the invasion was stopped in its tracks. Whether Brook and his colleagues hoped or believed that a fully-informed Eisenhower would prevail with Eden at the last moment, or that Dulles would prefer to see Britain humiliated at the UN and then thwarted by other means, must remain a matter of speculation. Neither Dulles nor Eisenhower told his story. The mandarins could only do their duty and let the consequences fall to others.

The final stages of collusion were decided in Paris on 23 and 24 October.[27] Lloyd had been sent to the Security Council to engage in one kind of deceit; after the Chequers meeting on the 21st, Eden all but hauled him off the return flight from New York and sent him to Paris for the consummation of another kind. These meetings form the basis of several accounts which purportedly expose collusion. What has not hitherto been revealed is the one element in these Paris discussions which puzzled the French and Israelis. This was British preparation for a bombing campaign which, over a six-day period, seemed designed for civilian rather than military targets. The Israelis, in particular, feared that Eden would order

Air Marshal Barnett, commanding the RAF Squadrons assigned for *Musketeer*, to bomb Nasser's citizens rather than the two divisions at El Arish plus the line of communications and logistics between them and the Delta. Selwyn Lloyd and Patrick Dean, both in a state of physical and nervous exhaustion, made all kinds of pledges on the 23rd and 24th, but left the Israelis sceptical and the French once more disillusioned. If, at the last moment, Eden failed to deliver the Canberras according to Israeli requirements, his collusion would not only be futile but treacherous.

The CIA Station in London had a pretty complete picture of Eden's intentions by the last week in October. CIA knew of yet another switch by *Terrapin*'s planners from Alexandria back to Port Said; ground support for the airborne operation had again prevailed over logistic considerations. CIA knew of the conflict between Eden, obsessed with Nasser's destruction, and the French and Israeli governments, committed only to his military defeat (a commitment with which Allen Dulles and many others in Washington privately sympathised). Of comparable importance, CIA knew, so to speak, who knew, who would, if only in the final analysis, put the Anglo-American necessity for co-operation, even with Foster Dulles as Secretary of State, above Prime Ministerial temptations: 'Brook; Dean; the Chiefs of Staff; the heads of the intelligence and security services; Eden's Private Office; one or two others'. This was how CIA in London marked the card. All that the Station did not know was D-Day. Patrick Dean, after weeks of leading an unnatural life, was on the point of disclosing this last necessary clue, but, somehow, avoided doing so.

But it was the Director of Neabs during that last week of October who gave most away. Fergusson was about to arrive in Cyprus; the black propaganda broadcasts were ready. Sharkh el Adna was changed to 'The Voice of Britain'. This new approach to foreign policy by a supposedly major, democratic power was intended to start three days before bombing, during which leaflet raids would also be made. The Director saw these leaflets, crudely printed on cheap paper, threatening the Egyptian people with fire and sword. Destruction of their villages was the least of punishments to be inflicted on those who did not obey the British in the removal of Gamal Abdel Nasser from Egypt. Senior RAF officers in Cyprus were disgusted about the leaflets; the Director of Neabs was infuriated. He went on the air personally 'for the last time' to tell his audience that they would shortly be hearing lies and might experience bombing. They were not to believe the lies and must endure the bombs. These acts were not those of Englishmen who knew Arabia and cared for the Arab people. Then Neabs, as such, closed down – and remained closed. The Director found himself under house arrest, with an armed guard on the gate. His staff left in a body; their replacements, scraped together from the unemployed and feckless, unwittingly completed the Director's defiance; their Arabic was so poor that the Voice of Britain's audience had no difficulty in realising that something had gone seriously adrift with their old friend Sharkh el Adna. Fergusson was left in, rather than on, the air.

By 28 October, Ben-Gurion was prepared to wait no longer. Urged on by his Chief of Staff, Dayan – who had stressed to Lloyd and Dean that parachute troops dropping in the rear of the El Arish divisions supported by French air cover over Israel would justify a limited pre-emptive ground operation – Israel's Prime Minister gave the order to strike. At this critical moment the Israelis accepted that Canberra and Valiant bombers – Eden's secret weapons – would not be used in an interdiction role, one incidentally which would have 'separated the combatants' rather more effectively than aerial attacks on Nasser's citizens. Britain's Prime Minister had not only deceived his country; he had failed to support his ally-in-collusion. October 29 was a gloomy Fall day in Washington. Eisenhower returned from Jacksonville – where he had been on the stump, preaching racial equality – to learn that Israel had attacked Egypt and Britain was on the brink of doing so. By the time the first RAF raid took place on 30 October, Israeli forces were racing for their objectives – well short of the Canal. Israel's attack reflected one national obsession: security; the bombing reflected Eden's imperial ambitions. He gave no support to Israeli forces. Now even those in Whitehall who had been excluded from Eden's plans were in the know and enraged, above all in that Foreign Office he had led for so long and whose reputation he had done his best to destroy. One official, belatedly aware of Eden's aims, was asked for information by another, still in the dark. 'Don't ask me; ask that --ing madman over there.' It is a fitting, bitter comment.

Eden's 'Ultimatum' statement in the Commons on 31 October that Britain and France had intervened to separate the combatants was the last straw to an Eisenhower who had done his best, according to his lights, to give an old friend the final chance to regain his sanity. Dulles's plan to use the UN for stopping Eden was extended by a genuinely enraged President into a campaign designed to get Britain out of Egypt bag and baggage. Eisenhower could well have invoked Salisbury who, when he heard of Lytton's invasion of Afghanistan in November 1878, said: 'The time has been chosen with singular infelicity.'[28] Lytton also invaded a virtually defenceless state on the pretext of a threat – from Russia – to imperial interests. Salisbury was engaged in reaching an accommodation with Russia. Lytton stopped him. In 1882, after the bombardment of Alexandria and discovery of the deceit which preceded it, the House of Commons, with Churchill's father the leader in moral outrage, demanded explanation and heads on a political platter. Dominated by Bismarck, the courts of Europe demanded a place in the Egyptian – and African – sun. In 1956, and long before the Commons woke up to what was happening, Eisenhower demanded the full price. America had as much a place in the Arab sun as its economy required. But Eisenhower demanded Eden's head – and got it.

In July 1882 the Russian Government noted unctuously 'the happy coincidence that at the very moment when England, in her endeavours to get hold of the Suez Canal, has entangled herself in difficulties in Egypt, our Prince-Governor of Transcaucasia has started for Merv with the absolutely pacific object of organising the civil administration of that territory.'[29] In 1956, Eisenhower's rage with Eden was fundamentally due not only to shock at having been defied but alarm that the Suez adventure had distracted world attention from the Russian subjugation of Hungary. Whilst Eisenhower used the UN to destroy Eden, he was forced to watch helplessly whilst Khrushchev despatched troops to reorganise the civil administration of Hungary by methods even more brutal than Britain's bombing of Egypt.

If Eden had cancelled *Musketeer* once Israel attacked, Eisenhower would probably have ordered Dulles to drop his prosecution case against Britain at the bar of the United Nations. But for five days the Royal Air Force pounded Egyptian targets. The *Musketeer* invasion fleet steamed slowly through the Mediterranean, an elderly armada, manned by bored British reservists and conscripts who were either cynical or bewildered. Some enthusiastic regulars could be found, but most knew that the whole business was indeed, in Brook's words, a cock-up. Nasser's air force, as a potential threat to the invasion fleet, was destroyed in two days – by which time the Israelis had routed his army in Sinai – but Canberras and Valiants from Cyprus continued to bomb targets which were 'military' only in the sense that their destruction was intended to hasten Nasser's downfall. That in the event civilian casualties were, probably, below three thousand is a reflection on the ineffectiveness of bombing as a weapon of terror, not on Eden's supposed concern for Egyptian lines. One RAF pilot, to his honour, refused to bomb. His feelings were widely shared, but a Prime Minister retains his office until it is taken from him. Eden's orders were obeyed.

On 6 November a combination of American pressures imposed a ceasefire on Israel, Britain, and France. There was only one source for an ultimatum – the White House. The invasion force had been ashore at Port Said for thirty-six hours. Egyptian troops, police, and armed civilians surprised the invaders by the skill and courage of their resistance, but a move south along the Canal was about to begin. Nasser sank blockships at Port Said; *Musketeer*, not nationalisation, closed the Canal. On 1 November, during this week of international mayhem, Soviet troops began pouring into Hungary – and as yet another British Ambassador in Cairo burned his files, Dulles orchestrated moves at the UN which had been in train for many weeks. Unable to do anything about Hungary, alarmed at the possibility of Russian intervention in Egypt, gripped with the pains of incipient cancer, Dulles nevertheless conducted a two-front campaign against Britain with the savagery of a man whose opponent must, indeed, be pulverised. France was of no particular concern to Dulles. (Mollet, in fact, cut his losses, and ordered French troops out of Egypt well before a UN force arrived.) Whilst Hammarskjöld and his mainly American staff drew on America's logistic resources to put a UN force into Egypt, Dulles attacked Eden at his most vulnerable point – Macmillan.

'In the height of the Suez crisis Macmillan was to be seen in Trafalgar Square with the Dagenham Girl Pipers launching the Premium Bonds.'[30] That was in August. In the depths, Macmillan was to be found on the morning of 6 November in the Chancellor's office at No. 11 Downing Street, taking a telephone call from Dulles. Fifteen per cent of England's currency reserves had gone down the drain as a result of *Musketeer*. With Middle East oil cut off – Arab governments, as one, had supported Nasser – and only six weeks' stocks available Britain faced something more than the plague of petrol rationing. Dulles made his terms, as a corporation lawyer would: cease fire, and you get American help with sterling; no cease fire, and sterling can go down that drain and take Britain with it.

Macmillan explained, afterwards, 'there are times in a man's life when he has to make bold decisions.' Macmillan also said, at the time: 'It's ruin either way but it's better the quick way.'[31] The Greek obeyed the Roman. Eden, faced with a Cabinet revolt led by Macmillan, capitulated. At 1900 hours that night, General Keightley (*Musketeer*'s overall Commander) received the cease fire order. By 19 November the first UN troops arrived in Port Said. The UN executed American policy; the Romans sent their auxiliaries to keep peace, of a sort. By early December the men of *Musketeer* were on their way home – 'in time for Christmas' as one conscript subaltern with a sense of history remarked. Antony Head – who had succeeded Monckton as Minister of Defence when the latter resigned in despair on 18 October – was left to ponder the implications of Britain conducting potentially major operations with forces suitable only for internal security and guerrilla war.

As the dimensions of Britain's humiliation became crudely apparent, the political establishment relieved its feelings in recrimination and abuse. Eisenhower had been elected for a second term on that fatal 6 November. Khrushchev had destroyed a Hungarian rebellion against his imperial rule. In Budapest an observer from Broadway reflected that uprisings in Eastern Europe could now be wiped off the SIS and CIA list. Nasser was the hero of an Arab world whose xenophobia was stronger than its pride. Ben-Gurion and Dayan had got what they wanted. The American General Raymond Wheeler, for whom Selwyn Lloyd reserved the venom of a man who has had too much to bear, set about restoring the Suez Canal to full working order. He did so with impressive speed. But in Westminster and Whitehall charge and counter charge obscured these international realities. As usual, the House of Commons had been the last to know what was happening. Throughout November Eden was put on the rack. Members took their revenge.

Harold Nicolson, that reliable, despairing chronicler of his class and times, records for 16 November: 'I lunch at the Travellers. The Foreign Office are enraged. They were never consulted, nor were any of our representatives in the Middle East. The latter feel they have been badly let down, and that all their patient work during the last years has been destroyed in a night.'[32] Yes, indeed. The Director of Neabs, spokesman for those patient men, was flown back to Britain 'on medical grounds' and removed from the stage. Sharkh el Adna was closed for good. Several of its staff went to work for Cairo Radio, which thereafter had the propaganda field to itself. Trevelyan, his work in ruins, diplomatic relations with

Egypt broken, closed down the Embassy and recalled Nasser's words about Eden's Britain: 'You are suddenly acting in the sort of way we do.' But Nasser and his people had behaved well. Eden's temptation had given Nasser's people their dignity. Dulles gave them, at the end of 1956, another $54 million in aid, and showed most openly his support for Nasser by promising to send wheat and other food. Nasser's survival was ensured.

Eden had only a few more months of political life before him. A contemporary account says it all:

> The Prime Minister sprawled on the front bench, head thrown back and mouth agape. His eyes, inflamed with sleeplessness, stared into vacancies beyond the roof except when they switched with meaningless intensity to the face of the clock, probed it for a few seconds, then rose again into vacancy. His hands twitched at his horn-rimmed spectacles or mopped themselves with a white handkerchief, but were never still. The face was grey except when black-ringed caverns surrounded the dying embers of his eyes. The whole personality, if not prostrated, seemed completely withdrawn.[33]

From his seat below the gangway Winston Churchill sat in huddled silence.

Yet Eden was not completely spent. He still had strength for hatred. Before leaving for Jamaica to recover from the worst effects of his fevers, Eden ordered Nasser's assassination. The SIS Station Officer in Beirut 'packed up hurriedly and left for London'. Operation *Straggle* – or thuggery – was on the agenda. Eden left London – to stay in Ian Fleming's house. Life, as usual, had a laugh at our expense. But the Prime Ministerial order was disobeyed. SIS was not living in a James Bond world. White could well have echoed the remark of one embittered member of Eden's Cabinet: 'Even if Nasser goes, whom could we put in his place? We have run out of stooges.' An elaborate assassination plan was made, carefully arranged to fail. Nasser never did get the razor designed to explode when used. The old style SIS agents in Egypt disappeared, with some other illusions. The agents arrested by Nasser became beneficiaries of his clemency. When Britain and Egypt exchanged ambassadors again in 1961 after two years during which chargés d'affaires had represented the restoration of diplomatic relations, Nasser handed envelopes to the departing British diplomat. 'A present', said Nasser. Inside the envelopes were the names of those

SIS agents, expressions of an illusion, arrested by Nasser's intelligence service – and released by him.

5 · OUR MEN IN KUWAIT: ARABIAN OIL, 1961

In 1958 Macmillan expressed himself dissatisfied with the situation in which all the advice he received was loaded with the particular interest of the department concerned. Accordingly, he gave directions that a group representing the main departments of State should be set up to make some assessment of Britain's role about ten years ahead. With the strong support of Lord Normanbrook, Secretary of the Cabinet and Chairman of the group, Macmillan thus launched the first major attempt to review Britain's role since the Second World War . . . The Working Group was chaired by Sir Patrick Dean . . .

PHILLIP DARBY,
British Defence Policy East of Suez

When Harold Macmillan became Prime Minister on 10 January 1957 'he pinned up on the green baize door between the Cabinet room and the Private Office a quotation from *The Gondoliers* copied in his own writing. It said, "Quiet, calm deliberation disentangles every knot".'[1] Macmillan also told the Queen he didn't expect to be Prime Minister for more than six weeks; in the event, he ruled for six years, knowing, moreover, that Eden had recommended Butler to the Queen as his successor.

There was little calm or quiet in July 1962, when Macmillan sacked six of his Cabinet colleagues in a desperate attempt to stay in power. But in 1957 anything was better than Eden, a Prime Minister whose neuroses had caused Britain the biggest humiliation since Black Week in December 1899. Macmillan, who hated leaving the Foreign Office – 'the worst blow of my life' he said to the Under and Private Secretaries, with Lady Dorothy by his side, when the news came through that Eden had moved him to the Treasury – was determined to show the world how things should be managed on the international stage. But behind that determination lay a political ambition which was more important to him than re-establishing Britain's role in the world. Macmillan won a landslide General Election in October 1959 by carefully ignoring foreign issues and promising material rewards to the Man in the Street. Suez was expunged in 'never having had it so good'. The phrase was Macmillan's, uncharacteristically vulgar, revealing a psychological need to pretend that Britain remained powerful abroad and prosperous at home.

When Eden was collapsing under the strain of Suez, William Clark (Eden's Press Secretary) asked Macmillan to say something, anything, on his behalf in the Commons. Clark recalls that as he entered Macmillan's room the latter carefully put down the book he was reading to beguile a moment of leisure. *Pride and Prejudice* laid aside, Macmillan said deliberately: 'Anthony has had an easy time of it all his life: now he must have a hard time.' This, from the politician whom Lord Moran saw as Brutus when Churchill's resignation was mooted in January 1955, is one clue for defining Macmillan's approach to politics. To lose was the unforgivable mistake. 'Power for power's sake was what he enjoyed.'[2] John Wyndham who said this, served him devotedly for many years. Another clue is provided by Macmillan's hoaxing remark in the early days of Suez, when Eden's capacity as Prime Minister was first directly questioned. 'I could never succeed Anthony', said Macmillan: 'I am too old.' The one essential political gift was to ride a waiting race. Eden's tragedy was Macmillan's opportunity.

Macmillan, at sixty-two, was too old when he became Prime Minister. The scandals which marred his Government at its end showed how little he really understood what was happening at home. But Macmillan concealed the fact successfully because of his unabashed pleasure in the contrived culmination of a hitherto rather undistinguished political career. In order to act the part of the Queen's first Minister, Macmillan delegated to his Cabinet and to Whitehall responsibilities for the making, not merely the execution of policy. Free from detail and the chores of office, Macmillan played his Olympian part almost to perfection. The part would have suited Disraeli. Summitry with Khrushchev, friendship with Eisenhower, Commonwealth tours, the 'wind of change' speech accepting the challenge of African nationalism, were all part of a process, of a pretence that Britain was still a world power. A journalist with political ambitions once asked Macmillan: 'Would you say it is easier for a Prime Minister in this country to do one thing if he says he is doing something else?' Macmillan hedged his reply: 'It is a very common method, yes.'[3] It was not common until Macmillan became Prime Minister.

No doubt Whitehall found Macmillan a relief after Eden. The Permanent Government was given its head once more. In place of Eden's relentless insistence on Britain challenging a dictator, Macmillan might have murmured with Hilaire Belloc as he touched up the greasepaint: 'Decisive action in the hour of need denotes the hero but does not succeed.' Such action as might best preserve Britain's position in Arabia – indeed restore it *east* of Suez after the fiasco in Egypt – should be placed in the safe hands of officials. These officials were given the authority to devise a new Middle East strategy which depended on a series of assumptions. Suez had distorted more than Eden's perspective on events. Whitehall, having collectively opposed Eden during *Musketeer*, found itself pretending there had been no fiasco, merely an unfortunate accident, which must not be repeated. Britain's steadily increasing economic dependence on oil from the Persian Gulf area is one explanation for the east of Suez strategy which dominated so much of Whitehall's policies in the 1960s, but a curious – if understandable – desire to stay the hand of time also affected the deliberations of these zealous and experienced decision makers.

The dangers inherent in an east of Suez strategy based on assumptions about retaining local influence despite lack of resources was the one critical factor which escaped Macmillan's attention as he embarked on his otherwise impressive course of establishing a new relationship with America; reaching an accommodation with Russia; seeking membership of the European Economic Community for the United Kingdom; and giving independence to Britain's colonies. Macmillan had no private illusions about the end of Empire in his time. Behind the world-weary façade and the languid manner lay an acute intelligence and an imaginative grasp of international realities. Macmillan's real success in establishing a genuinely close relationship with the young President Kennedy was based on the fact that to one charged with enormous responsibilities he did not act a part.

Neither did Macmillan fail to move with the times, some of the time. Macmillan sacked Lord Salisbury from his Cabinet in 1957; the latter opposed independence for Cyprus. (The quirks of history were not lost on Macmillan, the scholar-politician.) During the Mau Mau rebellion in Kenya Macmillan repeatedly attacked knowledgeable and experienced Labour MPs for questioning the Colonial Government's handling of affairs. As Prime Minister, Macmillan gave Kenya independence. He acted likewise over Malaya – once the Communists had been defeated. Unlike Eden, who believed fervently in Britain's greatness to the end of his life, Macmillan knew that the only chance for the country to maintain a respectable position as a senior but no longer powerful member of the international community lay in the reduction of commitments and a concentration on economic priorities. Let the Romans take the strain; the Greeks must put their house in order.

What Macmillan failed to grasp was that his act, or charade of international statesman, deluded officials – and, which was of greater importance, senior members of the armed forces – into supposing that he shared their collective belief in the retention and execution of strategic commitments, above all in the Persian Gulf. Macmillan did not enter the looking glass world where the abolition of conscription was to be compensated by the advent of nuclear weapons. But Macmillan did not raise his prime ministerial stick and shatter the glass to dispel the illusion that the rudimentary British nuclear weapons system would deter or contain conflict. Macmillan stood, leaning on his stick, watching, or indulging in rhetoric: 'We must rely on the power of the nuclear deterrent or we must throw up the sponge.'[4] Eventually, he found himself forced to share the illusion, although in a political rather than a strategic context.

At Nassau, in December 1962, Macmillan was reduced to pleading with Kennedy to prolong the life of Britain's nuclear deterrent. Macmillan, who had taken the measure of Khrushchev's priorities and knew that Britain's international role was low on the list, asked Kennedy for the Polaris missile system simply and solely as a weapon of prestige. Macmillan had also learned that Kennedy, like Eisenhower, queried the role of a British deterrent. In 1963 de Gaulle would probably have vetoed the British Government's application to join the EEC whether or not the Nassau deal had been made. De Gaulle detested this apparent revival of the special relationship, but his opposition to Britain joining the EEC was mainly based on his determination that France should dominate it. However, Macmillan, by making the retention of a British nuclear deterrent a political priority and reducing Britain's application to join the EEC to second place, provided de Gaulle with a pretext. No more than Eden, or Bevin, was Macmillan able to escape from the past.

There is something particularly apt and ironic in the fact that it is to Patrick Dean that Macmillan primarily owed the evolution of a policy which ensured the retention of world-wide strategic commitments – on the cheap. By the same token, the Government's announcement in April 1957 that a complete, though crude nuclear weapons system was operational owed more to relentless lobbying by the Royal Air Force than to the beliefs of the Minister of Defence, Duncan Sandys. Nor did Sandys have any rooted objection to conscription, the abolition of which was announced at the same time. The Regular Army, collectively, disliked conscription, partly on the valid ground that it absorbed a disproportionate amount of time training men whose services thereafter with operational units was brief, largely because of an irrational prejudice against the youngsters whose courage in Malaya and Korea had enabled Britain's imperial and international roles to be prolonged. Sandys and the regular forces of the Crown agreed on one thing, however. Despite, or because of, Suez, the new Empire of the East, from the Persian Gulf to Hong Kong, was more important than the old in terms of a strategy of prestige.

There were a few perceptive officials and senior officers who saw the absurdities, not merely the dangers of the so-called Sandys defence policy, whereby Britain's nuclear weapons, no longer able to blackmail America, would impress minor powers. If these men had been able to get to Macmillan round the dinner table the real dimensions of Britain's overseas responsibilities and strategic capacities would have been rationally discussed. Macmillan might then have stopped talking in the House of Commons about Britain as 'a great nuclear power'. Macmillan would have drawn on the experience, rather than dispensed with the services, of Antony Head and a junior minister called Fitzroy Maclean. But Macmillan preferred the company of those whose views, however unrelated to what Britain could, and could not do, provided him with that romantic gloss on events which his essentially cautious Scottish soul required. Lord Home, as Foreign Secretary, attacking the United Nations for interference in the Congo; Julian Amery, Macmillan's son-in-law, warning of communist subversion in Arabia: these were the words which Macmillan heeded, not because of what was said, but because of who said them.

Amery achieved a position in the Conservative Party which Macmillan chose not to ignore. This position was not due to Amery being Secretary of State for Air, but because he said what others felt. Iain Macleod, as Colonial Secretary, followed a path in Africa which Gladstone rather than Joe Chamberlain would have approved. Macmillan and Macleod, two Scots, both members of a minority race in the British scheme of things, possessed an instinctive sympathy with African nationalism. Yet Macmillan allowed Home, over the Congo, to destroy much of that trust in Britain which the new African leaders were prepared to give. Julian Amery – 'My Minister for the Yemen', as Macmillan called him when a revolution there, with Albanian overtones, occurred in September 1962 – reflected opinions which ran directly counter to accommodation with Russia, or Nasser, anywhere. Sandys took a similar line, and when he became Commonwealth Relations Secretary in 1960 began rapidly to make Aden a new imperial outpost. The Yemen revolution appeared to justify the Sandys policy. SIS, on the spot, groaned as the old game was played again. Macmillan, demonstrably, did not have a kitchen cabinet; he was unable to rid himself of an imperial caucus, whose members were convinced that Britain must retain a place in the Arabian sun.

A 'delicate balance of terror' between America and Russia – or the absence of such a balance – did not receive much Whitehall attention. Until the Cuban missile crisis of October 1962, the balance between super-power nuclear deterrence and the almost unimaginable catastrophe of a nuclear war was maintained by the American and Russian governments concentrating virtually all their diplomatic and strategic efforts on Europe. British governments looked elsewhere. Britain had a nuclear Maxim gun, of sorts; others, East of Suez, had not. Neither Sputnik's orbital flight on 4 October 1957 nor Yuri Gagarin's journey into space on 12 April 1961 caused concern in the British governing establishment. 'Improvements' in nuclear weapons and advances in space exploration, and all the terrifying combinations of destructive possibilities therein implied, were matters for the super powers. When Gagarin visited Macmillan in Downing Street on 16 July 1961, the latter's Press Secretary, Harold Evans, observed: 'The P.M. felt at a loss for conversational gambits, but talked about his frolicsome week-end at Khrushchev's dacha.'[5] Exactly a month later the Berlin Wall was built.

Fortunately, across the river from No. 10, in the new SIS headquarters, some thought was being given to the cold war, concentrating on its geographical extent, where Britain was still in the front line, at what point the country might have to cry quits. Above all, White was determined that a professional SIS would not be expected by prime ministers and foreign secretaries to believe, let alone do, six impossible things before breakfast. The acquisition of raw intelligence, by properly trained officers; the maintenance, indeed the improvement of effective working relations with intelligence services with which SIS was in liaison; the penetration of hostile services: these were the requirements which White, during his eleven years as 'C', imposed on SIS. He was to have much success; suffer from insecurity in high places; see MI5 weakened by his departure; and find obsessions about the Middle East a challenge to the priorities which he laid down.

It is in the context of prime ministerial theatre, whose scene shifters were determined the play would go on, that the successful Kuwait operation of July 1961 must be set. Mounted and executed during the worst crisis between America and Russia since 1948, when Dean Acheson's State Department team was recommending offensive military action to relieve pressure on Berlin, the three months' occupation of Kuwait by British troops against a supposed threat from Iraq struck observers in Washington as an astounding irrelevance. The Washington mood, charged with the threat of conflict between super powers, excluded consideration of minor problems. Even the deepening tragedy of the Congo Civil War and the crises afflicting UN forces there – where Kennedy rather than Macmillan saw Khrushchev's hand at work – was left mainly to State Department specialists. Acheson, brought from retirement by Kennedy to help an Administration already beginning to look across the Pacific at Vietnam, presided calmly yet caustically over a group of officials who knew well enough that all the new-fangled theories of strategic missile deterrence and controlled resort to tactical nuclear weapons bore little or no immediate relation to a situation in Berlin where 4,000 refugees a day were crossing from east to west. The shadow of a nuclear holocaust nevertheless lay across every proposal and all decisions.

There was no panic in Washington; there was simply concentration on Khrushchev's crisis, coupled with a realisation that if he built a wall across Berlin, relations between America and Russia, already soured by the U-2 incident in May 1960 and the failure of either Eisenhower or Kennedy to repair the damage, would sink to zero. Despite the force of Acheson's recommendation, not much confidence was placed in the plan to send an armoured column from the American 7th Army in Bavaria along the autobahn to Berlin as a warning that the wall must not be built or, if built, must be destroyed. Nor did the proposal of Major-General Albert Watson, the American Military Commandant in Berlin, to hose the wall away before the mortar hardened, get more than a passing nod. Washington was preoccupied. Even Macmillan's plea to Kennedy – 'stay calm' – brought nothing more than acknowledgment. Kennedy and his Cabinet were too absorbed in monitoring the cold war's latest crisis to find time for irritation. Any British journalist talking about the situation in Kuwait during those June days, and seeking clarification of the American position, would have had short shrift. Compared to what Macmillan used to call 'the possible extinction of civilisation' in nuclear war, Kuwait was, indeed, irrelevant, a far-away country of which Americans knew little.

Yet the Kuwait operation has a particular place in Britain's post-war fortunes. If the Berlin crisis had not been so acute; if the overall American concentration on nuclear weapons as instruments of strategy had not become so strong; and if American interest in the Middle East had been based on good relations with Britain, Kuwait would have had its share of attention in Washington. A common policy for relations with Middle East oil-producing states, if not necessarily for the area as a whole, might then have evolved. But the American interest in the Middle East continued to be based on the simple premise that oil could be secured by paying increasing sums to the producing states. If this policy injured Britain, too bad.

The policy did cause injury. Throughout the late 1950s and early 1960s American governments, perceptive beneficiaries of access to cheap crude oil, actively backed Saudi Arabian demands, even to the extent of supporting territorial claims to the Buraimi Oasis, over which Britain, as *de jure* or *de facto* protecting power to the Trucial States and Oman, had a rather ambiguous authority. Treaties of protection undoubtedly justified British intervention in Buraimi, provided Oman's claim to the oasis could be established. The Saudi claim could only be understood by scholars, but in relation to Britain, gained some force from the treaty which Ibn Saud had made in 1927, by which the former agreed to a policy of 'non interference' in his domains.[6] British authority in Buraimi was nevertheless maintained in the 1950s by a series of minor campaigns, in which British officers commanded local forces, and where the mood of the North-West frontier was overpoweringly strong. The Saudis retired from Buraimi in 1957. Defeated in action, their resentment against Britain smouldered. The ambiguities of the Treaty of Jeddah, signed on 20 May 1927, enabled all varieties of interpretation to be made and sustained.[7] The State Department supported Saudi Arabia to the hilt. Saudi Arabia and Britain did not resume diplomatic relations until January 1963 – with Buraimi firmly in Oman's hands. America had Saudi Arabia's crude oil.

The harsh American approach to Britain in Arabia softened, but did not fundamentally change, on the sixth floor of the State Department. But there the enquiring British journalist would be asked: 'What is your government doing about the defence of Berlin, of the West?' The answer had to be 'not much'. The British Army of the Rhine decreased in size and declined in strength. Eden's pledge of four divisions was honoured in the breach rather than the observance. Dependence on tactical nuclear weapons increased. The Ministry of Defence instigated a press campaign, designed to fool NATO collectively into believing that the defence of Europe was the British Government's first priority. In fact, the only priority given was to a strategy designed to use tactical nuclear weapons from the outset of any conflict, however limited, and irrespective of whether the enemy had done so or not. As so often, the men on the spot saw reality more clearly than their superiors. One battalion commander in BAOR to whom a senior officer waxed enthusiastic about the ingenuity of this nuclear strategy replied scornfully: 'Do you think I'm going to chuck these things about like cricket balls?'

The nuclear weapons which Macmillan boasted about in 1957 were, in 1961, sitting in Cyprus, Aden, and Singapore. When Abdul Kerim Kassem, Iraq's dictator, accepted defeat over Kuwait in October 1961, Whitehall felt that a new era of British influence, indeed of 'friendship and mutual understanding' in the Middle East, was about to begin; senior officers at the Middle East Headquarters in Aden were thankful that the crisis had not reached the stage of outright conflict between Britain and Iraq; the staff of the British Embassy in Kuwait wondered if the lessons would be heeded; SIS suspected the lessons would be ignored. They were. Kuwait was *sui generis*, yet success there in 1961 bred a new set of illusions about British power and influence in Arabia which were not dispelled until Aden became the scene for full-scale urban guerrilla war; causing, in November 1967, an ignominious evacuation. Washington remained indifferent.

Kuwait in 1961 was of critical importance to the British Government: 40 per cent of all crude oil imported by Britain was produced in the State. That was not the reason for the despatch of forty-five warships (representing much of the Royal Navy's operational strength), and 6,500 troops between 30 June and 5 July, or for distorting the entire deployment of the armed forces, at home and overseas. The pretext was to test 'strategic mobility', and the capacity of the Strategic Reserve to do quickly what, apparently, British garrisons could no longer do at all in the post-Suez world. The real reason was to demonstrate to the world – or such parts of it as chose to notice – that Britain still counted. Kassem was not considered a serious threat to Kuwait. The most authoritative statement, based on an official report of the Kuwait operation is unequivocal on this rather basic point: 'HMG did not contemplate aggression by Iraq very seriously.'[8]

The act of deterrence, in which the nuclear weapons system played a central, concealed role, was directed against Nasser and, by extension, Russian ambitions in Arabia. Britain's Arab friends were encouraged to believe the stain of Suez had been wiped out. To some extent they did so believe. Randolph Churchill declared in November 1958, 'Britain can knock down twelve cities in the region of Stalingrad and Moscow from bases in Britain and another dozen from Cyprus. We did not have that power at the time of Suez. We are a major power again.'[9] The negotiations for Cyprus's independence were concluded in 1959. 'Sovereign Base Areas' were retained, under British control. A nuclear base was thereby acquired, from which a dozen cities, and not only in Russia, could be threatened.

The genesis of the Kuwait operation thus lies in Macmillan's determination to pretend that Suez went wrong because he was not in charge. For all his assumed calm and real cynicism, Macmillan reacted to Nasser much as Eden had done. Eisenhower noted in March 1957: 'Foster and I at first found it difficult to talk constructively with our British colleagues about Suez because of the blinding bitterness they felt towards Nasser. Prime Minister Harold Macmillan and Foreign Minister Selwyn Lloyd were so obsessed with the possibilities of getting rid of Nasser that they were handicapped in searching, objectively, for any realistic method of operating the Canal.'[10] Macmillan had to live with his obsession. In May 1957 he was driven by American pressure to accept Nasser's terms for re-opening the Canal. Macmillan briefly entertained the idea that he could still 'topple Nasser'. Eisenhower killed that idea, and stressed that Nasser would only open the Canal to commercial traffic if Macmillan put Suez behind him. Macmillan was forced to endure the taunt in the House of Commons that 'this was the greatest and most spectacular retreat from Suez since the time of Moses'. Lady Eden declared that the Canal had flowed through her drawing room; it seemed likely to engrave itself on Macmillan's heart. He thereafter 'readily identified Nasser with Hitler'.

Macmillan thus gave Dean his brief. For all Brook's support to members of the working group who sought limitation of overseas commitments and concentration on a European role, a combination of precedent, political factors, and service ambitions ensured that the final report 'confirmed Britain's world-wide interests and the requirement for a continued British involvement in the Indian Ocean area. The military assessment was broadly that both nuclear war and war in Europe were increasingly unlikely and that the major threat to peace was posed by limited conflicts in Africa, the Middle East, and Asia. Hence emphasis was placed on the development of strategically mobile forces.'[11] The report was presented to the Defence and Overseas Policy Committee of the Cabinet in mid-1960, by which time a revolution in Iraq appeared to justify most of the arguments. There is no evidence that Macmillan took much notice of the report, even although the Foreign Office, for which he had professed such affection and the Treasury, whose advice in November 1956 he had taken, argued strongly for the European role and against that East of Suez. The East of Suez role was nevertheless given an overriding priority. Britain's influence in Europe and in NATO continued to decline.

On the face of it, the report and review simply emphasised likely dangers and made sensible recommendations. In reality, the recommendations gave priority to solving problems by strategic means, but conspicuously ignored the fact that neither in the Mediterranean nor the Persian Gulf, and partly because of what had happened in 1956, were there bases from which limited, non-nuclear war operations could be mounted; reliable satellites; or a manpower reserve. Dean's working group did not pretend that Suez hadn't happened, but the Chiefs of Staff criticisms of Eden were replaced by a conviction that by the exercise of strategic mobility – and with the nuclear deterrent discreetly in the wings – Britain could continue to play a starring part on the international stage.

The reference to 'strategically mobile forces' made sense in a Far East context. Singapore was a major base, capable of supporting such forces. As a result, a decisive victory in limited war was gained against Indonesia between 1963 and 1966. There was no base in the Middle East, and there had been none since the decision to withdraw from Egypt in 1954. For political, geographical, and financial reasons, there was no possibility of establishing a major base in Cyprus, Aden, or Bahrein. 'Gibraltar, Malta, Aden – on this great string of fortresses long depended the power of Britain throughout the Mediterranean and the Middle East' wrote Macmillan with contrived nostalgia.[12] He was living in the past, when imperial resources, although often meagre, could be supplemented from India and the Colonies. By 1958, let alone 1961, the survival of the Empire of the East depended on coming to terms with the fact that Britain was no longer a major power. The requirement, above all regarding the Persian Gulf area, was intelligence of events; maintenance of economic strength by the supply of oil; and hence encouragement of local rulers who could also look ahead to the time when their relationship with Britain could be put on the basis of approximate equality.

SIS was not invited to comment directly on Whitehall's East of Suez deliberations. The Working Party engaged in strategic analysis and, by the Services representatives, in bids for cash. SIS, providing intelligence to meet the customers' requirements and tackling problems as they arose, played no part in these deliberations. In any event, once the worst of *Straggle* was over, White had concentrated on internal reform; the recruitment of a genuine post-war generation; new areas of possible conflict with Russia; and the improvement of working relations with the Foreign Office. By 1959, Controllers with regional responsibilities related to functions had replaced the Directorial system. Basing his approach partly on experience of the Malayan Emergency, where SIS and MI5 had worked together reasonably well, White started to look at Africa. Independence for the Gold Coast came in 1957. SIS was active in the Congo Civil War. Thereafter, Africa became a priority area for both services. Getting closer to the Foreign Office meant mutual acceptance of roles, a growing realisation that they were complementary.

Yet behind the Committees, behind Macmillan's façade, behind that establishment which he said had vanished but did so much to preserve, was a fixation which White would, perforce, have shared. In 1958 Britain still had an Empire, in fact, if no longer in name. America had not begun its colonial venture in Vietnam. Unless a member of the Permanent Government was an extreme radical he would take it for granted that Russia menaced that Empire at every point. White, for all his professionalism and his calm view of what was, and was not possible in the Middle East, accepted that the SIS role there became of paramount importance once Egypt was identified, so to speak, as a Russian bridgehead to the Middle East as a whole. Throughout the 1950s, and in language more trenchant than NSC 68, the annual Ministry of Defence Joint Planning Staff appreciation began: 'The Russian aim in cold and hot war is to establish a communist world dominated by Moscow.' Whereas NSC 68 and its successors concentrated on strategic aspects of the cold war – implying, after Hungary in 1956, and growing evidence of Russian success with the hydrogen bomb tests, the necessity for, not merely the desirability of, accommodation – the joint planners in Whitehall continued to stress the dangers to Britain's Empire from Moscow's belief in 'the historical inevitability of Marxism – Leninism'. Stalin's death in 1953 produced no revisionist views; Russia had always been aggressive, had always menaced Britain: so it would remain.

It is not surprising, therefore, that Eden's final words on Suez should strike a responsive chord. 'Everybody knows now what the

Soviets were planning and preparing to do in the Middle East. Russia supplied arms in such quantities, as has now been revealed, because she knew the Egyptian dictator's ambitions suited her own book.'[13] These words, spoken on Eden's return from Jamaica on 14 December, found no response in Whitehall. Checking Russia in Arabia remained a prime consideration of British strategy, but the latter must in future be one which would combine deterrence with economy. Eden went further. Referring to Suez, he said: 'I would do it again.' The Permanent Government was determined no prime minister would do it again; hence the search for a strategy which would combine deterrence with economy, caution with warnings. Whitehall knew, moreover, that this strategy, whatever its apparent justification in terms of deterrence to Russian ambitions in the Middle East, would find few backers in Washington. The political essence of the new East of Suez strategy lay neither in its assurances to Britain's Arab friends nor in veiled warnings to Moscow, but in the requirement to be independent of America without incurring American hostility. The Eisenhower declaration of January 1957, which stated that 'international communism is the greatest danger to the Middle East', was simply a piece of verbiage, rejected in London. Where were the American troops?

When Britain's old friend Nuri Said fled from Baghdad on Bastille Day 1958, was next day captured, dragged through the streets, then murdered as an unmistakable sign that the Middle East created by Cromer and Churchill had gone up in flames at last, American response was prompt – but brief. Alarm bells rang throughout Arabia. Where next would 'international communism' find a fire to light? The Lebanese Government asked Washington for help. Marines from the 6th Fleet poured ashore at Beirut in such numbers that their equipment was piled on the beaches in enormous heaps. The leading Marines drove noisily into the centre of Beirut, alarming rather than reassuring President Chamoun. His Army Commander ordered troops to put up road blocks and confine the main body of Marines to the jetties. Chamoun had invoked the Eisenhower Declaration. Within days he had, so to speak, revoked it. After three months the Marines departed. Lebanon, July to October 1958 marks the one independent American military intervention in Arabia.

Eisenhower remained content with his Declaration; above all, he accepted the CIA's appreciation that Nasser was his own man, not Khrushchev's. Nasser, although as much baffled by events on his doorstep as any Western observer, was always ready to trade on the American belief that Arabia's ills were due to its imperial masters. 'Really, I have no plan', Nasser used to say when asked for his revolutionary prescription. Such pragmatism may have destroyed his chances of ruling the Arab world; for nearly twenty years after Suez it suited the Americans nicely. Their pragmatism confirmed a policy of support for Nasser; eventually led to weapons for Israel; provided increasing oil revenues for Saudi Arabia; and was marked by indifference to Iraq and the Persian Gulf.

Matters were seen differently by the late imperialists. The emotions released by Nuri's death acted as a catalyst to some in Whitehall and many on the spot, fusing in one simple mood fear of change, suspicion that Nasser was behind every act of violence, conviction that the controlling hand was in Moscow and the Russian Embassy in Cairo. Nasser's photograph replaced King Feisal's in Iraq's government offices. The Iraq Communist Party came out into the open. Moscow, 'unfailingly guided by the principle of self-determination of peoples and with profound respect for the legitimate national aspirations of the people of Iraq', established diplomatic relations with the new regime.[14]

Nothing which happened in the ensuing years, none of the continued contradictions of Arab politics, affected the mood – in London – because emotions were a stronger influence on policy than evidence that the wind of change was blowing in Arabia also. Nuri's death, revolting and sudden, was a bigger shock than the murder of the Iraq Royal Family, women and men. Nuri was the candid friend whose advice and admonitions could be endured without resentment. He was the kind of man on whom the British in Arabia, when not indulging in fantasies about the Bedu, had utterly depended. For some years after July 1958, the last generation of British pro-consuls in Arabia sought another Nuri, indeed, as problems multiplied, a whole set of them. None was to be found. Nuri's death was the end of an old song.

When, however, a British parachute brigade, passing through Cyprus, landed at Amman airport on 20 July 1958 in response to Hussein's request for support, the stage seemed set for a new era. Hussein had spurned Eden in 1956; two years later he seemed to have accepted that Eden was right. A detached, experienced French observer of this new twist in Anglo-Jordanian relations commented: 'The West could scarcely have bettered this parade of its talents for the benefits of a wondering Orient.'[15] Macmillan would have agreed. But neither he nor his advisers publicly accepted the pointed complementary comment: 'But the Western gesture had been to some extent made in a vacuum. It did not affect or impinge upon the real issues in the Arab world.'[16] Whatever Macmillan thought, his public words mirrored his advisers' inner convictions that an East of Suez strategy was feasible in both political and military terms. The parachute brigade nevertheless left Jordan after three months – sitting around Amman airport throughout – and no serious effort was made to improve relations with Hussein so that he could bank on Britain's support in another crisis. Glubb's dismissal still rankled beneath the surface. It became necessary for the late imperialists to look further east than the Fertile Crescent. Refusing to accept that times were also changing in Arabia, Macmillan allowed his cronies to plan an Arabian counter-revolution.

The attempt to stop the clock led to some odd results, not least because the entire history of Britain in Arabia had lacked the consistency and coherence which is possible only with unambiguous imperial rule. Moreover, Suez had caused so much dismay to Britain's old Arabian friends and opponents that any consistent policy thereafter was virtually impossible. Britain was forgiven for Suez, but Nasser became the most potent figure in Arabia. Britain's Arab friends wanted two contradictory things: protection from Nasser, but without incurring the odious charge from nationalists in their midst that they remained British stooges. To cap it all, the enormously increased importance of Arabia in terms of world oil production and consumption required that the counter-revolutionary principle be sacrificed, or placed in suspended animation if, as in Iraq, the regime was both revolutionary and able to turn off the taps. Diplomatic relations with the revolutionaries in Baghdad were established with 'indecent haste'; the Iraq Petroleum Company was advised in December by the incoming Ambassador, Humphrey Trevelyan, to bend with the wind. Reluctantly and ineffectually, the Company attempted to do so.

No better man could have been found than Trevelyan to sense possibilities of compromise and restraint. Iraq's withdrawal from the Baghdad Pact in March 1959 (transmogrified thereafter into the 'Central Treaty Organisation'), followed by a campaign of abuse against it which rivalled Nasser's, was expected and accepted in London. Abuse was only to be expected from a regime which took its rhetoric from Moscow. What really mattered was the continued flow of oil. The IPC made some concessions, but none fundamental enough to satisfy nationalist demands. Nevertheless, Iraq's oil revenues increased. Russian arms were bought; the Moscow Norodny Bank in Beirut became a clearing house for IPC payments and Russian gold.

Resumed relations with Iraq were a stop-gap move, an experienced finger (Trevelyan's) in the revolutionary dyke. The basic strategy was to convince the conservative, indeed reactionary rulers of Kuwait and the Trucial States that their future depended on a British presence. What that presence should be was left conveniently vague; the vital element was its permanence, not its nature. There was nothing vague, however, about the fact that the Emir of Kuwait believed the time had come for his State to run its own affairs. Independence was the best antidote to Nasserism. There was nothing vague about the fact that Abu Dhabi's oil reserves – production due in 1961 – were, in the words of IPC's Managing Director, 'Equal to a couple of Kuwaits'. In the considered aftermath of Suez, SIS had been instructed to open a Station in Kuwait; in 1958 a Political Office (later an Agency) was established in Abu Dhabi.

These moves were politically inspired by Macmillan's ministerial colleagues but they were orchestrated by a Foreign Office with overall responsibility for re-establishing British influence in the Persian Gulf and a Ministry of Defence keen to test strategic mobility there. The first Political Agent in Abu Dhabi, Donald Hawley was, like most of his colleagues up and down the Gulf, a former member of the Sudan Political Service. Members of this enlightened service were well practised in dealing with intractable problems and opinionated sheikhs. Hawley and his successor Hugh Boustead – the latter last encountered in the Crimea,[17] his idealism now matured to the art of the possible – brought to Abu Dhabi an individual style and a firm hand in coping with the especially intractable Sheikh Shakbut, under whose variously demarcated territory lay enough oil to satisfy Britain's needs for decades to come. By 1961 Sir William Luce, the Political Resident for the Persian Gulf, could reflect, as he sat playing Mozart in his agreeable Bahrein drawing room, that 'East of Suez' had acquired new, and satisfying, characteristics. The Residency, white stone and cool lawns, sentries at the gate, evoked India. The occasionally mordant wit of Lady Luce, the style and assurance of her husband suggested an *imperium* which was capable of infinite adaptation to circumstance.

Neither Luce nor his predecessor George Middleton disposed of legions, only levies, of small size and doubtful reliability. The strategic need for a base, of sorts, was clear. Aden was selected. Between the closing years of the 1950s and the early 1960s, Aden became a kind of tropical housing estate for the mercenaries who were intended to defend the Empire of oil and stop the clock for a generation. Behind the Victorian cantonment façade and beyond the thriving port was built block upon block of colour-washed flats for the new kind of British regular, young, married, mobile. The whole area behind the housing in Ma'alla Strait and beyond the popular look-out of Steamer Point was to become a death trap when the South Arabian revolution broke out in December 1963, but in the years of Dean's working group and in the days when the V-bombers landed with a satisfying thud at all the places where the Union flag still flew, the Aden base was a visible symbol of counter-revolution in progress.

There was, however, one essential element missing in this strategy of delay. Aden could accommodate troops and aircraft, but there was neither space nor cash to construct adequate base facilities for the Royal Navy. Nature denied the Royal Navy space; Macmillan's nuclear weapons absorbed the cash. Reliance on Singapore, 4,000 miles from Aden, reflected an assumption that strategic mobility could dispense with naval support, or that a crisis in Arabia would mature with such convenient delays that the Royal Navy could take its time about arriving on the scene. A strategy which had been designed for the deterrence or containment of genuine crises would have been reflected in measures to provide the Royal Navy in Aden with facilities comparable to those in the port, readily available to the world's shipping lines and the major oil companies.

Thus the view from Steamer Point was often obscured by sunset haze, but *couleur de rose* was, in any case, preferred to the clear light of day. Aden, as a colony, could be ruled outright. Its hinterland was the domain of tribal rulers, whose incapacities and cupidities were, at the time, assuaged by bribes and by plans for a Federation of States, independent – and reactionary – under benevolent British tutelage. The working population of Aden, intelligent, educated, and polyglot, was regarded by the Governor and the chiefs – 'delightful rascals' – as nothing more than an enormous out-station for the Egyptian Intelligence Service. Action was taken accordingly. The American Consulate in Aden, a pleasant building by the sea, became a good place to hear another point of view.

Macmillan and his colleagues thus turned their back on Suez and looked to the Arabian Peninsula for greatness. SIS continued diligently to penetrate the weak points in Nasser's domestic regime. That hostile operation aside, Egypt, in counter-revolutionary terms, was ignored. It was to the East that the land looked bright. Yet not only was the vital strategic element of a major base missing from the counter-revolutionary plan and the reassertion of British influence east of Suez; there was a gaping hole in the map. Saudi Arabia had broken off diplomatic relations with Britain in 1956, ostensibly because of Suez, in reality because of the Buraimi Oasis dispute. Unless relations could be restored, hopes of a new British ascendancy in Arabia were doomed. Once the Suez dust had settled, considerable efforts were made to convince the Saudi ruling family and its advisers – several of the latter on close and confidential terms with SIS officers in the Middle East – that the era of counter-revolution was also one of renewed support for the Arab case on Palestine. By the 1950s the House of 'Al Saud had become more or less accepted in Arabia as guardians of Islam's holy places, Jerusalem in particular. During the 1920s Ibn Saud had defeated the rightful guardians, the Hashemites, in battle. Ibn Saud thereafter asserted a painlessly protective role towards Palestine, one which Roosevelt was quick to recognise. These factors ensured that Anglo-Saudi relations would remain distant. The Hashemites, Sherifs of Mecca, had been British protégés of a sort; Britain had been responsible for Israel, a State whose existence Saudi Arabia attempted to deny.

The Saudis were not appeased over Palestine; they were adamant about Buraimi. Diplomatic relations remained broken. The issue was not merely one of sovereignty, but of the long term future of all the States bordering Saudi Arabia. Ibn Saud had left his neighbours alone. With the exception of Iraq and Yemen, these neighbours were all under British protection, a relationship which Ibn Saud in the days of his poverty was content to accept. The discovery of oil and the establishment of America's dominant role in Saudi Arabia transformed this situation into one where continued British influence on the Peninsula was resented in Jeddah. Ibn Saud's successors, Saud and Feisal, saw themselves, with some justification, as arbiters of the Peninsula's future. This view was encouraged by the State Department in Washington, America's representatives in Jeddah and, above all, by the Arabian-American Oil Company (Aramco). Throughout the 1950s, Aramco's geological survey parties regularly encroached on British protected territory (the Eastern Aden Protectorate) in the assertion of non-existent Saudi rights. These acts – on one occasion causing casualties in the British commanded Hadhrami Beduin Legion – coupled with American support for Saudi Arabia over Buraimi meant that Britain was at odds with the two most powerful forces on the Peninsula.

Kuwait's and Abu Dhabi's arrival on the oil scene raised the stakes. American political influence was dominant in Saudi Arabia but non-existent among its neighbours. This factor was more than compensated by American shares in IPC (which also held the Abu Dhabi and Qatar concessions) plus Gulf Oil's 50 per cent stake in Kuwait. The American grip on oil concessions ensured that real power on the Peninsula would eventually go to a Washington-backed Saudi Arabia. Before the ink was dry on the Dean report it had become clear that there would be no point in reasserting British influence, practising the deterrent and mobility strategies, or fighting a counter-revolutionary campaign if the price of victory was surrender of more oil concessions. The restoration of the Shah had certainly been a pyrrhic victory. American oil companies dominated the Consortium which replaced Anglo-Iranian in 1954. Hostility from Saudi Arabia would have to be endured. If a firm line was taken over Buraimi, and a *coup de théâtre* attempted elsewhere, Britain's new East of Suez role might yet find political justification. Strategic justification would have to depend on circumstance. By 1960, the assertion of British interests in the Persian Gulf was given a higher priority in London than their defence against a real or supposed threat from Kassem's pro-Russian Iraq. The requirement was to find a ruler who would do as he was told.

Abdullah, Emir of Kuwait, was the ruler in question. He was not merely required to do as he was told, but to take part in a scheme whereby Kuwait, on becoming independent, would be tied more closely than before to Britain. The Political Agency in Kuwait was told by the Foreign Office to encourage Abdullah's desire for independence. White and his subordinates were given the task of convincing Abdullah and the 200-odd members of his family who formed Kuwait's governing system that independence without British protection was a prescription for disaster. Revolution in Iraq; the continued influence of Nasser throughout the Middle East; and Russia's increased role in the area gave plenty of opportunities to frighten Abdullah and subdue critics.

The ambiguity of Britain's relations with a Kuwaiti ruling

family which both sought and feared independence enabled the diplomats and SIS to execute a policy for their political masters which, elsewhere in the Arab world, would have been destroyed by rampant nationalism or the absence of effective military forces. The ambiguity, moreover, enabled those masters and, indeed much of the permanent government, to ignore Kuwait – once the political decisions had been made – and let the men on the spot get on with it. In London, Kuwait was seen through a mist of papers; East of Suez, enduring the intermittent sand storms and relentless heat, the agents of empire fashioned a policy of sorts.

Macmillan claimed that, over the Kuwait operation in 1961, 'The Cabinet left the whole management of affairs to me.'[18] Even for Macmillan, this assertion is absurd. Neither Macmillan nor the Cabinet was concerned with operational realities. The Foreign Secretary, moreover, was hazy about geography. Of Kuwait he declared, 'The defence of this island is vital to our interests.' The Cabinet 'failed to provide detailed instructions to cover all contingencies'. This failure 'revealed a lack of firm Government direction for the active use of its forces.'[19] Quite. A deterrent strategy which provides for ultimate rather than probable crises tends to lack clarity. In 1961 this ambiguity was of little comfort to Commanders and diplomats who were charged with executing a strategy of prestige. The management of affairs was left to Sir Charles Elworthy, Sir William Luce, and John Richmond. These three were the Commander-in-Chief Middle East, the Political Resident, and the Political Agent. Fortunately, Elworthy and Luce were fully conscious of the genesis and nature of this strategy.

Kuwait in 1958, when the new east of Suez policy emerged, was unique in being a State which contained enormous potential for enriching the West; a political structure which denied not only rights but citizenship to all save a small minority; a limited capacity for internal development; but a virtually unlimited one for providing financial help to its Arab brethren. The Sabah, ruling family for many generations, had shrewdly ingratiated themselves with the merchant class, and kept a nervous eye on the Arab foreigners in their midst: Egyptians who taught, the Palestinians who provided technical skills, and the Iraqis who laboured. The Persians, hewers of wood and drawers of water, were ignored. But it was in their relations with Britain and its imperial agents that successive Emirs had, until the late 1950s, shown most agility.

In 1899, the Emir sought British protection from an Ottoman

Empire scarcely able to maintain authority in its own dominions, but conscious none the less that the habitual rivalries of European powers were beginning to concentrate at the head of the Persian Gulf. In particular, the Kaiser was looking east. Bismarck's prediction that the Gulf would prove to be the world's wasps' nest was unknown to the Emir. But he and his forebears had ruled their trading and pearling State long enough for cunning to act as substitute for power. British protection was sought and, by the Foreign Office, unenthusiastically, granted.

The Emir insisted that there would be no interference in how he and his family ruled Kuwait. He made it quite clear that no interference would be tolerated from the Political Resident – in those days appointed by the India Office, and stationed at Bushire on the Persian side of the Gulf. The Foreign Secretary, Lord Lansdowne, left all the details to his officials. They found themselves embroiled in Arabian Nights tales of murder – the Emir, Mubarak, had killed his brothers to gain the succession – and kidnap: Mubarak claimed that the Germans had abducted him in order to extract an agreement to extend the planned Baghdad-to-Basra railway to Kuwait. The Foreign Office, after a fashion, sorted these problems out: the railway was not, and has not been extended. Mubarak and his heirs thereafter enjoyed the palm of protection without the dust of interference.

The ambiguities remained, however; as competition for Middle East oil intensified between Britain and America in the inter-war years, Kuwaiti Emirs began to display as much skill in playing off the competitors as they had in seeking protection. By a series of complex manoeuvres between 1925 and 1934, the Emir, Ahmed, succeeded in extracting an oil concession from Anglo-Persian which was not only favourable for the times but cut in a 50 per cent American interest in the shape of Gulf Oil. The Mellons who owned most of the Gulf stock had in those days a member of the family, Andrew, who was Ambassador to the Court of St James. With the Red Line Agreement notched on their rifle butts, well co-ordinated American political and commercial interests put such pressure on Ramsay MacDonald's weak Government that resistance was impossible. Once again, the Foreign Office found that relations with America were always bad when oil was on the agenda. The Political Agent in Kuwait (before the First World War the Emirs had made this token concession to a British role) was the amiable and astute Colonel Dickson. He saw which way the wind blew. He advised London there was little point in reminding

Ahmed that his first obligation in oil, or any other matter, was to Britain. Ahmed had been deeply influenced by Reza Shah's cancellation of APOC's concession. Letting Gulf in would provide an insurance policy. In December 1934 Ahmed, and Gulf, got just what they wanted. Britain got fifty per cent.

By the 1950s, by contrast, Abdullah was musing whether protection without interference was still a game which could be played. With 14 per cent of the 'free world's' proved oil reserves within his grasp – and with a great deal more undisclosed to that world lying beneath the hideous Kuwait New Town built on the oil revenues' proceeds – some kind of real protection from political demands and territorial claims might well prove necessary. By 1958 the American capital investment in Middle East oil was $1,850 million; Britain's, $805. Comparable figures reflected real power in terms of oil reserves and production. The position had been reversed in a decade. Yet America showed no sign of wanting to defend Kuwait or protect Abdullah and his brethren. Would Britain do these things?

Colonel Dickson had been gathered to his fathers; his successors had begun to transform a one-man Agency into an embassy in all but name – yet minus SIS. Abdullah knew that elsewhere in the Gulf the British, for all their protestations, were tightening rather than loosening their grip, removing ambiguities by interfering in local rule. The process began in the 1930s, a direct riposte to the American hold on Saudi Arabia. Sheikh Shakbut, in Abu Dhabi, could he heard muttering, 'We have always been pushed around by somebody.' By the 1950s not only was SIS operating from Bahrein, but MI5 was active throughout the Gulf, concerned with 'internal administration' – in a word, the prevention of subversion.

It was into Kuwait, this mirage of a State, this welfare wonderland with the highest per capita income in the world – everything free except freedom – that SIS opened a Station in 1958. One man, with a budget, a list of requirements, and a healthy scepticism about Kuwait, arrived from Bahrein. Kuwait was defenceless against a direct and sustained attack from any determined enemy or acquisitive neighbour. The Kuwaiti Army was long on gold braid, short on métier and experience. The British Army training team busily made bricks without straw, watching the Kuwaiti products of Sandʌurst lose initial zeal in dissipation and ennui. The Iraq Revolution, 'a matter of when rather than if', as the SIS Controller Middle East sagely minuted, did not, as might be expected, ease the Political Agency's tasks. Abdullah was quick to point out that neither Kassem, an obscure brigadier, nor his fellow conspirators had been spotted by the British Embassy in Baghdad. As with Nasser, the junior commissioned ranks and disaffected senior officers had escaped the supposedly all-seeing eye of British intelligence.

The priority requirement of SIS in Kuwait, therefore, was to establish a system which, in its comprehensive efficiency, would not only convince Abdullah that he would be spared Feisal's fate but also, in the range and sweep of its operations, would add emphasis to the Agent's warning that future protection might well mean the occasional presence of British troops. The system therefore required liaison with the Kuwaiti authorities, specifically the police, which ran a rather nebulous special branch, mainly consisting of little men in dark glasses, paid to do nothing except drink coffee, pick up, and relay every particle of gossip. They were instantly recognisable and absolutely useless, the laughing stock of the Egyptian Teachers' Mission (a kind of *de facto* embassy), Syrian Ba'athists, Iraqi communists, and Palestinian nationalists. SIS set out to penetrate these potential saboteurs. A dozen good agents were recruited within a year. An article of faith with the professional intelligence officer is that an agent can be recruited and effectively run from almost any combination of motives: money, the interest of the thing, the need for being wanted. The faith was justified in Kuwait.

SIS was also required, for sheer operational necessity, to penetrate the Kuwait Army, such as it was. Loyalty was as much in doubt as inefficiency was not. This counter-intelligence operation was put in train. But, above all, and by selection of the right man rather than recruitment of agents, SIS had to convince the ruling few that their fate was certain unless the hesitant shuffle along the independence path was changed into a purposeful march towards a new and enduring relationship with a Britain which was determined to stay East of Suez. On instructions from London, it was decided that the SIS Station Officer should declare himself in his true role. A senior Sheikh of the ruling family was told. This was a gamble, but a carefully considered one. Further, a Kuwaiti official, later to be a minister with a deserved international reputation for negotiating flair, was designated, rather to his surprise, as the day-to-day liaison between SIS and the ruling family. In addition to this liaison, SIS established comparable links with the Kuwait Army. By a combination of penetration and liaison, SIS – and, by extension, the Ministry of Defence in London – knew in detail what capacity existed in Kuwait for external self-defence. The answer was none. On the other hand, the internal security situation in 1958 and 1959 was threatening only to those who saw a communist or a Nasserite under every bed. These were diligently searched, but produced disappointing results. On such realities, SIS liaison with the Kuwaitis was rather nominal.

A virgin territory produced opportunities rather than difficulties. Moreover, the Ministry of Defence requirement given to SIS for co-operation in contingency plans for the defence of Kuwait was greatly eased by the willingness of staff seconded to the concessionary Kuwait Oil Company from British Petroleum (formerly Anglo-Iranian) to act as unofficial assistants. BP, after the Abadan experience and the restoration of the Shah, had a strong interest in the physical defence of its assets, whatever commercial depredations were made by American rivals. Similar moves were made with British expatriates working in key Kuwait government departments. Whilst Abdullah and his family were coming to accept that SIS might ensure their survival, the latter was establishing a system committed to the survival of an imperial role. SIS organised the visits in late 1959 – well before Abdullah formally asked for independence – of a party of civil engineers from Kenya. At least, this was the occupation written in their passports, and passports never lie. In fact, the visitors were the commander and staff of 24 Infantry Brigade, a formation in the Strategic Reserve. Derek Horsford, the Commander, a man not easily given to depression but much to sardonic humour, had something to grimace about when he surveyed the terrain. The only defensive feature was the crumbling escarpment north-west of Kuwait Town known grandiloquently as the Mutla Ridge. This heap of sand might, perhaps, stop an armoured column motoring on the Basra-Kuwait axis for twenty minutes.

But although SIS found itself immersed in military nuts and bolts, pressure on Abdullah provided both challenge and response. Without such pressure, a complementary operation in Bahrein, whereby new defensive arrangements between Kuwait and Britain were made, might well have proved impossible. Abdullah had to be persuaded if possible, or coerced if necessary, into signing a piece of paper which would enable British troops, 'by invitation', to defend Kuwait in circumstances left vague enough to justify intervention and the exercise of a deterrent strategy. Through the looking glass, it became clear that fear with the only coercive weapon available to British officials dealing with Abdullah. If a combination of Kassem, Khrushchev, and Nasser failed to alarm Abdullah, it might be necessary to make his flesh creep in other ways. The threat from revolutionary Iraq appeared to be remote. Kassem's irritating silence about Kuwait, his 'gratifyingly correct' relations with IPC (despite midnight sessions of cocoa and television, during which he harangued the latter's officials about their reluctance to surrender proved oil reserves to the Iraqi people), Khrushchev's patent irritation with the course of the Iraq Revolution, and Nasser's habit of falling out with his erstwhile allies, were all strong reasons for frightening Abdullah from within.

For the first three years of Kassem's regime he had nothing but praise for Kuwait. Abdullah's desire for independence was warmly welcomed. (It was the Hashemite rulers of Iraq who, in the 1930s, had hinted at the acquisition of Kuwait, a mere Emirate.) The Russian Embassy in Baghdad became increasingly puzzled by Kassem's 'bourgeois' attitude towards his opulent, capitalist neighbour. Russia, until July 1958, had ignored Iraq. Lacking embassy and with the Iraq Communist Party in hiding, the KGB was unable to run an effective intelligence operation. Kassem's advent and the establishment of diplomatic relations with Russia initially led to exaggerated expectations, all the greater given Nasser's readiness to bite the communist hand which continued to feed him arms and economic aid. But by late 1959, relations between Moscow and Baghdad were virtually non-existent. The KGB Station in Baghdad could well have quoted an appreciation which then enjoyed a restricted distribution in Whitehall: 'For reasons of prestige, or fear, the Soviet Government felt obliged to intervene as each Middle East crisis occurred, but her part was always that of an alarmed, puzzled, or even exasperated protector, who would have preferred a period of political stability in which long-term plans could gradually mature.'[20]

A supposedly revolutionary State which, after a mere two years, had driven the Communist Party back underground – Kassem never, in fact, legalised it – led that veteran Stalinist Anastas Mikoyan to exclaim at a press conference during a visit to Baghdad in April 1960: 'Must I really show an Arab that the policy of the Soviet Union and its attitude towards the Arab peoples differs from the policy of the imperialist powers?'[21] Mikoyan, 'visibly upset', was given the Arab equivalent of a raspberry by the assembled journalists. By June 1961, according to an expert witness, 'Soviet-Iraqi relations in the post-revolutionary period had reached an all-time low'.[22] But Russia had done one thing: the Baghdad-to-

Basra railway had been vastly improved. SIS in Iraq redoubled effort spent on the time-honoured task of closely observing trains.

But it proved difficult to put salt on Abdullah's tail. He and his like had resisted British persuasions successfully for so long that the Agency and Residency found themselves driven to encourage the notion of independence in order to reveal the dangers which it brought. Unwittingly, some rather tepid riots during 1960, in which Kuwaiti schoolchildren (by name, in fact idle and indifferent youths of nineteen and twenty) were encouraged to shout for Gamal Abdel Nasser, sufficiently alarmed the Family to hasten the processes of adjustment to British demands and needs. The rioters were knocked about; Iraqis were evicted; Persians, as before, ignored. The Egyptians were left alone, as were the Palestinians, whose role as technicians in keeping the Kuwait Army operational had reached the stage where the Sabahs, in conclave, seriously began to wonder who ran their state.

Working against time, Residency and Agency put together a treaty with Kuwait which gave it independence and ensured continued British protection. Kuwait's boundaries were defined, a process which intensely annoyed the Saudis, whose claim to some parts of their neighbour's territory was based less on ambiguities about the so-called 'Neutral Zone' – shared between the two States – than a desire to remind everybody that the house of 'Al-Saud was the arbiter of affairs. Boundary definition produced bizarre incidents. Colonel Dickson's shade was invoked as the authority on custom, writ, and possession. The key Chancery Staff in a well-known combination of the British overseas, a Scot and an Irishman, reassured Abdullah that Kuwait would emerge into the full light of independence and the warm embrace of the Arab League with frontiers both defined and secure. The Agency was translated into a Legation then, with a quick acceptance of Arab pretensions, elevated to an Embassy. On 19 June 1961, Kuwait became a nation. On the 25th Kassem verbally annexed it as Iraq's thirteenth province. On the 27th, the Military Attaché at the British Embassy in Baghdad signalled that an Iraqi armoured brigade 'intended' to move to Basra. On 1 July, by which time HMS *Bulwark* was lying off Kuwait, Horsford was on the spot, and 24 Brigade was in the air, Abdullah signed the other piece of paper, asking for British protection. It had been a damn'd close run thing. The original contingency plan for intervention in Kuwait was codenamed *Vantage*; its revised version was *Bellringer*. Once again some Ministry of Defence wit had been at work.

Kassem's motive for verbally threatening Kuwait remains unknown. Observers had always thought Kassem odd. John Strachey, who as Secretary of State for War in 1951 met him occasionally, thought him 'totally unbalanced'. An attempt on Kassem's life in July 1959 led to hallucinations. Perhaps he also saw Kuwait through the looking glass. At the time, however, Kassem's threat was both precisely what the new imperialists sought and the men on the spot feared. Richmond, 'too nice for this world, too upright' in the words of a sympathetic colleague, said sharply to London that no real threat had been made, or existed, or could be countered by sending British troops to where they were neither wanted nor needed. SIS in Baghdad said much the same, pointing out that until tanks were railed to Basra or unless the Iraqi Air Force was put in a state of readiness no specific threat could be identified. Train watching intensified; the Iraqi Air Force stayed on the ground. The morale of the Iraqi Army was patently low. The armoured brigade in Basra not only lacked tanks but officers. The summer leave season had begun. The soldiers wanted their pay. The Ministry of Defence in London nevertheless reported Iraqi troop movements. Richmond was told to keep quiet, Luce to arrive on the scene. The SIS Baghdad reports were duly noted, and confirmed by the Kuwait Station. But help was on its way, whether the Kuwaitis wanted it or not. Had they asked for it? A situation of opera bouffe developed in the early hours of 1 July as the awful possibility loomed that troops might arrive before Abdullah, formally, asked for them.

A providential duststorm delayed the arrival of *Bulwark*'s Royal Marine Commando. The Commanding Officer showed no enthusiasm for a premature arrival in hazardous conditions. The clock was stopped long enough for the rites to be observed. Run to earth in the Amiri Palace by the Head of Chancery, Abdullah 'requested' British troops. A civilian helicopter pilot was persuaded by SIS to guide the Commando to its positions. By D + 1, despite one fighter flying straight into the ground, two others landing at the civilian airport – occasioning much alarm to arriving passengers – and a Beverley transport crash-landing through suspected sabotage, Kuwait was well and truly defended, in terms of prestige. Kuwaiti merchants prudently put their sterling holdings into dollars. British troops from more units, formations and locations than one cares to remember were dug in on the Mutla Ridge, immobile and stricken with heat. The defence of Kuwait owed much to Dr Parry, Senior Medical Officer of the Kuwait General Hospital. He packed the victims of heat-stroke in ice, saving a dozen young lives. A sympathetic American, General Manager of the Kuwait Oil Company, was later given an honorary KBE for his determination to provide facilities for troops who had little to do off duty except frizzle in temperatures of well over 100°.

Bellringer, however, was a close-run thing in more than diplomatic terms. *Vantage* was based on two intentions: rapid reaction to an Iraqi threat; consolidation of a defensive position in Kuwait. The planned method linking these intentions was the despatch of a parachute battalion from Cyprus direct to Kuwait once the bells started to ring. Turkey would be overflown. On 26 June the Turkish Government stated that overflying permission had been refused.[23] Shades of Suez! The parachute battalion was stood down. Fortuitously – or not – *Bulwark* was in the Gulf. Her Commando replaced the parachute battalion. If *Bulwark* had not been in the Gulf and if a serious Iraqi threat had rapidly developed the new East of Suez strategy would have been put to the proof.

The defence of Kuwait would then have rested on two squadrons of rocket-armed fighters to attack Iraqi armour. There were *eight* such fighters immediately available in Kuwait; the remaining twenty-four were in Bahrein. Canberra crews were given targets in Iraq. In real terms, Kuwait could only have been defended from sustained attack by unacceptable means. Such an attack was unlikely; it was not absolutely impossible. Elworthy in Aden knew that *Bellringer* was a gamble, not a strategic option. Luce, once back in Bahrein, knew it. Horsford, like all others in Kuwait knew it only too well. The Royal Navy was a sitting duck – Iraq's Russian motor torpedo boats presented a genuine threat in those narrow waters – and left after three weeks, depriving Horsford's troops of air cover and radar surveillance. With tongue in cheek, that peripatetic correspondent Kim Philby reported to the *Observer* 'grey shapes are lying offshore'. The News Editor asked, with understandable suspicion and brevity: 'Couldst concretise grey shapes?' Alas, this could not be done. Far call'd, the Navy sailed away.

These awkward truths were lost in a flurry of diplomatic manoeuvres by the new nation, enlisting Arab League support, appealing to the United Nations. Abdullah had not wanted British troops. Once they arrived in Kuwait, he ignored them. Only a very old-fashioned warning from Elworthy persuaded Abdullah that Kuwait's empty schools (the pupils were on holiday) should become rest centres for his troops. By October they had gone. The Arab League force which replaced them was notable, the Sudan contingent excepted, for total inability to co-ordinate operations or maintain discipline. The Saudis dug and wired trenches, turned their front to rear, and threatened reprisals on unwanted visitors. Abdullah did not care. The defence of Kuwait was in Arab hands, indeed largely in Egyptian hands.

In London, Macmillan continued to stage-manage. 'On Christmas Eve I gave the necessary alert to our troops in case the Kuwait Government should once more ask for our support. On Christmas Day I heard that the expedition is all ready to start, as soon as I give the sign. I pray it might not be needed.'[24] Macmillan's prayers were answered, after a fashion. The same December Kassem expropriated the one part of IPC's concession which really mattered: North Rumaila, as rich a field as any in Arabia, proved but not yet in production. For three years IPC had successfully resisted Kassem's arguments about North Rumaila. Macmillan's strategy of prestige had put paid to those arguments, and there was not even HMS *Mauritius* to rescue the oilmen and their families.

On 8 February 1963 Iraq's Ba'athists finally murdered Kassem, a reach-me-down dictator. Today, the Head of the Russian Military Mission in Baghdad has no need to echo Mikoyan's words. In Kuwait, the Sheikh who objected most strongly to British troops is now the Ruler. Alone amongst conservative Arab States, Kuwait maintains diplomatic relations with Russia. Yet Kuwaitis remember what Britain did in July 1961, and some do so with gratitude and admiration. *Bellringer*, and the manoeuvres preceding it, made sense in a political and diplomatic context. Britain retained rights and privileges in the Gulf for another decade of increasing oil production and consumption. Strategically, *Bellringer* is, perhaps, best included amongst those operations from which the true lesson is rarely learned.

6 · MOST SECRET COUNCILS: MOSCOW – LONDON – WASHINGTON, 1962

'Members of SIS. I have been asked by the CIA to let you know of the absolutely crucial value of the Penkowsky intelligence we have been passing to them. I am given to understand that this intelligence was largely instrumental in deciding that the United States should not make a pre-emptive nuclear strike against the Soviet Union, as a substantial body of important opinion in the States has been in favour of doing. In making known this appreciation of our contribution, I would stress to all of you that, if proof were needed, this operation has demonstrated beyond all doubt the prime importance of the human intelligence source, handled with professional skill and expertise.'

'C', speaking in Century House in late 1962

The role played by SIS in hauling the world back from the brink of nuclear war in October 1962 has never been publicly acknowledged or, to Everyman, known. Dick White's message to his colleagues, given in the cinema at Century House after the Cuba missile crisis had been resolved, reflected President Kennedy's appreciation of what had been achieved, but beyond that SIS had to be content with the knowledge that failure to run Oleg Penkowsky for eighteen months might have led to that extinction of civilisation in nuclear war which Macmillan feared.

Throughout the last twenty years repeated efforts have been made to show that Penkowsky was a disinformation agent, used by the West to discredit Russia. *The Penkowsky Papers*, published in 1965, the work of those in CIA who opposed détente, provided apparent confirmation of this suspicion. Some in Britain and America who know the truth are still inclined to deride the value of Penkowsky's intelligence. Others, who agree about its crucial importance, assert that it was the CIA who ran this unusual member of the Russian establishment. In 1976 the Church Senate Committee on Intelligence referred to 'Penkowsky, the CIA agent in the Kremlin'. Skulking in the shallows and shadows of the American intelligence community may be found a few old timers who remain convinced that Penkowsky is the prime example of the KGB at its fiendish best.

White's emphasis on the magnitude of the achievement in providing Kennedy with intelligence of Russia's inability to attack America with intercontinental ballistic missiles, and with the time scale for emplacing medium and intermediate range launchers in Cuba, did not reflect chauvinism. White did not need to raise spirits after George Blake's treachery had been discovered in late 1960 and admitted by him in April 1961. White did want to stress the overriding importance of human intelligence to new members of SIS, and to put the value of other forms in perspective. But, beyond these considerations, White was determined to state clearly to his audience that the world revealed by the Penkowsky intelligence was the real world. It was a world of Russian fear and Russian backwardness; it was a world in which the nuclear balance was a necessity, not a choice, or an 'option' to be discarded by those in the Pentagon – or anywhere else – who believed in striking first.

White did not stand up and say that this real world differed from the looking-glass world. It is not 'C's' job to say such things. In any case, and, ironically, almost as White spoke, Macmillan was concluding a deal with Kennedy which prolonged Britain's role as 'a great nuclear power' – on the private understanding that the weapons would never be used in anger. Nevertheless, no member of SIS listening to White that day could fail to have drawn a distinction between the real strategic requirements of the times and Britain's independent nuclear role as projected by the Prime Minister. Amongst those requirements was the acquisition and distribution of intelligence capable of increasing international security rather than asserting the national interest. The Penkowsky operation not only met that requirement, and indirectly contributed to the improvement in relations between America and Russia which characterised the 1960s and 1970s; the intelligence operation as a whole showed that the adventurism of Suez and the opportunism of Kuwait already belonged to the past. Indirectly, the Penkowsky operation thus enlightened the permanent government about the strategic realities of the nuclear age; the impossibility, not merely the futility, of genuine nuclear independence for Britain; the fact that retaliatory power – and hence true deterrent capacity – depended on American goodwill.

White left details of the Penkowsky operation to the Controller Soviet Bloc and his subordinates. The Washington Station was in the safe hands of a future 'C'. There was a professional quality about the operation which sustained SIS as a whole and convinced its members that the 'horrors' – and absurdities – were over at last. Alas, this was not entirely true, but what was achieved in Africa throughout the 1960s and attempted in Ireland during the early 1970s reflected fundamental change. Above all, relations between the Foreign Office and SIS showed that agreed objectives and complementary methods were essential, not merely desirable. From the early 1960s onwards, the two services began to work together in a world in which Britain's survival depends on human skills being used by governments in the most intelligent way possible.

The Penkowsky operation is thus the unique example in recent history of intelligence as the servant of foreign policy, as a resource and not merely an expedient or a technique. The intelligence played a direct and vital role in the execution of foreign policy and military strategy. SIS, and indeed that part of the permanent government concerned with international security, made a contribution to Kennedy's policies which his advisers were initially inhibited from making through disagreements over Russian intentions and capacities. That contribution was made, between April 1961 and October 1962, as Macmillan schemed to keep the independent deterrent in being despite Kennedy's expressed fear that he was 'haunted' by the spread of nuclear weapons.

The ironies and contradictions need not be pursued, although they are legion. Moreover, the circumstances in which Penkowsky made his overtures and the methods by which he was, eventually, run provide examples of human idiosyncrasy, courage, absurdity, and acute perception, which stand in sharp contrast to the further evidence of treachery revealed by Vassall, Blake, Houghton and Lonsdale – and of laxity by John Profumo, a member of Macmillan's Government. Whilst SIS was running Penkowsky, Macmillan's Secretary of State for War was sleeping with tarts who slept with Russian intelligence officers. In January 1963 Philby reached the end of the road; he arrived in Moscow, eluding with embarrassing ease the SIS officer sent to bring him home from Beirut. White wearily signalled all stations to revise procedures. Otherwise that chapter was closed, after twenty-five years.

Theories of massive retaliation and roll-back had received their political quietus four years before Kennedy won the Presidential election of November 1960. Eisenhower had waged peace. In March 1959, during yet another Berlin crisis, he had stated flatly: 'We are certainly not going to fight a ground war in Europe.'[1] Nevertheless, Eisenhower had allowed the CIA to conduct an intelligence war with gadgets which had grown in intensity once Eastern Europe was finally abandoned to its fate and reliance on human assets was replaced by an addiction to electronic and other forms of scientific intelligence. Not everyone in Washington believed in a super-power nuclear balance, based on mutual fear of annihilation. The U-2 first flew in 1955; Eisenhower was initially kept in the dark. Richard Bissell, Allen Dulles's special assistant, was put in charge of the aircraft's flights over Russian territory – despite intense objections by General Curtis Le May, Chief of the Air Staff. He wanted, at the right moment, to convince Eisenhower personally that Russia not only had hydrogen bombs but the intercontinental missiles to carry them. Le May believed that the

Air Force, not the CIA, should decide the strategic priorities.

But it was Dulles who used the U-2 to advance his cold war arguments. Kennedy fought his election on assertions of a 'missile gap' which was opening between America and Russia; the latter was already ahead in the missile race. The CIA's annual National Intelligence Estimates by 1960 had become a more potent text than NSC 68. The habit of preferring capacity to intention – maybe unavoidable in a society which makes gods from machines – led, by an unfortunate progression, to the NIEs becoming texts for those who argued that Russia intended, sooner rather than later, to attack America.

Kennedy was no intellectual, and did not spend either his working days or spare time pondering the subtleties of nuclear strategy. Kennedy's reactions to developments and events were intuitive and imaginative. But he respected, collectively, the new intellectual élite, whose theories of nuclear deterrence were attacked by the cold warriors throughout the last years of Eisenhower's Presidency. Once Kennedy became President he forced the protagonists to argue their case in front of him. In particular, Kennedy asked his Defence Secretary, Robert McNamara, and Allen Dulles's successor, John McCone, to discover the truth about the alleged missile gap. This was a taxing requirement, made more difficult to execute by the insistence of the deterrence theorists and the State Department that Russia's intentions must be considered before its overall strategic capacity was assessed.

The problem was further complicated by the fact that the CIA was unable to acquire reliable political intelligence about Khrushchev's motives and methods. Christian Herter, who had succeeded Foster Dulles just before his death on 24 May 1959, had nothing to put in place of either cold war or Eisenhower's search for accommodation. Kennedy's Secretary of State, Dean Rusk, listened to what his officials said. There was no consensus. 'The pacific and lethargic nature of American foreign policy during the Eisenhower administration' had to be replaced.[2] But by what?

Khrushchev's hand would have been difficult to read even if Kennedy and his advisers had agreed about their policies. Macmillan was convinced that Khrushchev bragged more than he threatened, and did so to conceal weaknesses in the Russian communist system which acute Western eyes might spot, and react to accordingly. But Macmillan was impressed, possibly intimidated by Khrushchev's boasts in the later 1950s that Russia had 100-megaton bombs and the 'rockets' to deliver them. Macmillan pointed out to Eisenhower, with understandable apprehension, that bombs like this would devastate Britain at one blow. Neither in Russia, nor anywhere else, could SIS discover whether Khrushchev's jest that he had not ordered these particular bombs to be tested 'because they would break all the windows in Moscow' was a joke, or concealed the awful possibility that such a threat to Britain did, in fact, exist.[3]

Allen Dulles and Le May, rivals over the U-2, were united in their determination to assert that Khrushchev threatened with a purpose. They were not much concerned with threats to Britain, but when Khrushchev said, 'I shall not be revealing our military secrets if I tell you that we have long range rockets, rockets of intermediate range, and close range rockets'[4] the hard-line Washington reaction was: We told you so. When Khrushchev said, at the January 1959 twenty-first Party Congress, 'War in the nuclear age is absolutely inadmissible',[5] Dulles and Le May said, 'Tell us another'. Khrushchev's visit to America in September 1959 alarmed Dulles and Le May. Would Khrushchev reveal that he knew all about the U-2? Khrushchev had other things on his mind. China was no longer willing to listen to Moscow, preferring an independent foreign policy. Eastern Europe was stirring; even Albania had broken ranks. 'Hoxha had let go with an assault on Khrushchev that surpassed anything the Chinese had yet said, and he combined it with an emotional eulogy to Stalin, a wise Marxist-Leninist statesman slandered by the current leadership of the CPSU.'[6] Khrushchev's manifold cares and preoccupations were lost on a Washington which chose to accept what the U-2 photographs, seemingly, revealed. 'To the Air Force every flyspeck on a film was a missile. At various times ammunition storage sheds in the Urals, a Crimean War monument, and a medieval tower were identified as the first Soviet missiles.'[7]

Gary Powers's abrupt descent over the Northern Urals on May Day 1960 can now be seen as a blessing in disguise. Powers, 'the shoemaker's son from the coal-mining village of Pound, Virginia, and one of the straightest fellows I ever knew' (in the words of a senior member of the CIA, John Maury) had been ordered to fly U-2 number 360 from an airstrip on the Afghan-Pakistan border on a route across Soviet Central Asia to photograph the missile test centre at Tyura Tan near the Aral Sea. From there Powers was to fly over research establishments near Chelyabinsk and Sverdlosk in the Urals. That mission accomplished, Powers was due to fly west to photograph the naval bases at Archangel and Murmansk. En route, Powers was ordered to photograph Plesetsk, believed to be the site of a fully operational ICBM base. If all went as planned, Powers would land at Bodo, in Norway, nine hours after his 0626 take-off. But over Sverdlosk, Powers's U-2 took a 'near miss' from a SA-2 missile, close enough to wreck the aircraft's control surfaces – and to destroy a Mig 19 sent up to intercept. Powers was thus shot down, Washington supposing him dead, and glumly accepting the fact that 70,000 feet was no longer a safe height to spy from.

The resulting exchanges between Eisenhower and Khrushchev wrecked a planned mid-May four-power summit meeting in Paris – 'approached by American officials in the spirit of a young girl being asked out for the evening by a well-known seducer, previous encounters with whom had led to scandalous propositions rather than honourable declarations'[8] – but on which Macmillan had pinned great hopes; forced Eisenhower to cancel the U-2 flights; and led the CIA to increase its dependence on SAMOS satellites. Unfortunately, of five launchings between October 1960 and December 1961, only two managed to get into orbit. Another device, the 'Discoverer Biosatellite', was, however, more successful. Shortly after its initial launch in August 1960, CIA officials claimed: 'We have photographed the Soviet inventory'. It was on the basis of such assertions that Kennedy accepted the 'evidence' of a missile gap.

In fact, Gary Powers's capture and the poor quality of satellite photographs – invariably dark and lacking definition – led to a situation where Kennedy's advisers were virtually forced to begin a debate about Russian nuclear and missile strength. Khrushchev meanwhile shifted his braggart emphasis from ICBMs to the intermediate and medium range variety. Such a move, a virtual admission that America could not be devastated as Western Europe might be, would have been quickly and accurately assessed by an Administration which had settled to its tasks and had achieved agreement on basic issues and the assessment of intelligence. Khrushchev won a major intelligence victory when Powers was shot down. If the U-2 flights had continued for much longer even Dulles and Le May might have been forced to admit that Khrushchev's threats were empty.

Indeed, despite the establishment of an effective defensive system against aircraft, Russia lay open to an American first strike by missiles, and could equally be the victim of retaliation should Khrushchev attempt anything against America's NATO allies.

The American intention to strike might be wanting; the capacity to do so was not. Le May and the Air Force knew this. What John Foster Dulles had threatened in the early 1950s and then abandoned in 1956 after failure to intervene over Hungary became, at last, a distinct possibility. But for Le May to have admitted it would have destroyed his case for pre-emptive attack. He continued to urge the case for threatening to strike first as a strategic necessity. America must close the missile gap and take the lead. Only then would it be possible to destroy Russian cities and missile sites.

Two factors for long inhibited consideration at the Presidential level of whether Khrushchev, and others, might be lying: the debate between Kennedy's advisers strayed into the metaphysics of nuclear strategy; Khrushchev, from early 1960, put Cuba on the chessboard, determined that 'the road to Berlin should lead through Havana'. In February 1960, Mikoyan went to see Fidel Castro who, from January 1959, had been the unquestioned communist ruler of an island ninety miles from the American coast. Since March 1958, when the Eisenhower Administration stopped sending arms to the Batista regime in Cuba, Castro's eventual victory there had been assumed by Washington. With a sneaking feeling in Washington that even a communist could hardly be more trouble to any American Administration than Batista had become, Castro was allowed to entrench himself.

In February 1960, Hawthorne and Wormald – the SIS 'P' officer and the unofficial assistant so ingeniously created by the author of *Our Man in Havana* – would not, in February 1960, have aroused was busy selling sugar to Russia; 'Machines looking like giant vacuum cleaners', of Wormald's imagination – and Graham Green's prediction – would not, in February 1960, have aroused interest in Washington. By the end of the year, however, Cuba ranked in importance with Berlin. Indeed, to many Americans who believed in a kind of nuclear Monroe Doctrine for the second half of the twentieth century, Cuba was their Berlin. On 17 March 1960, Eisenhower ordered the CIA to plan guerrilla war against Castro. On 8 May, a week after Powers was shot down, Khrushchev's Russia and Castro's Cuba established diplomatic relations. On 9 July Khrushchev turned the screw: 'I should like to draw attention to the fact that the United States is obviously planning perfidious and criminal steps against the Cuban people. It should be borne in mind that the United States is not now at such an inaccessible distance from the Soviet Union. Figuratively speaking, if need be Soviet artillerymen can support the Cuban people with their rocket fire, should the aggressive forces in the Pentagon dare to start intervention against Cuba. The Monroe Doctrine is a thing of the past.'[9]

Khrushchev could hardly have known how deeply his taunt about the Monroe Doctrine struck at historic American susceptibilities. Not only did Khrushchev imply that America would be too scared to fight. The taunt made nonsense of much that the new school of nuclear strategic analysts had been propounding for several years. Henry Kissinger's *Nuclear Weapons and Foreign Policy* was published in 1957; Albert Wohlstetter's article, 'The Delicate Balance of Terror', appeared in the January 1959 issue of *Foreign Affairs*; Herman Kahn's *On Thermonuclear War* was published in 1960. Other works and many seminars attracted public interest, which even reached across the Atlantic. In Britain, a group of like-minded intellectuals – Alastair Buchan, Denis Healey, Richard Crossman prominent amongst them – began cautiously to ask whether a similar spirit of enquiry about the dangers of nuclear war would be welcomed by the Government. Whitehall at once provided a freezing rebuke. If you've never had it so good, it is obviously bad form to enquire whether you are going to have it all. The middle years of Macmillan were not a good time for people in Britain who asked awkward questions about survival.

America ordered these matters differently. Kissinger weighed pros and cons with deliberate care; a cautious defence of tactical nuclear war was made. Wohlstetter pondered how many nuclear devils could balance on the point of a pin. Kahn advanced a thesis of positively Wagnerian gloom, in a prose of teutonic complexity. Once nuclear war began, the participants were on an escalator; at the top, everything went – boom! 'Those bloody Germans', as Patrick Blackett, the elder statesman of strategic analysis in the nuclear age – and, unknowingly, their mentor – called them, earned from Le May the good, red-blooded American's final dismissal: 'Gobbledygook has become the union card of defence intellectuals.' Le May's derision reflected his regret at the impending departure of Allen Dulles on grounds of age and his likely replacement by a man new to intelligence. Le May opposed Dulles in Washington's bureaucratic maze; they agreed on fundamentals. Dulles had used the National Intelligence Estimates with great skill; a successor might lose his way in the maze. There were plenty of people in the CIA who disliked the entire NIE approach, and, for good measure, not only opposed dirty tricks but believed that the acquisition of raw intelligence from agents should have remained the CIA's major task. Prominent amongst this group was Richard Helms, by 1960 a strong contender to be Deputy Director of Plans in succession to Frank Wisner. The DDP was a key appointment. Wisner and Bissell made the Directorate into a dirty tricks department where changing a foreign government by assassinating the head of it was not the least of their ingenious ideas. Helms had little time for Wisner and Bissell and less for the 'number crunchers' who produced the NIEs.

Le May had a point when he tilted at the intellectuals. The language of nuclear strategy is absurd because its euphemisms are designed to disguise the horrors of mass destruction; its jargon is often meaningless to the layman because those who use it rely on abstract arguments to discuss urgent questions. That said, the new intellectual élite was a necessary, almost an inevitable antidote to the John Wayne simplicities of Le May and his fellow generals. But Kissinger and his like conspicuously failed to discuss what kind of world Americans were actually living in. Shorn of the jargon, most of their arguments boiled down to a plea for America to do a nuclear trade with Russia which would ensure that the country could safely remain too proud to fight. Peripheral problems – Cuba, Berlin – and entangling alliances, NATO in particular, were considered of less importance than establishing, against the facts of geography and the factors of politics, a new Monroe Doctrine. Ignorance of the facts – assuming these could be discovered and communicated – only stimulated a determination to fit those which could be gleaned to theories bred from solitary thought and earnest conclave. These were seductive arguments in Republican ears, to men who disliked alliances, entangling or otherwise. Kennedy's advent as a Democrat who declared 'Ich bin ein Berliner' compounded the necessities for choice.

Thus when the men from Harvard and MIT, the Rand Corporation and Brookings came trooping into the State Department and the Pentagon in the winter of 1961, those early days of a forty-two-year-old President, they brought with them not only a spirit of enquiry and the American academics' desire to pit theory against practice. The men from the strategic backwoods were determined to find out about the missile gap. If Le May was right and Russia was ahead in the missile race, theories of graduated deterrence and controlled response were so much eyewash. If Le May was wrong – if he could be *proved* wrong, a singularly American thing to want to do – there was a chance that, from supposition and theory, mathematical analysis and judgment about human probability, a strategy of deterrence could be re-established, to be communicated to friends and enemies alike. The Washington atmosphere became charged with intellectual excitement. Intellectual arrogance was not lacking, and it could be intoxicating; not until the Berlin Wall was built did some people sober up. Even after the Cuba missile crisis had been solved by concentration on facts derived from various intelligence sources, theories continued to proliferate. Not many academics were put on the Penkowsky intelligence distribution; theories of controlled response in the early 1960s were based on the fact that the Cuba missile crisis had been peacefully solved, not on the reasons why it had. Only McNamara and his colleagues, John Maury and a select few in Washington, realised that SIS alone had the full story.

Kennedy put McNamara in charge of a kind of nuclear Council of Trent. The President, who saw the new Defence Secretary as a good management man, well able to trim the sprawling Pentagon and its vast budgets into shape, had made the right choice. McNamara, behind the executive glasses and outside the executive hours, saw nuclear war in Khrushchev's terms: inadmissible. For all the talk of 'counterforce' (retaliatory strikes on a military target), McNamara and his advisers knew that such an attack would put some sixty warheads on Moscow. There were two ways to agree with Khrushchev: prevent nuclear war or, if deterrence failed, fight it by degrees, not via 'spasm', or simply by issuing warnings that, at some unspecified point in the conflict, the ultimate horrors would be visited on an enemy. McNamara totally rebutted Kahn's theory of the escalator; rational men did not seek annihilation, nor did a limited nuclear war, should all diplomatic and strategically conventional methods to prevent it have failed, presage Armageddon. McNamara therefore argued that to improve America's nuclear capacities did not imply an intention to use them. This was an idea too difficult for most Air Force minds to grasp. Even more difficult for such minds to accept was McNamara's argument that quality was more important than quantity, that deterrence on the basis of 'mutual assured destruction' (the acronym was quickly seized on by the Tom Lehrers of this world) required the capacity to respond, not the necessity to initiate.

McGeorge Bundy, who became Kennedy's Special Assistant for National Security Affairs, had a similar outlook. The tycoon and the academic – McNamara had been President of the Ford Motor

Company, Bundy was from Harvard – were otherwise dissimilar in manner and outlook. McNamara's wartime experience had been in Air Force logistics, Bundy's in intelligence, but of a highly specialised kind. What they shared, and could articulate convincingly to all but the most resolute sceptic or cynical Congressman, was a moral commitment to preventing nuclear war and a belief that the co-ordinated employment of human intelligence was the best way to do so. Both men were to become very close to the President. Shortly after his appointment, Bundy sent a note to the White House which said: 'A general nuclear exchange would be so great a disaster as to be an unexampled failure of statesmanship.' Kennedy hardly needed to be told this. What he needed was a CIA able to help him make decisions which would be statesmanlike rather than suicidal. Kennedy had McNamara and Bundy to argue one case. Roger Hilsman, Director of Intelligence at the State Department, an official who was temperamentally and intellectually close to the academic strategists, could be relied on to support it. But what about the Joint Chiefs? What about Allen Dulles's CIA?

When Kennedy met Khrushchev in June 1961 Le May was still powerful in Washington. The capital was beginning to be dotted with signs which said 'Fallout Shelter'. Kennedy took a team to Vienna which reflected his uncertainties. Three months as President had merely demonstrated that nobody in the Administration knew what Khrushchev was up to, nor what he had in his nuclear armoury. But of far greater importance for Kennedy, politically and personally, mid-April had seen the Bay of Pigs fiasco, when 1,400 Cuban counter-revolutionaries, financed, armed, and trained, after a fashion, by the CIA, had been scooped up with contemptuous ease by Castro's Militia a few hours after they struggled ashore. The Director of Plans, whose Deputy was responsible for this escapade, engaged in drastic reorganisation; Allen Dulles offered his resignation to the President. Adlai Stevenson, America's Ambassador to the United Nations, was made to look a fool in a forum where, by 1961, the new majority suspected America of dirty tricks and did not want evidence to prove them. Dulles's resignation was accepted, but Kennedy's chagrin at the fiasco was such that he went to Vienna anxious to conciliate Khrushchev if possible – but lacking any tactics to employ should the latter take advantage of his adversary's mistakes. In the meantime Kennedy appointed a middle-aged businessman, and a Republican, as Dulles's successor. McCone was to prove a fortunate choice. As Chairman of the Atomic Energy Commission, McCone understood Washington.

If Kennedy had known that SIS began to run Penkowsky almost at the moment of the Bay of Pigs he might, perhaps, have reckoned that he was about to learn something of value. More probably, he would have seen the information as just another example of the intelligence community's propensity to spin yarns. A long road would have to be travelled before Kennedy became convinced that in Oleg Penkowsky America in particular and the West in general had acquired 'the single most important spy' in the history of the cold war.[10] Bissell's parting shot before he was sacked after the Bay of Pigs was: 'How do we know this guy's on the level?' There were plenty of important people left in the CIA to echo Bissell's words. By 1961 the CIA had become a very large, unwieldy, and politically divided organisation. Between the advocates of the National Intelligence Estimates at one end of the spectrum and the enthusiasts for dirty tricks at the other, those who knew how to run agents and assess their intelligence had a hard time. Bissell's abrupt departure led to a campaign by his friends to put the agent runners in their place.

In Vienna, Khrushchev did take advantage of a young and inexperienced President. 'We will extend to the Cuban people and its government all the necessary aid for the repulse of armed attacks on Cuba.'[11] That was Khrushchev as statesman on 18 April. On 22nd he let fly: 'Aggressive bandit acts cannot save your system.'[12] Thus the Vienna meeting was characterised by what the hawkish but experienced Paul Nitze described as 'hours and hours of abuse from Khrushchev, emphasising that he, the steel-worker, knew how to run a super power and Kennedy, the nice kid, was not fit to run anything at all'. Nitze had written much of NSC 68; in October 1949 he had succeeded George Kennan as Director of Policy Planning at the State Department. Kennedy appointed Nitze Assistant Secretary of Defence for International Affairs, a seemingly artificial job which, in fact, enabled Nitze to exercise much influence throughout Washington.

Nitze never raised his voice; he simply made his point. He regarded attempts, Presidential or otherwise, to reach accommodation with Khrushchev as a total waste of time. Nitze never indulged in Le May's crudities, indeed his arguments were essentially political rather than strategic: Kennan had stated the case for containment, and nothing which had elapsed in the intervening decade had faulted it. President Kennedy's job was to convince

Khrushchev that Russian adventurism would be contained. If Russia established satellites – like Cuba – in the American sphere of influence, they must be removed.

Khrushchev's tactics, both at Vienna and in the months following appeared in every way to confirm the accuracy and shrewdness of Nitze's argument. The building of the Berlin Wall – all other factors apart 'a gross violation of the Potsdam Agreements' – was followed a month later by the resumption of nuclear tests in the atmosphere. Kennedy was particularly upset at this move. He had half hoped, and Khrushchev had half hinted, that a super power moratorium on such tests might be possible. By October, Khrushchev's Defence Minister, Marshal Malinowski, was asserting that Russian ICBMs were more accurate than the medium range variety. It was no comfort to an increasingly divided Administration that Foreign Minister Gromyko at the same time indulged in hyperbole about the Vienna meeting: 'How happy I was to have participated in it! One had to see with one's own eyes what happened in Vienna in order to carry for the rest of one's life the memories of this event in which one was fortunate to participate. If the Soviet Union and the United States united in the cause of peace, who would dare and who would be in a position to threaten peace? Nobody. There is no such power in the world.'[13]

Kennedy's team remembered Vienna rather differently. That Khrushchev was more concerned about Russia's open breach with China, and the awful possibility of an eventual Washington-Peking axis, than the problem of Berlin, and that Gromyko's words echoed his master's fears should have been appreciated by some members of an Administration whose own Asian involvements were already beginning to go wrong. McNamara thought clearly about nuclear strategy; neither he nor his colleagues and subordinates did so about deterring or containing minor conflicts in far away countries. In 1961, Vietnam was just a place on the map, where experiments with lives could be cheaply conducted. The Counter-Insurgency School at Fort Bragg, North Carolina, was in late 1961 the centre for theories of war in the shadows both ludicrous in their political naivety and alarming in their ignorance of guerrilla war. Men who had actually fought in or reported on recent conflicts, in Malaya or Kenya, were acceptable if they equated insurgents with communists, but were regarded with grave suspicion if they did not. Fortunately, the President had little time for Fort Bragg; his mind was elsewhere. As the glory of the Fall gave Washington an air of deceptive calm, Kennedy and his advisers were rather feverishly wondering what Khrushchev would do next. An armoured column had not thundered down the autobahn to Berlin. Khrushchev had won a clear round there. Where would he strike next? And what, literally or figuratively, would he strike with?

It was thus into a Washington of conflicting views and contested theories that the Penkowsky intelligence first arrived – to a very mixed reception. Not only the controversial nature of the intelligence but the form in which it was initially sent from SIS ensured a fierce debate inside CIA. Was it genuine? If it was, who should get it? SIS sent a summary of Penkowsky's first batch to the CIA Station in London, which signalled it to headquarters. The raw intelligence followed later. By the Fall, the transcripts of Penkowsky's all-night sessions in London with SIS were also on their way. By then the flow had become a flood. We must step back, in time and space, to understand why.

Penkowsky had endured four years' frustration before he found a Western intelligence service which was prepared to run him. Posted in 1955 to Ankara as the equivalent of an Assistant Military Attaché, Penkowsky, virtually from the time of his arrival, tried to convince his opposite numbers and their civilian counterparts from Western embassies that he could provide intelligence of Russian plans concerning the area for which he had been responsible as a staff officer during his previous appointment at the Glávnoye Razvédyvatelnoye Upravléniye (GRU, or Directorate of Military Intelligence) in Moscow: the Near and Middle East. Penkowsky found no takers. The intelligence proffered was low grade, and Penkowsky's habit of 'haunting diplomatic functions and buttonholing all and sundry' did not inspire belief in his commonsense or credibility. The CIA Station was warned by Headquarters in general and James Angleton in particular to leave Penkowsky alone. Angleton, as Director of Counter-Intelligence, was a potent voice. The Agency trace revealed that, as a regular soldier with a good war record and steady progress up the ladder of promotion, Penkowsky was marked for higher things. Such did not become traitors. That, at all events, was the CIA assessment. It was distributed to NATO embassies in Ankara and accepted. Penkowsky was rebuffed.

In 1958 he was back in Moscow, and at this point something must be said of a man who rejected sanctuary when it was provided; refused cash when it was offered; and paid for his services to the West with his life. Penkowsky, who was thirty-seven in

1958, came from the kind of bourgeois background, the salariat, which even revolutions find difficult to destroy. Penkowsky's father, a junior officer in the White Army, died in the Civil War, but the family recovered well enough for the 18-year-old Oleg to become a cadet at the Kiev Artillery School in 1937. He joined the Communist Party, and although his front line record in the war was respectable, he did not see much active service until 1943. The cultivation of contacts in the Communist hierarchy, not least through marriage to a general's daughter, and a political general at that, went hand in hand with regimental and staff appointments.

The post-war years followed the same pattern; Penkowsky's staff appointments were notable more for social *réclame* than military significance. By 1958 Penkowsky was the very model of a prospective, modern major-general, an adequately equipped professional with a keen eye for the main chance. He had succeeded, above all, in steering a careful course between the various intelligence and security services which are such an enduring feature of the Russian system, past and present, and which are characterised 'by a fairly bitter enmity towards each other'. Penkowsky knew whom to know.

That was Penkowsky on the surface – and, indeed, beneath it. The SIS officers and Ministry of Defence scientists who spent so many hours with Penkowsky in London were never able to decide what made him open his country's Pandora's box. To this handful and to Greville Wynne – *fidus Achates* indeed – Penkowsky was the best of fellows, high-spirited, a gallant rather than a womaniser, good company, undoubtedly the bravest of men. Wynne, himself a man of outstanding courage, who also paid heavily for his service to the State, was in a good position to know Penkowsky. But he was not in the best position. Penkowsky's motives remain obscure. His repeatedly expressed hatred of the communist system hardly explains the measure of his betrayal. Penkowsky was a beneficiary, not a victim of the system. Penkowsky's father died when he was four months old. Penkowsky may have wanted to avenge the death; he followed in his father's professional footsteps in becoming a gunner, always a service of esteem in the Russian military caste. Pique at occasionally deferred promotion has been put forward by CIA members who stood up for Penkowsky when Angleton and Bissell were deriding him. Vanity, a desire – or a compulsion – to do the most treacherous thing possible has been suggested. We shall never know the truth.

In 1958 not only were Penkowsky's motives unknown; back in

Moscow he was, for the first time, a subject of investigation by the KGB. Promotion to full Colonel was being considered by his superiors in the GRU. The rank is of greater importance in the Russian Army than in those of the West, and should be equated with brigadier. Once more promoted, to major-general, Penkowsky could reckon on the elevator of communist nepotism replacing the ladder of diligent application. He was on his way to the top, to the executive suite, so to speak, of that vast, sprawling, backbiting, corrupt, occasionally murderous, corporation known, by name only, to the outside world as the Soviet Communist Party. Penkowsky's past, not only his record, was investigated. The White Russian father was, figuratively, unearthed. Penkowsky was questioned. Maybe this was the turning point. Haunting embassies in Ankara had been futile. Now Penkowsky had to convince. In order to do so, raw intelligence so important that no Western embassy would reject it, whatever the source, was essential.

Penkowsky's chance came in November 1960. The KGB had cleared him; promotion had followed. In September 1958 Penkowsky attended a course for senior gunner officers on missile technology at the Dzerzhinskiy Military Academy. This useful familiarisation process completed, Penkowsky in June 1959 was posted back to the GRU Fourth Directorate as the equivalent of a Brigadier General Staff. A year later Penkowsky was transferred to the Third Directorate, concerned with Western Europe. He was also appointed to sit on various inter-GRU committees. As is the case everywhere, loyalty was measured in bureaucratic terms. Penkowsky was as clean, and as secure, as it is possible to be in Russia. At once he began to haunt Western embassies again. This time he had something to offer. The GRU Central Registry allowed access only to a limited number of officers. Penkowsky was one of them. All senior officers in the GRU had to do their tour as duty officer. Weekend duty in Moscow, as anywhere else, was unpopular. That good fellow Penkowsky was already ready to stand in for a comrade who wanted to get away. (He was senior duty officer when Powers was shot down, and later gave a diverting account of the incident.) At last, Penkowsky was in a position to deliver the goods.

He was rebuffed again, and again. He became a bore. In November 1960, however, Penkowsky went to a reception at the Canadian Embassy, steered a senior member of it into a corner, produced a bundle of papers, said 'take them', and walked out.

Alarmed rather than curious, the official took the papers to the Station Officer. The latter had the wit to contact his opposite number at the British Embassy. This officer, behind his diffident, bank manager's appearance and rimless spectacles, made the first, and vital decision in the long running of Oleg Penkowsky. The stuff was Greek to the Station. London would have to make sense of it. Penkowsky must wait. That was arranged. He agreed. For five months he had to speculate about the result of his final throw.

When Penkowsky's papers reached London they were sent to people in Century House who could make sense of them. The Ministry of Defence unit in SIS got to work. The response was simple: 'More please.' No such simplicity was possible for White's subordinates. Yet one stark fact was undeniable. No Russian counter-intelligence operation, designed to plant a double agent, would use material which was both genuine and of the utmost importance. There are easier ways to do these things. All the suspicions bred from Penkowsky's importunities evaporated in face of that intelligence fact. The SIS trace on Penkowsky was pondered. SIS rather prided itself on a good filing system. One of its members' complaints about MI5 was that you could never find anything. The trace showed Penkowsky as potentially pure gold. Here was a prospective agent in place, in the one place which really mattered, the place which no Western intelligence organisation, none anywhere, could reasonably expect to penetrate. The Controller Soviet Bloc, once revelation overcame incredulity, was 'up to the Chief in a flash'. This was not some mouldy old Middle East ruler to be bribed or squared. This, dear CIA, *was* pure gold. The dog-like sixth sense, the instinct that this had to be right, had triumphed over the tendency to agree with what Washington said.

For White, however, matters remained complex. On 7 January 1961, the KGB's Conon Molody, known to history as Gordon Lonsdale, the Krogers, and their British associates Harry Houghton and Ethel Gee, had been arrested, not through good work by MI5 or the Special Branch but because of an alert member of the Dorset Constabulary. This team of spies for Russia had concentrated their efforts on naval establishments. Their success had been limited, but capture and trial revealed continued weaknesses in the British security system as a whole. By May George Blake, once regarded as about the most promising member of SIS, was awaiting trial, having 'admitted to having passed to his Soviet contact every important official document which had come into his hands'.[14] Blake's gift to the KGB of the name and location of virtually every SIS officer in the field and much else of interest besides completed what Philby had begun. Blake not only blew SIS officers, but agents operating in the Federal German Republic and Berlin. A defector to the West from the Polish intelligence service put paid to Blake in turn, and may have had something to do with Lonsdale's arrest. The damage caused could not be made good by reliance on defectors. Macmillan instituted various enquiries, locking the stable door long after the horses had bolted.

Blake's arrest, although it removed from active life one of the most resourceful KGB double agents ever to have penetrated Western defences, was a reminder to White that SIS remained on notice to recover from past horrors. The secrets of the Underwater Weapons Research Establishment at Portland might now be safe from Lonsdale and his team, but the whole story of treachery and laxity ran back five years and more to that piece of business which most people in SIS preferred to forget: Buster Crabbe. Was there just the faintest possibility, a scintilla of one, that the Russian intelligence system would be prepared to run Penkowsky in order to further deepen CIA suspicions that MI5 never caught anyone in time, that SIS harboured traitors – and that neither was up to the job?

In his own mind, White knew three things for sure, where much else was murky. His controllers rarely insisted on an intelligence source being unique – and essential; Penkowsky was the exception. MI5, whoever was Director-General, would continue to make mistakes until the entire service was drastically reformed. CIA suspicions were due to personalities and politics rather than evidence. The occasional failures of the FBI in the 1950s to catch Russian spies and assorted folly over Cuba showed clearly enough that Americans made mistakes also. Certainty about Penkowsky, or any other agent, was impossible. If SIS ran him, it would be a major operation, with the CIA fully involved. Indeed, by the terms of the 1946 Agreement between Attlee and Truman, CIA would be involved in any case. If Penkowsky turned sour, the blame could be shared. If Penkowsky turned out to be a winner, the kudos to SIS would be enormous.

What White really thought, in his few private moments, about MI5 and an establishment where the only crime was to be caught, he kept to himself. Roger Hollis, White's successor as Director-General of MI5, had been his Deputy. He worked long hours and kept calm when the Press was shouting its head off. These attributes were virtues to White, who remains convinced of Hollis's innocence. Yet White also knew that there was something rotten in the state of the Establishment which would one day be publicly known.[15] In the meantime SIS had requirements given it and intelligence to produce. In April 1961, without then fully appreciating the strategic significance of the Penkowsky intelligence, White told his subordinates to run him.

This proved to be a major undertaking, and it had better be said here and now that the methods will not be found in these pages. Greville Wynne's accounts are misleading – sometimes for good and sufficient reasons – in many important respects, and the *Penkowsky Papers* are valueless except for some known facts and as an exercise in the practice of selective innuendo. What can be said is that once Penkowsky had been contacted, Wynne played a brave and essential part. But the burden of the operation fell on the diffident man with the appearance of a bank manager. Penkowsky insisted on physically removing material from the GRU, pages of it, volumes of manuals, sheaves of drawings, the works, so far as he was able to get his hands on whatever struck him as worth purloining.

It is a misuse of words to say that SIS ran Penkowsky. It did so but, in a very special sense, he ran himself. Well before the customers were clamouring for more, and a system for processing, not only assessing the intelligence had been set up in London, Penkowsky was ready to unload. He was impatient to do so before the SIS Station in Moscow had worked out live and dead letter boxes. Only Wynne, as an unofficial assistant, was organised and in place before the Penkowsky operation began, and his value depended solely on carrying on as what he was – a British businessman who visited Russia and the bloc countries in order to organise trade fairs and, in general, improve commercial relations between capitalists and communists. Haste would mean muddle; it would probably lead to disaster. From the start the risks were commensurate with the prize. As was noted in Century House, 'Even the KGB can't watch people all the time'. But Penkowsky was about to risk his life, and do so daily. Protection by SIS of an agent is always limited. In this case, it was negligible. The Moscow Station also knew that something more than a diplomatic incident would occur if the Embassy was caught with its hand in the GRU till.

Penkowsky's insistence that he would produce originals, not summaries or microfilms, posed particular dangers. Had the stakes not been so high, it is likely that SIS would have insisted on a slower, safer, rate and method of delivery. But the stakes were of the highest, and Penkowsky had cards which he was determined to play in his double game with the GRU and SIS. Penkowsky's task in the GRU was to assess NATO's military potential, particularly in the field of missiles. That task, in the view of Penkowsky's superiors, could best be carried out by providing him with a cover which would enable him to visit Western Europe in a perfectly legitimate fashion. The cover was Secretary of the Scientific Research Committee, a body charged, amongst other innocuous activities, with the establishment of friendly relations with learned societies, technical bodies, and well disposed souls in that West which Khrushchev despised, feared – and envied. When Penkowsky told Wynne, the cut-out for verbal communication with SIS, that he would be able to visit London occasionally, the whole operation took on a new dimension. If a safe house could be provided, Penkowsky could talk the night away. By the summer of 1961 there was a great deal which the customers wanted to know.

Penkowsky's original intelligence had convinced SIS – once its nature and importance had been explained – that the usual procedures for acquisition, production, and distribution would have to be drastically changed if the value of the material was to be properly appreciated. SIS does not say 'this is good' or 'we don't think much of what X says'. SIS concentrates on satisfying the requirement to produce. But in mid-1961, the importance of the Penkowsky intelligence was felt, rather than known, to be supreme. The decision was taken to expand the Ministry of Defence unit in Century House so that initial internal assessment was rapidly followed by distribution to those in research establishments who could interpret, comment – and ask for more – on the basis of expert knowledge.

The experts knew that Macmillan's nuclear 'deterrent', that crude, first-strike affair, would not be affected by anything Penkowsky produced. Nor was Britain able to produce a genuine deterrent, a force capable of retaliation. British missiles, other than the ground-to-air variety, flew no further than the drawing board. But even 'Bloodhound' and 'Thunderbird' could only shoot down aircraft. The Russian missile would always get through, and would certainly hit something vulnerable. Any future deterrent would come, if at all, from America. Nor would intelligence about the Warsaw Pact order of battle add much to what was already known All who were involved knew that there was only one real customer for the Penkowsky intelligence: the American Government. The CIA would have to decide what to distribute, and to whom. But, from the start of the operation, White ensured that the British Embassy in Washington was on his distribution. The political importance of the Penkowsky intelligence was well appreciated in London. Other intelligence services with which SIS was in liaison were not included on the London distribution, although some later received enough by way of summary to keep their governments happy, or quiet. Penkowsky was, all the way, an Anglo-American affair.

Thus Wynne's announcement that Penkowsky would visit London caused a reaction comparable to Mahomet coming to the mountain. Mahomet would *talk*; moreover, he would be safe, relatively, in London. When senior Russian citizens travel abroad they are not, contrary to popular imagination, followed about endlessly by the KGB. Penkowsky would have official duties to perform in London as part of his cover. Visits to factories and trade exhibitions would occupy his days. The nights were his own affair, provided he used normal care and discretion. Several rooms in a London hotel notable for its size, anonymous character, and popularity with the middling rank of foreign visitors were turned into a most unusual safe house. The Berkeley had been chosen for Abas Kupi during the Albanian escapade. Penkowsky had to make do with a two-star hotel. Whatever the venue lacked in style, it compensated by a battery of equipment designed to record all that Penkowsky said and to make certain that only those who needed to know heard it.

Penkowsky was to pay several visits to London in 1961 and 1962, and one to Paris, but it was the first which caused most interest. Even the Controller Soviet Bloc, an officer not normally given to expressing his feelings, wondered aloud how the visit would go. Penkowsky's security was not the problem; it was the danger of exaggerated expectations and the problem of who should interrogate this single most important spy which dominated the planning sessions on the tenth floor of Century House. Although the distribution of Penkowsky's intelligence had been kept to the absolute minimum, and even the Prime Minister had received only the most cryptic summaries, the range and variety of the material now being sifted in London and the Ministry of Defence research establishments meant that a good many people wanted to ask questions. Nor could the CIA be ignored. The London Station would certainly send a representative from Grosvenor Square to that two-star hotel. There was quite a crush in the hotel bedroom but a more select company can hardly be imagined.

In the event, this first visit combined expectation, reward, surprise, and anti-climax in about equal proportions. When Penkowsky arrived for the first session, SIS and their colleagues met a burly, voluble soldier who was determined to talk his head off. It soon became clear that Penkowsky was not content, perhaps not able, simply to answer questions. When the rock was struck, the spring gushed forth. But it also became rather dismayingly clear that Penkowsky's knowledge and understanding of military technology in general and missiles in particular was rudimentary. The expert interrogators expected a man who could talk their language. They found a gunner who had taken his courses and passed them, just. The men from the Ministry of Defence did not find a technical wizard. Wynne remarked once that he believed 'Oleg's information was very important but I never knew what it was'. Penkowsky was rather better informed, but not in the sense which enabled him to talk technicalities. When Penkowsky was asked the key questions about the guidance systems of Khrushchev's and Malinowski's vaunted ICBMs he replied: 'They couldn't hit a bull in the backside with a balalaika.' This answer, although vividly expressing the truth, was not much help to experts. Nor was it any comfort to those responsible for Britain's civil defence. Britain's backside was such an easy target that even a Russian ICBM could hit it: America was an entirely different proposition. Listening to these exchanges the SIS representatives realised that Penkowsky would have to intensify the effort he was making to rifle the GRU of every document on missiles. Over eighteen months, approximately ten thousand pages were handed over to SIS and the CIA.

Penkowsky had several all-night sessions in the safe house. There were two reasons for this. The CIA was keen to hear all Penkowsky had to say about low life in the Russian hierarchy. SIS, fairly bored by this aspect of Penkowsky's disclosures, nevertheless realised he had to talk scandal in order to feel at home. Talking openly, endlessly, to representatives of a world he undoubtedly believed to be free was the equivalent of confession, a kind of emotional night on the tiles. Nobody tried to stop Penkowsky. Even his requests were, up to a point, humoured. Could he be made a Colonel in the *British* Army? This was a facer. The short answer was 'No, he could not'. The more tolerant – and canny – response was to provide him with a uniform, ready-made, properly badged as to rank. Could he meet 'C'? This one had already been pondered. The idea had possibilities. On the other hand, better not. Penkowsky was turned down.[16] Finally a real surprise. 'Can I meet the Queen?' Consternation. *No*. 'Why not? Surely we trust each other?' People began to realise that Penkowsky was a maverick, probably a manic-depressive. Very firmly, but using all the art which is needed to run an agent successfully, Penkowsky was told that enormous gratitude and admiration was felt for his services. His job lay in Moscow. Keep up the good, the vital work there. And don't take stupid risks. Penkowsky returned to Moscow, perhaps slightly crestfallen, but determined to complete what he had begun.

In Washington, late that Fall, the battle lines over the Penkowsky intelligence were drawn. The Chief of Soviet Operations in the CIA, John Maury, knew that any intelligence which revealed evidence of Russian military weaknesses, above all in the missile field, would cause intense controversy. Unlike White's SIS, Dulles's CIA was a service in which political convictions were freely expressed, and where the execution of tasks often reflected Congressional pressure rather than the requirements of national security. Angleton did not play politics, but his ingrained suspicions about Russian machinations struck a responsive chord in the Congress. Angleton's ambivalence towards Britain – affection and dislike tugging in opposite directions – reflected the feelings of many in Washington.

Maury was both a professional intelligence officer and a politically aware member of the Washington world. Once raw Penkowsky intelligence began to arrive on his desk Maury took a decision which was to prove as important as White's in April. Maury refused to commit himself about Penkowsky as a source or about the material which he produced. Maury shared the SIS conviction that Russians don't feed high-grade material as a counter-intelligence operation. But Maury, inclined to accept Penkowsky as a source, was determined to reinsure. One man would first read this raw intelligence, the lot, in the original. That the individual who was selected happened to be serving with the National Security Council Staff, had been a protégé of Allen Dulles, expressed strong views on strategy – and had a wife of Russian parentage – was irrelevant to Maury. This man met the requirement. His summaries of the first substantial batches of Penkowsky material from SIS would form the basis of Maury's next critical decision: whom to put on the distribution.

To read, over several months, thousands of pages of mostly

technical material dealing with what the only known enemy could, or could not, do to destroy one's country was a daunting business. With the exception of some rather low-grade intelligence about the Warsaw Pact, and a good deal of miscellaneous items, Penkowsky's material was concerned exclusively with capability, not intention. The reader chosen by Maury was intellectually more inclined to look for motive than method. He was well aware, however, that the analysts who wrote the National Intelligence Estimates and the 'wizards' responsible for electronic warfare at the National Security Agency were sceptical of all but their own conclusions. These conclusions were known, public, and political. There was a missile gap – in Russia's favour. Yet the Penkowsky intelligence showed that Russia was experiencing increasing problems with every aspect of its missile programme, particularly with 'long range rockets' (ICBMs) and, above all, with guidance systems. The material was raw in the most literal intelligence sense. A manual for the emplacement of intermediate and medium range missiles specified, for example, the number of theodolites needed, the number of men required to prepare the sites and the time the whole operation should take.

By the end of the year the material had convinced one man in Washington that there was a missile gap – in America's favour. This blockbuster of a contradiction between America in peril and Russia defenceless was put firmly back in Maury's lap. He read the new summaries. He became convinced that Penkowsky was a reliable source, producing genuine intelligence. Conviction did not provide a solution to a problem which was political in at least two senses: within the intelligence community; inside the political cauldron known as Washington. A political balancing act was imposed on Maury once he accepted that Penkowsky was genuine; the distribution would have to balance likely supporters against two sorts of committed sceptics: those who believed, or chose to believe that the missile gap was in Russia's favour; members of the CIA, headed by Angleton, who believed in rejecting any gifts brought by the Greeks.

Circumstances nearly thwarted Maury at the turn of the year, when the distribution, other than a laundered version to some fairly junior grades in the research establishments, was still being composed. In late December 1961, Anatoli Golitzin, a KGB officer stationed in Helsinki, defected. He came into Angleton's hands. Prolonged interrogation, by a kind of inevitability, fished up Philby from the depths of Golitzin's trained intelligence memory. Other suspected traitors surfaced also – including at least one senior CIA officer – but Angleton's concern was to prove or, failing that damagingly to demonstrate, that SIS could not be trusted to run a whelk-stall. It was no consolation for White that further circumstantial evidence of Philby's treachery should be found at just the moment when the unique source which SIS had acquired at the heart of the Russian establishment was delivering intelligence of crucial importance.

Fortunately – for us all – Maury was well able to separate the wheat of civilisation's survival from the chaff of melodrama about traitors. The Golitzin story would keep Angleton happy for a time. Nothing could remove or reduce his phobias about SIS sources and MI5's lackadaisical ways, but a really well-planned distribution of the Penkowsky intelligence would neutralise most of the harm which his hostility might otherwise cause. With great care, and hastening slowly, Maury began to distribute the essentials of what his reader had discovered and confirmed. McCone and his immediate subordinates had obviously to be on the list. The new DCI was, fortunately, an outsider, with no strong views except on the necessity of ruling with firmness and moderation the Service which Allen Dulles had created. Bernard Brodie, a long-time friend of the CIA, whose *Strategy in the Missile Age* had succeeded in convincing even Dulles that nuclear bombs weren't just bigger ones, was judiciously included on the distribution. The State Department would be a sympathetic recipient of the intelligence, not just an obligatory customer for it. Roger Hilsman certainly would ensure that such men as 'Chip' Bohlen, who insisted that Khrushchev feared an American first strike, and who had strongly criticised NSC 68, would read the material. In Moscow, Ambassador Llewellyn Thompson, who had similar views to Bohlen, was already in the picture. Bundy, on the President's behalf, saw what he needed to see.

The new Defense Intelligence Agency in the Pentagon – a kind of watchdog for the three armed forces intelligence directorates, which proved to be one of McNamara's few management mistakes – raised question marks about distribution. Would the DIA prove an ally or not? Relations with the Joint Chiefs of Staff in general and with Le May in particular had not yet been defined by McCone. To restrict distribution and hasten slowly remained Maury's text for the early months of 1962. In any case, he had other matters to tackle. On 10 February on the Glienicker Bridge over Lake Wannsee, separating Potsdam and West Berlin, Gary

Powers was exchanged for the KGB Emil Goldfus (Colonel Abel), caught by the FBI in June 1957 when he was head of the regional station for North America. The exchange was the first of several in coming years, an attempt at détente by default.

As Washington's winter turned to spring, Kennedy's questions, posed so urgently shortly after his inauguration, remained unanswered: was there a missile gap? What was Khrushchev up to? Neither McNamara nor McCone had yet digested the full implications of Penkowsky's intelligence. Kennedy and McNamara at intervals throughout 1961 had hinted that the missile gap in Russia's favour concerning ICBMs might have 'evaporated'. No such assurances were given about MRBMs and IRBMs. The Defence Secretary, for all his innate convictions and recourse to intellectual analysis, was still at the stage of reorganising the Pentagon. Missile technology continued to advance, but crabwise, raising new questions rather than answering them. In early March, a Nike Zeus missile destroyed a Nike Hercules in an anti-ballistic missile test. Some drew the inference, unsupported by any evidence, that Russia possessed effective defences against American ICBMs. McNamara pondered these matters, but his mind was elsewhere, methodically working on the issue of human, not missile survival. Not until May did he fire the first shots in a campaign designed to convince sceptics that nuclear continence was a necessity, not a choice. McCone was at a comparable stage. The directors responsible for the National Intelligence Estimates were still influential.

Bundy in the White House and the National Security Council as a whole had other matters, of seemingly greater importance, to attend to. A year earlier, McNamara had received from Walt Rostow, the architect of counter-insurgency at Fort Bragg, the following scribbled note: 'Bob: We must think of the kind of forces and mission for Thailand now, Vietnam later. We need a guerrilla *deterrence* operation in Thailand's north east. We shall need forces to support a counter-guerrilla war in Vietnam: aircraft, helicopters, communications men, special forces, militia teachers, etc. WWR.'[17] At the time, Vietnam was still that far away country. A year later, American involvement in Vietnam was providing a stark contrast, by its method rather than the motive, to controlled thought and policy about nuclear deterrence.

The British Embassy had not yet made its mark. The Ambassador, David Ormsby-Gore, was not only a relation by marriage of the President and Macmillan but a close personal friend of the former, an intimate of the White House, regarded even by Anglophobes as having a special relationship with the Kennedys. But, for the moment, Ormsby-Gore was the postman for Macmillan's homilies to 'young Jack', who combined, in one of the elderly actor's happier phrases, 'that indescribable look of a boy on holiday with the dignity of a President and Commander-in-Chief'. There was not much of a holiday atmosphere in Washington during early 1962, but to some observers Khrushchev's threats and boasts had subsided. When Walter Lippmann went to see McNamara on 23 May he found the latter more concerned with mutiny in NATO than any Khrushchev-inspired crisis. State Department briefings on the situation in Cuba were excessively bland, even referring to missiles as if they were wholly defensive weapons.

Throughout the months which followed, two crises – Cuba, and the control of nuclear weapons by the super powers – dominated the President's thoughts and actions, and those of the men close to him. At the heart of Kennedy's and McNamara's arguments about strategy in the missile age was a conviction that there could only be one centre for Western nuclear decision-making: the Oval Room of the White House. Specifically, McNamara, Kennedy's spokesman on these issues, succeeded to his own satisfaction (but rarely to that of his audiences) in combining a case for non-proliferation with refinements of a nuclear Monroe Doctrine. If Britain retained and France built nuclear 'deterrents' – in McNamara's mind, with his insistence on *retaliatory* capacity, a misuse of language – not only would Khrushchev be alarmed, and might react with a surprise attack on Western Europe, but it would be impossible for a rational dialogue with the Russian Government to be created. Khrushchev could always claim there was only one centre for decision-making in the Warsaw Pact. If the Federal German Government got its finger on the nuclear trigger, as Chancellor Adenauer and Defence Minister Strauss patently desired, Khrushchev's reaction would certainly be to act decisively against a weak NATO member. If such an act assumed nuclear proportions America could be dragged into a conflict demonstrably not of its own making.

These issues may seem peripheral to the Cuban missile crisis, let alone to the central part played by Penkowsky's intelligence in resolving it. The issues are not peripheral, or incidental at all. Kennedy and McNamara, together with advisers who kept their nerve, looked at the confrontation with Khrushchev steadily and looked at it whole. The central issue was the place of nuclear weapons in a world of super powers. At the mid-May NATO meeting in Athens McNamara said: 'Weak national nuclear forces with enemy cities as their targets are not likely to be sufficient to perform even the function of deterrence. The creation of a single additional national nuclear force encourages the proliferation of nuclear powers with all of its attendant dangers. Limited nuclear capabilities, operating independently, are dangerous, expensive, prone to obsolescence, and lacking credibility as a deterrent. Clearly, the United States' contribution to the Alliance is neither obsolete nor dispensable.'[18] McNamara made a final point: 'The United States cannot and will not carry the enormous burden of the Alliance, and face the catastrophic dangers of a thermonuclear war if, within the Alliance, it has lost the initiative and the ultimate responsibilities, on the issues of peace and war.'

Little of this was at all clear to McNamara's NATO colleagues. Harold Watkinson, Macmillan's Minister of Defence, sat through McNamara's stark warning wearing an inimitable expression of aggrieved incomprehension. Intellectual gifts are as rare in politicians as in airmen who believe in dominant weapons. Where McNamara's words were clear, they were resented. When he repeated them publicly in America on 25 May – having converted Lippmann, with all that this implied for the communication of Administration policy – and 16 June protests from London and Bonn, although muffled in tone, conveyed nevertheless unmistakable hints of rebellion. De Gaulle maintained a contemptuous silence. Thereafter McNamara resolved to urge on Kennedy the absolute necessity for a dialogue with Khrushchev. Super-power agreement on the inadmissibility – and horrors – of nuclear war would ensure that whatever 'additional national nuclear forces' were preserved or designed, decisions on their use, so far as humanly possible, would rest with the President of the United States. By the summer of 1962 McNamara, like Bundy, was still only aware of the broad implications of the Penkowsky intelligence. But both men were acutely aware of the fact that the nuclear ambitions of America's allies were both a threat and a challenge to Khrushchev.

The challenge came and the threat was posed a month after McNamara's speech at the University of Ann Arbor. In July, Khrushchev decided to put medium- and intermediate-range missiles into Cuba. At about the same time, Penkowsky's file at the KGB was re-opened. As a matter of routine, his foreign travel permit was withdrawn at the end of 1961. Even in Khrushchev's relatively relaxed Russia (compared with Stalin's) foreign travel remained a privilege, to be granted and withdrawn at regular intervals. Despite advice from SIS and Wynne, Penkowsky not only demanded the return of this privilege, but pulled strings to get it. Pique may explain this stupid act; a growing need to talk probably accounts for much. Penkowsky got his permit back. Reaction slowly set in. Why was Colonel Oleg Penkowsky so keen to visit the West? The ponderous machinery of state surveillance ground into action.

The four months from July to October 1962 thus have a particular, a unique place in post-war history. Any recollection of the Cuban missile crisis by the men who advised John Kennedy communicates this uniqueness powerfully and directly. Where the advisers were close to Kennedy, from friendship or intellectual sympathy, the recollections have their own quality, sombre rather than tragic. The Cuban crisis was faced and overcome by Americans not only acutely, agonisingly conscious of the world's peril, but sustained by Kennedy's leadership. This, in turn, was strengthened by crucial intelligence, but without Kennedy Armageddon might have come during that October of 1961. We are so used to verbal exaggeration and distortion today that to write 'the world stood on the brink of nuclear war' can sound both commonplace and unlikely. But the world did so stand, and the men with Kennedy knew it. Khrushchev, the Supreme Praesidium, and the Politburo also, if belatedly, knew the dimension of the crisis.

There is no means of knowing, in terms of historical probability, precisely what these men thought, and felt, but although Khrushchev's anguished message to Kennedy on 26 October was not a 'nightmare cry', it did express, in his characteristic idiom, what the crisis really meant. 'We and you ought not now to pull on the ends of the rope in which you have tied the knot of war, because the more the two of us pull, the tighter the knot will be tied, and the moment may come when the knot will be tied so tight that even he who tied it will not have the strength to untie it, and then it will be necessary to cut that knot . . .'[19]

The moment nearly came, but the knot was not cut. Nuclear holocaust was averted by the efforts of men in Washington and Moscow who knew, but only near the brink, what each other knew: that America possessed, overwhelmingly, the strategic advantage. The severity of the missile crisis lay just in this fact, and its choice for Khrushchev: to accept defeat or play another, desperate card. Khrushchev was, it must never be forgotten, the gambler – the 'high-roller' as the CIA called him – in a nation of chess players. But there was another man in Moscow, desperate, as he put it, 'to finish what I have begun'. On 22 October, Penkowsky was arrested – a fact known within hours to SIS and communicated immediately to the Embassy in Washington; much later tried – a show trial to discredit Wynne and the West; subsequently shot. Penkowsky's intelligence, in the assessment of those in the best position to know, 'allowed the CIA to follow the progress of Soviet missile emplacement in Cuba *by the hour*'. Penkowsky was there, to the end, even when he had gone beyond the help of his friends in SIS, who understood what it was all about.

Kennedy did not fully accept the significance of Penkowsky's intelligence until the evening of the 23rd. Even then he continued with preparations for both bombing and invading Cuba, with the ultimate objective of destroying Castro as Khrushchev's most valuable satellite. To the end of the crisis on the 27th Washington was preparing for nuclear war, and there were men in the capital who were prepared to initiate it, despite – or because of – Khrushchev's virtual admission on the 26th that his gamble had failed. Kennedy's eleventh hour understanding of what Penkowsky meant, not only to the West but to Russia, led to further efforts by those who asserted that the intelligence came from SIS – an unreliable source. Russia should be struck before another crisis of confusion struck America.

Those four months of creeping crisis thus saw a Washington conflict between the hawks who wanted to persuade Kennedy into violent action and the doves who urged restraint. The Penkowsky intelligence, and the complexities of its distribution throughout Washington, can be compared to the nervous system of a creature whose brain receives conflicting messages. The conflict was due to disagreements which went far beyond the credibility or otherwise of a source and his intelligence. The conflict reflected disagreements about the objectives and methods of America's cold war strategy, above all about the purpose of nuclear weapons. At an even deeper level, the conflict was between political and military authority, an American version of the Whitehall struggle in the First World War between politicians and the soldiers, the 'frocks' and the 'brass hats'. Kennedy was said to 'loathe' Le May. The emotion was probably mutual.

McNamara's feeling about Le May was less intense, but more complex. The airman's instinctive dislike for an interfering civilian led the Defence Secretary to state frequently and explicitly just what the delicate balance of terror really meant. Everything which McNamara said was intended to be heard – in the White House, the Pentagon, by Congress, across the country, throughout the world. His words – and, above all, his acts during the crisis and beyond it – reflected a belief in undivided control, in restraint, in using the imagination to see what was happening on the other side of the hill. McNamara during this time was determined above all that his words should be heard throughout NATO, and that the actions of his President should be understood by governments with ambitions to maintain, build, or procure 'independent' deterrents. Bundy, temperamentally poles apart from McNamara, had precisely the same intellectual – and moral – approach to the issue of national survival in a nuclear world. Neither man knew much about Dick White's SIS, even less about Penkowsky and the decisions which White had taken about his role. Unwittingly, Bundy and McNamara were deeply in White's debt. So too was Robert Kennedy, who came to believe that what his two colleagues said made sense in a world which often struck him as insane.

There is, and there will remain, an equivalent conflict of circumstantial evidence about the reasons for Khrushchev's decision to put medium- and intermediate-range missiles into Cuba; what roles, if any, Castro and his brother Raúl played; exactly when the first launchers arrived; or where in Cuba they were stored whilst sites, slowly and with difficulty, were prepared. All that can be established with reasonable certainty is that not until mid-August did some men in Washington begin to see a distinct threat to the survival of America from these moves. The State Department's January announcements about missiles in Cuba merely referred to SAMs. Although McCone argued before the crisis, and others have done so since, that SAMs were only deployed to protect offensive missile sites, it was known at the time that they had various roles, tactical and strategic. Castro had reason to fear an American invasion. Such an operation was being planned; camps in Florida were being prepared to accommodate troops whose task was to succeed where the CIA and their desperados at the Bay of Pigs had failed. Operation *Mongoose* was as freely discussed in the bars of Havana as in the back streets of Miami. The operation would begin with bombing attacks. The SAMs reflected Castro's determination to resist and his assurance from Khrushchev that Russia would help him to do so.

The decision to send SAMs to Cuba was relatively straightforward. Throughout the next twenty years these useful weapons, in their Russian modes, turned up in the armed forces of all kinds of Third World countries. Even the guerrillas fighting in Rhodesia had them. The decision to emplace forty-two MRBMs and sixteen IRBMs was made in a different context, reflecting Khrushchev's irrational conviction that he could use these hideously destructive weapons like cards on the poker table. The missiles were credible, compared with Russia's ICBMs; in Cuba, even if detected, perhaps *especially* if detected, they would theoretically increase the strategic choices available to Russia, whether or not a first strike was required or retaliation in the event of an American attack on Russia was possible.

It is doubtful if Khrushchev was able or willing to ponder strategic arguments or technical details. Khrushchev's aim was political, in the most dangerous sense, lacking balance and judgment. The notion of devastating American cities had a certain crude appeal. Like others before and since, Khrushchev separated in his actions what was rationally 'inadmissible' from what was politically – and psychologically – tempting. He alternately despised Kennedy for failure over Berlin and pusillanimity at the Bay of Pigs, and feared him for a growing bellicosity about America's missile potential. During 1961 and 1962, America's ICBM programme had been accelerated. On 27 March 1962, Kennedy was quoted in the *Washington Post* as saying: 'In some circumstances we might have to take the initiative.' The following month, shortly before Raúl Castro visited Moscow, Khrushchev met and overcame criticisms from his advisers that sending any type of offensive missile to Cuba was dangerous.

Between April and July Moscow was the scene of a conflict which mirrored that shortly to break out in Washington. The senior officers whose secrets Penkowsky continued to steal knew that emplacing missiles, even in unhardened sites, was a lengthy business in Russia or Eastern Europe. Cuba, a tobacco republic, lacking the infrastructure needed to support modern weapons, would present acute technical and political difficulties. Preparing sites would be the work of a pick and shovel brigade. Unlike America, Russia could not emplace its missiles in a matter of weeks with the help of advanced construction technology. (This was a difference in material assets between the super-powers which many in the CIA found hard to accept.) The labourers disguised as soldiers would have to be Russian, several thousand strong. A Russian bridgehead in Cuba would also require infantry. The Russian High Command had no intention of defending the bridgehead with Cuban troops. For their pains, Generals Mosalenko and Golikov, commanders respectively of 'Strategic Rocket Forces' (and a deputy defence minister) and the 'Main Political Administration' of the armed forces, were sacked. The technical yogi and the political commissar had pointed out that it was dangerous to gamble with rockets, above all in strange places. In sacking such men, Khrushchev convinced himself that he could take Kennedy to the brink and there wring concessions from him.

Not until early September were intelligence assessments, derived from U-2 flights over Cuba, able to say with certainty that deployment of missiles there might occur. By then evidence of site preparation for launchers was too strong to be ignored. Yet on 4 and 13 September Kennedy publicly stated: 'There is no evidence of the presence of offensive ground-to-ground missiles, or other significant offensive capability, either in Cuban hands or under Soviet direction or guidance. Were it to be otherwise, the gravest issues would arise. The United States would act if an offensive military base of significant capacity were to be established.'[20] If Kennedy had known that on 7 September Khrushchev told the American poet Robert Frost 'democracies are too old to fight', he might have declared there was one quite young enough to do so. Strong domestic political pressure was imposed on Kennedy to talk toughly about Cuba. The pressure also came from the top of the Washington establishment. Few of its members believed the Moscow statement of 11 September which asserted that 'the armaments and military equipment sent to Cuba are designed exclusively for defensive purposes'.

Several times throughout August, John McCone had told Kennedy that 'he suspected the Russians of placing offensive missiles in Cuba'.[21] McCone based his argument on the undisputed evidence of SAMs. He did not then, or later, give Kennedy summaries of the intelligence on which his assertion was based. What McCone did do was to use direct access to the President as a means of putting an idea in his mind. This was his duty and he would have failed in it if he had avoided the issue or minimised its gravity. The tone of the messages was calm and moderate, that of an intelligence officer, not an advocate for toughness. Nevertheless, McCone's direct access and the arguments which he put complicated the handling of the crisis in Washington from the outset. McCone was not playing politics when he left Kennedy with the suspicion that Khrushchev thought him a weakling, for all his style and charisma. Others thought it too. Calling off the

Bay of Pigs operation had won Kennedy no medals from Le May. The impending mid-term Congressional elections would be a time for patriotism rather than statesmanship. It was no comfort for Kennedy to recall Adlai Stevenson's words: 'Perhaps we need a coward in the room when we are talking about nuclear war.'[22] It was a common Washington jibe about America's man at the UN that 'he's not soft on communism; he's just soft'.[23]

Kennedy could well have reflected that Ambassadors to the UN might be in the arena but combat there was only with paper lions. The Oval Room was in the front line. As Truman used to say, 'the buck stops right here'. Within weeks of Kennedy's cautious public remarks, the buck had done just that. On 24 August Hilsman described the Russian aircraft and patrol boats arriving in Cuba as 'The sort of stuff you would use to strengthen your coastal and air defence systems'.[24] On 14 October, Bundy, on a television programme stated: 'I *know* there is no present evidence that the Soviets are attempting to install a major offensive capability in Cuba.' Bundy knew precisely the opposite – in terms of Russian *intentions*; but he also was convinced that installation of the *capability* would take months rather than weeks. The Penkowsky intelligence enabled a calculation to be made of sixteen months. (Years later, the CIA tacitly acknowledged that emplacement of the launchers on their sites would have taken eighteen.) Bundy believed America had *time*, because he had become convinced by Penkowsky's intelligence; he also believed Kennedy had to be in a position where he could distinguish between what was essential about Cuba and what was problematical.

Both McCone and Bundy threw down their gage; Kennedy picked up neither. Instead, he revamped the role of the NSC, at just the moment when planning for *Mongoose* was nearing completion. McCone's reorganisation of the CIA had increased his authority and influence. Maury's distribution had convinced the 'addressee only' recipients that the President should be given the facts. By the time that the 'ExComm' (Executive Committee of the National Security Council) met in the White House Cabinet Room on the morning of 16 October the issue of survival had become the subject of contention.[25] After further reflection, McCone had raised the *ante*. On the desks in the Cabinet Room lay the kind of evidence the modern American accepts as gospel. Thousands of feet of film had been processed. What in September had appeared as clearings half-hacked from the jungle were now sites for emplacements, launchers, and all their associated wonders. The Cuban missile crisis had begun. October's days were marked on the back of the silver calendar which Kennedy gave to those who enjoyed his confidence during the crisis: the 16th to the 27th were embossed. It was then, as Kennedy said, 'he earned his salary'.

At no time during those twelve days did McCone or anyone else in the CIA say that offensive *missiles* had already arrived in Cuba. (None did.) But the supposition that missiles had arrived was stronger than the evidence that they had not for most members of ExComm. One reason why Bundy and McNamara had to battle against scepticism when they urged the U-2 intelligence should be weighed and considered was because they refused to assume that sites being prepared, even the evidence for launchers' eventual emplacement, meant the missiles had already arrived. The difference between capability and intention divided a group of men who ardently looked for certainty. They divided not only as individuals, but because the complexities of the Washington system prevented agreement on the very nature of intelligence, the one resource in those twelve days, much of it from that curious outfit called SIS, which was vital to the survival of America – and its NATO allies. That resource, in all its complexity and diversity, was not automatically available to all members of ExComm; not all of them understood it when explanations were made, or offered; no two members interpreted the intelligence in exactly the same way. Behind ExComm and beyond the White House were dozens of experts, each with a point of view. Across the Potomac lay the Pentagon; at its centre sat the Joint Chiefs, with their view of a nuclear world.

Intelligence from agents in Cuba was generally discounted; that from U-2 flights was accepted; Penkowsky's was the subject of contention, not only because of the source, but because when the diagrams in the manuals which he produced were compared with the U-2 film even his critics were forced to acknowledge an exact match. But the film did not give time-scales for the processes from site selection and clearance, through the many stages of emplacement, to launch, re-load, and launch. The film did not, by itself, enable the CIA to define the categories of medium- and intermediate-range ballistic missiles. Penkowsky's intelligence was definite, except on one point which critics could validly use. At any rate, they did so. The MRBM could be used in a mobile role. The film indicated emplacement and hence the MRBM's deployment in a static role, but this did not absolutely preclude mobility.

The MRBMs, designated as T-1, or 'Sandal' had a range of 220 miles, and a re-load rate of 'several hours'. (The exact time remains classified.) The IRBM's range details were less specific; this was a more advanced type of missile than the MRBM. Penkowsky had been unable to meet all the customers' requirements. Estimates of the IRBM range varied. The CIA estimate was 2,200 miles; virtually every city in America could be destroyed from Cuba. The Ministry of Defence estimate was 1,300 miles. Britain was safe from an IRBM attack unless Khrushchev moved these weapons into the German Democratic Republic. *Nobody* outside Russia knew whether the missiles which supposedly had arrived in Cuba – or might have arrived – would have, or had, nuclear or conventional warheads. Expecting trouble, it was natural for ExComm to be pessimistic. Even a conventionally armed MRBM, if mobile, could be used as long-range artillery, against an invading force.

By the 16th the basic intelligence issue had already become not so much what to accept as what Kennedy should be told; in what form; when; and by whom. This last factor is the most important, because only McCone, as Director of Central Intelligence, had direct access to the President with raw intelligence. Until the 16th, nobody was very keen to commit Kennedy to a decision on the basis of intelligence reports. Nor was Kennedy anxious to be committed. The President was essentially a cautious man. McCone could, if necessary, show the President raw intelligence rather than the summaries provided by Bundy. All other intelligence agencies, and those working for them, distributed their material through the complex Washington system. The sheer volume of material, on any subject and from all sources, forced those responsible for distribution to rely on summaries to indicate essentials. The CIA, moreover, unlike SIS, wrote 'assessments', giving individual or collective views about the intelligence received and the conclusions which might be drawn from it. To a degree, the same freedom was exercised by the National Security Agency and the Defense Intelligence Agency. All summary is selective; summary plus assessment can, unwittingly, present a distorted picture. The unique value of Penkowsky's intelligence lay in the source, the nature of the material, and the form in which it was produced. Above all, the value lay in detail.

These factors are directly relevant to the Washington system. The Director of the DIA reported directly to the Joint Chiefs of Staff, not to the Defence Secretary. McNamara was, in effect, by-passed for receiving raw intelligence, despite the fact that the

CIA's Deputy Director, Major-General Charles Cabell, USAF, reported to him. Rusk was better served than McNamara; Hilsman could provide raw intelligence, thus by-passing some of the traps lying deep in the Washington maze. Maury, to a limited extent, had also been by-passing the system during the eighteen months of Penkowsky's great endeavours; the addressees had become the spokesmen for restraint. By 16 October, it had become clear to all concerned that if the Penkowsky intelligence was accepted *tout court*, above all by Kennedy, the crisis would assume a new dimension: Khrushchev might be engaged in a colossal bluff, poker at its crudest – or most subtle – hoping to frighten Kennedy into concessions or watch him over-react. To over-react by invading Cuba would earn Kennedy world odium at no expense to Russia.

This realisation disposed of no problem; it raised the *ante* again, to the level where acceptance, rejection, or making use of the Penkowsky intelligence, posed the issue of whether the crisis could be confined to Washington's ruling few or would become a major international issue. Nor could domestic politics be ignored. Kennedy's attempt to censor the crisis until the 22nd, when he broadcast to the nation, not only reflected a concern for security; it was acknowledgment that the congressional mid-term elections were taking place. Kennedy went to the brink with his eye on the polls, as a good democrat must. A bogus brink would have exposed Kennedy to more than international condemnation; it would have meant political ridicule at home. For all their love of tough talk, most American voters in 1962 wanted to sleep in their beds, not retreat to the nuclear fall-out shelters.

Unavoidably, with matters not only complex in themselves but subject to legitimate – and biased – differences of interpretation, from survival to prestige, we have gone a little ahead of the story. It is again necessary to stand back for a moment and see where the American participants found themselves. Above all, it is essential to realise that, given the nature of collective action and individual difference, even acceptance of Penkowsky's intelligence on 16 October would not have solved the crisis. The intelligence, to those who accepted it, was sufficient evidence of limited capability and hence, by an inference which owed something to hope as well as reason, limited intention. Khrushchev did not intend to bury America, not least because the capability to do so was less than America's power to bury Russia. But the Penkowsky intelligence was not even circumstantial or inferential evidence of what other options were available to Khrushchev. If he was prepared to bluff so dangerously, so suicidally, it was reasonable to suppose that he might still be prepared to go to the brink, if not necessarily with missiles in Cuba. Maxwell Taylor, Chairman of the Joint Chiefs of Staff, and a soldier with a deserved reputation for thinking before he spoke, was a strong supporter of *Mongoose*, arguing, as did Acheson from behind the scenes, that decisive action in the hour of need was the only kind which Khrushchev would understand. The Penkowsky intelligence worked two ways. As the sceptics began to give ground on details, they regrouped to argue a case for decisive action before it was too late to discover if Khrushchev could be called or not.

Between the 16th and 22nd, ExComm was mainly concerned with whether the missile sites – and much else in Cuba – should be bombed, or ships known to be on their way from Russian ports to Havana stopped and searched by the Navy. There was a strong possibility that missiles for MRBMs would arrive before sites had been completely prepared. The Penkowsky group knew that they had to get to the President with their intelligence in order to convince him that a sensible interpretation of it would lead to the conclusion that whether Khrushchev was bluffing or not, an air strike would be the worst decision possible. If Khrushchev was bluffing, America would be in the international dock. In 1962, such a place was still abhorrent to American governments. If Khrushchev was not bluffing, an attack on the MRBMs and IRBMs in Cuba would almost certainly produce a retaliation. Success in Cuba would be dearly bought if it led to the loss of Berlin. In 1962, every NATO contingency plan assumed a decisive and sudden attack at any point where Russia enjoyed obvious and overwhelming advantage.

Throughout the looming crisis those on the Penkowsky distribution had been far more conscious of the wider international implications than the men who wanted to bomb the living daylights out of Russia – and Cuba. But the Penkowsky group had not got through to Kennedy. Nor, directly, had McNamara read the material. The Deputy Director's direct access to the Defence Secretary was an administrative device, of no practical use. Moreover, General Cabell, as an Air Force intelligence specialist, was not bowled over by Penkowsky, preferring the evidence provided by satellite and camera. Bundy, however, as the President's right-hand man on matters of life and death, had not only read enough to be convinced; he was determined that those involved in the crisis would be convinced also. Bundy formed ExComm on the 16th, and he did so determined to keep the military men with their nuclear *machismo* well below the salt. They remained there during the days which followed because, by degrees, Kennedy came to believe that he had a margin of time in which to reach the brink.

The crisis divides into three periods: from the 16th to the 22nd, the 22nd to the 26th; and Saturday the 27th, a cool, sunny day in Washington, when exhausted men nearly cut the rope. The first period when, by relentless argument and not a little arm-twisting, the case for blockade (or 'quarantine') of freighters approaching Cuba was made and won, did not often involve Kennedy directly. He remained available, but went on the stump, and received a variety of foreign visitors, ranging from Ben Bella of Algeria to Uganda's Milton Obote. Congress was discreetly told what was in the wind. Walter Lippmann and his peers knew enough to keep quiet. The rest of the press was kept, almost, in the dark.

The second period, beginning with Kennedy's broadcast announcing the quarantine, and denouncing Russian adventurism, moved swiftly from naval activities to Khrushchev's virtual, but not total, climb down on the 26th. There was melodrama in the Security Council. Ships heading for Cuba turned back; others hove to, awaiting orders; one was searched by a US Navy boarding party. Kennedy talked to Macmillan, but listened to Ormsby-Gore. De Gaulle and Adenauer were told. Kennedy was determined not to take America to the brink alone. The 27th was the day of Khrushchev's second, threatening, message, the loss of a U-2 over Cuba, the D-2 of *Mongoose*, the imminent despatch of the President of the United States and his closest advisers to their own special bunker.

This was no looking-glass world, and the men in ExComm acquired a sense of realities which remained. The story has been told before – and well – but from the perspective of twenty years and with a little knowledge of some of those involved, it is possible to appreciate how ExComm, as a group, clung to the belief in American power as the arbiter of 'eyeball to eyeball' confrontation, not only the superpower global balance. The available intelligence fortified that belief, but it posed most starkly the necessity for probably ultimate choice. Therefore, the case for quarantine was made not only in terms of time but with the sure knowledge that

America's naval strength could immediately be deployed in a classic demonstration of how to keep a crisis within manageable proportions.

Bundy and McNamara worked on their colleagues' natural desire to postpone ultimate decisions and their equally natural pride that the US Navy could do the job. The two men of restraint were well supported by Rusk, Robert Kennedy, and Ted Sorensen. McCone stuck to his job, and thus demonstrated that a DCI could do so. The members of ExComm who wanted to bomb dwindled in numbers and lost appetite for drastic solutions. The Joint Chiefs were in attendance on ExComm, and in favour of bombing and invasion. Only Taylor was a member, and he was out-manoeuvred. After Le May's direct challenge to Kennedy on the 17th, he quit. 'Le May argued strongly with the President that a military attack was essential. When the President questioned what the response of the Russians might be, General Le May assured him there would be no reaction. President Kennedy was sceptical. "They no more than we, can let these things go by without doing something. They can't, after all their statements, permit us to take out their missiles, kill a lot of Russians, and then do nothing. If they don't take action in Cuba, they certainly will in Berlin".'[26] The case for bombing was lost; the decision for blockade was confirmed.

By the 22nd all was in train. The naval task force of 180 ships was sailed to form a line 800 miles east of Cuba. A case of Jack Daniels was promised to the first crew to locate a Russian submarine. Such a distinct threat to the US Navy was a factor in the situation which caused more concern to Admiral Anderson, the Chief of Naval Operations, than stopping and searching freighters. The great naval ports of the eastern seaboard were alive as they had not been since the Second World War. Florida became an armed camp, with two major operations – aerial surveillance of Cuba, and preparing to invade it – under way simultaneously. When Kennedy spoke to an America which abandoned most other evening activities to watch him, the Navy in which he had so bravely served was already on station. Although no maximum nuclear alert was ordered, America's forces around the world were also at a high state of readiness. The next move was up to Khrushchev.

Kennedy, in his broadcast, had been particularly careful to distinguish between sites, launchers, and missiles, and had concentrated on the dangers of Khrushchev's lies rather than the menace of his weapons. Kennedy did not directly say that offensive missiles were already in Cuba. Kennedy spoke calmly of Gromyko's direct and personal lie to him on the 18th, repeating the Moscow statement of 11 September, and his stark warning to Khrushchev was a masterpiece of controlled response: 'It shall be the policy of this nation to regard any nuclear missile launched from Cuba against any nation in the Western Hemisphere as an attack by the Soviet Union on the United States, requiring a full retaliatory response upon the Soviet Union.' Apart from ambiguity about 'requiring', Kennedy's message was clear. He did not assert that offensive *missiles* had arrived in Cuba, and he did not declare that Russia must remove weapons. Kennedy called on the United Nations to act. This was both a good diplomatic move (although it alarmed Congress and infuriated the Joint Chiefs) and a skilful tactical one.

By the 23rd ExComm had acquired momentum and character. There was no unanimity; there was a working consensus. Kennedy's broadcast went down well. The *frisson* was felt in Europe rather than America. On the 24th, the *Daily Telegraph* and the *Daily Mail* in London, twin champions of Suez, sounded alarm bells, not NATO rallying calls. Kennedy would have appreciated the irony that two right wing papers, strong supporters of Macmillan, thought his broadcast provocative rather than prudent. The *Daily Mail* said that 'The President may have been led more by popular emotion than by calm statesmanship'. The *Daily Telegraph* thought the blockade 'greatly mistimed'. Macmillan supported the blockade, but was not above telling 'young Jack' to exercise the maximum restraint. Macmillan was rattled, and his memoirs reveal this fact quite plainly. During the Cuba missile crisis Macmillan learned what deterrence actually meant. Yet Kennedy welcomed his transatlantic telephone talks with Macmillan. They were a relief from hideous possibilities: a Prime Minister who could consider issuing a Royal Proclamation, calling out the Reserves, and warning the Governor of the Bank of England to safeguard sterling (shades of Suez!) because the world might blow up certainly lived in a different one from ExComm. It was from Ormsby-Gore that guidance came.

The Ambassador was so close to Kennedy that he had become within days an unofficial member of ExComm. Ormsby-Gore was the only diplomat in Washington who had been promised a place in the President's Appalachian hideout if the worst was about to happen. In mid-October, the Embassy knew more about the critical intelligence factors than the CIA. Visitors from London, ostensibly in America to attend a conference, strengthened the SIS presence. When Ormsby-Gore went to dine with Kennedy on the 23rd he knew as much as the members of ExComm about details; he knew more about essentials. Penkowsky's arrest on the 22nd had fundamentally changed the situation. Khrushchev's bluff had become a hideously dangerous gamble, inviting an American offensive. Until the 22nd, Kennedy had possessed a margin of time. Now he had to give Khrushchev a margin so that he could respond to Kennedy's broadcast knowing that Penkowsky had given America the strategic advantage.

The Kennedy clan motto was 'Don't get mad, get even'. That admirable political prescription had to give way to one of John Kennedy's strongest convictions: 'Never put your opponent in a corner from which he can't escape.' At one moment during ExComm's arguments about the quarantine its proponents were sufficiently alarmed that Kennedy might succumb to the case for bombing that he was called on an insecure outside line and urgently asked to pause. Now on the 23rd, having in the words of his hero Winston Churchill 'armed to parley', he was urged to pause again. Ormsby-Gore became the means whereby Kennedy was convinced about the double importance of the Penkowsky intelligence. The task of giving Kennedy the 'hour by hour' intelligence not only fell to the British Ambassador; he had to urge further restraint on Kennedy. The quarantine line should be 'shaded', from 800 to 500 miles. The Russian ships were slow-steaming. Three hundred miles would add a day, probably more, before the US Navy was forced to fire a warning shot.

There had been much argument about distances when the quarantine was being organised. There was a case for a distant blockade and for a close one. Even America's naval strength could not provide adequately for both. Eight hundred miles had been a compromise. Ormsby-Gore's case for further delay could be translated into an order from the Commander-in-Chief without arousing suspicions that he was losing his nerve or being told what to do. The order was given. For the next three days most of ExComm's members and much of the Pentagon remained absorbed in the quarantine. The dangers and uncertainties added stress to men who were beginning to forget what going home at the end of the day felt like. McNamara and Anderson had 'a flaming row' on the 24th. Anderson said that 'the Navy had known all there was to know about running a blockade since the days of John Paul Jones.'

McNamara replied distinctly: 'The object of the operation is not to shoot Russians but to communicate a political message from President Kennedy to Chairman Khrushchev. The President wants to avoid pushing Khrushchev to extremes. The blockade must be so conducted as to avoid humiliating the Russians; otherwise Khrushchev might react in a nuclear spasm. By the conventional rules blockade was an act of war and the first Soviet ship that refused to submit to boarding and search risked being sent to the bottom. But this was a military action with a political objective. Khrushchev must somehow be persuaded to pull back, rather than be goaded into retaliation.'[27]

It was in such terms that Kennedy wrote to Khrushchev on the 22nd, and again on the 25th. Kennedy stressed the insanity of nuclear war and ignored Khrushchev's reactions to the quarantine – 'outright banditry'. Khrushchev by mid-week was so concerned with the danger of holocaust caused by miscalculation – his – that he initially paid little attention to the olive branch held out to him by Kennedy when the quarantine limit was reduced from 800 to 500 miles. Even when Khrushchev did react, Kennedy was forced to reiterate that insanity and state necessity could not be separated by verbal ingenuity. Khrushchev was left in no doubt that America would prefer an insane decision to surrender if the missile sites were not dismantled. As he approached the brink Kennedy was shadowed by temptation and fear. A pre-emptive nuclear attack remained one option; fear that America would never forgive him for failure – might indeed impeach him – could not be shaken off.

Thus the quarantine was central to Kennedy's strategy. McNamara's characteristic rebuke to Anderson mirrored a situation where Khrushchev began, almost too late, to accept defeat. Desperate, his methods were bizarre, producing confusion, and reviving doubts about a gambler who seemed to believe he always had one more card. Foy Kohler, Thompson's successor in Moscow as Ambassador, had reported on the 16th that Khrushchev was in a conciliatory mood – on matters in general. Russian weapons were in Cuba for defensive purposes. There was, as Khrushchev put it to Kohler, a 'Caribbean crisis' – of America's making. In any case, he – Khrushchev – had no desire to embarrass the President during an election. On the 24th Khrushchev had a talk with William Knox, president of Westinghouse International. The meeting was one of those pointless exchanges in which Khrushchev, both ignorant about and envious of Western technology, loved to indulge. Knox noted that 'Khrushchev was calm, friendly and frank – without any histrionics – although he did appear very tired.' Khrushchev avoided talk of Cuba, except to hint that the quarantine was a game at which two could play.

Khrushchev was more than tired. He was frightened, fortunately for us. Between the meetings with Kohler and Knox the bottom had fallen out of Khrushchev's world. There was no point in boasting about 'rockets' to an America which knew the truth from Penkowsky – and might act on it in search of a final solution. By the 24th Khrushchev had checked with the Russian Embassy in London to confirm the worst about the man from the GRU. Khrushchev was told the worst. As an odd bonus, he was told that the British Government was not too happy about developments. Khrushchev knew that already. He needed help, not useless information. Within hours of his meeting with Knox, Khrushchev's messages were flying in all directions. With an effort which seems admirable in retrospect, Khrushchev had put up a front to the Western tycoon. Now he had to salvage the wreckage of his Cuban adventure. He also had to salvage his own reputation with comrades who had grown tired of his adventurism.

Khrushchev's first move was to order ships approaching the quarantine line to turn back. Kennedy, despite the dreadful temptation to force the issue, had already shaded the distance and ordered the task force to shadow, not intercept, Russian submarines. On the 25th, while Adlai Stevenson in the Security Council flourished the CIA's photographs of the Cuba build-up Khrushchev was writing a letter to Kennedy, 'long, rambling, and confused', to the ExComm sceptics who read it but, in fact, sane, pithy, and honest. By the time that day the USS *Joseph P. Kennedy Jr* had sighted the freighter *Marucla*, Khrushchev's letter was ready. Khrushchev had also ordered Alexander Fomin, the KGB Station Commander in Washington, to contact Rusk indirectly with an offer to deal: the Russian Government would dismantle the missile sites if the American Government promised not to invade Cuba. Within the UN, a labyrinth possessing its own very individual characteristics of infinite delay and endless half-measures, the possibilities of another deal were being fabricated: American missiles to be removed from Turkey, Russian from Cuba. Behind the façade of Stevenson's rhetoric, the deal acquired momentum. Walter Lippmann aired it in the *Washington Post* on the 25th. Unfortunately, Anatoliy Dobrynin, the Russian Ambassador in Washington, assumed Lippmann's article to be a White House trial balloon, and told Khrushchev so.

Kennedy's margin had been given to Khrushchev. He had used it. Now Kennedy needed time. He was to be given a few hours. Operation *Mongoose* had lurked behind every ExComm meeting from the start. By the evening of the 25th, D-Day was little more than 48 hours away. The planners, aided by the hawks and every department and agency concerned, began to pass the word that the SAM sites were just about operational. The shadow of the fear that some of the 42 MRBMs might be mobile, could be armed, possibly with nuclear warheads, began to creep into the minds of men whose capacity for clear thought was beginning to dry up. By the time that Kohler started sending Khrushchev's letter late on the 26th, every member of ExComm wanted above all the crisis to end. Khrushchev's offer, never made public, to remove 'missiles' – as distinct from aircraft – from Cuba if America ended the quarantine and gave assurances that no invasion would take place was transmitted over a period of several hours. Before the letter lay on Kennedy's desk hope for a rational solution had nearly died. By the time that Kennedy and his brother had read the message of a beaten man hope had begun to revive.

Throughout the night-hours of the 27th until dawn the President, his brother, and Dean Rusk, together with Bundy, McNamara, and Llewellyn Thompson, sought to make sense of Khrushchev's letter. At 0700 on the 26th, *Marucla* had been stopped, boarded, searched, and allowed to proceed. According to *Marucla*'s manifest the cargo was 'electro-measuring instruments, truck parts, sulphur and newsprint rolls'. *Mongoose* had reached the stage where 125,000 troops had sent last messages to sweethearts and wives. 'Kennedy ordered the State Department to proceed with preparations for a crash program on civil government in Cuba to be established after the invasion and occupation of that country.'[28] Every member of ExComm was told to expect heavy casualties. Kennedy said that Russian 'missiles' would cause them. He did not elaborate. Discussion about detail was losing momentum because fate appeared to be overtaking choice. Time was running out.

By mid-afternoon on the 26th Fomin had contacted Rusk, through Joseph Scali of the American Broadcasting Corporation, who knew him, and knew Hilsman. Khrushchev's letter, ending another twenty-four hours of tension and speculation, 'looked like the real thing'. On the 26th Kennedy had ordered a leaflet raid by the Tactical Air Command on Cuba. The message, in Spanish, blamed the Russians for putting Cuba in 'mortal danger'. Now, as the night hours of the 26th and 27th passed, Kennedy concentrated his mind on the mortal danger facing America. What impressed Kennedy as he read Khrushchev's letter was that despite the very real fear which underlined every word, the man at the other end of the rope was using a language common to them both. They shared the same dilemma.

'We must not succumb to petty passions or to transient things', wrote the tired man, 'but should realise that if indeed war should break out, then it would not be in our power to stop it, for such is the logic of war. I have participated in two wars and know that war ends when it has rolled through cities and villages, everywhere sowing death and destruction.'[29] This was not language which could be understood, let alone accepted by hawks. Zbigniew Bryzinski, a hawk of the academic kind, and in Jimmy Carter's Presidency chosen to sit in Bundy's chair, had that day said to Kennedy's friend Arthur Schlesinger: 'Any further delay in bombing missile sites fails to exploit Soviet uncertainty.'[30] By 26 October there was no secrecy or censorship left in Washington. Kennedy stood on the brink watched by his fellow Americans. Acheson, the most experienced member of ExComm, remained a sceptic and had become a critic: 'We have the thumbscrew on Khrushchev, we should give it another turn.' Kennedy disagreed. He ordered nuclear warheads on the Jupiter missiles in Turkey to be defused.

Fortunately for survival, Kennedy did not want to exploit anything or anyone. His brother Robert, probably by this stage the biggest influence on Presidential decisions, argued that when Khrushchev went on to write, 'Only lunatics or suicides, who themselves want to perish would seek to destroy your country', he was appealing to imagination.[31] This faculty governed what these two Kennedy brothers believed in and decided to do. Khrushchev's proposal – to dismantle the sites in return for a pledge by Kennedy not to invade Cuba – was taken seriously because it went far beyond the scope of mere bargaining. Fomin had made the proposal during the 26th; Rusk had authorised a temporising reply: 'I have reason to believe that the USG [United States Government] sees real possibilities and supposes that the representatives of the two governments in New York could work this matter out with U Thant and with each other.'[32]

But even at Khrushchev's eleventh hour he could not resist a final gamble. He said that missiles had already arrived in Cuba. He referred to the Bay of Pigs. He compared plans to overthrow Castro with American attempts to destroy the Communist revolution. Rusk's decision to tell Fomin that the proposal was basically acceptable began to look premature. Hilsman's analysis, supported by one of the few members of his staff who had also read the Penkowsky material, had been that the letter was genuine. Others, who disliked the State Department and all its works, were not so sure. Saturday came with the knot tighter than ever. Rusk had told Fomin 'time is very urgent'. There was practically no time left. By early morning the FBI reported to Robert Kennedy that Russian diplomats were destroying papers. When Kennedy arrived at the White House he found that Khrushchev had sent yet another letter. Moscow radio was broadcasting it. There was neither imagination nor wisdom in this one: 'We will remove our missiles from Cuba, you will remove yours from Turkey . . . The Soviet Union will pledge not to invade or interfere with the internal affairs of Turkey; the United States will make the same pledge regarding Cuba.'[33]

John Kennedy was exhausted by now. In the last few days he had become totally involved in every aspect of the crisis. He had neither time nor strength left. He read Khrushchev's second letter. 'Now it can go either way', he said to his brother.[34] It was not the trade on missiles as such which gave Kennedy another turn of the screw; he had been thinking of removing the Jupiter missiles in Turkey for the past eighteen months. The Jupiters, first generation missiles, were rather like the Russian IRBMs, 'liquid-fueled, slow to fire, and sluggish in motion'.[35] The Turkish Government had not wanted them – they were a provocation rather than a deterrent – and McNamara did not believe in them. He wanted submarines armed with the Polaris missile system to be put on station in the Mediterranean. What turned the screw was Khrushchev's tone, utterly removed from that of a man on the end of a rope. The demand suggested that Kennedy would do anything to loosen the knot, even if he was impeached in the process. In the intensity of their fear Dobrynin and Khrushchev had forgotten that no trade over Jupiters could be made openly by Kennedy, least of all during an election. Democracies, old or young, have such problems. A pledge not to invade Cuba could be kept secret – for a time. *Mongoose* could be postponed. But removing the Jupiters from Turkey would be a visible and outward sign of inward and invisible *détente*. This was not a state of grace with any appeal for Congress.

McCone chose this Saturday morning to report, inaccurately,

that 'the Cuban MRBM installations would be completed this very day; bunkers are being erected for nuclear warheads.'[36] McCone had reached the dangerous stage of equating capability with intention. ExComm sat through this and other, half-digested, partly accepted items. The knot was agonisingly tight. If McCone was right, a Russian nuclear strike on the invasion force was more likely than not. Attempts at drafting a reply to Khrushchev's letter of the 26th were frustrated by exhaustion, doubt, and approaching despair. By the time McCone had finished reading from his 'CIA Seal/The Crisis/USSR – Cuba' folder, ExComm was told a U-2 had been shot down over Cuba – by a SAM. The pilot, Major Rudolf Anderson, had been killed. This news had hardly been accepted as true, as inevitable, when the State Department passed to ExComm an even more numbing report. Another U-2 had overflown Russian territory, had been intercepted and escorted out of national air space. The President, not yet drained of bitter humour, remarked: 'There's always some so-and-so who doesn't get the word.'[37] He said nothing about the despatch of other American aircraft to escort the errant U-2 back to base. American and Russian fighter aircraft flew within miles of each other. The radar screens showed pictures hitherto reserved for nightmares.

At this point, when Dr Strangelove would have pressed the button and many in Washington were adamant that the President should do so, Robert Kennedy stood up to the Joint Chiefs and to the State Department. The Attorney-General, a highly-strung, irritable man, was nevertheless determined that the mind and the imagination would prevail over the solar plexus. The Joint Chiefs, silenced for twelve days, demanded an air strike within twenty-four hours. The State Department representatives, possibly envious of military simplicities, argued that Khrushchev must be told to remove the 'missiles', without conditions. The President's refusal to finally commit America to war tied a knot of tension which his brother suddenly cut. Ignore the second Khrushchev letter, he said; offer to deal on the basis of the first one. The sites must be dismantled first. Then we will agree to leave Cuba alone.

Robert Kennedy got his way – by compromise. Standing on the brink, looking into the abyss, he agreed that if Khrushchev refused to accept the offer, the air strike would take place. Dobrynin would be told this. He was so told, John Kennedy meanwhile replying in his brother's terms to Khrushchev's first letter. Whether the President would have ordered the strike remains pure speculation. Robert Kennedy believed that he would have resisted the Joint Chiefs, faced them down, dismissed them rather than cut the final knot. We will never know. Whilst Robert Kennedy was watching the preliminaries of the Washington Horse Show with his daughters the following Sunday morning (a date which neither they nor he saw any reason to cut) Rusk telephoned him. Dobrynin, whom Kennedy had seen earlier, had been on the line. 'Khrushchev had agreed to dismantle and withdraw the missiles under adequate supervision and inspection . . . everything was going to work out satisfactorily . . . Mr Khrushchev wanted to send his best wishes to the President . . .'[38] Khrushchev virtually demanded that invasion plans be abandoned. Kennedy never openly agreed to do this but displayed political acumen and magnanimity in calling off *Mongoose*. Llewellyn Thompson, who had understudied Kennedy during the day by direct contact with Moscow, said this *was* the real thing. Robert Kennedy went back to the White House. The brothers talked for a long time. The last words should be with the wise counsellor: 'As I closed the door, he was seated at the desk writing a letter to Mrs Anderson.'[39]

The crisis was over. The sites were dismantled. *Mongoose* was put in cold storage. The Jupiters passed into history. Many senior officers of the Russian High Command, the GRU, and the KGB were sacked or demoted – a belated tribute to the comrade who had betrayed them. Generals Mosalenko and Golikov were reinstated – the first warning to Khrushchev from his comrades that adventurism was not a permanently operating factor. But before ExComm finally dispersed, the President had one more task to complete. He called McNamara: 'Get Le May here, and come too.' The President sat his Chief of the Air Staff down and said: 'Now listen General. Let me tell you what really happened.' Kennedy traced the course of the crisis; Le May heard him in silence. Kennedy finished his tale and then said: 'There won't be deliberate nuclear war with Russia. War would come by miscalculation. You won't miscalculate. Khrushchev nearly did. He thought he could bluff concessions out of us. Now he knows you can't do that in the nuclear age. If there is an accident, if a Russian bomber crashes here, even a missile, you don't retaliate. You come here, and we talk about it. That's what Secretary McNamara means by a controlled response.'

7 · A CONFIDENTIAL WAR: NIGERIAN OIL, 1967

'I left it to the men on the spot.'

MICHAEL STEWART

On 26 January 1903, Sir Henry Campbell-Bannerman wrote to James Bryce: 'The truth is we cannot provide for a fighting Empire, and nothing can give us the power.'[1] Campbell-Bannerman was leader of the Liberal Party; in 1906, after the virtual electoral annihilation of a Conservative Party led by Salisbury's nephew Arthur Balfour, Sir Henry became Prime Minister. Bryce was a supporter of Campbell-Bannerman in the anti-imperialist wing of the Liberal Party. Later, as Ambassador to Washington, Bryce succeeded in persuading sceptical Americans that the Liberal Government had learned the lesson of the South African War, and would no longer attempt to settle local or regional issues on the African Continent by force of arms.

Sixty-four years later the truth and the implications of Campbell-Bannerman's statement were brought home to the Permanent Government when civil war broke out in Nigeria, British Africa's largest, richest, and most populous country. As a member of the Commonwealth, the Nigerian Government expected a positive British reaction. But Britain did not intervene to prevent, limit, or end the war. Harold Wilson's Labour Government left the resolution of the war to the men on the spot. The latter, and their compatriots in Whitehall, could well have echoed Campbell-Bannerman's words; the historically-minded amongst them – a fair number concerning Africa – probably did so. They knew that although the Empire had been transformed into a Commonwealth, with the white nations in a minority, Britain was still expected, in defence of its own interests, to do something to protect those of the black African races. By 1967 African affairs had assumed an international dimension; a new scramble for the dark continent was an option debated in both Moscow and Peking.

But the men in Whitehall and on the spot knew for the same reason as in 1903 – and all the years between – that whatever was done by Britain would be limited, and mostly covert. Such men also knew that whatever they did would expose their political masters to abuse or ridicule from those who believed all Britain's policies in Africa to be dominated by self-interest. In the event, and although the civil war's essential issues, in terms of British interests, were settled in the first six months, it dragged on for another two years of death and destruction. In those years, members of the permanent government in general, including SIS, struggled to limit the war's effects, and to maintain their candidate, Yakuba Gowon, in power. No British troops were involved; other means were used. Throughout this period Wilson and his colleagues were engaged in a very different exercise: an apparent confrontation with Ian Smith, a white rebel leader in the colony of Southern Rhodesia. The men of the permanent government (and one foreign secretary) lived in the real world; Wilson and his like in the looking-glass world.

The real truth of Campbell-Bannerman's statement, in fact, had less to do with the factor of Britain's limited strategic resources or the dislike of Liberal governments for war – it was Balfour who remarked, 'We are a fighting but not a military nation' – than with the fact that imperial policy in Africa was governed from the outset by the interests of the white races, concentrated, with few exceptions, amongst those who wanted to exploit the continent's mineral resources without awkward Whitehall questions being asked about methods and profits. The South African or 'Boer' War between 1899 and 1902 merely emphasised the truth that these white races had a common objective, which was to dominate the black man north and south of the Limpopo and, if possible, north and west of the Zambesi. The Treaty of Vereeniging in May 1902, which effectively ended the South African War, gave the *Boers* most of what they had been fighting for: continued domination of the black races. Campbell-Bannerman's Liberal Government, despite its high moral tone and anti-imperialist wing, did nothing for these blacks in South Africa, and little for the Indian and coloured peoples either.

An illusion nevertheless persisted that Britain had a special relationship with the black African races which, where a conflict with white interests occurred, would determine the issue. The legal abolition of slavery in the early nineteenth century and its suppression thereafter in West Africa established a tradition which indifference to the Arab slavers of East Africa and white practices to the south did nothing to weaken. Throughout the late Victorian division of the African spoils amongst European contenders, and those years dominated by world war and their major international repercussions, belief in a British power to support the black races was buttressed by missionary zeal and political declaration. In 1923 a Conservative Colonial Secretary stated that, 'The interests of the African natives must be paramount, and that if and when those interests and the interests of the immigrant races should conflict, the former should prevail.'[2] The Colonial Secretary was the Duke of Devonshire, Harold Macmillan's father-in-law. The young *arriviste* in the circles of aristocratic paternalism stored the words away for later use.

But in that same year and by the same Colonial Secretary Southern Rhodesia was given the status of an internally self-governing colony; power was vested in a white immigrant minority which had no intention then, or later, of regarding the Devonshire Declaration as anything more than verbiage – which it was. Nevertheless, even verbiage can reflect realities. Where British governments could advance the interests of black African races without detriment to the paramountcy of white settlers they would do so. Nigeria and its neighbouring colonies of the West coast, wisely governed and often devotedly served by generations of imperialists, reached by 1939 a state of stability and relative prosperity which owed more to the firm control kept on white enterprise than to the ability of native rulers, allowed to retain much symbolic and some real authority. East and Central Africa remained in limbo, due to the absence of direct racial conflict, and the presence of many enlightened whites. Southern Rhodesia and South Africa were left free by the imperial government to pursue racialist policies which varied from the savage to the disingenuous.

Throughout the Second World War Franklin Roosevelt and Cordell Hull continued to demand the end of European imperialism, everywhere. The British Empire and Britain's 'veiled protectorate' in the Middle East aroused stronger feelings in Roosevelt and his Secretary of State than the Dutch, the Belgian, or even the French colonies. Churchill, in daily receipt of Roosevelt's version of the special relationship, passed these threats to his Colonial Secretary, Oliver Stanley. By 1945 the British Government devised a temporising formula: India would become independent; some colonies, mandates, and protectorates, and the like could reckon themselves independence candidates; a third category, however, would remain dependent indefinitely, 'because of their inherent inability to govern themselves'. Stanley did not particularise, but in fact he meant to include the larger Caribbean colonies and Malaya in the second category, most of those in Africa in the third. This formula ingeniously, and deliberately, obscured the fact that Britain's African empire south of the Sahara consisted of thirteen dependencies, of which those on the West coast alone were already well advanced to internal self-government. But this empire also included the protectorates of Bechuanaland, Basutoland and Swaziland. All three protectorates were firmly within South Africa's economic orbit. The Mandate of South West Africa was in the same position. This territory was a legacy of the League of Nations, legally and morally the responsibility of British governments. In practice, South West Africa was ruled from Pretoria.

Strategically vital colonies – Gibraltar, Malta, Cyprus, Aden, Singapore, and Hong Kong – were also put in the third category, and there was no disposition by the post-war Labour governments or their Conservative successors to change the *status quo*. The Labour Government in 1949, inheriting the Liberal tradition, deposed the accepted claimant to the ruling chieftainship in Bechuanaland, and did so in deference to the South African Government's protests at his marriage to a white woman. In July 1954 a junior minister, Henry Hopkinson, speaking for the Government, declared that Cyprus could never expect to become 'Sovereign'. The Colonial Secretary, Oliver Lyttelton – whose wartime experience as first Minister of State in the Middle East led him to see Cyprus in purely strategic terms – was even more specific. Cyprus could never be independent. The first post-war decade, which saw many illusions about Britain's empire in the Middle East dispelled, did not, in No. 10 or Westminster, produce a realistic policy for the colonial empire.

In 1951 the politicians who had deposed Seretse Khama of Bechuanaland produced a plan for a Central African Federation, of Northern and Southern Rhodesia and Nyasaland, which would have completed what white settlement had begun and the Devonshire Declaration had underwritten: a white dominated State of economic potential to match its neighbour South Africa, and that conveniently forgotten responsibility of South West Africa, rich in diamonds, and uranium. The idea of a Central African Federation – Cecil Rhodes's vision of white rule from the Congo to the Cape brought to life by a Labour Government – had a distinct appeal to Pretoria. South African Governments held good cards in their dealings with British governments. Walvis Bay, on the South West African coast, is one of the finest natural harbours on the continent. The Royal Navy Station at Simonstown (near Cape Town) was an integral element in the strategy of protecting trade and communications by sea. As oil tankers grew in size, and increasingly by-passed the Suez Canal, Simonstown grew in complementary importance; no British Government until the 1970s was prepared to assert that the Station should be given up in order to remove one ace from South Africa's hand.

Many in the Labour Party and some in the Conservative Party opposed the Central African Federation. The white settlers, in Southern Rhodesia above all, opposed it effectively. They attacked the Federation's milk and water provisions for black rights so thoroughly that even Conservative governments were loth to grant such racialists the formal independence they desired. In 1963, dismembered skilfully by R. A. Butler (as Macmillan's Foreign Secretary) the Federation represented no more than a confidence trick which had been played on black nationalists. But the damage had been done; despite sheer force of circumstance – recognised by Macmillan in his 3 February 1960 'Wind of Change' speech on the inevitable advent of black nationalism, written by Norman Brook and delivered to a bemused South African Parliament in Cape Town – which led to independence for most of the African dependencies, the eve of the Nigerian Civil War in July 1967 found Wilson's Labour Government in no position to act, overtly and with confidence, as the friend of black Africa.

To write this preliminary comment is, in no sense, to minimise the skill with which the Macmillan governments transformed a white man's empire into a multi-racial Commonwealth; the importance of independence; or the enthusiasm with which it was greeted in Accra or Lagos, Nairobi and Dar es Salaam – and, indeed, wherever the imperial sun had set at last. Independence eve ceremonies were moving occasions, the final lowering of the Union flag at midnight watched with as much emotion by all races present as the sight of a new flag, of an independent State, being hauled to the masthead by a Sandhurst-trained subaltern. Something new, and hopeful, came out of Africa with every independence day. A thunderstorm of more than tropical intensity broke almost on the eve of Nigeria's independence, 1 October 1960. The storm cleared magically just before the ceremonies, so baffling to the outsider, so essential to men guided or governed by emotion, were graced by Princess Alexandra and, apparently, sanctioned by the heavens.

Throughout the last dreary years of the second Macmillan Government and its twelve months' successor, led by Sir Alec Douglas Home, faith in the new Commonwealth was strengthened. [3] Despite the absurdities of Macmillan's nuclear deterrent, his failure in January 1963 to join the European Community, economic malaise, and further revelations of security scandals which had stalked the establishment for years, independence for black Africa reassured sceptic and cynic alike that Britain still had something to show the world in the arts of leadership. And the sceptic and the cynic were right to be reassured. Ghana in 1957; Nigeria in 1960; Tanganyika (Tanzania) and Sierra Leone in 1961; Uganda in 1962; Kenya in 1963; Nyasaland (Malawi) and Northern Rhodesia (Zambia) in 1964. These were milestones on a road which appeared to lead towards a new place for Britain in the international sun, one of mentor, if no longer of master.

South Africa's withdrawal from the Commonwealth in March 1961 – virtually an expulsion at Nigeria's insistence after a stormy conference at Lancaster House – seemed to mark a more radical process, an agonising reappraisal for Britain of where its true interests lay on the dark continent. But the economic realities which also governed British policy in Africa were unchanged by Commonwealth opposition to South Africa's racial policies. British capital investment in South Africa continued to increase throughout the 1960s; South African governments accelerated the processes of *apartheid* and the denial of political rights to the black majority. These governments confidently expected that no British government would even try to stop them. They were right in their expectations. Moreover, Macmillan and Home did not confine their support of white economic interests to South Africa. They covertly backed the secessionist Moise Tshombe in his province of Katanga when the Congo became independent from Belgium in June 1960.

The reason for such support was simple: 'Katanga supplied in 1960 nearly 10 per cent of the world's copper; 60 per cent of its cobalt and most of its radium, plus large quantities of zinc, industrial diamonds, germanium and other metals. Katanga produced half of the metal used in making jet engines and radar equipment in the non-communist countries.'[4] One company owned this wealth: the Union Minière du Haut Katanga. Belgian interests predominated, but British, American – and South African – holdings were also substantial. South African and Rhodesian mercenaries fought for Tshombe, but apart from the Belgian Government his strongest support came from Macmillan and Home. British governments' opposition to United Nations involvement in the Congo was partly a delayed reaction to Suez but, at deeper levels than emotion, reflected a determination to support white economic interests in Africa. Tshombe, opposed by the United Nations Secretariat, the United States Government, and a majority of African countries in the General Assembly, was backed by British governments because he did as his white economic masters told him. In 1964 Tshombe became Prime Minister of the Congo.

In the real world and the world of *Realpolitik* governments are judged by their capacity to evolve and execute policies which have some likelihood of being utilised by their successors. The Macmillan and Home governments, concerning Africa, must be judged by this criterion. Not only was there a basic flaw in post-imperial attitudes to Africa – the same racialist flaw which had disfigured the imperial scene – but Britain's capacity to intervene there by any definable, and overt, means finally disappeared just before the moment when Harold Wilson took his place on the stage vacated by Macmillan and Home. In January and February 1964 British troops were sent at short notice to suppress mutinies in the armies of newly independent Tanzania, Uganda, and Kenya. A limited military operation, mainly depending on the Royal Navy's presence off the East African coast, was executed with great skill; the mutineers were returned to barracks during two months of almost bloodless campaigning. The Presidents of the three countries had asked for help; they were suitably grateful when it was given; but Whitehall made it clear that in future covert assistance only would be provided. The requirements laid on SIS increased accordingly. Liaison was established with the British trained intelligence and security services of these new Commonwealth members, and SIS and MI5 did much thereafter to keep their governments in power. Between them, the two services provided 'security liaison officers', whose tasks remain demanding and arduous.

Whitehall drew definite conclusions from the suppression of the East African mutinies. The Chiefs of Staff did not say in so many words that Africa was no longer a strategic commitment. Whitehall reorganisation in the late 1950s and early 1960s was designed, on paper, to reduce the advisory role of the Chiefs of Staff. There was more shadow than substance in this change. The Chiefs did not consciously echo Campbell-Bannerman's words, or utterly repudiate all that Patrick Dean had urged in his post-Suez strategic survey. But the Chiefs closed the Africa account none the less. They did so because the increasing cost of the nuclear weapons system bought from America after the Nassau meeting in

December 1962 not only cut the British Army to a size which precluded world-wide campaigning but denied it the arms and equipment necessary to fight effectively in more than one place at a time. The Chiefs also terminated commitments in Africa because military operations there depended on airfields and related logistic facilities being readily available at short notice. These facilities were maintained throughout the 1960s for the retention of commitments east of Suez, namely in the area from the Persian Gulf to the Far East. Island staging posts in the Indian Ocean were established (later, to become a quasi colony, the 'British Indian Ocean Territories'), and proved to be strategically effective and financially economical.

By contrast, air staging across the African Continent was involuntarily terminated by the refusal in 1962 of the Nigerian Government to provide routes, and facilities *via* Kano. The Nigerian Government also refused to make a defence agreement with Britain. This was a decision which the Federal Nigerian Government of 1967 regretted, but which was not forgotten in London. Facilities in Kenya, which had been crucial to the success of the Kuwait operation, were being run down by 1963. El Adem, in Libya, ceased to be a staging post in 1964 because although King Idris was prepared to allow his British-commanded troops to defend the BP oilfields in Cyrenaica, he was determined not to cause trouble with Nasser by providing facilities for forces sent from Britain to fight a colonial war in the Federation of South Arabia. In 1964 the Chiefs argued that British forces could only engage in conflict up to the level of limited war if a major base, unequivocally at their disposal, was in the theatre of operations. Singapore was the one base which met this requirement, and it did so less by virtue of its physical characteristics than because of the political factor that the independent Malay and Singapore governments were Britain's allies in an undeclared war with Indonesia. Nevertheless, the war was fought by British, Gurkha, and Malay troops with obsolescent weapons and inadequate equipment, and it was no comfort to these men on the spot to know that V bombers from Singapore (armed with 'conventional' bombs) could easily reach Indonesian targets. This subaltern's and platoon sergeant's war was won by troops whose units were under strength, made up to the order of battle by cross posting on a scale which revealed the strain on Britain's most valuable strategic resource: trained men.

The attempt to sustain counter-revolution in Arabia and to do so from Aden met with no local support. A revolution in Yemen in September 1962, and an intensification of tribal war in the South Arabian Federation during 1963 were instantly, and correctly, attributed by Macmillan, Home, and those with whom they chose to dine as mainly the work of Cairo Radio. The Arab soldiers of the Federation, those quite exceptionally unreliable imperial levies, certainly fought revolution with a rifle in one hand and a transistor radio, tuned to Cairo, in the other. The radio proved mightier than the rifle. But the real fact of the matter is that the game in Arabia was almost over. The Federation lacked all semblance of political cohesion; tribal levies were more disposed to fight each other than the revolutionary (and supposedly communist and Russian-backed) enemy which, from December 1963 onwards, taxed British resources and again ruined Britain's reputation for sense and style in dealing with Arab affairs. Campaigning in the rugged and romantic terrain which extends from fifty miles north of Aden up to, and across, the Yemen border became, between early 1964 and the final débâcle in November 1967, an affair for the connoisseur of the absurd.

Macmillan's attempt, executed by Julian Amery and a clutch of his old Albanain cronies, to fight the good fight in Yemen, was tacitly opposed by SIS because, all other factors apart, it degenerated into a matter of bribes to the wrong people – £30 million, to be exact, laundered through the Colonial Development and Welfare Acts, ostensibly paid into the South Arabian Federal Treasury, then handed out to tribal rulers on both sides of the border. The rulers in South Arabia and Yemen took the cash and let Britain's credit go. Some rulers turned to Cairo, more to Jeddah. Few in South Arabia remained loyal to Britain, because none saw how British governments could support a Federation which had no political identity. By the end of 1964 the Federation was struggling to survive, and although Nasser lost more than he gained by his intervention in the Yemen, a revolution, of sorts succeeded there. White made no attempt to turn SIS into an organisation which recommended what should be done; he and his officers stuck to the job of acquiring intelligence and executing counter-intelligence operations. Nevertheless, as the South Arabian Federation slid into chaos, White's men in the area were forced to suggest that loyal – and non-tribal – politicians of moderately radical views be given a chance.

Attempts were belatedly made in Aden, but none in the tribal hinterland. Even there moderate men could be found, but the suggestion that they be given a chance to weld tribal warriors and Aden's trades unionists – employees at BP's refinery and in the Port – into a broadly based political organisation, committed to genuine independence from Britain, were instantly rejected by the Federation's High Commissioner, Sir Kennedy Trevaskis, and the Conservative Government which he so faithfully served. Aden was a major base, in theory. Aden represented the permanence of Britain's role in Arabia. Offer the Federation independence, the right to choose whether to retain or abandon the base in treaty relations with Britain, and another bit of the imperial arch would crash. Shorn of rhetoric about loyalties and obligations Macmillan's imperial caucus wanted to keep Aden because its members believed in occupying a base from which military operations in the Persian Gulf could be executed at any time in an indefinite future.

When Harold Wilson became Prime Minister in October 1964 (with a majority of four in the House of Commons) he thus inherited policies which reflected the fact that Macmillan, for all his skill and the measure of his achievements in black Africa and Malaya, had failed to escape from the illusion of Britain playing a major role on the international stage. The attempt at counter-revolution in Arabia had failed. Exclusion from the European Economic Community left the arbitration of political and economic affairs to de Gaulle. Britain's strategic nuclear forces were being retained by courtesy of America – and with an American finger not only on the procurement of vital components but, for all practical purposes, on the trigger. Wilson, however, also inherited a legacy of Macmillan's relationship with Kennedy and Lyndon Johnson which is more relevant to his stage-managed role in African affairs than was obviously or immediately apparent at the time. The real nub of the deal which was made after three days of hard bargaining at Nassau in December 1962 had less to do with nuclear weapons than with an historic shift in Washington's view of Britain's place on the international stage. By late 1962 Britain's Empire had gone; by contrast, America had acquired one, of sorts, in Vietnam.

One ironic consequence of this reversal of roles was that Britain also acquired a new international status in American eyes, but one which was not matched by the strategic resources needed to maintain it. The irony was both acute and subtle. On paper, the Nassau Agreement committed Britain to assigning the Royal Navy's new, retaliatory, American nuclear missile weapons to NATO except in conditions of 'supreme national emergency'.

Because everyone at Nassau knew that this emergency would be one where Britain had been abandoned by America there was no need to define or articulate it. By the same token, all the participants in the Nassau deal knew that Kennedy and McNamara not only opposed the nuclear blackmail arguments of the 1950s, but had no intention of providing a British government with weapons which would drag America into a war of Britain's making. Macmillan was forced to rely on David Ormsby-Gore's post-Cuba relationship with Kennedy to assure him Britain would not use strategic nuclear weapons *first*. The Polaris system, being retaliatory and not first strike, lessened that danger, but did not entirely remove it. Britain remained – and remains – so vulnerable to immediate and total nuclear destruction that possession of even a retaliatory weapon was, and is, merely another gesture. Everyone at Nassau also knew therefore that 'supreme national emergency' was a form of words, a concession to British national susceptibilities, and that there were no imaginable circumstances – and no possible way – in which Britain would, in strategic nuclear matters, act independently from America.[5]

The subtle irony lay in Kennedy and McNamara seeking from Britain an independent, non-nuclear strategic role which would complement American endeavours in Vietnam. No member of Kennedy's Cabinet was more determined than McNamara that Britain should lose its nuclear independence, by *force majeure* for preference, in some form of NATO deterrent under overall American command as a second best option. But no member of Kennedy's and Johnson's Cabinets was more insistent than McNamara that Britain should hold the line – sometimes hard to draw and often impossible to define – in South East Asia. Only Robert Kennedy, a liberal casuist, was able to oppose Britain's war with Indonesia whilst defending his country's conduct in Vietnam. McNamara, Dean Rusk, the American Chiefs of Staff, and the CIA, saw in the war with Indonesia convincing evidence that Britain's subjection to American nuclear dictates – in practice, although not in the pretence of independence – did not mean its entire renunciation of international responsibilities.

The framers and makers of American foreign policy and strategy in the Johnson years also began to walk through a looking glass, wherein they found a Britain which seemed to be, and in fact sometimes was, making rather a good job of limited war and the like. But Johnson's men did not look at Arabia – in economic terms, firmly within America's grasp and hence in their view, immune from communist threats – and, strategically, took little notice of Africa once the Congo civil war was over. Ironically, in view of traditional American attitudes towards the British Empire, Johnson's Washington showed no enthusiasm for the new Commonwealth. In British Guiana (Guyana), where communist slogans were thought to mean Russian influence, the CIA was active in a crude kind of way, reflecting the traditional American belief that the Caribbean was within its sphere of influence. When the Colony became independent in May 1966 the Governor-General at once sharply reminded the CIA officer sent from Washington to keep an eye on things that he had no business to be there in the first place. No agreement had been reached on intelligence liaison. The officer was unmoved by the rebuke, and pressure from Washington ensured that he remained on the spot.

Denis Healey, who was Wilson's Defence Secretary for six years, simplified and rationalised these varying demands on Britain's strategic capacities. Governed by the economic factors which were the sole interest of almost every member of Wilson's Cabinets until his defeat in the 1970 General Election, Healey succeeded in achieving compromise on future commitments with the Chiefs. Healey and Whitehall spoke a common language, based on close study of what was, and was not, possible with diminishing strategic resources. Commitments in the Far East could be sustained for a decade or so; in the Middle East they should be terminated as quickly as possible. Healey believed strongly in close Anglo-American relations. He rejected much in Patrick Dean's recommendations and dissolved dreams of empire based on Aden and the Persian Gulf. But Healey fought the Indonesian war with all the non-nuclear resources at Britain's disposal. These resources were inadequate, but Healey did not stint them. Good marks were earned in Washington.

However, Healey, despite – or because of – his close association with McNamara, Bundy, and their advisers, failed to provide his Prime Minister with an objective appreciation of what was possible in real strategic terms. Healey and McNamara spoke the same language of strategic analysis, one which was simple in concept but elaborate in exposition. Wilson spoke the language he thought Lyndon Johnson wanted to hear. Healey understood about controlled response and a single centre of nuclear decision-making in NATO. Healey realised that the British Government's support for America's war in Vietnam (and the encouragement given to those staunch Commonwealth members Australia and New Zealand for participating in it) was less important in Washington than Britain's success in containing the Indonesian conflict. Wilson saw none of this. In August 1965 he said, 'Britain's frontiers are on the Himalayas'. This was the kind of remark Macmillan would have relished but, by 1965, would not have made. Healey knew that the remark was particularly absurd. Wilson made it in the immediate aftermath of a war between two other Commonwealth members, India and Pakistan, which had been settled by *Russian* mediation. Russia's frontier remained north of the Himalayas, but Moscow's influence in the sub-continent could no longer be contained by the rhetoric of a British Prime Minister. Yet Wilson indulged in rhetoric because he believed that Johnson was responsive to it. America of the middle 1960s was a patently less self-confident and assertive power than in the days of Kennedy's brief Presidency.

The six years of Wilson's first two governments (he was returned with a convincing majority in March 1966) saw a steady deterioration in the American capacity to arbitrate world events to their President's liking. John Kennedy's assassination on 22 November 1963 marked the end of an era; Churchill's death on 24 January 1965 ended the imperial age for Britain. Kennedy had succeeded in demonstrating that power could be used with restraint. When Johnson met Khrushchev's successor, Alexei Kosygin, at Glassboro (New Jersey) on 23 June 1967, American armed forces in Vietnam were chiefly demonstrating their power to destroy. At Glassboro Johnson ordered McNamara, in the middle of a crowded, bibulous lunch, to explain his strategy of controlled nuclear response. With controlled anger, the abstemious McNamara did his best to do so, but failure to convince Kosygin was implicit in the time, the place and the atmosphere. By the time of the Glassboro meeting the concept of nuclear restraint, for which the Kennedy brothers, McNamara, and Bundy had fought so hard, was being abandoned in favour of national proliferation. During the 1960s, France and China became nuclear powers.

Despite his intellectual commitment to American nuclear paramountcy, Healey carried on where Macmillan left off. McNamara and Rusk failed to establish a NATO nuclear force under American control. Healey accepted such control for the Royal Navy's Polaris system (although the 'twelve Russian cities' of 1957 first strike strategies remained, and remain, the target) but nevertheless spent much time and billions of dollars on improvements which reflected technological innovation rather than strategic necessity. De Gaulle built a simpler system, exclusively from French resources and, as he took pains to stress in January 1963 when about to veto Britain's application to join the EEC, 'at our own disposal'. To pay for the Polaris system, the British Army was forced to fight with weak units and obsolescent weapons and the Royal Navy abandoned the classic task of guarding the sea lanes, on which Britain's real security has always depended. The Navy's fleet carriers were progressively scrapped. Frigates and anti-submarine vessels continued to be built but in steadily diminishing numbers.

Given these factors of change and decline, it was, perhaps, inevitable that Wilson should seek to demonstrate a power of independent strategic action which would nevertheless cost nothing in terms of strategic resources. Africa absorbed Wilson – in terms of time and cultivation of the international statesman role – between 1966 and 1970, during which America sank into the Vietnam morass, another Arab-Israeli war was fought, and the Czechs saw their brief flash of human freedom vanish beneath Kosygin's tanks. In none of these events could Wilson play more than a rhetorical part. He could do nothing to prevent or riposte to de Gaulle's second veto in May 1967 on another attempt by Britain to join the European Community. In Africa, however, despite the legacies of history and the lessons drawn by Whitehall from East Africa in the first two months of 1964, there seemed room for political manoeuvre.

Between October 1964 and March 1966 Wilson was, understandably, concerned to survive. After the latter date he had room for parliamentary manoeuvre, given the relative unity of his own Party and the disarray of an Opposition led by Home, a politician constitutionally averse from rough and tumble. Macmillan's Cabinet butchery in July 1962 and the Profumo affair in June 1963 had openly shaken a Party traditionally well able to quarrel in private. Macmillan had hoped to preserve an image of the country house and the grouse moor for the resolution of what he called 'matters of high importance'. The Profumo scandal ensured that the image left in the mind of the public would be that of the massage parlour.

Profumo belonged, by cultivation, to the looking-glass world re-created by Macmillan after Suez. In such a world a pose was more important than a policy; the Kuwait operation, for which Profumo, as Secretary of State for War, had a direct Ministerial responsibility, could be hailed as a master stroke of imperial strategy. In this looking-glass world the only crime was to be caught. Profumo had been caught, had lied, had been forced to confess by the men in his Party who preferred to sacrifice one transient office holder than have questions asked about graver scandals or face demands for a real investigation into security lapses by officials, and others.

Macmillan ordered regular investigations into these affairs during his last years as Prime Minister, but these were exercises designed to prove that all was for the best in the best of all possible Conservative worlds – except for the malpractices of journalists, two of whom were sent to prison in March 1963 for refusing to divulge their sources when the Press again tackled the wider implications of the Vassall affair. Macmillan not only denied all knowledge of Profumo's liaisons, but took a cavalier attitude towards the laxity of a former junior Admiralty minister, Thomas Galbraith, Vassall's political master and friend. Despite Macmillan's denials, the Conservative Party collectively felt, and implied, that he should have known – and maybe knew more than he chose to say. Macmillan did not exactly resign in October 1963 because of scandal – a genuine illness was also a great convenience – but Nigel Birch, a former minister and his most bitter critic, chose Browning's lines to speed him on his way

'. . . let him never come back to us!
There would be doubt, hesitation and pain
Forced praise on our part – the glimmer of twilight
Never glad confident morning again!'

In such circumstances, with Home a patently stop-gap leader menaced by the sombre figure of Edward Heath as rival, Wilson had an easy time in the Commons. For several years after Macmillan resigned the Conservative Party publicly conducted an internal feud. Questions about Britain's place in the world were left to a minority of MPs who felt about it strongly or who took the trouble to ask whether commitments were being honoured or abandoned. Wilson was adept at evading questions, Healey – a bit of a bully at the despatch box – good at reminding the Opposition of past mistakes. Neither Wilson nor his colleagues faced sustained Parliamentary criticism after the two major African crises of Southern Rhodesian rebellion and Nigerian civil war erupted in December 1965 and July 1967. Despite the importance of the issues and the emotional commitment to them of much of the

British people, Parliament treated rebellion and war with relative calm. This factor reflected Wilson's Parliamentary strength, not the realities of the African situation. In neither Southern Rhodesia nor Nigeria did the Wilson Government as such have the slightest influence on events.

In Southern Rhodesia, Ian Smith was able to plan, execute, and sustain a rebellion against the Crown because he knew that British forces would not intervene. Smith knew the Chiefs of Staff in London had indicated with sufficient clarity to the Government that if there was one place in Africa where intervention was not only strategically impossible but politically unacceptable it was Southern Rhodesia. The Rhodesian armed forces had close connections with their kith and kin in Britain (the Royal Rhodesian Air Force played a useful role during the Kuwait operation), and the Chiefs said plainly to Wilson that any order to suppress rebellion in the white settler colony would put the gravest strains on the loyalty of the forces they commanded. The Chief of the Defence Staff and Chairman of the Chief of Staffs' Committee during the later 1960s was Sir Charles Elworthy, who had coped with the Kuwait operations and its implications. Healey accepted what Elworthy said about Africa.

Macmillan and his colleagues had grasped the political danger of intervention by British troops when the break-up of the Central African Federation led to demands from Southern Rhodesians for final independence. When Northern Rhodesia and Nyasaland became independent in 1964 (whites in the former accepting black rule knowing well their privileged economic position would be enhanced rather than otherwise) Southern Rhodesian demands became hard to resist, except on the basic principle that political *apartheid* did not accord with the precepts advanced by Macmillan in his 'Wind of Change' speech. But no real resistance was offered; Wilson merely happened to be Prime Minister when the inevitable happened. Frantic efforts were made thereafter to convince the world, the United Nations, even the British electorate that what the *New Statesman* loyally called 'the smack of firm government' was heard throughout Africa. For over a year, a British Governor, Sir Humphrey Gibbs, continued to fly the Union flag in Salisbury.

Southern Rhodesia was blockaded – by Order-in-Council. Royal Navy frigates patrolled the Beira Strait. Their task was to prevent oil tankers reaching ports from which Southern Rhodesia could be supplied. In practice, oil products, Southern Rhodesia's one indispensable economic need, continued to flow with undiminished ease by way of South Africa and Botswana (Bechuanaland), saved from Pretoria's grasp by the hurried grant of independence in 1966 but remaining economically dependent on its white southern neighbour none the less. SIS in Rhodesia duly reported the flow of oil by road and by rail from South Africa; train-watching was again the order of the day, the Station Officer in Salisbury, a careless young man, being declared *persona non grata* by the Smith regime for his pains. Despite the SIS reports, and much else besides, the Wilsonian illusion persisted that the rebellion would be defeated by blockade, world opinion, his diplomatic bouts with Ian Smith, the whirligig of time. In the meantime, Smith and his rebellious settlers flourished as never before. When not otherwise engaged, they gave full support to what the Wilson Government was also pleased to call the rebels in Nigeria. Such support would have been impossible without the flow of oil into Southern Rhodesia; the Company most directly involved was Royal Dutch Shell.[6]

Wilson was also impotent in Nigeria. Yet Britain's particular involvement in events there from the time the first violence began in 1966 was sustained and partisan. Above all, without a regular and mounting flow of arms and ammunition from stocks in Britain in the later stages of the war, the morale of Gowon's troops would have sunk to a dangerous level of disloyalty. But neither the scale, extent, nor nature of the involvement owed anything to political initiatives from No. 10 and little to the calibre of Wilson's foreign secretaries in 1964 and for much of 1967. Patrick Gordon Walker had been responsible for exiling Seretse Khama in 1949; as Foreign Secretary in Wilson's first Government he represented nothing more than the debt party politics owes, and sometimes pays, to loyalty.

Michael Stewart, who replaced Gordon Walker in January 1965, had the root of the matter in him; he understood not only the forces of history but also the realities of a post-imperial age, in which members of the permanent government and their colleagues in the field would make and execute as much of a foreign and commonwealth policy as Britain could afford – and, in Africa, the international business community would allow. But Stewart was replaced by George Brown in August 1966. This, however, was only a brief interlude in the execution of British foreign policy by Whitehall and the men on the spot. Brown's ability to fire some of his advisers with enthusiasm was not matched by a willingness to concede that the Foreign Office, collectively, knew more about the world than he did.

In March 1968 Brown resigned. Stewart returned to his former post, and made it clear to Wilson in his dry, clipped fashion that he was more than content to leave the Government's role concerning the Nigerian Civil War in the hands of his officials. These officials were well able to distinguish what was politically desirable from what was strategically possible and economically acceptable. Such delegation of authority left Stewart free to concentrate on dismissing vocal but unco-ordinated critics in the Commons and, as the war went into its second year, amongst his own Party. Stewart's hand was strengthened by three factors, apart from a conviction that his appreciations and decisions were correct. First, Dean Rusk stressed that Nigeria was not America's affair. 'We regard Nigeria as part of Britain's sphere of influence' settled the matter so far as Washington was concerned.[7] The American Government refused to supply arms to either the Federal Nigerian Government or the secessionist regime in what came to be known as Biafra. Commercial arms suppliers were refused export licences. Even an active Russian presence in Nigeria left Washington unmoved. The American Ambassador in Lagos took his cue from the High Commission, whose members looked at Russian activities dispassionately.

Second, Wilson convinced himself that he, and the Commonwealth, could play the peacemakers, an illusion which Stewart was careful not to dispel. In reality, such Commonwealth initiatives as occurred were mainly due to the organisation's Canadian Secretary-General, Arnold Smith. Wilson's belated visit to Nigeria, in March 1969, nearly two years later after the war broke out, was only notable for the fact that he carefully avoided meeting the 'rebel' leader, Odumegwu Ojukwu. Wilson had a series of meetings with Gowon, but the latter was more concerned to assert the justice of his cause than to express gratitude for the British Prime Minister's support. Various members of Wilson's Government visited Lagos during the war, and did so in increasing numbers as public protests in Britain about the supply of arms and the sufferings of the Biafrans were dramatised by the media. None of these visits affected the course or the conduct of the war.

The third factor which enabled Stewart to deflect public criticism at home and abroad was the increasing authority which changes in Britain's traditional international roles had given Whitehall in the making and not merely the execution of policies.

Stewart had no objection to being attacked in the Commons or by the media. He reckoned that as part of the job, allowing the permanent government to carry on unscathed, indeed usually unnoticed. Stewart's tactics succeeded, moreover, because the Foreign Office, between 1964 and 1968, absorbed the Colonial and Commonwealth Relations Offices. This merger indicated in bureaucratic terms that, because the Empire had been replaced by the Commonwealth, only one centre of Whitehall decision-making was required to help keep it in being.

The merger, however, was directly relevant to what Whitehall and, in particular, the men on the spot did before and during the war. Events in Nigeria between 1966 and 1969, and especially throughout 1967, can only be fully understood by a Nigerian or, at all events, a black African who belongs to or comprehends the nature of tribal systems, trying to survive in the context of 'nations', born from colonies established with arbitrary frontiers by imperial powers. But to the extent that the outsider can understand, and comprehend why Britain's agents, and others, were active in Nigeria before and during the war, appreciation of the importance of a bureaucratic structure designed to put many roles under one roof is essential.

The new Foreign Office (formally called the Foreign and Commonwealth Office from 1969) brought together divergent views about Nigeria and achieved, eventually, a synthesis from them. But SIS also changed. In 1967 White retired, and was replaced a year later by Sir John Rennie. He came from the Foreign Office but despite responsibility for the Information Research Department between 1953 and 1958 lacked that close connection with and understanding of SIS which distinguished many of his colleagues. The appointment was not welcomed in Century House, partly because Rennie's heart was not in the intelligence business, but also due to the belief of the men on the tenth floor that a professional SIS could find 'Cs' from its own ranks. Rennie did his best to work amicably with his new confrères but the appointment inevitably meant that relations between the Foreign Office and SIS changed still further from the mutual suspicions of the 1950s and the cautious cordiality of White's years as 'C'. Rennie did not consciously intend to weaken SIS or subordinate it to the Foreign Office. But Rennie's advent as 'C' meant that the Foreign and Commonwealth Office collectively came to regard SIS as part of Whitehall rather than as an independent service.

From the late 1960s, the duties of the Controller Africa in SIS were seen by his opposite numbers in the Foreign Office as a reflection of the policy which they made. The Controller Africa – still a relatively new position in 1967, reflecting changed priorities – found that the Foreign Office rather than the Ministry of Defence began to lay down the requirements. With direct military intervention in Africa ruled out, Joint Intelligence Bureau requirements were bound to decrease. In any case, the Defence Adviser at the High Commission in Lagos had his own, and very direct, line to the Nigerian armed forces. The Controller Africa was thus circumscribed in his tasks by the new authority of the Foreign Office and the diminished role of the Ministry of Defence. Rennie's arrival in Century House only completed a change which was bound to occur. Occasionally strained relations between the new Foreign Office and SIS were eased by the fact that the Permanent Under-Secretary for most of the war, Sir Paul Gore-Booth, had deputies who did know SIS and did appreciate what it was for.

The synthesis achieved about Nigeria has been popularly represented as one where the views of the old Colonial hands in the new Foreign Office were adapted with a few modifications here and there. These views can be summarised in a word: 'unity'. Nigeria had been given independence in 1960 on the basis of 'one country', not a collection of tribal factions. By 1963 nevertheless, these factions, poorly disguised as political parties, were threatening to split Nigeria wide apart. Although the High Commission in Lagos did not directly intervene in the hopes of reconciliation, its representatives continued to insist that unity for Nigeria – even when it took a federal form – was essential if the new nation was to survive. Nigeria should stay one country, because if it split into tribally dominated regions the inevitable result would be another Katanga. Unlike their political masters, most senior members of the Colonial Office had supported the idea of Congolese unity, indeed of African attempts to establish nations. Nigeria must not be 'Balkanised'. These views were misguided rather than disingenuous. Nigeria until independence and after it was dominated not only by the tribal factor but by the power of the huge Moslem Northern region over all other areas.

Critics of Colonial Office policy for Nigeria had always said that officials favoured the north, because of its superior culture, ability to produce good soldiers, and the cordial feelings of its rulers towards most things British. By contrast, the assorted tribes of the other regions were said to be regarded by Sanders of the River and his like as a bunch of money-grubbing traders or, on a more charitable view, simple sambos who had to be told what to do. The unity advocated by imperialists was, allegedly, no more than a device to ensure continued Northern domination. Although there is some historical foundation for this crude interpretation of the imperial rule in Nigeria, the fact of the matter is that by the 1960s economic considerations had replaced sentiment. These considerations governed the policies of the High Commission and the recommendations about unity which it made to London. Not only did the multinational trading giants, above all the Anglo-Dutch Unilever, continue to dominate Nigerian commercial life; by 1966 oil, discovered in the 1950s, was being produced at around 400,000 barrels a day.

This oil had three characteristics: it was produced mainly by BP and Shell, in partnership, but with Shell as the operating company; it was a new, non-Middle East source for the West's growing energy requirements; it came from the south and east of Nigeria. The Northern Region lost its dominating position once the oil began to flow. The Christian Ibos of the Eastern Region, scene of Shell's main activities, began to lift their heads from the Muslim yoke. The High Commission view of unity was adjusted accordingly. The Hausa-Fulani tribal confederations of the North, splendid in their isolation and pride, began to look like back numbers.

The violence of January 1966, which returned in May and July, and again in September and October, reflected a basic struggle for power between Hausa-Fulani and Ibo which was bound to break out eventually. In the first round the Ibos had their day, massacring the leaders of the former Northern ascendancy. Thereafter, the Hausa-Fulani took their revenge. Whatever the number of Ibos massacred in September and October, the one material fact is that the survivors fled to their tribal sanctuary of the Eastern Region and there found in Odumegwo Ojukwu – appointed Governor in January when elements in the Army staged the first military coup – one of their number who was less a soldier than an ambitious and envious contender for the control of Nigeria and of its increasing wealth from oil. By the time that Ojukwu's fellow Ibo had found sanctuary, a rump of the Army's surviving senior officers had appointed the minority tribesman Yakuba Gowon as Head of the Federal Military Government.

Whatever the tribal rights and wrongs of the issues which rent Nigeria in 1966 the essential political elements were the rivalries between Ojukwu and Gowon and their struggle to retain or acquire control of the oil revenues. Gowon was the High Commission's man, because he represented a unity which might be imposed from Lagos on regions by virtue of the fact that Shell paid its royalties and taxes to the Federal Treasury. But Gowon was the High Commission's man only for so long as he controlled the oil and secured those revenues. By early 1967, 10 per cent of Britain's oil imports came from Nigeria. Should another Middle East war break out and the flow of crude from there cease, that 10 per cent would become crucially important to the British economy.

Throughout 1966 the High Commission engaged in a process which can best be described as 'wait and see'. In early August Gowon, just installed on a precarious throne, saw the British High Commissioner, Sir Francis Cumming-Bruce and the American Ambassador, Elbert Matthews. Gowon was, and is, everybody's ideal of the nice African boy who becomes more British than the British in manner and turnout. He had impressed his British colleagues in the Nigerian brigade which served under the UN flag in the Congo civil war as a straightforward character and a competent soldier.[8] Gowon's manner, diffident yet direct, appealed to Cumming-Bruce, as it did to his successors. But Gowon had absolutely no illusions about British policy for a Nigeria which was producing crude oil. Gowon had also been convinced since the political manoeuvres of 1963 and 1964 that Ojukwu would eventually take the Eastern Region out of the Federation and turn it into an independent state, capable of surviving if it kept the oil revenues. Gowon saw Cumming-Bruce and Matthews with one simple question to ask: 'What will your governments do to help me if Ojukwu rebels?'

The directness of the question forced Cumming-Bruce and Matthews to prevaricate. They said the question was hypothetical. Ojukwu had shown no signs of rebelling. He had denounced the Federal Government's control of oil revenues, but had done nothing to stop Shell paying them directly into the Federal Treasury. High Commissioner and Ambassador, pressed by Gowon, were forced to reply with the cliché about Nigerian unity. Pressed further, prevarication crumbled. The truth came out: 'Preserve unity, and we can help you; abandon, or lose it, and you won't get a penny, or a cent, in economic aid or any other kind of support.' By the time this crucial meeting was over Gowon knew what Cumming-Bruce and Matthews meant: lose control of the oil and the revenues and you will be abandoned as far as Britain and

America are concerned.

In January 1968, Gowon and Ojukwu met at Aburi in Ghana in an attempt to work out a new constitution for a federal Nigeria. The need was to end tribally dominated regions; to devise new regions, which would enjoy reasonable autonomy from Lagos; and to allocate oil revenues in such a way that the Federal Government retained ultimate rather than immediate or automatic control. On paper, agreement on these necessities was reached. Whether Ojukwu ever intended to honour the 'Aburi Agreement' or whether Gowon was determined to crush him if he did not is rather academic. Nothing could alter the fact that although oil exploration was taking place throughout Southern Nigeria and production had begun west of the Niger, the Eastern Region held the key to the country's entire future.

During the war, Ojukwu succeeded in convincing many people that he was an idealist, only seeking independence and freedom for 'Biafra', as, from Aburi onwards he described the region of which he was Governor. In reality Ojukwu was Gowon's rival; with his 'people' behind him and Shell's revenues in his pocket, Ojukwu reckoned he was the man to wear Nigeria's crown. His point of view is understandable, but it is important to realise that Biafra's leader, who ran away to safety in the Ivory Coast at the end of the war and left his people to shift for themselves, was more interested in his ambitions than concerned with ideals.

In February Cumming-Bruce's successor, Sir David Hunt, arrived in Lagos, and the stage was set for a play of personalities which mirrored the conflict which broke out five months later. Hunt, appointed by Wilson – whom he had known since Oxford – with the injunction 'keep in touch' was an assertive character, very different from Cumming-Bruce. A career of unusual diversity – don, Chief Intelligence Officer to Field Marshal Alexander in the Second World War, a private secretary to Churchill, High Commissioner in Uganda and Cyprus – had given Hunt the not unreasonable conviction that he knew his way about the world, above all the one in which the permanent government played such a central role. Wilson's choice of Hunt cannot be faulted; Whitehall approved it. Here was a diplomat, with much experience of a Commonwealth which had been evolving since independence for India and Pakistan. Hunt had served in Nigeria before; he would be able to judge just how much, and how little Britain could afford to be embroiled in Nigeria's affairs. Malcolm MacDonald, Wilson's roving ambassador in Africa, did what he could behind the scenes to make the Aburi meeting succeed.[9] MacDonald was active throughout the Nigerian civil war in expressing the liberal spirit of painless goodwill. Hunt had the job of making bricks without straw.

The High Commission, which Hunt came to dominate with a personality not only assertive but masterful, uniquely represented the post-imperial age in terms of delegated diplomacy, aid projects, and public relations. Only the gunboats were lacking. The fourth largest British diplomatic mission (Washington, Delhi, and Paris exceeding it) Hunt's High Commission occupied a skyscraper in the middle of Lagos. All the embassies and the other Commonwealth High Commissions were downtown. Together with the Deputy High Commissions in Kaduna, Ibadan, and Enugu, the hundreds of officials serving under Hunt complemented an expatriate population of some 15,000, most living in the high colonial style. No mere routine decision ensured that an exceptionally pleasant if somewhat ingenuous Third Secretary joined Hunt's staff in 1967. Prince William of Gloucester was the first member of the Royal Family to become a bureaucrat. His posting to Lagos reflected Whitehall convictions that royalty could help to fly the flag. Soon, Prince William was dashing about Nigeria in his own aircraft. He showed a slightly touching interest in SIS. This interest was adroitly deflected: the Prince went to every party, picking up gossip which was occasionally more relevant to the political situation than Hunt and his senior chancery staff liked to admit.

Despite impressive public relations, the High Commission was a white elephant or, if not exactly that, a curious hybrid, an attempt to balance pomp with circumstance. The real British presence in Nigeria was commercial; Nigeria's problems reflected a personal struggle for power, to be settled, if conciliation failed, by force of arms. Hunt's High Commission could only exert a marginal influence on commercial issues, little on conflict between Gowon and Ojukwu. Hunt did not altogether accept these limitations, but they were realities none the less. The centre of Britain's commercial presence was the Shell offices and refinery at Port Harcourt, in no way answerable to the High Commission in Lagos. Shell at Port Harcourt had created an African Kuwait, an industrial society in a community of fishermen and peasants.

Shell, unlike BP, had rarely heeded the word of British governments or its official representatives, a fact of which Hunt was well aware. Over the years BP had established a particularly close connection with Whitehall, not excluding SIS. The latter's reports, sufficiently detailed, but only as to content, were distributed to the company's senior staff. The same connections could be found overseas. Shell executives, wherever they worked, avoided anything more than the most formal contacts with Whitehall, embassies, and high commissions. This independence was rooted in the past; both before and after the First World War, British governments had made strenuous efforts to buy a controlling interest in Shell. These efforts had been rebuffed. Shell went its own, commercially imperious way.

Thus the outcome of a civil war in Nigeria – by early 1967 the possibility was being freely discussed in Lagos – would be decided by factors which neither the High Commission nor Whitehall could directly change. Robert Scott, Defence Adviser in the High Commission, had been Gowon's Company Commander at Sandhurst and, in a paternal fashion, was a friend. Scott and 'Dear Jack' were, indeed, able to communicate in ways which eluded – and came to exasperate – Hunt. But Scott could deliver few of the goods which Gowon required. Moreover, because of his knowledge and experience of the Nigerian Army, and his easy access to it, Scott doubted its capacity to fight a short, decisive civil war. The sanguinary events of 1966 had robbed the Army of experienced senior officers. Advice on how to help Gowon would have been difficult for Scott to give even if the means to do so had been available.

The SIS factor in these equations complicated them. Two basic political requirements were laid on the Station in Lagos by the Foreign Office. The first requirement was intelligence about the attitude of the Federal Government towards British policies in Southern Africa. The second requirement was intelligence about Britain's two main rivals for political influence in Nigeria: Russia and France. The first requirement could, by and large, be met overtly by the High Commission Chancery, or a journalist of average ability. The Nigerian Government thought poorly of Britain's Southern African policies and measured its relations with the British Government accordingly. The High Commission, collectively, reported throughout the late 1960s that no Nigerian government could do other than despise and, where possible, oppose Wilson's conciliatory treatment of Ian Smith and South Africa. (Despite Wilson's refusal to supply South Africa with arms for 'internal security', his Minister of Technology, Anthony Wedgwood Benn, as he then was, arranged in 1969 for uranium to be bought from the Rio Tinto Zinc Corporation Company in South West Africa in order that Britain's nuclear weapons programme could be sustained.)

The second requirement begged several questions and, indeed, was based on various assumptions. Whitehall tended to exaggerate the threat from Russia and France to British interests in Nigeria. Yet Russia could not threaten Britain's commercial position in Nigeria, because no offer could match Shell-BP's achievements. France's theoretical power to injure Britain commercially was considerable, but threats would only become serious if de Gaulle's determination to weaken the grip of 'Les Anglo-Saxons' on the world of oil could be translated into effective action. In June 1964 Couve de Murville, de Gaulle's Foreign Minister, had written a four-page *aide mémoire*, in which the aim of weakening the grip was given as the priority French foreign policy. The BP office in Paris had acquired a copy of this xenophobic document. The Foreign Office, perusing it, found little of substance. French missions in the oil-producing States of the Middle East doubted that de Gaulle could do anything to change the oil scene. French oil companies were large and enterprising, but they could not compare with Shell or BP, let alone with major American concerns. In 1967 no fears were entertained in Whitehall about French designs on Nigerian oil despite the presumed influence – in the Organisation of African Unity and elsewhere – of the Francophone bloc.

So much for the paramount commercial factors. Broad political considerations were, of course, important, but there was little evidence to suggest that Russia could present much of a threat. There were few in Whitehall by January 1967 who could convincingly argue that any success had been scored by Moscow in penetrating West Africa. Initial, and superficial successes which came in the wake of independence for British, French, and Belgian colonies had been followed by a marked loss of political assets. Patrice Lumumba had been independent Congo's first Prime Minister, and Moscow's protégé; he had died at Tshombe's hands. Russian efforts to support Antoine Gizenga in Orientale, another Congo province with secessionist trends, had been thwarted by various means, including some robust operations in and beyond the Congo by SIS. Gizenga never received his gold from Moscow; it disappeared in Khartoum *en route*. The Station Commander in Léopoldville (a lady who, today, is a distinguished member of Oxford's academic establishment) was good enough at her trade for the Russian Embassy to report that there was little to be gained by supporting Gizenga, or any other opponent of the Western-backed Congolese politicians.

Moscow had made progress for a time in Guinea, but President Seké-Touré's refusal during the 1962 Cuban missile crisis to allow Russian aircraft to stage through the country on their way to support Castro had extinguished that hope for a West African bridgehead. Thereafter Moscow sought to penetrate by proxy; the German Democratic Republic Security Service took a hand, and began to do so in the middle 1960s in other supposedly Francophone states. Kwame Nkrumah in Ghana had been seen as an ally in the liberation of Africa from white commercial imperialism – it was thus that Russian ambassadors on the continent passed the word – but his fall from power on 24 February 1966 ended that relationship also. Russia had certainly been active in Ghana, and Nkrumah, from motives of caprice rather than considered policy, had given facilities for building airfields and the covert deployment of Russian military personnel which went a good way beyond diplomatic courtesies. When Nkrumah went so did these Russians.

One Whitehall argument which did have an airing after Nkrumah's fall was that so great a loss to Moscow would have to be compensated elsewhere, and next door but one if possible. Nigeria in turmoil would be seen by Moscow as something more than a target of opportunity; a Balkanised Nigeria would present singular opportunities for penetration. It did not escape Whitehall's attention that the Ibo – ostensibly the cause of Balkanisation fears – were Christian by faith and Roman Catholic by practice. They tended to favour native skills, from reasons of tribal background, and, because of missionary endeavour, a bourgeois and free enterprise approach to life rather than one derived from Marxist-Leninist doctrine. But neither did it go unnoticed in Whitehall, as the early months of 1967 presaged deepening crisis, that the Russian Ambassador in Lagos was Alexsander Iosisovich Romanov. After three years *en poste* Romanov understood Nigerian politics more than adequately.

That, however, was not the point. Romanov was an extremely experienced diplomat, whose three spells in London between 1948 and 1964 had given him a grasp of British policies which probably no other Russian official could match. When not in London, Romanov had specialised in British Commonwealth affairs. He had impressed all in London as innately shrewd enough to realise that Russian penetration in and of the Third World (a third of whose members also belonged to the Commonwealth) would have to be carried out by adaptation to the circumstances of the local scene. In Lagos, Romanov impressed those who chose to listen to him with his honesty in distinguishing between theoretical opportunities for Russia and the realities of Nigerian politics.

Nevertheless, Whitehall equated Romanov's appointment to Lagos with Moscow's selection of Nigeria as a priority target; after Nkrumah's fall this equation became an axiom. Hunt reported that Romanov was 'a good fellow but a bit rough on the tennis court'. This, in Whitehall's view, got one precisely nowhere. What did Century House have to say? The answer was unambiguous: Russian – and French – missions in West Africa must be targeted. The production of raw intelligence – above all on Russian objectives and methods in Nigeria – became a requirement which reflected much common ground between the Foreign Office and SIS.

Alexander Goschen, the Station Commander in Lagos, did not share, or accept, London's assumptions and the conclusions drawn from them. He did not agree with his Controller in London that the overall Whitehall appreciations about Romanov produced a requirement to carry out counter-intelligence operations against him. Goschen reminded the Controller that not only SIS but MI5 was represented in Nigeria; and that his deputy had been declared to the Nigerian Intelligence Service (which SIS had trained), and hence to the authorities in Lagos. These people could look after such operations. *His* job, as he saw it, was to acquire intelligence, by various means, about Nigeria as such; to provide intelligence which would enable the British Government to assess the overall Nigerian situation, and to reach a reasoned conclusion about likely developments. Goschen had no objection to hostile operations; he had taken part in a few. But he argued strongly, and repeatedly, that the intelligence requirement was for a detailed picture of Nigeria's internal politics; Romanov was, in effect, a distraction and an irrelevance.

Much latitude was allowed to Sandy Goschen, well described by one colleague as a man with 'a face battered by life'. His birth, background, war record, African experience, and rapport with Nigerians of all degree made him respected, and sometimes feared in Century House. A capacity for drink, for enormous hard work, combined with an endearing loyalty to all things British meant that the heresies of disputing a requirement and then advancing arguments in refutation of it were treated more leniently than would normally have been the case. Goschen said, in so many words, that Britain's job in Nigeria was to back the right man; the Russian factor was not important. If Gowon's intelligence service targeted Romanov's Embassy, well and good. If SIS could help, so be it. But Gowon would keep his counsel. What mattered was the civil war, which was going to come, and the outcome of which was important for Britain. The Station Commander did not trouble himself with the oil factor. Gowon, not Ojukwu, was Head of the Nigerian Federal Military Government. Lack of good intelligence about Ojukwu and his aims – reflecting the different roles, and skills, of SIS and NIS – may have contributed to this uncompromising attitude.

Eventually, after two years of argument, this idiosyncratic intelligence officer was told what to do, and it was done. But in early 1967 such trenchant views on the limitations of Britain's power to influence events; this virtual dismissal of the Russian factor; and these assertions about requirement for intelligence of *Nigerian* affairs were distinctly irritating to a High Commission whose Chancery members reckoned they knew a good deal about the local scene without the Station Commander putting his oar in. Hunt reckoned he knew something of Nigerian politics, and could play his part in resolving a crisis. Hunt, at Gowon's request, went to see Ojukwu in Enugu towards the end of March. Hunt met Ojukwu with the praiseworthy objective of averting war; he represented the full weight of the permanent government, *circa* 1967. But it was a paper weight, no more effective than Wilson's political government, because it could not decisively affect events. Hunt's High Commission reflected degrees of opinion, not a consensus for action.

Hunt could reason with Ojukwu; he could not coerce him. Hunt reflected that Ojukwu was 'the only Oxford man in the Nigerian Army'. But this graduate-soldier was also known to be inspired by Nasser. The chances for conciliation looked poor. They proved to be so. Ojukwu, on the brink, rebuffed Hunt, and prepared for secession, enlisting what support he could from Africa and elsewhere. On 27 May Gowon, after a series of 'final appeals' to Ojukwu, issued a decree, dividing Nigeria's four regions into twelve states; he also declared a state of emergency. On the 30th, Ojukwu announced secession and the establishment of 'the Republic of Biafra'. Thereafter, relations between Lagos and Enugu swiftly deteriorated, both sides seeking pretexts for coercive action, and increasingly taking it. Before war broke out on 5 July,

Ojukwu had an army, of sorts (most of the technical and support services in the Federal Army were recruited from Ibo, but few of the latter were found in the infantry), a rudimentary air force, and a natural conviction that if he could seize Lagos by marching across the Niger the crown would be his. In these opening moves Hunt and his High Commission played a role best described as 'hope for the best'.

Shortly after his Enugu meeting with Ojukwu, Hunt made certain recommendations to London. But these were more temporising than his published account of immediate and outright support for Gowon suggests. London heeded Hunt's caution, and temporised also. The Minister of State concerned, George Thomas, and his senior adviser, Sir Morrice James, were forced to procrastinate by circumstances dominated by the oil factor. When war broke out, 'wait and see' was still the order of the day. Gowon was the High Commission candidate – but Ojukwu sat on the oil. Shell's General Manager at Port Harcourt, Stanley Gray, was almost a confidant of Ojukwu; in the heady atmosphere of pre-secession Biafra, with Ojukwu asserting his right to power, the streets of Enugu full of marching soldiers, and trenches being dug by the roadside, Gray and the rebel leader remained in close and cordial contact. In April Gowon saw Hunt with Matthews and asked a direct, specific question: would Britain or America supply 'some old fighters and bombers'? Ojukwu, with $20 million in foreign exchange available, had acquired two obsolete American B26 bombers from the second-hand arms market. Gowon was well aware what a few bombs on Lagos might do to a Federal Government which was clinging to office rather than exerting authority. Gowon needed fighters and a few, retaliatory, bombers.[10]

Hunt had to think quickly. Would Gowon go to France or Russia if his plea was refused? If he did, what would the political price be? The Russians might hope for little (Hunt tended to agree with the Station Commander on this score) but French arms could hardly be supplied without the *quid pro quo* of an oil deal. Hunt was certainly prepared to back Gowon diplomatically; after his March meeting with Ojukwu, Hunt had instructed the Deputy High Commissioner in Enugu, James Parker, to tell the former that if Gowon attempted to embargo the Eastern Region's trade and freeze its assets, the British Government would support him. But at the April meeting it was clear to Hunt and Matthews that diplomatic support was not enough. An outright commitment was demanded.

Playing safe Hunt said, 'No'. Matthews had already said his Government declined to intervene. Gowon insisted that Hunt clear the issue with London. Inside twenty-four hours Gowon had been told: 'You will not get aircraft from Britain.' After hearing this message from Hunt, Gowon saw him to his car, saying: 'I will get them from the devil if necessary.' The devil proved to be Romanov. Gowon had no desire to let the French in. Romanov, betraying surprise rather than showing pleasure, asked for time to consider. Within a week Moscow said, 'Yes'. There was no catch; the arms were paid for. By August a small number of Russian aircraft had arrived in Nigeria. Russian technicians were sent also; the aircrews were Egyptian. It was left to the Station Commander to salve something from the derelict state of Anglo-Nigerian relations, which were not improved by rumours that the British High Commission would be defended from Ojukwu's bombers by Bofors anti-aircraft guns sent post-haste from home. The Ministry of Defence in London agreed to find some Royal Air Force personnel who, for a consideration, would be prepared to become civilians on Gowon's payroll. These mercenaries were given the task of flying Gowon's few British training aircraft in an operational role. Nobody in Lagos had much faith in the capacity of Egyptian aircrews to shoot down Ojukwu's bombers or hit Biafran targets.

Whilst the Lagos High Commission was digesting these various problems, and as Ojukwu's levies marched along singing, 'If you've never been a soldier you will never ever be happy', a six-day war had been fought between Egypt and Israel, raising the world oil stakes to a level which made immediate British support for Gowon virtually impossible. The war, between 5 and 11 June, not only blocked the Suez Canal, but caused the Arab oil producers once more to boycott crude destined for Britain. North Rumaila was finally and totally seized by the Iraq Government. At a stroke Nigerian oil assumed critical importance. Some journalists in London, who rushed along to BP and Shell for a background briefing, found the latter's Supply Department calmly monitoring the situation, confident that the Cape route would more than compensate for the Canal's closure and that increased Iranian – and Nigerian – production would meet the shortfall caused by what was correctly assessed as a boycott of limited duration. By the time the Nigerian Civil War broke out, Shell in London and Port Harcourt was firmly of the opinion that Ojukwu was the man for their money.

The first months of the war thus imposed a degree of equivocation on the Permanent Government which accurately, if unwittingly, reflected the dilemma of backing the right man. Fortunately for Britain, rather than Nigeria, the early months saw Ojukwu lose the oil war through an odd, if fortuitous, combination of anger on his part and strategic perception on Gowon's. Both men fancied themselves as strategists, but Ojukwu had the big ideas whilst Gowon believed in husbanding his resources. Ojukwu's attack across the Niger, which began on 9 August, had the double objective of capturing Lagos and employing the Trojan horse of the Ibo minorities west of the river. But Ojukwu was too late. Pre-empting him, Gowon ordered an amphibious operation in late July which, on the 25th, resulted in the capture of the port of Bonny. Port Harcourt was sealed off. Ojukwu might lay his hands on Shell, but no oil could be exported from Biafra whilst Bonny remained in Federal hands and the Federal Navy blockaded the coast. The capture of Bonny and the blockade (both owing something to the discreet support of Royal and Indian Navy personnel) settled one major strategic issue, and did so for the duration of the war.

Ojukwu, however, was determined to seize revenues which Shell would normally have paid to Lagos at the end of September. Hard cash would buy more bombers. On 27 July, Ojukwu arrested Shell's General Manager, Stanley Gray; incarcerated him (in some comfort) in the Presidential Hotel in Enugu; and threatened punitive action against Shell employees, if sums, variously estimated at between $500,000 and $five million, were not immediately paid. Gray knew Ojukwu well enough to realise that he could turn very nasty indeed. Wisely, he signalled London for support. Just over three weeks later a Shell Managing Director, Frank MacFadzean, arrived in Enugu, with a cheque in his pocket. In Indonesia, during the 1965 civil war which ended Sukarno's rule, MacFadzean had seen Shell employees in acute danger 'from violent men with whom I had some sympathy but whose demands I had to resist.' He had no intention of caving in to Ojukwu; but neither had he the slightest intention of putting the interests of the British Government, or of Gowon, before those of his Company and the men – and families – who were on the spot.

After Gray's arrest, MacFadzean sought the opinion of Britain's foremost international lawyer, Elihu Lauterpacht, who stressed that, 'Payments made under duress to a *de facto* regime do not breach contracts'. Armed with this opinion, MacFadzean confronted the Foreign Office, rejected appeals to bear 'wider considerations' in mind, and flew to Lagos. He saw Gowon, whose pleas were similarly ignored. MacFadzean did not see Hunt – 'a waste of time'. Forty-eight hours after leaving London, MacFadzean was sitting in Gray's hotel room. He had not, as the BBC reported, 'struggled through the jungle'. He had flown to Enugu in a Shell aircraft. But MacFadzean, although an old campaigner, was preoccupied. The stakes for Shell were as high as they were for Nigeria and Britain. If Gowan won, Shell would be needed in the new Nigeria – provided Lagos had received revenues for oil actually produced, *or* if MacFadzean had outwitted Ojukwu. If Ojukwu won, Shell, co-operating, would be pre-eminently in a favourable position. If Ojukwu won without Shell's enforced co-operation, he would remember who had been his friends and who had not. There were other oil companies to which Ojukwu could award prizes. The cheque in MacFadzean's pocket was for $47 million, due to the Federal Government for the entire third quarter tax and royalty payment, not for a calculable 'Biafran' share, or a sum which might keep Ojukwu quiet, buy arms – and produce the release of Shell's employees and their families.

MacFadzean did not have long to wait. Shortly after midnight Ojukwu arrived, conveying an air of menacing affability. Banalities were exchanged; MacFadzean was determined not to be drawn. But he was tired. Without thought he referred to Ojukwu's 'rebel regime'. The balloon went up. Ojukwu jumped from his chair, towering over MacFadzean, a Scot built like a bulldozer. 'Nobody calls Biafra a rebel regime. It is a sovereign state. You will see.' Ojukwu then slammed out of the room. 'This is it', thought MacFadzean. 'He'll want the lot, and he'll want it now.' Four hours later, Gray was summoned to Ojukwu's headquarters. MacFadzean refused to go. Gray was back in the hotel in no time. 'We're to get out now, all of us, with a safe conduct to Port Harcourt. He says we're out, for good.' MacFadzean had one question: 'What about the money?' 'Didn't mention it; still too bloody angry, I suppose.' Twenty-four hours later all Shell staff and families had left Ojukwu's territory. MacFadzean's cheque was still in his pocket. Back in London he again went to the Foreign Office. 'They were quite pleased.' Britain could back Gowon, after a fashion, but with growing conviction that Ojukwu's real assets had vanished in that flash of rage. Gowon had enough foreign currency to pay for the war; in January 1968 he changed the

Nigerian note issue; 'Biafra's' currency was, with few exceptions, rejected by the outside world.

And that, in a sense, was that. Ojukwu had neither oil to sell nor cash with which to buy arms. Federal forces outnumbered Biafra's, and although Ojukwu's 'Directorate of Propaganda' persuaded international liberal opinion, South Africa, Southern Rhodesia, Portugal and four African states (Gabon, Ivory Coast, Zambia and Tanzania) to support him, Gowon more than countered by gaining the overwhelming backing of the Organisation of African Unity. The Nigerian Intelligence Service, with a little help from its mentor here and there, penetrated the OAU Secretariat, enabling Gowon to assess which member states supported him and who needed persuasion or conciliation. From the 14th September 1967 OAU summit Kinshasa (formerly Léopoldville) onwards, Gowon consistently outmanoeuvred Ojukwu in repeated and protracted negotiations with the one organisation which could be said to represent African hopes and fears. Liaison between SIS and NIS provided London with a better picture of pan-African developments than could be gained from any other source. One piece of intelligence thus acquired, and somewhat ruefully digested in London, was Nasser's influence in an OAU with which he had been associated from its founding in 1963, and in which he played an elder statesman role with growing success. Gowon, not Ojukwu, learned from Nasser how to manage an international gathering. The OAU's members were not interested in Gowon's Christian sincerity; they wanted him to win the war, once the essential issue of oil had been settled, because they genuinely feared African Balkanisation.

Whitehall at last read the signals correctly, basing its policies on a deepening conviction as the war ground on that British support must be confined to the supply of arms and ammunition; the OAU factor; the covert role of ex-RAF personnel; and the improvement, where possible, of the Federation Army's operational standards in the field. In September 1968, despite blockade, heavy Biafran casualties, and a Federal offensive across the Niger, stalemate on the ground led to a scheme whereby British military intelligence officers were attached to Federal formations. These officers were sent to Nigeria in order to inject experience into a large uniformed force which was an army only in name. The decision to support the Federal Army by this method reflected not only lack of real strategic resources but also de Gaulle's belated support for Ojukwu.

In August 1968 de Gaulle, although continuing to recognise the Federal Government, ordered Biafra to be supplied with arms as part of the policy summarised three years earlier by Couve de Murville. Ojukwu made promises to the partly State-owned Compagnie Française des Petroles; secret deals were concluded in Paris; lovers of mystery had a field day. The SIS Stations in Paris and Lisbon reported that the arms were insignificant in number and type, but the prolongation of the war which they caused and the suffering which ensued forced Scott's hand. He reported on the inadequate performance of Federal forces; in London, the Foreign Office, SIS, and the Ministry of Defence organised the intelligence officers. An International Military Observer Team of senior officers from Britain, Canada, Sweden and Poland furnished suitable cover – unwittingly so for the neutral members.

Yet Biafra fought on; a year after French intervention Ojukwu appeared to be gaining new friends. President Nixon was making the kind of noises associated with big business and international politics; French oil interests were looking into crystal balls; the Federal Army, despite its covert support from Britain, was still bogged down in the scrub and jungle of Western Biafra. The war was an enormous human tragedy for Nigeria; to the world outside it had become, after two years, a wonderful opportunity for the stage army of the good, a great temptation for those who like to get their fingers into pies. But the end, in fact, was at hand. One man's ambition, his people's courage, and vested interests had sustained a struggle for national rights – or a rebellion – during two and a half years of inconclusive, inexpertly waged war. Reduced to their heartland, short of food – but not starving – the Biafrans retreated upon Enugu. But there was to be no last-ditch struggle. On 11 January 1970 Ojukwu decamped to the Ivory Coast. Betrayal hastened defeat. On the 12th, Major General Philip Effiong, 'Officer administering the Biafran Government', surrendered to Gowon. The war was over.

There was neither recrimination nor retribution. Gowon could afford to be generous. In restoring unity to Nigeria he rewarded rather than punished. Shell-BP flourished, rebuilding Port Harcourt, training Nigerians. But there was a delayed, a very late grinding of the mills. In June 1979, BP and Shell jointly warned Lord Carrington, the Foreign Secretary, that unless British Government policy on Rhodesia was totally changed their company in Nigeria would be nationalised. Nigerian governments had come and gone; the commitment to ending white rule in Southern

Africa had not changed. The warning was ignored. During the Commonwealth Conference of the following August, the Nigerian Government did nationalise. British Government policy changed, too late for the oil men.

8 · A BITTER KINGDOM: IRELAND, 1972

Some day we may recover the builder's eye which we lost a hundred years ago. Some day we may acquire, what as a race we have never possessed, the historian's eye. Is it worth acquiring? I think it is. Any serious and liberal habit of mind is worth acquiring, not least in an age which the increase of routine and specialism on one side, the extension of leisure and amusement on the other, is likely to make less liberal and less serious. But if I needed another argument, I should say: look at Ireland. There we have the great failure of our history. When I think of the deflexion and absorption of English intelligence and purpose by Ireland, I am inclined to regard it as the one irreparable disaster of our history; and the ground and cause of it was a failure of historical perception: the refusal to see that time and circumstance had created an Irish mind; to learn the idiom in which that mind of necessity expressed itself; to understand that what we could never remember, Ireland could never forget. And we live in an age which can afford to forgo no study by which disaster can be averted or eluded.

G.M. YOUNG, *Victorian England*

Come all you young rebels
And list' while I sing,
For love of one's land
Is a terrible thing.
It banishes fear
With the speed of a flame
And makes us all part
Of the Patriot Game.[1]

The one sustained attempt during the last decade to confront head on the enduring tragedies of John Bull's other island reached a climax on 7 July 1972. In a tall Chelsea house by the Thames and in a drawing room hung with paintings by those Edwardian masters Greaves and Sickert, eleven men sat round a table to talk. William Whitelaw, the British Home Secretary in a Conservative Government, supported by Foreign and Home Office officials (one of the former a senior SIS officer), met five leaders of the Provisional Wing of the Irish Republican Army and one from the Provisional Sinn Fein.

Whitelaw and his advisers did not meet with gunmen in the same spirit as Lloyd George and his colleagues had met with Irishmen in London fifty-one years before. Then the British Prime Minister had planned, and made, a deal whereby the twenty-six southern counties of Ireland, overwhelmingly Roman Catholic in religious observance, achieved quasi-independence from the British Crown. In return, Arthur Griffiths, Michael Collins and their Sinn Fein colleagues accepted that the six northern counties would not only remain under the Crown, but would do so on a constitutional basis which was intended to deny, and did for fifty years deny to the Roman Catholic minority political rights, religious toleration, and economic prospects. The six counties which became known officially as Northern Ireland, had always been called Ulster by the Protestant two-thirds majority. In those two names, and the latter's historical associations – the ancient province of Ulster comprised nine counties, three of which are now in the Republic of Ireland – lies much of the reason why Britain's last colonial campaign is still being waged.

The meeting in July 1972, although in direct historical descent from the deal, the 'Treaty', made in December 1921, and indeed from all the events preceding and following it, was held in response to Irish demands, to an insistence by the Provisionals that they should be allowed to state their case directly to the British Government. The meeting was originally intended to comprise only one member each of the Provisional Sinn Fein and IRA. Once other, more militant figures demanded a place, most British officials involved in Northern Ireland saw the meeting as no more than a gesture. But there were also officials who wanted the meeting to take place in order to discover whether some Irishmen, who lived by the gun and gloried in their race's tradition of violence and martyrdom as symbols of a nation, might be persuaded to accept that the six counties could be transformed from a battleground into another, quasi-independent state, with equal rights for all. These officials were also members of the Permanent Government. Their service in Northern Ireland, dating from late 1969, a year after another cycle of violence began, had convinced them that such a transformation was possible – if the Provisionals and the Ulster Protestants handed in their guns.

There was a further premise which these officials shared rather than articulated: they had played a crucial, covert role in the formation of a democratic political party, the Social Democratic and Labour Party, which they saw as an acceptable alternative to the Provisionals, and one which would be accepted by Northern Ireland's Catholics. In short, Whitelaw's official advisers who were of a moderately optimistic bent did not believe that the Provisionals spoke for their suffering fellow Irishmen; the latter could be weaned from their enforced support for a terrorist organisation.

The nominal backing for these efforts came from Edward Heath, a Prime Minister whose interest in Ireland at the time was slight, and whose convictions about it rested on the proposition that, after 800 years, British governments should be quit of a commitment which was expensive, humiliating and, in the last resort, impossible to sustain even by the one method on which British authority had always rested: coercion. 'It cannot be denied that simple repression remained a standard instrument of British rule in Ireland throughout the whole period of the Union (1801–1921).'[2] This historical truth applied to conditions in Northern Ireland, *circa* 1972, and had been appreciated by the Labour Government Home Secretary in 1968, James Callaghan. It was he indeed who set in train the processes which were to evolve behind a foreground of violence and brutality. The processes were utilised by the Conservatives, Heath and Whitelaw. To Heath, a Prime Minister who had, a bare six months before the July 1972 meeting, brought Britain into the European Community – realising a personal ambition of many years' standing – the entire situation in Northern Ireland reflected the anachronisms, not the accidents of history. Heath shared with his advisers the illusion that Ireland was a problem not a tragedy, and that, in consequence, common sense could be applied to issues there.

The meeting was a failure, if seen in the perspective of Irish history and that hope for a united Ireland which few Irishmen wholly reject and which so few Englishmen can even begin to comprehend. The violent men found the demands which they made were unacceptable to the politicians – above all for the phased withdrawal of British troops. They found Whitelaw's demeanour hostile, their claims to speak for Ireland derided, and then rejected. The provisionals, who had been brought from Northern Ireland in some secrecy and at considerable risk to all involved, returned to their version of a holy war. By mid-July Whitelaw had publicly admitted the meeting taking place, thereby alienating Ulster Protestants and the Dublin Government in roughly equal proportions. The Protestants also have gunmen, and they could claim a bloody, 300-year-old history of asserting their hatred of Roman Catholicism and the supposed disloyalty to the British Crown of its Irish adherents. Like the Provisionals, the Protestants' reaction to the meeting in London was violent.

In the light of events during the following eighteen months, culminating in the Sunningdale Agreement of December 1973 and the 'Power-Sharing Executive' for Northern Ireland which was thereafter established, the meeting was not a complete failure. Men of courage and goodwill in Northern Ireland, and even in that Republic of Ireland which had achieved its final and total independence from the British Crown only in 1948, met with Heath to plan a future for the six counties which was to be based on equal rights for all citizens – and the guarded hope of eventual unity. Governments in Dublin, committed enemies of the IRA, Provisional or otherwise, were unable to resist the dream of a united Ireland even if they doubted its realisation. Prime Minister Jack Lynch and his successor Liam Cosgrave, heirs to the men who made the 1921 Treaty, had learned that compromise was not possible with nihilists. Nevertheless, the men of goodwill were not deterred. The Sunningdale Agreement was a peculiarly Anglo-Irish achievement.

Thus for eighteen months, indeed until May 1974, hopes for the future were entertained, seeming to be stronger than fears that the violence wrecking Northern Ireland would destroy it. The hopes proved false. It was the Power-Sharing Executive which was destroyed by a mass Protestant strike in May thus bringing Northern Ireland to a standstill. There was neither power, water, nor sewage once the men came out. In February Heath had fought and lost a General Election brought about, such are the other ironies of history, by a total failure to grasp what was happening in the world of Middle Eastern oil and his uncharacteristically panic-stricken conviction that the British economy was about to be wrecked by the combined, if unconcerted, efforts of oil producing countries and the National Union of Mineworkers. A combination of increased oil prices, some decrease in supplies from the Middle East following the October 1973 Arab-Israeli war, and a miners' strike put Britain on a 'three-day week'. Heath asked the electorate's support for tough measures. He failed to get it. Heath was succeeded by Harold Wilson, who had striven late in 1971 and early in 1972 to throw new light on Irish problems. But in 1974 Wilson led a weak Government and a troubled Party, neither of which had the temper for a fight with Ulster's armed, militant strikers. The strike – a proletarian rebellion against the Crown – could have been broken only if Wilson had been prepared to take immediate, punitive action, bring power workers and maintenance staff from Britain, use the Army, and risk the consequences.

Men of goodwill were thus reminded that bigotry is as effective a prescription for Irish, or Ulster, patriotism as the bullet and the bomb. There were precedents enough. It was not necessary for historically-minded Irishmen (and who amongst them is not?) to go back those 300 years to the siege of Londonderry by the Catholic James II. The siege had been raised by the Protestant William of Orange. Before and after the 1921 Treaty the 'Orange pogrom' against Northern Irish Catholics had matched in ferocity anything occurring elsewhere in this island. Orangemen had declared before and during those years that, as in the 1880s, 'Ulster would fight and Ulster would be right'. In 1912, a Conservative politician, Bonar Law, had assured his fellow Ulster Protestants of Scots Lowland descent: 'You hold the pass for the empire.'[3] Law, when in opposition, reminded a Liberal Government that Ulster would fight to remain outside a 'Home Rule' Ireland and for the right to stay within the protection of the British Crown. It may be permissible to doubt the reality of a united Ireland; it is not a useful historical exercise to doubt the reality of Ulster nationalism. The motto of the old Orange Order was 'a barrier to revolution and an obstacle to compromise'.

Since May 1974 the sectarian civil war in Northern Ireland – and it is essentially that, not a war simply to destroy or preserve the British connection, and unite or keep separate North and South – has fluctuated in intensity. A long period of relative stalemate in the later 1970s was followed by renewed violence, and in 1980 and 1981, recourse by the Provisional IRA and Sinn Fein to that most hallowed of martyrdoms, the fast to death. Unable to maintain political standing amongst the Catholic community, defeat the British Army in Northern Ireland by guerrilla war, or mount terrorist operations there and in Britain on a scale to weaken the resolve of British government and the British people, the Provisionals have reverted to type, to a version of Irish history which demands from the true believer that the accumulated wrongs of the past stand witness for the violent acts and agonising deaths of the present.

Men, women and children continue to die violently and be maimed horribly, but it is the ritual death and the sanctified burial – the Provisional firing party over a comrade's grave using live ammunition – which wracks all with a fragment of reason left, yet continues. 'I wish to God it was all over. The country is gone mad. Instead of counting their beads now, they're counting bullets; their Hail Marys and Pater Nosters are bursting bombs . . . and their creed is, I believe in the gun almighty, maker of heaven and earth – an' it's all for the glory o' God an' the honour o' Ireland.'[4] O'Casey's philippic on his countrymen and his times applies today.

Pseudo-religious hysteria is no stranger to Ireland. But its manifestations always harden the Englishman's heart against a people with whom understanding has rarely been possible. When fighting for their rights, the Irish have been called rebels, and treated accordingly. To Queen Elizabeth 400 years ago, who so described them, the remedy was 'Thorough': coercion savage enough to be remembered today. Under another Queen Elizabeth, the same description is given and similar treatment recommended whenever violence returns or intensifies. But when to rebellion is added an hysteria which can even influence hard men in Dublin, the English become contemptuous and dismissive. The Irishman, from being an amusing rogue, a music hall joke, feckless, dirty, and improvident (an assortment of racial prejudices which has no parallel for inaccuracy), becomes a foreign devil. The English and Irish today are alienated as never before.

The July 1972 meeting and its twenty-two month aftermath do

not reflect a complete illusion. These attempts by a British Government to move forward into an era of reconciliation and adjustment – and on a matter which for at least a century has had an international dimension and a direct bearing on Anglo-American relations – did reflect Heath's acceptance of a changed role for Britain in the making and execution of its foreign policies. The men of goodwill were not peddling dreams. Neither members of the Permanent Government between 1969 and 1972, nor their successors serving in Northern Ireland, have suffered from illusions about the problems to be faced and the opposition to be met. Failure between 1972 and 1974 was not inevitable. But the belief that commonsense could prevail – up to a point – and that compromise was a necessity which only a fool, if not a fanatic, would deny, was widespread. To see why this was so, and to grasp why some basic illusions about Britain's capacities – rather than its roles – persisted it is necessary to summarise aspects of Irish history. We must then consider the attempts at negotiating compromise in a context where the Northern Irish Catholic and the Ulster Protestant are at least united by the conviction that the Englishman is imprisoned by history. Like Catholic rebel and Protestant patriot he cannot, or does not escape.

The imperial mind is an official mind. Rule has been by division, whether to conquer, coerce, concede, or reconcile. Since 1945 British imperialists have accepted division in India, Palestine and, in effect, Cyprus. A theoretical belief in unity has never prevented a bureaucratic conviction that divided dependencies could become client states. The Central African and South Arabian Federations were established on the basis of this conviction. In the imperial high noon, Nigeria and many other colonies were divided between a small area of directly ruled territory, which formed a hinterland to Government House and the Secretariat, and the protected but usually indirectly ruled areas which lay beyond. Kipling's 'Lesser breeds without the law' meant tribes living beyond this small area of absolute imperial rule. The precedent was the fourteenth century 'Pale' (literally, fence) in Ireland, within which English rule was absolute, beyond which chieftains, elevated to barons and earls, swore fealty to a Plantagenet King but retained control of tribes dimly conscious, if at all, of their imperial overlord.

Comparisons with modern Ireland are relevant, if only in the British bureaucratic mind and are not, historically, far-fetched if one remembers the seventeenth century Ulster 'Plantation' – the deliberate planting by Stuart kings of Scots settlers less than twenty sea miles from their own shores. One should also remember the fact, so often forgotten, that the oddity of an Irish Parliament with authority to debate but none to decide was opposed in the eighteenth century as much as it was accepted, and utilised, by Catholic and Protestant Nationalists alike. But neither could agree on what form opposition should take. A mere century ago, Lord Randolph Churchill's discovery of genuine Ulster nationalism convinced both his Party and Gladstonian Liberals that the latter's 'Home Rule' was a prescription for dividing the loyal Protestant from the malcontent Catholic. In the process, British Governments also discovered that Irish nationalists were themselves divided between those who sought independence by Parliamentary, by constitutional means – and hence were prepared also to accept a divided Ireland – and the gunmen, 'the bold Fenian men' who were determined on nothing less than unity.

Thus it is neither surprising nor unnatural that the Permanent Government in the late 1960s and early 1970s should have believed in divide and rule, and related it to a policy, belated enough, of coercion, conciliation and compromise. Irish unity remained an aspiration at Sunningdale, not an element in policy. Shaw's quondam priest, Keegan, makes the point: 'There is a saying in the Scripture which runs – so far as the memory of an oldish man can carry the words – let not the right side of your brain know what the left side doeth. I learnt at Oxford that this is the secret of the Englishman's strange power of making the best of both worlds.'[5] When the English Broadbent – not unlike Edward Heath in his hard-hearted moral earnestness – rebukes Keegan for misquoting Scripture, for confusing brain with hand, the Irishman is unabashed. No Englishman will believe he can be wrong, especially about Ireland. The Englishman, in effect, sees division as a rational compromise – which a rational Irishman can accept. The Englishman's search for rational Irishmen – as he would define the adjective – has been a long one.

But for a more particular precedent to illustrate this singularly English mixture of coercion and blandishment, this unique English belief that he can see into the mind of the other fellow – even an Irish mind – we must look at what happened between 1912 and 1921. In those nine years, Asquith and Lloyd George achieved a compromise which appeared to justify the prescription of divide and rule. The two prime ministers were aided by much of the British Army's support for the armed Protestant Ulster Volunteer

Force; the Orange pogrom; thugs in a version of British uniform – the 'Black and Tans'; and an intelligence organisation rooted in the fact that coercive rule since the Union had depended on a gendarmerie and an official magistracy capable of penetrating subversive organisations and producing informers. Lloyd George in 1921 destroyed the fragile unity between constitutionalists and gunmen which the Dublin rebellion of Easter 1916 had appeared to forge. The Easter Rising proclamation, 'read aloud to a sparse and almost completely uncomprehending audience', spoke nobly: 'In the name of God and of the dead generations from which she receives her old tradition of nationhood, Ireland, through us, summons her children to her flag and strikes for her freedom . . . We claim the right of the people of Ireland to the ownership of Ireland and to the unfettered control of Irish destinies to be sovereign and indefensible . . . The Irish Republic is entitled to, and hereby claims, the allegiance of every Irishman and Irishwoman.'

Six years later, the leaders of that rebellion executed or exiled, the constitutionalists signed a Treaty which seemed to confirm the truth of Lloyd George's belief that Irishmen would accept division to escape persecution. Perhaps, claiming as he did, the insight of a fellow Celt, Lloyd George was right, but the civil war in the South which followed the Treaty revealed that attempts actually to destroy the idea, or ideal, of a united Ireland only breed fresh horrors. The IRA fought their erstwhile Sinn Fein allies by ambush and assassination, by methods which ensured that when the 'Irish Free State' emerged into the light of 1923 its rulers would repress those who had not accepted the Treaty with a severity equal to anything achieved by the British. That free state had so emerged by fighting a civil war in which the decisive military element in the initial stages had been the discreet, but outright support of the British Government.

No Prime Minister of the Free State was harder on the IRA than that 'constitutional Houdini' Eamon de Valera, whose participation in the 1916 Rising, equivocations thereafter, and desertion of his colleagues is not forgotten in the combined mythology and demonology of modern Irish history. The sixteen years of de Valera's rule (1932–48) were marked by two factors, neither of which has had the attention it deserves: suppression of the IRA was prosecuted so vigorously that its members were driven increasingly to mount and execute terrorist operations in Northern Ireland and Britain; liaison between the British and Irish intelligence services survived Ireland's declaration of a Republic in 1938, flamboyant neutrality in the Second World War and the final, constitutional break with Britain – withdrawal from the Commonwealth – in 1948. This political reality of an independent Irish Republic was accepted by the Attlee Government in 1949, with the proviso that any exploration of the possibility of a united Ireland would only be made with the consent of the Northern Ireland Parliament.

The period between 1948 and 1968 was, superficially, one of those cycles of relative stability in Ireland, during which a new generation of gunmen is bred and the old processes of blandishment and coercion continue unchanged and unchecked. Irish governments began a slow pursuit of economic development. The power of the Irish Roman Catholic Church – always inimitably difficult for the foreigner to define or establish – appeared to lessen. The IRA remained a proscribed organisation – as it is today – its members hunted and imprisoned. Northern Ireland existed, in reality, as a self-governing colony where the jackbooted, armed policeman was a more familiar sight than tolerance or progress. Despite minor IRA campaigns in the 1950s, the Royal Ulster Constabulary, Protestant almost to a man, kept the security lid screwed down. What simmered beneath was ignored. The British soldier, after fighting in Korea, Malaya, Kenya, or Cyprus, called Northern Ireland 'Happy Valley'. Not more than a brigade at any one time in those twenty years was stationed there. British governments also ignored Northern Ireland, and the existence there of Catholic British subjects, all but a few of whom lacked votes, decent jobs, and hope.

Yet during this long, deceiving time the processes of history continued to work inexorably. All political parties in the Republic declared unity to be indefeasible. In the North, a new generation of lower middle class Catholics who had benefited from some improvements in education and living standards (R.A. Butler's 1944 Education Act, which raised the school leaving age from fourteen to sixteen, has also much to do with the formation of the Social and Democratic Labour Party) slowly began to ask themselves whether they must forever remain a depressed and coerced minority.[6] Northern Irishmen in the IRA emerged from the shadows of a Gaelic past. The North had bred revolutionaries in that past, but now, for the first time, a distinctive type emerged: born in a slum in Londonderry or Belfast, or raised in the no-man's land of South Armagh: Catholic by parental influence but caring little for priests or Papacy; a true Northerner, different in revolutionary sentiment from his nominal compatriots in the South. The latter had become careful, increasingly prepared to accept the Government in Dublin or turn their intermittent energies to propaganda work for the legal Sinn Fein and attempt to put some colour in its rather threadbare rhetoric. The Northern revolutionary had urban poverty to give an economic, neo-Marxist edge to a bitterness feeding on alienation and despair. This was, this is, a new factor in the history of the Irish revolution from imperial rule, and it is one which caused the IRA internal convulsion in 1970 and its offshoot – the Provisionals – dissension in 1972 and thereafter.

Northern Ireland governments continued to be an amalgam of Anglo-Ulster gentry and Belfast businessmen, dominating Parliament at Stormont Castle and well able to ignore the Catholic Members which a gerrymandered constitution ensured would remain but a handful. The different Orange lodges reflected these Protestant social divisions, but unity was effectively maintained by the necessity to equate ascendency for their faith with repression of the Catholics. But, by the middle 1960s, a new type of Protestant politician was beginning to emerge. In Brian Faulkner, a rich bourgeois who was believed actually to know some Catholics, observers could detect further signs of change.

Nevertheless, such observers, able to mark these almost imperceptible changes in the monochrome pattern of Northern Ireland life, were to be found neither in the Royal Ulster Constabulary nor in the bureaucracy of Stormont. Unlike their forebears of the Royal Irish Constabulary and the Resident Magistrate, the RUC and the bureaucrats were almost totally ignorant of the nature of subversion, let alone the identity of revolutionaries. The RUC Special Branch files on suspects had one simple characteristic: virtually all were Catholics. The possibility, even to a professionally inclined Special Branch officer, that terrorism should not necessarily be equated with one community simply did not exist. Extreme Protestant resentment at Faulkner and his like and the conflicts which might result were ignored by policemen who, on the kindest view, suffered from sectarian myopia.

Acute violence erupted in Londonderry on 5 October 1968; neither the Government of Northern Ireland nor its executive officers were prepared or comprehending. The historian of the IRA has written: 'Nationalism in Ireland is like electricity flowing through a covered flex. It is powerful and unseen until someone frays the covering.'[7] But on that October day in Londonderry the covering to the electricity of Northern Irish Catholic nationalism, flowing through a flex of many strands woven tightly together by the forces of history, was frayed by intolerable circumstance, not deliberately cut. The frayed flex revealed the strands; the coercive authorities of the Northern Ireland Government were unwilling to recognise what had happened; to the extent that they did so, no resources were available to cope positively with the event. Coercive authority always assumes conspiracy, relies on precedent, hopes to identify and prefers to attack the doer rather than analyse the deed. The Civil Rights Association march on that October day reflected frustrated nationalism but it also expressed, in a crude and bewildered way, the longing of ordinary people for the ordinary things of life – jobs, homes, children growing up in a community, not herded into a ghetto.

These things were as important as, arguably more significant than, the nationalism. James Callaghan and Whitehall then, and later, recognised the truth. Members of the Permanent Government, also trapped in the past, never quite realised the implications of their energetic, persistent, increasingly covert attempts to give Northern Ireland's Catholics the chance to live as free men, but the achievements greatly outweighed the failures. The Northern Ireland Government, collectively, was indifferent to the truth. So too were the IRA and the Sinn Fein. The Provisional dissenters from these widely discredited movements came to recognise the complexities of protest because they knew Northern Ireland. But, as revolutionaries, republicans, heirs to nihilism, much influenced by contemporary theories of liberation, guerrilla war, urban conflict, and terrorism, the Provisionals made the classic mistake of savagely coercing the Catholics of Belfast and Londonderry into, briefly, supporting them. Seamus Twomey and his kind would not have been allowed even to pack the explosives in a properly organised liberation movement, much less to use them.

The Civil Rights Association was formed in 1967. This was a year of dissent and disorder throughout much of Western Europe and the United States, only to be exceeded by the events of 1968. The CRA's origins were due to resentment at housing discrimination in favour of Protestants finding a spokesman in a young Stormont MP, Austin Currie. A beneficiary of the Butler Education Act and, that rare thing, a graduate of the Protestant Queen's University of Belfast who represented Catholics in Stormont, Currie in 1968 lacked pronounced political ideas and was immune from republican influence and motives. Nevertheless the

CRA acknowledged some help in its formation and the establishment of moderate political objectives from the National Council of Civil Liberties. This quintessentially English organisation, heir to Victorian liberalism rather than twentieth century radicalism was, and is, regarded with dislike and suspicion by MI5 and the Metropolitan Police Special Branch as the home not merely of barrack room lawyers but as a kind of staff college for political agitators.

From its inception the CRA was seen by the Royal Ulster Constabulary Special Branch in Northern Ireland as the Council's poor, but equally demagogic relation, not merely liable to infiltration by republicans but actively welcoming their support. The fact that Northern Ireland's Prime Minister, Terence O'Neill, was, in these restless years, slowly moving towards proposals for ameliorating the Catholics' economic condition – without fundamentally changing their political lot – convinced the zealots of his Ulster Unionist Party that in resisting their leader they must also crush the CRA. Between its formation and October 1968 the CRA had undoubtedly become a political movement, seeking amongst other unexceptional demands (or what would be seen as such elsewhere in the United Kingdom) 'one man, one vote'. In Northern Ireland, in 1968, the Government controlled a voting machine which not only denied votes to Catholics but ensured plurality to Protestants.

When, therefore, Currie, in protest at a particularly flagrant piece of housing discrimination, organised the 5 October march, the RUC was ready and waiting with batons and jackboots. An earlier march had gone off peacefully. Londonderry was to be different. Even an apologist for Ulster and all its Protestant loyalties was moved later to write that 'members of the Royal Ulster Constabulary and the Special Constabulary lost their heads and shamed their uniform'.[8] Many policemen, in fact, behaved with courage and restraint in the face of undeniable provocation. It would be naive to suppose that decades of grievance culminating in a 30,000-strong march would not attract the *agent provocateur*. But the Special Constabulary, a part-time gendarmerie which was virtually the private army of Ulster Unionism, needed little to provoke its collective hatred of the minority. Without rhetoric it can be said that history frayed the flex on 3 October 1968. The march became a battle, further repression and mounting agitation the only victory. The RUC was mauled also, and it became at once clear to O'Neill and his colleagues that Ulster could no longer govern itself.

O'Neill sought help from Wilson's Government because he lacked both coercive and political authority. The RUC and Special Constabulary could only intimidate a cowed minority; a militant one, whether penetrated by agitators or not, was beyond their means. O'Neill lacked political authority because his Party opposed even modest reform. Faulkner, for all his ability to ride two horses, had no intention of breaking his political neck by supporting O'Neill. The latter's appeal to Wilson at once put the Government of Northern Ireland in commission, in fact if not in name. Wilson was quickly aware of this truth. In delegating authority to Callaghan – who, as Home Secretary, was constitutionally responsible for Northern Ireland – Wilson, in effect, delegated it to the Permanent Government.

Although Callaghan at once showed great energy and determination in forcing O'Neill and his Cabinet to accept change as the price of survival – specifically British troops to provide a disciplined internal security force – the logic of events imposed effective executive authority on those from the Foreign and Home Office who, by October 1969 were well entrenched in Stormont. By then Northern Ireland was, indeed, a battleground. Catholics and Protestants were at war. The IRA was hesitant and uncertain, but a Protestant bigot, Ian Paisley, had begun to emerge as the one politician in Northern Ireland able to sway a mob or stamp on compromise.

Callaghan, in his lucid and objective account of these events and developments, makes the point.[9] From the outset, he contemplated the imposition of direct rule, and let the increasingly harassed O'Neill know that this was no empty threat. Lloyd George's deal with Ulster's Unionists had provided for the loss of self-government *in extremis*; this state had arrived. That a Labour Government which was taking sides in an African civil war should seek impartially to arbitrate the issues in an Irish one was a political contradiction lost on the Cabinet at Stormont. Congenital indifference and inherent hostility to reform had rendered the Cabinet impotent. Such a condition aroused the strongest feelings in those members of the Permanent Government who had been sent to this most recent of Britain's colonies. Sir Philip Allen, Permanent Under Secretary at the Home Office, was credited with saying of O'Neill and his colleagues: 'None can be trusted; all are second-rate.' This was neither true nor fair. Under pressure, the necessities for constitutional change became the mother of political invention. But Allen's remark reflected the shock of men who simply had not realised what Northern Ireland was like.

Whilst Allen and his colleagues began the implementation of change – modest enough, but drastic by Ulster standards – Callaghan planned two other, more basic reforms. The Foreign Office would provide the equivalent of a Resident, with a Deputy, to act as the Government's or 'United Kingdom' representatives. This move was designed to enlarge the scope of the British Government's intervention, and to prepare for more drastic moves, above all the encouragement of Catholic political activity as at least a partial antidote to an expected republican campaign. Such moves would inevitably mean appraising the intentions of the Government in Dublin. Several times Callaghan had to remind Stormont that it was Her Majesty's Government which was responsible for relations with the Irish Government. The Foreign Office was, therefore, the obvious source for a new kind of man on the spot. Those who were sent, beginning with Oliver Wright, pro-consular in appearance and, occasionally, in manner, soon found their hands full. Neither diplomatic nor colonial experience provided much by way of precedent. O'Neill's enforced resignation in April 1969 made matters no easier. His successor, James Chichester-Clark, another Anglo-Irish Guardsman, was, fairly obviously, no more than a caretaker Colonial Premier. There was no longer room for gentlemen in Ulster politics.

The imposition of Whitehall, quasi-imperial authority aroused considerable feelings in political and bureaucratic Stormont. Ulster politicians' loyalty to the Crown was in inverse ratio to the latter's authority over them. Real opposition, however, was reserved for Arthur Young, appointed by Callaghan in October 1969 to be Inspector-General of the RUC. Young, who at the time of his appointment was Commissioner of the City of London Police, had great presence, much post-war colonial experience, liberal ideas, and was liked and admired by Callaghan. None of these attributes, found both necessary and sympathetic by the men from Whitehall, endeared Young to the RUC and its Stormont compatriots. Callaghan's insistence that the Special Constabulary was a menace and must be disbanded caused a major row. The 'B-Specials', Protestants to a man, their weapons kept at home, their capacity for selective vendetta unlimited, were the linchpin of the entire Ulster system. Callaghan had his way. By the beginning of 1970 there were 8,000 troops in Northern Ireland, nearly thrice the number in 1968. Callaghan left Chichester-Clark in no doubt that he would take these troops out if he was opposed. The 'B-Specials' went.

Callaghan's intervention and the activities of his advisers posed a direct, if subtle challenge to the IRA. Between 10 January 1970 when, at a meeting in Dublin, both the IRA and Sinn Fein split and 7 July 1972, the Permanent Government at Stormont and the Provisionals in Northern Ireland fought a campaign as intense and deadly as that waged by a British internal security force increasingly committed to guerrilla war. Catholic militants turned parts of Belfast and Londonderry into staunchly defended citadels, providing sanctuary for a Provisional force of approximately 1,300 men, well-armed and trained, poorly led but heavily financed from bank raids throughout Ireland and by sympathisers in America. Indiscriminate bombing and calculated murder was preferred by the self-styled 'Sean MacStiofain' and his comrades to political indoctrination or selective attacks on British Army units. The Protestants built their citadels also but until the first appearance in August 1971 of the Ulster Defence Association – mirror image of the Provisionals – concentrated on riotous mobs to pay off scores on Catholics or tie down the Army. The latter rarely penetrated the Catholic citadels, but when it did so the arms and munitions discovered there provided evidence enough of the Provisionals' aims and strength.

Heath's advent as Prime Minister on 14 May 1970 made no difference to the level of violence, or to the determination of Northern Ireland's *de facto* colonial government in its pursuit of change. But there were two fundamental shifts in momentum. In 1970, Heath appointed a General Officer Commanding who, like the United Kingdom Representative, was ordered to report to him direct. In 1971, Heath also decided that SIS must start to operate in Northern Ireland. These two moves were to have considerable impact on the political and intelligence factors which governed the period in question. In particular, the moves were made when British and Irish intelligence was paying particular attention to the division of the IRA and Sinn Fein into conciliatory and militant camps. In November 1969 the official IRA had decided to 'recognise' the Governments in Dublin, London – and Belfast. The Irish Intelligence Service came to the conclusion that this decision indicated not only a fundamental change in republican politics by the IRA's senior officers but would also lead to a virtual rebellion against it by the younger elements – the future Provisionals. These men would concentrate on Northern Ireland, whilst retaining links with the South. Improved co-operation between Dublin and London became urgently necessary.

Once the Army was committed to active operations – throughout 1969 and 1970 primarily to containing violence by separating the antagonists – the intelligence requirements became paramount. Foreign and Home Office officials had decided views on these requirements, differing in some important respects from those of the Army. Soldiers and civilians agreed on one point, however: the RUC Special Branch had poor intelligence, in terms of calibre, method, and result. Late in 1970 Heath approved the appointment of a detached, reflective Scots Guardsman, Vernon Erskine Crum, as GOC. He died from a heart attack shortly after his arrival in Northern Ireland. In Erskine Crum's place, during February 1971, was appointed Harry Tuzo, an extrovert gunner. Commanding an infantry brigade in the undeclared war with Indonesia, Tuzo had operated with the confidence sprung from the acquisition and rapid distribution of first class intelligence, much of it due to the Special Air Service Regiment. SAS penetration of Indonesian territory was one of the keys to success in a war waged by the Wilson Government resolutely and at great financial cost.

Tuzo and his subordinates, like their civilian counterparts, could not but be affected by recent experience. The British Government's representatives had also risen to senior rank during the long post-war years of de-colonisation and its aftermath of covert British involvement in former imperial territories. But the combined experience thus committed to Northern Ireland reflected latent differences of conviction and approach to the business of preparing people for independence or keeping them in that state afterwards. The anomaly of Northern Ireland, reduced to utter dependence on the British Government, sharpened these differences. The Whitehall civilians, from the outset, believed that a political solution required, indeed largely depended on, political intelligence in both the broad and technical sense. The formation of the SDLP in September 1970 provided a basis for political action, none, on the face of it, for political intelligence. The civilians were determined to remedy this deficiency – as they saw it – and use the SDLP for contact with, not penetration of, the Provisionals.

The Army, whose senior ranks were not devoid of men given to political theory, argued that in fighting a guerrilla war political and military intelligence was indivisible. By extension – rather than definition – the Army's Command and Staff thus tended to believe that intelligence should be their concern and co-ordination of it their responsibility. The urgent need not merely to contain violence but to end it brought the differences into the open. Arguments about intelligence ensured that a Prime Minister who believed in giving orders would decide to appoint either a GOC or a Representative who, in co-ordinating security operations would, in effect, control them. The arrival of MI5 on the Northern Ireland scene – primarily because Provisionals had targeted Britain for bomb attacks – complicated the issue. Heath, before making his decision, turned to SIS. By early 1971 some new ideas were badly needed.

Sir John Rennie was still 'C' when Heath turned to SIS. Rennie, however, was not only due to retire in two years, but was unsuited, from lack of experience and inclination, to add Northern Ireland to the Red Book. His Deputy, Maurice Oldfield, dealt with the requirement – and with a Prime Minister given to command rather than consultation, Rennie signed the directives in the green ink exclusive to 'C', but his Deputy did the work. Oldfield, in 1973, became the first 'C' to be appointed from within the Service, a man from whom writers of fiction greatly benefited but, in fact, an interesting enough individual in his own right: 'Moulders' to the Office, Maurice to his intimates – never a large number – a scholar by inclination and training, an intelligence officer through the fortunes of war. The Derbyshire farmer's son who rose from a sergeant in field security to 'C' had, however, no interest for Heath. But he saw in a fellow bachelor a like professionalism. There was no co-ordination of intelligence in Northern Ireland. The establishment of an SIS Station within the Representative structure would ensure that there would be.

This ruling was, in a crude way, a victory for the civilians, a fact which the soliders deplored rather than resented. The Army continued to conduct intelligence operations which went well beyond the military field. Until SAS committed a squadron to Northern Ireland in 1974 these operations were conducted neither with imagination nor success. But even SAS found Northern Ireland totally different from Malaya, Southern Arabia, Borneo, or Oman. Cross-border operations in Ireland seemed a challenge to be met rather than a political factor to be considered. The Irish Government was more than willing to co-operate with British security forces provided they showed some understanding of the need for intelligence, in both senses of the word. Tuzo and his brigadiers saw the point; others did not.

Initially, Oldfield presented a reasoned case to his Prime Minister that SIS should not operate in Northern Ireland, part of a United Kingdom which was the preserve of MI5. He said, with some point, that SIS did not operate in England, Scotland, or Wales. A bad precedent would be established if it began to operate in Northern Ireland. Heath was indifferent to these niceties – as they must have seemed to him. Heath was much impressed by SIS penetration of the EEC and its members, but was otherwise never happy with its seemingly ambiguous place in the scheme of things; his years as Prime Minister were marked by occasional brushes with Oldfield, some faintly comic, some distinctly odd. On one occasion SIS was ordered to search the remote island of Socotra because of reports that Russians were about. SIS duly reported that Marco Polo's isle was inhabited by date growers and fishermen. Heath was not convinced. Two officers were sent back to find some Russians. Again they reported all was well. Eventually Heath accepted the fact, perhaps arguing to himself that as he was free from obsessions about Russia SIS could well be right. Heath was indeed tolerably free from such obsessions, and Oldfield's objective grasp of Russian aims and methods was something to appreciate in critical matters. Northern Ireland was critical enough – 'the gravest problem which the Government had to face' as one of Heath's few confidants has said – but at no time did the Russian bogey distract attention from the search for clues to a solution.[10]

Possibly, Heath's clarity of vision about Northern Ireland convinced Oldfield that opening a Station there would not create a precedent. By the Spring of 1971 SIS was on the ground. A very large, pipe-smoking Arabist, a veteran of Suez and the Sudan, was the first to arrive. He was, fairly quickly, replaced by officers whose intelligence experience was matched by diplomatic gifts. They executed tasks both overtly and covertly within the 'United Kingdom Representative' structure, a further indication that, in the 1970s, the Foreign Office and SIS began working as part of the same team. Although nothing approaching effective liaison with the Army, the RUC – or MI5 – was achieved for many months, the arrival of SIS did have one crucial effect. It added to the Foreign Office strength on the ground, and this was to mean that not only the overt acquisition of political intelligence but the mounting of covert counter-intelligence operations could be justified as requirements by the overriding necessity to find a political solution.

Oldfield sent officers who understood the nature of political intelligence, were persistent in its acquisition, and were capable, above all, of recognising that Northern Ireland was, indeed, a place apart.

The issue which brought argument about intelligence to a head was internment without trial, debated for nine hours by the Cabinet on 5 August, decided not only through the unusual process of vote but by a majority of one. Home and Lord Carrington (the Foreign and Defence Secretaries, and thus directly involved in Ireland at all points) opposed internment. Reginald Maudling, the Home Secretary, supported it, arguing, in Chichester-Clark's words of some months earlier, that 'the Provisionals had declared war on the British Army'. 'An acceptable level of violence', in Maudling's characteristically offhand language, could no longer be contained. But the Army strongly opposed internment – as did the Permanent Government members at Stormont – knowing that the only intelligence source which could 'justify' seizure of those suspected of harbouring Provisionals or secreting weapons was the RUC list of Catholics. An operation which interned Catholics and ignored Protestants would produce a reaction not only violent in itself but of great advantage to the Provisionals.

These views were very strongly put to Heath by Tuzo's fellow gunner George Baker, the Chief of the General Staff, a man of considerable stature in every way. Nevertheless Heath, reluctantly, agreed to internment. In March 1971 Chichester-Clark had resigned, forced from office by the same pressures which had been applied to O'Neill. Faulkner became Prime Minister and, menaced by Paisley, proceeded at once to demand from Heath that war, in effect, be made on the Catholics. In the summer of 1971 Heath was still avoiding the central issue in Northern Ireland: direct rule. For the first – and last – time he gave way to Faulkner. Internment followed.

Operation *Demetrius* – the Army's role in rounding up those on the RUC list – was carried out on 9 August. There were two entirely predictable results: the Provisionals escaped, a leading member, Joe Cahill, taking great pleasure in boasting of the fact. Violence intensified, with the Army for the first time suffering casualties on a scale which put Northern Ireland in front of every British family. If a referendum on retention or withdrawal of troops had been held in Britain during late 1971 there is little doubt what the result would have been. Other results were less predictable but, in retrospect, were all but inevitable. Support for the Catholics in Northern Ireland became international, enabling the Provisionals to increase their funds, imposing on every Irish-American the duty to remind the British Government that past wrongs and present miseries were alike evil and unacceptable. Senator Edward Kennedy called Northern Ireland 'Britain's Vietnam'. This was a misleading comparison, but the emotion which lay behind the words was genuine enough.

Of greater importance than American rebukes was the effect of internment on the SDLP. Its members had become increasingly critical of the Army's role as 1971 ran its bloody course; in July 1971 the Party withdrew from the Stormont Parliament in protest at the deaths of two Catholics, shot by British troops. The SDLP reaction was a blow to the Representative and his colleagues. It was small comfort to these hard-pressed officials to know that G2, the Irish Intelligence Service, had co-operated on *Demetrius* or that twelve of those interrogated after internment had provided useful intelligence. Heath, to his credit, ordered interrogation by methods barely short of torture to be stopped, but further damage to Britain's international reputation had been done. The intelligence yield was absolutely no compensation and, in any case, had little value in determining the extent to which the Provisionals had created, or could create, a militant political movement in the Catholic population as a whole.

What was entirely unpredictable and unexpected was the way in which the Provisionals then proceeded to miss a unique opportunity. No movement involving a majority of Northern Ireland's Catholics in revolutionary activities was created – and none exists today. In a situation which a Castro, or a Makarios, could have exploited, the Provisionals continued on their mindless course of bombing and revenge. 'The IRA's profound disregard for civilian life', as one of the bravest and most perceptive journalists covering Northern Ireland at the time has written, was only exceeded by the Provisionals' total inability to comprehend the nature of the conflict or the longing of Catholics for peace and security.[11] There were men in the Provisional Sinn Fein who, although given to violence on occasion, saw what was at stake and sought to educate their terrorist compatriots. David O'Connell, then Vice-President of the Provisional Sinn Fein, a schoolteacher of some acuteness and possessing surprisingly wide contacts, knew that Twomey and MacStiofain were the worst possible advertisement for Irish nationalism. O'Connell's colleague Ruari Braidaigh took much the same view, although, as an older man, he was unable to escape from the conviction that legitimate political business could not be carried on with a British government.

Such politically-minded Provisionals lived in the Republic, were, indeed, Southern Irishmen. The difference in background and outlook between Northern and Southern revolutionaries increased as the former killed the innocent and the latter argued for compromise. Even within the ranks of the Provisional IRA men could be found whose feelings were not wholly blunted. But these men were gradually eased out of command and went south. In their place came the utter fanatics, the founders of the Irish National Liberation Army. These assassins made contact with similar groups in Europe and the Middle East, but did so when police, intelligence, and security services in many countries were beginning to work closely together in the fight against terrorism. In the process, the tragedy of Northern Ireland became confused in some minds with 'international terrorism' and the hidden hand of the KGB. No such confusion existed in the minds of those fighting Northern Ireland's battles.

Given these factors the Army's action in Londonderry on Sunday, 30 January 1972 in shooting thirteen unarmed men in twenty minutes during a banned march by the Civil Rights Association can only be explained by the reasons given and discovered after the event. The British Army unit engaged in Londonderry on that day was a battalion of the Parachute Regiment, which had been ordered to contain violence and arrest trouble makers because of its particular training, experience, and discipline. The battalion, on being warned for this operation, was told that individual commanders and soldiers could exercise an 'independent' interpretation of the standing order, based on English common law, that fire should only be *returned*, or, alternatively, opened on a reasonable supposition of being attacked. The subsequent enquiry – which exculpated the Army as a whole from unnecessary coercion, and specifically exempted the soldiers who fired from disciplinary measures – nevertheless showed conclusively that they had, indeed, interpreted the standing order 'independently', and that unnecessary civilian deaths were caused as a result.[12] Equally there is little doubt that some members of Heath's Cabinet and some Senior Army commanders in Northern Ireland favoured a policy towards Catholics there in their presumed general support of the Provisionals which was, if not punitive, near enough to it to be regarded as such by men and women who simply wanted to live in a community based on some semblance of justice and opportunity.

In January 1972 neither the United Kingdom Representative and his staff nor the British Government realised that Catholic support for the Provisionals was limited, and was waning. If they had known it, they would have urged Heath to stay the Army's hand, a factor of which some of the latter's more zealous formation commanders were well aware. Army attitudes had hardened since internment; the military cemetery outside Lisburn was the scene of regular firing parties.

For the Representative (Howard Smith) contact with Catholics remained limited, compared to an enforced relationship with a Protestant Northern Ireland Government which was still functioning after a fashion. Despite the determination of the Representative to look for political clues as an alleviation of Northern Ireland tragedies, his day-to-day work was primarily implementation of the various changes which had been framed by Callaghan and accepted by Chichester-Clark. Faulkner was unwilling to co-operate with the Representative on these matters; the latter had his work cut out to make any progress at all. Even on security issues, Faulkner claimed a role which was denied alike by events and responses to them. The SDLP's opposition to the Army's role was not only a blow to co-operation but further reduced contact with Catholics at the level which mattered – the harrowingly drab, shattered streets of the citadels. SIS had not yet made headway. In January 1972 the Representative and his staff, whose predecessors had been ordered by Callaghan to 'bring a very direct influence to bear on the politics of Northern Ireland', were still operating in the dark.[13] Over two years had passed but little had been achieved. The UDA and Paisley remained an obstacle to compromise.

The 'Bloody Sunday' of 30 January remains a tragedy which no amount of analysis can defend. The burning of the British Embassy in Dublin on 2 February reminded Lynch that there were limits to co-operation. Members of Trinity College, young men of impeccably bourgeois antecedents and inclinations, members of a class which prefers Ireland prosperous to militant, destroyed more than a beautiful house; symbolically, both Lynch and Heath were reminded that the deep Irish hatred of British wrongs was burning again. Unless something drastic was done, and pretty quickly, even the Provisionals' total failure to understand the issues would become irrelevant; the Catholics of Northern Ireland would fight their own war and would seek help from any group, or government, prepared to offer it. 'Ministers went back to first principles on Ireland. A completely new policy had to be devised.'[14] On 24 March, direct rule was belatedly, reluctantly, but unambiguously imposed not only on Northern Ireland but on a Faulkner whose summons to London was made solely to strip him of office. Whitelaw became the first Secretary of State for Northern Ireland. Faulkner was allowed to resign, as was his Cabinet. The Stormont Parliament adjourned, after fifty-one years of inglorious life. Northern Ireland continued to be represented at Westminster by directly elected members but, for all practical purposes, a new dependency of the Crown had been established.

Fortified by Heath's courage in facing the central issue, the Representative and his Deputy decided to take some special political action on their own account. With Whitelaw's arrival the office of 'United Kingdom Representative' ceased to exist, but the same men carried on. Operating with great caution, employing the various overt and covert resources available, contact was sought and obtained with Catholic individuals and groups beyond the known areas of authorised protest and dissent. On one occasion a member of the SIS was constrained to remind his IRA contacts: 'If you shoot me there will be rather a row.' The point was taken, but this covert search for political compromise remained dependent on unusual resources of courage and imagination.

Contact was also renewed with the SDLP. The objective was to assess whether the Provisionals, north and south of the border, were open to persuasion and compromise. At least one of Tuzo's brigade commanders, Frank Kitson, was hostile to these moves: 'We beat the terrorists before we negotiate with them.' This was a prescription which had been successfully applied in Kenya; it was not applicable to Northern Ireland. Whitelaw's officials in touch with the SDLP said firmly that the British Government was not out to beat anybody but to seek workable compromise by the most appropriate means. Belatedly, in the Spring of 1972, the Permanent Government began to make decisions, above all to operate within the Catholic community, specifically to locate and penetrate the Provisionals. Whitelaw by this time had become what the Army rather sourly called the 'Court of Appeal' on all security and intelligence issues; although it was a court which rarely sat, contact with the Provisionals had the Secretary of State's tacit consent.

The SDLP was the intermediary in the early stages of this operation, not only because its members knew where to find the Provisionals but because Currie and his colleagues had to re-establish good relations with Whitelaw's Office in order to regain political credibility with a British Government which was collectively still lukewarm about Roman Catholic problems and arguments. Currie concentrated on contacts in the Republic; Paddy Devlin and John Hume on Londonderry and Belfast. These three frustrated politicians had been arguing for months that if a cease fire could be made and honoured, the Provisionals would talk. The intransigent would find their pretensions exposed; the conciliatory would make offers. In order to achieve such contact Whitelaw's Office and the SDLP knew that the Provisional Sinn Fein was more important than the bombers in the citadels. Hence Currie's, and others', visits to the Republic. Hence also the decision to co-operate with Lynch and the Irish Intelligence Service – but only up to the point where new, overt political initiatives for Northern Ireland might be described and discussed. Those working for Whitelaw knew that the Irish Government, as a matter of principle, neither negotiated with terrorists nor co-operated with governments which did so.

At what point contact becomes negotiation is, of course, a matter for subjective interpretation. The SIS appreciation by mid-June was that 'the fish had to be taken from the water', namely that the Provisionals' inability to wage effective guerrilla war should be exposed – but that an offer to negotiate with them should nevertheless be made. This view reflected intelligence from reliable sources – SIS operating covertly – that 'Chairman Mao would have discerned a perceptible cooling of the water in which his fish of revolution swam'. The Catholics in the citadels who told SIS about the evils of Provisional terrorism had not read Mao on revolution and did not use such language. There was no need; the evidence of failure was clear. But, by the same token, the Catholic population was waiting for leaders who could fight their battle. The SIS task, therefore, was to take advantage of the Provisionals' failure but also, and concurrently, to use direct rule for an entirely new approach to Northern Ireland. Obviously this was Whitelaw's objective also – once the full implications of direct rule sank in – but most of his time in the first three months as Secretary of State was spent in persuading Faulkner and the Unionist Party that no deals with Catholics were in train.

A cease fire was the first requirement. An earlier attempt, in September 1971, had broken down after a few days. Success in another attempt required the SDLP, SIS, the Provisional IRA, the Provisional Sinn Fein, and the British Army in Northern Ireland to work together, overtly and covertly. Another of Tuzo's brigade commanders, Anthony Farrar-Hockley, who operated on the principle 'in strange territory it's as well to have guides', played his part in renewing contacts with the Provisionals. Concentrating on Londonderry, meeting at night in safe houses, risking their lives, the parties to this positive conspiracy succeeded, on 22 June, in negotiating a cease fire. The order to MacStiofain and his fellow commanders came from Dublin. It was not well received, but it was obeyed. The cease fire was a remarkable achievement for all concerned. Yet it led those on the British side to believe that the Provisionals were a totally discredited organisation, its leaders not only rejected by the Catholics in the citadels but of poor quality as revolutionaries.

There was little of the usual British failing to appreciate the Irish mind in this case. As often happens when antagonists are driven to unusual forms of contact, personal relationships, intermittently cordial, in one instance of mutual respect, developed between men of utterly disparate background. 'Goodbye, good luck' – the invariable conclusion to telephone talks – became more than a formula. But it is possible that a subtle mind on the British side would have realised the necessity to be deft in negotiation for a political settlement, not merely intelligent and persevering in arranging a cease fire. The Provisionals' acceptance of a cease fire had been contingent on a meeting with Whitelaw. This demand had been accepted by Whitelaw and welcomed by some of his advisers. Unfortunately, others tended to assume that because the Provisionals were discredited they compensated for failures by total intransigence in making demands. A deliberately planned approach to the meeting with Whitelaw would have, or should have, produced proposals on the British side which the Provisionals might have found hard to reject. Such an approach would have given the Provisional Sinn Fein the chance to remind their compatriots in the north where power in the revolutionary movement really lay. In 1972 the Provisional Sinn Fein was the source of the Provisional IRA's funds; the former could provide sanctuaries in the Republic, or deny them.

A further barrier to a successful meeting was the attitude of the Secretary of State to negotiations with terrorists. He showed no relish for the encounter. Whitelaw, a man 'whose heart ruled his head' as those about him agree, was prepared to make concessions in order to encourage hopes for a cease fire, but agreed to meet the Provisionals only at their insistence. Whitelaw also lacked a clear mandate from Heath to spell out the implications of direct rule. Whitelaw had not told the Protestant community that a new era began in Northern Ireland when direct rule was imposed. If Whitelaw had been able to convince Protestants that times had changed it is possible that all but the most extreme amongst them would have supported him. Whitelaw would then have had a negotiating card. Whitelaw was quite capable of generous emotions about political causes – he became a Zionist from serving as a young soldier in Palestine, not by studying the arguments – but was unwilling or unable to involve Heath directly in the immensely difficult business of taming the Protestants, conciliating the Catholics, and offering a card to the Provisionals. Heath had imposed direct rule; let that rule be imposed. Whitelaw, an energetic, open man – a conservative Callaghan, minus the guile – was in the position so familiar to British ministers when dealing with Ireland: responsibility without power, the power of prime ministerial, Cabinet, party political backing.

Whitelaw was only partially involved in negotiations for a cease fire. He disliked subterfuge. He was no Lloyd George. Above all, Heath's determination to exclude Lynch from any role in a wider political settlement limited the choices facing Whitelaw in any meeting he might have with the Provisionals. Heath, using an agent of his own, a distinguished retired soldier, an Irishman of old-fashioned loyalties and unusual intellectual depth, reckoned, at the time, that the Irish dimension could be confined to ruling the North with justice and mercy. Yet the Irish Government's simple opposition to the IRA, official and Provisional, extended rather than diminished the British Government's requirement to make choices about Northern Ireland.

In July 1972, however, Heath and his Cabinet had not yet accepted the fact that getting a good price for the termination of a commitment there – the cost of direct rule was reckoned to be one million pounds a day to the British taxpayer – depended on an open approach to Dublin. Because Lynch would have rejected negotiations with the IRA it does not follow that he would have opposed discussions with Heath about Ireland's future. There is some irony in the fact that in the early months of 1972 the British Government allowed its official representatives in Northern Ireland to negotiate with the Provisionals – with terrorists and revolutionaries – but refused to contemplate discussions with a legitimate Irish Government.

Plans for the 7 July meeting in London, therefore, were made from conclusions about the situation on the ground rather than by a reasoned appreciation of the wider problems. There was no certainty that a cease fire – which the Ulster Defence Association and Provisionals were respecting up to a point – would hold; without a distinct political initiative the cease fire would certainly be broken by the Provisionals, leading not merely to renewed but to intensified violence. Yet a political initiative not only required Whitelaw to make concessions but to announce a programme. Concessions were made by releasing some Catholics from internment and according, although in dangerously ambiguous terms, political status to prisoners. This half-hearted conciliation merely strengthened Paisley's hand. Behind Paisley stood much harder men. Whitelaw followed in Callaghan's wake concerning reforms in housing and local government, was at all times available and at no time concealed his detestation of Protestant bigotry. But nervous of Protestant tactics and lacking a mandate for radical change – above all, a political structure for Northern Ireland which would give Catholics something more than promises for a fair share of the vote and of the seats in a new Stormont – Whitelaw was denied the chance to offer the Provisionals any share in the future.

The permanent government, in fact, for all that its members in Northern Ireland had shown resolution, imagination and courage, had hustled Whitelaw into a premature meeting. No politician likes to be hustled; British politicians loathe it. There was a gap between the permanent government's appreciation of the need for momentum and Heath's refusal to look at Ireland as a whole. The gap was not large; it could have been bridged but only by a Secretary of State for Northern Ireland who was prepared to take risks. Lloyd George's meetings with the Sinn Fein had been 'shrouded in melodramatic secrecy'.[15] Secret arrangements were made – but from necessity – when Whitelaw met the Provisionals. This kind of thing made no appeal to Whitelaw, and he shook hands with the Provisionals on 7 July in a mood of dislike for the entire proceedings which was patent to all but himself. Doubtless Whitelaw knew well enough that if he took risks, took a conciliatory line, looked ahead, the Provisionals might co-operate. But they might not do so. Lacking a mandate, lacking the temperament for quasi-colonial horse-trading, Whitelaw dug himself in behind the table.

Yet in the two days of concentrated, secret preparation for the meeting, the British officials and members of the Provisional movement involved did have some hopes and even came to share them. The enlarged Provisional team represented internal compromise: O'Connell; MacStiofain; Twomey; Martin McGuiness; Ivor Bell; and Gerry Adams. The last named was released from internment for the meeting on the idiosyncratic ground that, as an undergraduate, he might be able to state the Provisionals' case more clearly than his supposedly proletarian comrades. A Dublin solicitor, Myles Shevlin, accompanied the team as *rapporteur*. Strictly speaking, only O'Connell was genuinely interested in a deal – partly because he believed in outflanking the SDLP – but MacStiofain, although suspicious and contemptuous, had come to accept that his movement had reached the end of the road. Twomey and his three subordinates – McGuiness and Bell, his commanders in Londonderry and Belfast, together with Adams – represented intransigence, but in 1972 only the leader of this group was committed wholly to terrorism. Twomey came to keep an eye on O'Connell.

British officials hoped that O'Connell and MacStiofain might see a ray of hope in the fact of the meeting taking place at all, and reckoned, cautiously, that if Whitelaw showed his hand these two Provisionals would use combined authority to exert pressure on their comrades. But there was no love lost between O'Connell the quiet man and MacStiofain the hard one. One of the two British officials who were to be present at the meeting – because he had become directly and covertly involved with the Provisionals – nevertheless hoped that a statement from Whitelaw on radical change in Northern Ireland might provide a starting point for rational discussion on wider issues.

Prospects for success were not improved by several potentially explosive and one farcical incident as the Provisionals were collected and flown to Britain, or by degrees of tacit understanding between some Army units and the UDA. MacStiofain's personal account, although biased, is accurate on the facts, conveying drama about the risks and doubts over the venture. An acid humour etches his picture. MacStiofain took the precaution of seizing hostages before a journey which was only made possible by the enforced co-operation of the Royal Air Force and the Metropolitan Police Special Branch. MacStiofain, half-English – and indeed a victim of the *déraciné*'s isolation – was above all conscious that it was over fifty years since any kind of contact had taken place between a British Cabinet Minister and Irish revolutionaries. MacStiofain had failed as a guerrilla leader, but that sense of past wrongs which is never absent from Irish issues strengthened his conviction that he could match what he saw as British arrogance with a determination not to repeat the mistakes of 1921.

O'Connell, temperamentally poles apart from MacStiofain, and perhaps flattered by contact with Heath's own agent, hoped merely that he might get a word in about Braidaigh's ideas for 'a democratic, socialist republic of a thirty-two county Ireland, governed on a federal basis of the four historic provinces – Ulster, Connaught, Munster, and Leinster'. Such ideas were not new. Lloyd George, and Asquith before him, had heard the same. O'Braidaigh had recently revived the federal idea; Lynch's Government showed no interest in it. As so often in Irish history, the best was the enemy of the good, a theoretical commitment to unity preferred to a thoughtful case for compromise. The Provisionals reflected on the past, their British fellow passengers on the future. SIS must live in the present, but those officers who were in touch with the Provisionals knew well enough what was passing through the Irish mind on this strange journey.

An early start had been necessary to fly the party by helicopter to Aldergrove (outside Belfast), to the Royal Air Force Station at Benson in Oxfordshire, thence by road to London. Delays and tension made the formal exchanges between Whitelaw and the Provisionals stiff and cold. Whitelaw, 'smooth, well-fed and fleshy' – in MacStiofain's unkind description – began the proceedings with a general statement. This was anodyne, not positive or specific. There was no reference to equal political rights in the only terms which the Provisionals would accept, even within the artificial context, to them, of Northern Ireland – changes in constituency boundaries – and there was no mention of those historic issues so dear to an Irishman's heart. Whitelaw summarised the situation in Northern Ireland as if he knew what was best for colonial subjects.

The atmosphere did not improve, in fact it deteriorated appreciably when MacStiofain read a statement summarising the Provisional case. This compromise affair called on the British Government to recognise publicly that it was the right of the people of Ireland acting as a unit to decide the future of Ireland; called on the Government to declare its intention to withdraw all British forces from Irish soil, such withdrawal to be completed on or before the first day of January 1975; insisted that before such withdrawal British forces must be removed immediately from sensitive areas; called for a general amnesty for all political prisoners in Irish and British jails, for all internees and detainees, and for all persons on the wanted list.

Shades of 1921! Whitelaw knew that the Provisionals would make a statement, that it would sound like a demand, and that the language would be designed to force an admission – or a denial – from him that Ireland was one and indivisible. A subtle man, an imaginative politician, given a lead by his Prime Minister and under less immediate pressure to curb violence might have fielded this characteristically worded and harshly delivered statement. Whitelaw might have asked the supposedly articulate Adams to comment. Even humour, not at pretensions but boldness, might have given this meeting some relief. It was not to be. Feeling boxed in, hustled – as indeed he was by a MacStiofain who was determined to dominate the proceedings – Whitelaw retreated on the formula of 'constitutional guarantees to the people of Northern Ireland' – the one phrase in the Labour Government's 1949 Act which Conservative ministers were prepared to quote with approval. Impasse. Whitelaw's advisers had hoped for a general discussion before anything specific arose. They were dismayed by the Provisionals' insistence on withdrawal of troops being divorced from the security context in which this could occur. But, above all, they realised that premature and gratuitous references to 'the people of Ireland' would not so much irritate Whitelaw as enable him to evade the issue of basic changes in Northern Ireland's electoral structure and political system.

The parties took a break. Despite the language of the Provisionals' statement, O'Connell and MacStiofain were prepared to let it lie on the table. No immediate response was demanded. Having got the statement off their chests these assorted Irishmen were quite prepared to talk generalities, then to bargain on details, specifically an extension of time for the withdrawal of troops. Having actually met Whitelaw, the Provisionals began to see the dangers of returning empty-handed to an Ireland which had rejected them. They hoped Whitelaw would open up. It was not to be. After the break Whitelaw raised the stakes. He may have perceived that a faint air of legitimacy was stealing into the proceedings, that the men bunched together opposite him might soften their demands if he widened the scope of the discussion. Shades of 1921! Whitelaw played for speed, not time: 'You have forty-eight hours to agree to negotiations. If you don't agree all bets are off.' In short, this was a demand that the Provisionals surrender their positions in Belfast and Londonderry, after which some kind of a deal might be struck. This was essentially the

Army's case, one with which Whitelaw instinctively agreed.

The fleshy man and the lean men had found no common ground. The existence of Ulster Protestant proletarian nationalism – as a fact, not an argument – was ignored. Whitelaw's reliance on 'constitutional guarantees' was subjectively interpreted by MacStiofain as an excuse to avoid the issue of Irish nationalism. If Whitelaw had broached the issue of an Ulster nationalism equivalent in strength of conviction to MacStiofain's it is just possible that both men would have openly admitted the real nature of the tragedy. It was not to be. The meeting ended. The Provisionals were returned to Ireland – Adams to internment – those British officials who had silently witnessed this sterile affair hoping nevertheless to keep their lines of communication open. They succeeded; for the past decade the Provisionals, and others, have always known whom to meet on the British side. SIS has established a role in both overt and covert diplomacy which was neither sought nor welcomed, but which has given the most secret of services a strengthened place in Whitehall. Politically, however, MacStiofain's immediate decision to tell the world about the 7 July meeting and give his version of it forced an admission from Whitelaw, enraged Lynch, and strengthened the convictions of those behind Paisley that all bets were indeed off. The truce broke down and violence increased to a pitch which reflected the conviction of fanatics in all camps that one final devastating horror would force Heath to come down on their side. The Army confronted extreme 'loyalist' private armies, but these, in practice, concentrated on sectarian murder rather than outright battle.

On Friday, 21 July, Twomey's men exploded twenty bombs in Belfast, killing nine civilians and injuring well over a hundred. All were totally innocent victims. Six days after 'Bloody Friday', a day no more easily found in the revolutionary calendar than any account of subsequent events, 4,000 extra troops arrived in Northern Ireland, bringing the total to 21,000. On 31 July, in operation *Motorman*, troops entered and, in practice, occupied the Catholic citadels. There was little opposition. 'Bloody Friday' had killed the Provisionals as a political force to be reckoned with. As the remaining Protestant barricades came down, the Army sought intelligence from Catholics only too willing to co-operate. The Provisional IRA command structure was penetrated and destroyed. The SIS role in penetrating in order to negotiate produced a fortuitous reward for the Army. MacStiofain and his like faded from the picture, to be picked up intermittently by Irish governments, to be replaced by a generation of gunmen even less able than those who opposed Whitelaw on 7 July 1972 to face the problems of the future.

Thus, by late 1972, Heath found a vacuum in Northern Ireland's affairs. The Provisionals had eliminated themselves as an effective terrorist and political force; in Heath's mind, if in few others', the way lay open to a compromise solution. Two years after becoming Prime Minister, Heath addressed himself, with all his unusual powers of concentration, to the Government's gravest problem. Northern Ireland, for a time, had supped its fill of horror. Heath even met Lynch; there were chilly, probing exchanges, but seeds were sown. There was a macabre, appropriate scene for one meeting: the Munich Olympics, where Israeli athletes were slaughtered by Arab extremists. Lynch had grown to political maturity in a Republic which not only retained clear memories of violence but where governments wasted no time with those who caused it. Heath was a Prime Minister who had risen to the top in the years following Suez. Eden's Chief Whip then, Heath had become the modern management politician, not a post-imperial statesman. Yet in the aftermath of Bloody Friday Heath began to react to Ireland, to think about it, to plan a future for a country which might be united by consent. Another meeting with Lynch at the United Nations left both Prime Ministers mistrustful. But the processes of contact were maintained.

There were many false starts and trails in the months which followed *Motorman*. The SDLP came into its own as the one movement which could legitimately represent most Catholics in Northern Ireland, but despite efforts by a small minority of moderate Protestants grouped together in the Alliance Party, the great mass of Ulster unionism remained unresponsive to Heath's advent and Whitelaw's revived energies. Until October, when the Army shot its first Protestants, the UDA and the utterly militant Ulster Volunteer Force refused any confrontation – thus, in their view, maintaining a common, 'loyalist' identity with the forces of the Crown – but the progressive determination of Whitelaw and Tuzo to find and seize Protestant terrorists forced all Unionists to ask themselves whether to co-operate with Heath in his search for a genuine solution or oppose him every inch of the way. Neither the Orange lodges nor gunmen in the UDA and UVF were in doubt, but Faulkner's realisation that the destruction of the Provisionals as a serious security threat had created a new situation, potentially of distinct advantage to the Catholic cause, led him to reconsider the future for the Ulster Unionist Party which he led and for whose survival he was responsible.

Faulkner saw that Heath, Prime Minister of the United Kingdom of Great Britain and Northern Ireland, was a man slow to acquire convictions but steadfast in retaining them. To Heath's logical mind opportunities for the SDLP demanded a response from moderate Unionism. The Protestant fanatics had to be outmanoeuvred by a compact between moderates in all parties. This requirement, to Heath, complemented the establishment of principles about what kind of Northern Ireland should be created. Heath found it hard to make a compact or define the principles. His gifts lay in closed-door negotiation rather than open diplomacy; Faulkner never established *rapport* with him. Nevertheless, the British Government's proposals of March 1973 marked an historic shift of attitude about Northern Ireland, and were well received by both Faulkner and Cosgrave, who replaced Lynch as the Republic's Prime Minister just as the proposals were published.

Heath found Cosgrave easier to deal with than Lynch. Nevertheless, Heath could not answer Cosgrave's inquiry: 'In what relationship to the Republic should Northern Ireland now live?' Heath fenced on this fundamental Irish political issue of unity, convinced that more urgent matters must be taken care of first. In a way, Heath was right. Cosgrave was deeply sceptical about unity. No Irish politician in the Republic dare voice the scepticism and hope for office. Cosgrave had no choice but to ask the question. But Heath's biggest mistake, in an otherwise impressive political initiative, was one he shared with Whitelaw and his officials. They all ignored that section of Protestant militancy which carried neither guns nor bombs, depending on trades union solidarity as an expression of Ulster nationalism. At union meetings it was the flag of Ulster, the Red Hand, which draped the speakers' table, not the Union flag of the United Kingdom. To such men, in their tens of thousands, the British Government's March 1973 Statement was a complete betrayal.

Ian Paisley, whose extremism did not rob him of shrewdness, was the only politician in Northern Ireland to see that Heath's neglect of trades unionists would lead him, or a successor, into worse trouble than Whitelaw's abortive confrontation with the Provisionals. Paisley and those about him were not deliberately excluded by Heath from the all-party Conferences in September 1972 and December 1973. This common assertion overlooks

Paisley's determination to go his own way, his instinctive realisation that the only way in which Heath could succeed in the aim of creating a viable 'Power-Sharing Executive' would be by either eliminating extreme Protestantism or by converting it. Neither course was attempted. Despite a change of attitude after July 1972, the Army was always reluctant to tackle Protestant gunmen with quite the vigour it applied to the Provisionals. Few Protestants were interned.

Whitelaw's officials never gave to Ulster nationalism the same enquiring mind and absorbed attention that they focussed on the IRA and Sinn Fein. Men with names like Barr, Boal, Craig and Murray, residuary legatees of the seventeenth century Scots Plantation, were active in Belfast's great shipyards, amongst power stations and in the labyrinth of the city's sewers. The possibility of converting such men to moderate ways never arose because their place in the scheme of things was never considered. Their organisations and unions, their para-military forces and cabals remained immune from penetration, yet another irony when one considers the zeal with which MI5 and the Special Branch elsewhere in the United Kingdom seek intelligence of allegedly subversive activities. For all their skill and courage, Whitelaw's officials brought to Northern Ireland's issues much of the old imperial outlook. The Provisionals were enemies with whom one could fight or negotiate. Belfast's Protestant workers were beyond the pale. Even Brian Faulkner, an Ulsterman who had matured into tolerance and vision through harsh political circumstance, was able to ask about the striking proletariat in May 1974: 'Where do they come from? Who elected them? What is their authority?'[16] Faulkner supposed the strikers spoke only for themselves. He was wrong. The strikers represented the same spirit of nationalism which in 1921 had forced Lloyd George and Churchill to surrender England's oldest colony to Griffiths and Collins.

The strenuous efforts of the eighteen months following Heath's direct intervention can, therefore, be represented as men busily making bricks without straw. Such a judgment would be false. Although the Darlington Conference in September 1972 was a failure (neither the SDLP nor any member of the Irish Government was present) the gathering at Sunningdale in December 1973 was a major triumph for Heath. By the exercise of unstinting pressure and a capacity to arouse respect for his convictions even from the most obdurate Irishman present, Heath overcame suspicions and antipathies which reflected generations of conflict. Heath brought together the men and the parties from the Republic and the North to agree a set of principles, based on the March 1973 Statement, which were designed to form the basis for genuine power-sharing. The language of the Statement and of the Sunningdale declaration is anodyne to the point of parody. No self-respecting Irishman could have written it. But the principles there set down are as honourable as anything in Ireland's long history and have more right to be recalled than rhetoric in the patriot vein.

The principles still provide the only rational basis on which Irishmen of imagination and goodwill can work together. Northern Ireland would remain with the Crown until a majority of its citizens decided otherwise; until that time, a Northern Ireland Assembly of seventy-eight members would be elected by proportional representation, from which would be drawn an Executive reflecting the balance of parties, and empowered to pass all laws other than those concerned with the overriding responsibilities of the British Government. There would be a Council of Ireland, bringing together, albeit in limited fashion, Dublin, Belfast, and London. The Council would consist of a Ministerial group drawn from seven members of the Irish Government and seven members of the Power-Sharing Executive, and an Assembly of sixty members drawn equally from the Irish Parliament and Northern Ireland. Extremists and fanatics mocked these proposals. Politicians like Cosgrave and Faulkner backed them. To Heath they were a combination of enlightened self-interest and common sense.

Elections for the Northern Ireland Assembly took place in June 1973. The Sunningdale Agreement served partly to ratify these elections, but mainly to bind the parties. Sunningdale also involved the Irish Government openly and legitimately in the North's affairs. Despite intimidation and derision by extremists, above all Protestants, the election took place in a mood of anxious hope which Northern Ireland had not before experienced. But no democratic election had ever been held in this strange, anomalous territory, neither Ulster nor Northern Ireland – if the facts of history and geography are respected – once a self-governing colony by bargain, now a dependency from the circumstances of violence.

Brian Faulkner, who again became leader of affairs after an electoral contest in which the parties and their professed religions were fairly represented, did believe by the time of the Sunningdale meeting that, at last, something new was coming out of Ireland. He was wrong. His coalition with the SDLP was from the outset menaced by extremists inside and beyond the Assembly. Whitelaw and his successor Francis Pym remained as a benevolent presence but Heath, for all his convictions about Sunningdale, lost his grip on events. Harold Wilson was Prime Minister of a coalition in all but name. The desire to remain in office was stronger than the will to rule. In May 1974 it would have taken an old-fashioned imperialist to have broken the Ulster workers' strike. Britain had gone beyond the possession of such men. In stepping back from the looking glass Britain had also renounced the power to rule.

CONCLUSION

'I declare it's marked out just like a large chess-board!' Alice said at last. 'There ought to be some men moving about somewhere – and so there are!' she added in a tone of delight, and her heart began to beat quick with excitement as she went on. 'It's a great huge game of chess that's being played – all over the world – if this *is* the world at all, you know.'

LEWIS CARROLL,
Through the Looking Glass And What Alice Found There

In February 1974 Edward Heath lost a general election; Harold Wilson lost perhaps the best chance for peace in Northern Ireland. In both cases, although in such different circumstances, Heath and Wilson failed to meet that direct challenge to authority which British governments had invariably resisted. In neither case was failure due to lack of resources; in both, to want of resolution. In neither case was a British Government attempting to delude itself into playing an exaggerated role, but in both cases the legacy of assumptions about power and responsibility proved to be a burden, not a strength. In both cases, although the issues were ostensibly domestic or local, their international repercussions were as important as the immediate consequences: the advent of a weak Government, and the extinction of hope amongst Northern Irishmen of goodwill.

Britain's capacity to govern had rarely been doubted by friends and enemies elsewhere in the world, whatever opposition its policies and pretensions might have caused. Asquith and Lloyd George made concessions to Ulster nationalism but never lacked for coercive will or capacity over Ireland as a whole. In 1974 doubts were voiced about Wilson's commitment to the Sunningdale Agreement and the Power-Sharing Executive; Ulster's Protestant proletariat challenged him; he was defeated; Britain's international standing declined as a result, because Ulster's nationalists challenged the authority of a British Government during a period of overall decline. Throughout the years between 1974 and 1979, the years of the Wilson and Callaghan governments, Britain's reputation as an enlightened minor power continued to diminish, not least in that Commonwealth which Westminster had done so much to create and enlarge. James Callaghan, the architect of change in Northern Ireland, was forced to rely for survival in the House of Commons on the votes of Ulster Unionist members – thus further reducing chances for compromise in Northern Ireland; things had come to a certain pass. Reliance on such support effectively dispelled the notion that British governments were independent.

Loss of independence imposed on Whitehall the impossible task of governing Northern Ireland by coercion. Merlyn Rees, Harold Wilson's first Secretary of State for Northern Ireland, was no Welsh wizard but an amiable, average politician. Despite the success of the Ulster Workers' Council strike against the Power Sharing Executive and all that it stood for, Brian Faulkner and his colleagues still hoped to sustain some kind of dialogue with London and Dublin. Rees rejected Faulkner, and did so in the naive belief that a return to direct rule would bring the province's industrial proletariat to its senses.

Rees's advisers knew, from contact with the IRA, that direct rule would produce a violent reaction, not so much from the Provisionals as from the Irish National Liberation Army and other, barely identified groups. The latter's fanaticism, access to explosives, and international terrorist connections ensured that targets could be selected at will, above all in England. Between October 1974 and March 1976 33 people were killed and over 300 injured in London and other cities. These attacks, although belatedly checked by improved intelligence and resolute action, produced a situation where the idea of political initiatives for or in Northern Ireland became something of a sick joke. British courage in adversity did not provide a solution for Wilson's political impotence.

Irish governments also proved unable to cope with a situation where terrorism, in destroying hopes for political compromise, hardened traditional prejudice. On 21 July 1977 the newly appointed British Ambassador in Dublin was killed when his car blew up on a mine. Christopher Ewart-Biggs died because the Irish security authorities were caught off guard – and, as some British officials believed, because they regarded a British Ambassador much as they did his embassy, expendable. Jack Lynch, once more Prime Minister, responded to Rees's statement of 5 March 1976 that the British Government 'did not contemplate any important new initiative for some time to come' by asserting on 8 January 1978: 'I reaffirm my commitment to the reunification of Ireland and I call upon Britain to withdraw from the North.'

A week after Lynch's statement about reunification it was repeated by Dr Tomas O Fiaich, Archbishop of Armagh, Primate of All Ireland – and a native of Crossmaglen, the most violent and dangerous Republican stronghold on the border. Dr O Fiaich differed in all respects from his predecessor Cardinal Conway, with whom the British had enjoyed both conciliatory and courteous relations. Lynch's advisers rejected his statement on reunification but Charles Haughey, his successor in 1980, had no hesitation in bringing it to the British government's attention. In this millionaire politician were found all those lurking sympathies for extreme action which British governments feared so much and fought so hard.

Between Rees's admission of political impasse in 1976 and an Irish rejoinder in 1978, the Queen had paid a visit to Northern Ireland which alienated her Catholic subjects to the degree that it heartened her Protestant ministers. Roy Mason, Rees's successor in January 1978, had broken another power workers' strike the following May by a combination of steady nerves, good intelligence, and the provision of troops who knew about turbines. Mason, never lacking in courage although short on understanding of Irish susceptibilities, believed that a visit by the Queen could only do good. On 10 August 1977 the Queen was played as a socialist British Government's last card. Unionists welcomed the visit as 'a reaffirmation of the link with Britain'. The Social Democratic and Labour Party, whose efforts at reconciliation and compromise in the early 1970s had so starkly reflected the hopes of Irish politicians and British officials, virtually boycotted the Queen.

The wheel had turned again. Despite co-operation between SIS and the Irish Intelligence Service, the later 1970s were marked by a steady refusal of Irish governments to co-ordinate cross-border security procedures with the British Army and the Royal Ulster Constabulary. Irish governments also refused to extradite terrorists for trial in Britain. A decade of violence in Northern Ireland ended with over 2,000 dead, thousands more maimed or stricken in their minds, the population sullen, the economy in ruins. Although terrorism changed from indiscriminate attacks on the innocent to selective assassination of the famous or influential, direct rule in Northern Ireland brought neither security nor hope to Catholic or Protestant. The shadow of a gunman was the only symbol recognised by all subjects of this British province.

Margaret Thatcher's Government in May 1979 thus arrived on a scene of despair. Lord Mountbatten's murder by an INLA group and the ambush of eighteen British soldiers on 27 August did nothing to break the Anglo-Irish impasse. Mountbatten, uncle to the Queen, was murdered in the Republic; the ambush mine had been remotely controlled from across the border. The Irish Government tightened internal security procedures – and Mrs

Thatcher met Mr Haughey in Dublin on 8 December 1980. The meeting was notable only for contradictory statements afterwards on what was discussed. Mr Haughey believed something on the lines of the Power Sharing Executive had been mooted; Mrs Thatcher flatly denied it. Northern Ireland's future was no concern of the Republic. Throughout 1982 critics of the British Government's proposal to 'devolve' certain powers, exercised under direct rule, on a new Assembly for Northern Ireland stressed that the virtual exclusion of the Irish Government, indeed of Irishmen south of the border, was a prescription for failure.

Thus behind the tragedies lay at all times the longer, darker shadow of discord and misunderstanding between two nations. Britain, sliding ever more rapidly into the economic abyss, could still produce servants of the State, civilian and military, who saw Ireland in terms of nationalism, not commitments. The British people, in the face of terrorism, remained calm and sane. The House of Commons on 11 December 1975, when violence was at its peak, could still refuse to vote the death penalty for convicted terrorists. But British governments, clinging to an imperial past which was gone and an international role which was diminishing, refused to conclude the major national task and give the Irish people their country.

The years between 1974 and 1979 would have tested the capacity of any British government to define and establish a credible international role. Wilson and Callaghan suffered from particular problems caused by the loss of American authority and prestige over Vietnam. Whether accepted or denied, the basic factor in British foreign policy since 1945 had been relations with America. During the six years in question, America endured the final Vietnam humiliation and, in at least partial reaction to this unprecedented event, sought an international role which was based on maintenance of the super-power strategic balance and a limitation of commitments. 'Camp David' took place in September 1978 during a year when Strategic Arms Limitation Treaties (SALT) with Russia promised much. The Shah fell in 1979, and Afghanistan was invaded, finally, from the north. All these events have a common denominator: America as a super-power which sought to reduce its international commitments. Where not demonstrably isolationist, American foreign policy was based on a pursuit of the national interest rather than on an international balance of power. Egypt and Israel were encouraged to seek peace: no help was given to Afghanistan or the Shah.

Détente with Russia continued to be the main aim of American foreign policy until Ronald Reagan's election as President in November 1980, but Congressional opposition to an extension of SALT in the months preceding reflected more of a desire to be quit of multilateral responsibilities and entangling alliances than fear of nuclear war. Neither the fall of the Shah nor the Russian invasion of Afghanistan goaded America into providing for the Middle East an alliance structure on the lines of NATO, which in the 1950s had established a secure Western partnership.

American foreign policy reverted to the commercial and economic priorities which, disguised as the Marshall Plan and aid programmes, had also distinguished the 1950s. The Arab-Israeli war in October 1973 witnessed a notable display of personal diplomacy by Henry Kissinger (President Nixon's Secretary of State) as he used the United Nations to patch up yet another armistice. The really significant event of that year, however, was the fourfold increase in prices made by Middle East oil-producing governments as an excuse for their refusal actively to support Egypt's President Sadat in his touch-and-go war with Israel. This price increase, although it caused a world economic slump which is with us to this day, did no harm to American business and its stake in the Middle East. The major American oil companies had no objection to higher prices – or expropriation of their assets – provided they could continue to buy crude oil on better terms than their competitors. The melodramatic, and largely artificial, increase in crude prices was only the logical culmination of a process which the American majors had pursued in the Middle East for twenty-five years.

In marked contrast to this American concentration on commercial deals, of which the weapons so lavishly provided for the Shah between 1974 and 1978 was only the most grandiose example, British governments finally withdrew troops from Bahrein in 1974 – but fought a war in Oman. The aim was to ensure that the Straits of Hormuz were not closed to oil tankers by communist subversion or a Russian strategic presence based on Aden. The Oman war has a certain historical interest: the Special Air Service played a part remarkably similar to the Special Operations Executive in the Second World War, propping up a Sultan in Oman who ruled because the British had put him there; Britain's Middle East role ended in 1979 as it began a century earlier, in the protection of commercial and strategic interests, not the lives, welfare, and future of native races.

This surgical approach to the end of Empire proved impossible in Africa. A sense of responsibility for the native races, one which was often futile and hypocritical, nevertheless forced Wilson and Callaghan to treat Rhodesia as a colony in rebellion. Despite the ease with which Ian Smith defied Wilson and Heath, Wilson and Callaghan between 1965 and 1979, British government, political and permanent, continued to fabricate schemes for ending rebellion by compromise. Even Edward Heath, as keen to wind up colonial legacies in Africa as in Ireland, was unwilling to accept a white-dominated Rhodesian regime as a government in all but *de jure* recognition. British sanctions against Rhodesia remained in force during Heath's three years as Prime Minister. Ministerial delegations came and went. The oil continued to reach Rhodesia.

When Wilson became Prime Minister for the third time in 1974, he accepted Britain's strategic impotence in Africa, but sought nevertheless to curb Smith by invoking the United Nations in pursuit of tougher sanctions. In 1977, Callaghan's Foreign Secretary, Dr David Owen, went further. He tried to get UN agreement for an international force for Rhodesia, committed to ending the guerrilla war which Smith's black enemies had waged since December 1972. British attitudes to the UN had changed since 1964, when a peacekeeping force was established for service in Cyprus. British troops formed – and form – an integral part of UNFICYP (United Nations Force in Cyprus). This force, committed to limiting strife between Greek and Turkish Cypriots, unwittingly ensured protection for the Sovereign Base Areas. In July 1974, Callaghan (as Foreign Secretary) gave outright, covert support to UNFICYP. He ordered twelve Phantom aircraft of the Royal Air Force to be flown from Britain to Cyprus as a direct warning to the commander of Turkish forces which had invaded the island that he should not attempt to seize the capital. UNFICYP was prepared to defend Nicosia by force. The Turks stopped at the city walls. The United Nations gained one of its rare victories.

The UN was rebuffed by Smith. No force was established. Henry Kissinger had been ignored. In 1977, President Carter tried goodwill in the person of Mr Andrew Young, his black Ambassador to the United Nations. Neither pressure from the Commonwealth nor appeals by the Organisation of African Unity made the slightest dent in the white bastion of Rhodesia. By the late 1970s, however, the guerrilla forces (known collectively as the Patriotic Front) which were attacking Smith's regime from sanctuaries in Mozambique had forced him into measures not only punitive and defensive, but costly in terms of economic strains and white emigration. In June 1979 General Peter Walls, Chief of Staff of Rhodesian Security Forces, admitted that a white military victory 'is not on at all. It just can't come'. The end of Portugal's African Empire in the mid 1970s, resulting in independence for Angola and Mozambique, provided African nationalist guerrillas with their one essential strategic asset: sanctuary. From Angola, guerrillas carried the war into Namibia.

Smith shifted his ground. By the time of Margaret Thatcher's election as Britain's first woman Prime Minister in May 1979, the so-called 1977 'internal settlement' in Rhodesia had produced, like a black rabbit from a white conjurer's hat, Bishop Abel Muzerewa, leader of the 'United African National Council'. He too became a Prime Minister, whose white masters used him and his black colleagues as witness to the purity of their multi-racial intentions. Meanwhile, the Patriotic Front, despite heavy manpower losses, and dissension between the tribal rivals Joshua N'komo and Robert Mugabe, intensified the war. Whitehall knew little about the Patriotic Front but a good deal about Smith's manoeuvres. The Foreign Office believed that Muzerewa, if not exactly a winner, might prove a stayer, even capable of gathering genuine black support. SIS funds supported Muzerewa; the Foreign Office collectively succeeded in convincing itself that black stooges could be found in Southern Africa who would not only denounce the bullet and applaud the ballot box, but accept the reality of continued white economic domination.

A constitution for Namibia was produced by the South African Government in March 1977. The terms were similar to Smith's internal settlement. White lawyers in Pretoria, however, inserted a provision in the Constitution that 'the private enterprise' system would remain inviolate in an independent Namibia. Uranium and diamonds would not pass into black hands. The Foreign Office, otherwise engaged with the United Nations in an exercise to provide independence for Namibia, covertly supported the South African Government, and did so in political, not merely economic terms. An independent Namibia must rest on the basis of an 'acceptable' constitution, not the bloody sacrifices of the Patriotic Front's fellow guerrillas, the South-West Africa People's Organisation.

The Rhodesian internal settlement was a fraud, accepted by Whitehall anxious only to close the political account in Africa. Mrs Thatcher found the settlement more of an embarrassment than a convenience. She approved the settlement, and, during and after her election campaign, did so publicly. But as the Rhodesian guerrilla war entered its sixth year, it became apparent even to a British Prime Minister congenitally hostile to having her mind changed that acceptance of the internal settlement and *de jure* recognition of Rhodesia would not merely damn Britain in the eyes of the Commonwealth – a prospect Mrs Thatcher viewed with equanimity – but would destroy British commerce in Nigeria. This was a prospect which the Foreign Secretary, Lord Carrington, viewed with dismay. Nigeria possessed two characteristics: governments had not wavered in their opposition to the Smith regime; imports from Britain accounted for an enormous proportion of the latter's overseas trade. Lord Harlech, who, as David Orsmby-Gore, had been a key figure in the Cuba missile crisis, and who had become by 1979 an elder statesman of the Conservative Party, was sent by Carrington in May to sound African opinion. Harlech told Mrs Thatcher that her formal acceptance of the internal settlement was a prescription for disaster.

The Commonwealth Conference, or 'Heads of Government Meeting', in Lusaka from 31 July to 8 August 1979 brought the Rhodesian issue to the boil. A caucus of Commonwealth activists, Australia's Malcolm Fraser, Jamaica's Michael Manley, Tanzania's Julius Nyerere, Zambia's Kenneth Kaunda (host to the Queen and the Conference in his own capital) spoke for their fellow premiers in forcing Mrs Thatcher to abandon conditional acceptance of the Rhodesian internal settlement and pledge herself to elections on the basis of a new, one man one vote constitution. Extreme pressure was applied; the threat of Britain's expulsion from a Commonwealth of over forty members was never openly made because it was known to lie on the table. Britain was completely isolated, a fact which was not made more acceptable to Carrington by Nigeria's nationalisation of Shell-BP. He joined forces with the majority, abandoning his Prime Minister in order to coerce her. Nobody who was present at the Conference will readily forget the drama of the conflict between 1 and 3 August when Mrs Thatcher, driven to a written statement (drafted during long night hours by a Foreign Office Under Secretary, Sir Anthony Duff, acutely alive to what was at stake), at last repudiated the notion of white power in Rhodesia. On the 3rd, Mrs Thatcher, head bowed over her statement, speaking quickly and in determinedly neutral tones, told her silent majority of fellow Prime Ministers that a constitutional conference would be held in Lancaster House to settle the Rhodesian issue, for good. Ian Smith could come; the Patriotic Front was invited.

But that was not quite the end of the affair. The Lancaster House Conference between 10 September and 21 December has some importance for any student of British foreign policy in an age of illusions. For over three months of continuous negotiation and relentless bargaining, much of Britain's political and permanent government united in one last attempt to preserve white power in Rhodesia behind a façade of constitutional change and a democratic election. Such an election would obviously produce not only a black victory but one for leaders hostile to the white economic power so eagerly accepted by Muzerewa. The British Government therefore sought by all possible means to prevent N'komo and Mugabe from participating in the election except on terms which would cripple their armed followers' chances of getting to the polls. Carrington, as Conference Chairman, imposed a timetable which, although repeatedly extended, manoeuvred the Patriotic Front leaders into accepting terms for a cease fire which not only confined their forces to 'Assembly Places' but put them at the mercy of the Rhodesian Security Forces – on whom no restrictions were placed on freedom of movement or operational deployment.

The source of the Assembly Places plan was General Walls, not only present at the Conference with the head of the Rhodesian Security Service and the 'Rhodesian Diplomatic Representative in South Africa' (Kenneth Flower and Air Vice Marshal Hawkins), but in constant touch with his opposite numbers and close friends in Pretoria. Walls was determined to preserve white power in a country whose copper and coal were part of the South African economic 'constellation'. Walls said plainly that if Patriotic Front forces moved from their Assembly Places during the Election, his Rhodesian Security Forces would open fire on them. Walls said this on 23 November; the Conference had been in almost continuous session for ten weeks; Walls had become an essential element in the British cease fire proposals and the conduct of the election. By the end of November, Smith had quit and Muzerewa was totally discredited. Walls and his henchmen remained, the last white men and the only ones who counted.

This attempt to preserve white power in Rhodesia failed. Acceptance of the cease fire ended rebellion against the Crown. A

Governor was again appointed: Christopher Soames, Winston Churchill's son-in-law. The stage was set. Failure lay in the realities of the drama which followed. The Patriotic Front, despite the Assembly Places, lack of election cash and facilities compared with the Smith-Muzerewa organisation and, above all, the Rhodesian Security Forces' subjective interpretation of the cease fire, won a landslide victory on 29 February 1980. Out of 100 seats contested (including 20 virtually reserved for whites), Mugabe won 57; N'komo 20; Muzerewa 3. Walls made one last throw. He personally appealed to Mrs Thatcher – another friend, by association, who had said, 'keep in touch'. Walls asked Mrs Thatcher to cancel the election result and rule directly through a Council of Ministers. But Mrs Thatcher had learned wisdom. Walls was given his *congé* by Rhodesia's Deputy Governor, Sir Anthony Duff, and retired to South Africa. In May the colony of Rhodesia became the independent nation of Zimbabwe, and a member of the Commonwealth.

There were two reasons for white failure. One was the tide of history. Ian Smith and his supporters, brave but blind, had lost none of the will but much of the capacity to rule a landlocked country the size of France, where less than a quarter of a million whites were pitted against seven and a half million blacks. Direct, militant South African intervention in Rhodesia had always been doubtful. By 1980, it was impossible. South Africa was fighting its own, messy, 'no win' war in Namibia. In Rhodesia, Muzerewa was simply a stooge. But, as Britain discovered at Suez, there were really no stooges left. The Patriotic Front, in retrospect, was bound to win, despite internal dissensions, whatever the curbs, however great the provocation presented by the Rhodesian Security Forces and their SAS-type irregular soldiers, the Grey and Selous Scouts.

The second reason is one which reveals that the British capacity for pragmatism and flexibility, for sense and moderation had not been entirely destroyed by the cynicism and opportunism which had disfigured the African scene for so long. At the Commonwealth's collective insistence, but with discreet support from some quarters in Whitehall, the Lancaster House Conference decisions were redeemed from a total bias in favour of white Rhodesian power by the establishment of two groups, one to observe the election, the other to monitor the cease fire. The observers had their problems, but the tasks of the Commonwealth Monitoring Force would have been impossible to execute but for the courage and imagination shown during over two months' very active service by 1,400 British, Australian, Fijian, Kenyan, and New Zealand troops. The Force brought a desperately needed sense of security to 22,000 men and women of the Patriotic Front who accepted the cease fire terms and the one-sided plan for the Assembly Places. Peace was kept by a disciplined military presence.

Carrington initially resisted the entire concept of the Monitoring Force. In this, he acted for Smith and Walls. Gradually and skilfully, proponents for the Force argued their case, finding spokesmen not only in the Marlborough House headquarters of the Commonwealth Secretariat but amongst the British and Commonwealth soldiers who were concerned in the details. The Foreign Office was forcefully and frequently told that unless the numbers of troops were increased from the original handful and the Force provided with a sound operational aim, there would be no cease fire and no election. Although the Force was denied power to intervene when the cease fire was broken and was at all times in widely dispersed positions of acute danger, operation *Agila* represented a triumph for those who believed that the welfare of the native races was the paramount British responsibility in Africa. As Major-General John Acland, the Force Commander remarked, 'God, for once, was on the side of the small battalions'. Acland's brother, Chairman of the Joint Intelligence Committee, could well have said the same.

Thus the final days of Rhodesia and the emergence of Zimbabwe was a period when Britain's historic concern for balance in affairs, for active intervention to maintain it, and recourse to imaginative, sometimes original methods in consequence, was shown to be capable of resuscitation. This was not before time. Although Zimbabwe's independence may seem a small matter in the spectrum of history, it came after many years, the post-war and post-imperial years, during which British governments all too often refused to accept the realities of declining national resources and changing international politics. In a sense, Britain lacked a foreign policy in those years. British governments made do with the leavings of imperial policy. Success, in various ways, nevertheless came to them, compensating for if not explaining the mistakes, the absurdities, the illusions. But such success was likely to reflect the capacity of Whitehall and the men on the spot to stay on the right side of the looking glass. Political government (Prime Ministers and Cabinets) was a victim of history rather than a prisoner of the fact that declining resources inexorably limit freedom of action.

Through the Looking Glass is not a testimonial to the permanent government as such, nor to that element which works in the shadows. SIS, although strictly speaking an organisation for the production of intelligence, not for the assessment of its value, has had its share of absurdities and illusions. Elsewhere in Whitehall the imperial legacy has been hard to wind up. The pursuit of that great illusion, strategic independence based on nuclear weapons, absorbed people in high Whitehall places, not only in Number Ten and the Cabinet. But the case has been made, soberly enough, that as time passed, the permanent government in general and SIS in particular did come to grasp the nature of the contemporary world and to accept that Britain must live intelligently with and in it. Whether British governments have yet understood and accepted this reality is, perhaps, something for the reader to judge.

POSTSCRIPT: THE FALKLAND ISLANDS

'National honour can rarely be redeemed on the cheap.'

JOHN BIFFEN,
Lord President of the Council and Leader of the
House of Commons, 7 June 1982

The Falklands' conflict between Britain and Argentina, which dominated both countries' domestic politics and produced some international repercussions between April and July 1982, will for long be a matter of controversy as to its immediate causes and wider effects. Yet the basic issues are clear enough, and although some of the facts remain in dispute the impartial reader can judge for himself whether or not the conflict and its aftermath reflect the persistence of illusions about Britain's place in the world.

Although, for Britain, the conflict is not a case of guilty men or *J'accuse*, history is likely to record that the invasion of the British Crown Colony of the Falkland Islands on 2 April 1982 by the forces of Argentina's military regime was due to mistakes by Whitehall rather than by the Government. But the historical record will be false if this verdict is given. Mistakes of judgment were certainly made by individuals in Whitehall, but they pall beside those made by governments since 1945 whose members deluded themselves that since the Falkland Islands could not be defended – or, rather, would not be, with resources suitable for the requirement – they would not be invaded. Yet Argentina's claim to 'Las Malvinas' was not only known but, to a degree, accepted by British governments. Thus the Falkland Islands conflict demonstrates that illusions persisted, two in particular: lesser breeds – and British subjects who should have known better called the Argentinians by unflattering names during the conflict – would not fight; if they were minded to do so, verbal warnings from Britain would deter them.

In fact, but for the courage, discipline and skill of Britain's armed forces in fighting an enemy who was possessed of every advantage except morale the conflict could well have ended as it began – in humiliation. The word is Lord Carrington's, who resigned as Foreign Secretary on 5 April because he inherited, and upheld, the tradition that the buck stops at the Minister's desk. The margin between victory and defeat was always narrow, at times indeed so finely drawn that only Mrs Thatcher's undoubted and singular brand of absolute determination to fight rather than negotiate enabled operations to be sustained. The Royal Navy was sent to war in ships whose obsolescene, inadequate defensive armament, and poor design reflected economies imposed on the Services for decades by the always increasing costs of making or buying nuclear weapons. If there are guilty men it is those exponents of nuclear 'independence' for Britain who ignored the reality of historic commitments and genuine responsibilities. Understandably, these men are not mentioned in the inquiry under the Chairmanship of Lord Franks, which was set up by the Prime Minister once the fighting stopped to find scapegoats and make ritual sacrifices.[1]

John Nott, as Mrs Thatcher's Secretary of State for Defence, privately recorded during and after the conflict that it was an 'aberration', something unique in the strategies of deterrence and of limited war: lessons could not be learned or comparisons made. In one, political, respect Nott is right. No future American Administration is likely to give even the tepid support which President Reagan gave the British Government once the latter had abandoned all pretence at negotiating a compromise with General Galtieri and his regime in Buenos Aires. Reagan's support, reluctant, belated, and brief, nevertheless strained America's relations with its Latin American neighbours to a degree which only months of patient diplomacy restored to something like their original state. But Nott, an arch disciple of nuclear 'independence' for Britain, abuses language in regarding the Falkland Islands conflict as an aberration in strategic terms. It was in fact all but inevitable once an Argentinian Government saw Britain abandon even the pretence of defending the Islands.

There are other places in the world where military regimes – and democratic governments – threaten countries or colonies for which Britain retains responsibilities which, however 'residual', can only be honoured if adequate forces are available. Venezuela has claims on Guyana, Guatemala on Belize. On the other side of the world, Brunei, which is due to join the Commonwealth as an associate member late in 1983, will certainly expect Britain to answer any call for help. The Chinese Government aims to regain control of Hong Kong, diplomatically for preference, by force if necessary. Mrs Thatcher postured absurdly in the immediate aftermath of the Falkland Islands conflict, and her genuine belief that 'Britain's Empire once ruled a quarter of the world, Britain now will not look back from her victory'[2] reflects an illusion about an independent almost an imperial role comparable to that which regards nuclear weapons as deterrents to every variety of threat.

Britain's capacity for *independent* strategic action at the conventional level continues remorselessly to shrink; Mrs Thatcher's words would only mean anything if Britain's nuclear weapons programmes were abandoned, and would only amount to an alternative strategy if ships and aircraft were built which could be fought with a reasonable chance of success against a determined enemy. Before examining the background to the Falkland Islands conflict it might be remembered that if the Royal Navy had lacked the Harrier VTOL aircraft the task force could not have been formed. Even with the Harriers the force remained acutely vulnerable. This aircraft, now in service for a decade, was opposed by its original customer, the Royal Air Force, because it appeared to have no role in 'probable' – that is nuclear – conflict in Europe. The one effective sea-to-air missile with which *some* British warships were equipped – 'Sea Wolf' – has been coming, slowly, into service for fifteen years. If Britain is to retain real international strategic responsibilities, defence policy must be radically changed; if it is not changed, those responsibilities should be abandoned. Belated response over the Falklands did not, and has not changed this reality.

With these strategic factors in mind we can look at the political background to the conflict. The essential factors are few and simple. The validity or otherwise of Argentina's claim to the Falklands is a matter for the historian and international lawyer. The claim is, however, long standing, and even in the 1920s and 1930s, the cruisers of the Royal Navy's South American squadron were required to pay periodic visits to Port Stanley. Claims were given some kind of recognition by the United Nations in December 1965, and from this date onwards no British government was left in any doubt about the need either to abandon or defend the Falkland Islands. The Foreign Office view was that since the Islands could not be defended except at great cost the inhabitants must be persuaded to accept the inevitability of Argentina making its claim good by one means or another.

The Falkland Islanders, however, totally refused to compromise. Despite declining population in the 1970s, poor living standards – measured in crudely material terms – and conditions of employment by the Falkland Islands Company which may best be described as peonage, the people as a whole remained obdurate.[3] They did not want, and do not want, Argentina to rule over them.

(It was to be this xenophobic characteristic which caught the imagination of Mrs Thatcher, hitherto indifferent to the issues, when Argentina invaded. Thereafter, Britain's unique Prime Minister, spoiling for a fight and still smarting from the humiliations imposed on her at Lusaka in August 1979, identified with these white Islanders to a degree which divided her Cabinet and alarmed the Chiefs of Staff.)

The Conservative Government which took office in May 1979 initially gave scant attention to the Falklands. Rhodesia, Ireland, the EEC, these were the foreign policy issues which preoccupied Mrs Thatcher's Cabinet. Above all, and despite the Prime Minister's rhetoric about Britain's place in the world, economies were relentlessly sought in 'conventional' defence expenditure. Even a few million pounds was welcome if it could go towards the inexorably increasing cost of nuclear weapons. Between June and December 1981 yet another defence review led to major economies – 'cheaper' warships, fewer advanced aircraft for the Royal Air Force – and minor savings. Amongst the latter was the planned withdrawal of HMS *Endurance* by mid-1982, guardship, of a sort, for the Falkland Islands and, with the exception of less than one hundred Royal Marines, the sole expression of Britain's defences in the area.[4]

Lord Carrington personally and the Foreign Office collectively protested at the *Endurance* decision, but the former was defeated in Cabinet and the latter thereafter began to argue that a major effort must be made to do a deal with Argentina. Abortive discussions in the 1960s and 1970s had always ended in bad blood and, by Argentinian spokesmen, accusations of bad faith. Carrington realised he was 'boxed in', as he put it, by intensified Argentinian claims, continued obduracy from the Islanders – and the imminent withdrawal of HMS *Endurance*. A deal was essential. If it was made sufficiently attractive in economic terms, and if Argentina could be persuaded to drop its threats, the Islanders might become less obdurate. If they did not, it would be necessary to remind them that no British government could indefinitely be thwarted by 1,800 sheep farmers 8,000 miles away. Hitherto, British ministers had assured the Falkland Islanders that their wishes were 'paramount'. This provided the Islanders with a veto against fruitful discussions with Argentinian governments, and an acceptance of the one issue which the latter considered non-negotiable, an eventual transfer of sovereignty.

Ironically, the first two months of 1982 saw a British, right-wing Conservative Government, which was considering the virtual abandonment of a crown colony, confronted by an ostensibly reasonable proposal from Buenos Aires. Costa Mendez, the Argentinian regime's civilian, and experienced, Foreign Minister proposed the equivalent of a permanent joint committee to settle outstanding issues in, of course, 'a spirit of compromise'. One writes 'of course' because at almost the same time as exploratory talks were concluded on this proposal, SIS reported the first clear indication of a firm Argentinian intention to invade the Falkland Islands – at a convenient moment rather than at a specific time. By the end of February the Argentinian Embassy in London and the Mission to the United Nations had replied to a question by Costa Mendez: 'What would the British Government do if we invaded?' The answer was: 'break off diplomatic relations, and impose economic sanctions'. The inference was clear: Britain would not vigorously respond to an invasion.

This key intelligence did not immediately reach Carrington, either raw, in summary, or by way of assessment. Ministers cannot see everything, and their advisers must decide the priorities, and the distribution. At the Joint Intelligence Committee level, however, the SIS report was considered sufficiently important for the Chiefs of Staff to be informed. The latter's reaction, particularly that of the Chief of the Defence Staff and the First Sea Lord, was that the only rapid response to what was clearly a threat by *intention* would be the despatch of nuclear powered submarines. Capable of a sustained speed of 30 knots, these submarines could be detached from their NATO stations and arrive in the Falklands area not more than two weeks later. The CDS, however, and his fellow sailor were advised by their staffs that the risk of damage to, possibly loss of, such valuable boats, equipped with advanced, secret detection and destruction systems, was unacceptable in a context where there was no hard intelligence that Argentinian forces were about to invade. The nuclear powered submarines were regarded as elements in the deterrence of major war, not the limitation of minor conflicts. Yet there was nothing else readily available. The Captain of HMS *Endurance* had signalled an appreciation that an 'invasion atmosphere' was detectable in Southern Argentinian ports. Not only SIS but other sources were reporting in similar terms. The submarines remained on station.

Nothing is easier than being wise after the event. If anybody in Whitehall had seriously believed an invasion was *imminent*, the issue of whether or not to send submarines would have reached the

Cabinet. But the *probability* of an invasion had always been discounted. Moreover the inherent difficulty of reporting Argentinian invasion movements must not be forgotten. SIS resources in Argentina are limited: the National Security Agency's satellites and other devices provide intelligence of ship movements and the like. But nothing can alter the fact that an invasion force, of sorts, could be embarked and sailed not more than twenty-four hours after an opportunist, last minute, spin of the coin decision by Galtieri and his colleagues had been taken. (This is what did happen, resulting, such is fate, in eventual defeat for the invaders. The Argentinian troops, so hurriedly assembled and embarked, were mostly untrained conscripts. A strong force of regulars, trained to invade the Falklands and then defend them, would have given British troops something to think about.)

Three weeks elapsed between the SIS reports and the Cabinet receiving an assessment that an invasion appeared more likely than not. On 29 March the Cabinet Defence and Overseas Policy Committee woke up to the fact that Britain's bluff had been called. Carrington persuaded the Committee to send those submarines whose sensitive strategic role had weighed so heavily with the Chiefs of Staff. With thirty years' ministerial experience behind him, Carrington used his own methods to orchestrate diplomatic manoeuvres and contingency plans which would ensure a positive British response, however belated. Carrington, a realist, something of a pessimist, saw more clearly than his Prime Minister and Cabinet colleagues what, at last, was happening. He was under no illusions about the causes of the crisis, but believed that a vigorous response, clearly signalled to Galtieri, could still deter invasion. He was wrong. The Argentinian regime gambled, and enjoyed the brief experience of a bloodless victory.

Without Carrington's mordant assessment of the situation in the four days preceding invasion even the combative Mrs Thatcher would have hesitated to commit Britain to an expedition more risky than Suez and mounted to redeem – what? Only a politician of unique single-mindedness could have ignored the wider issues and concentrated on what she saw as the only point of principle: Britain must count in the world. But as news of the invasion reached London Mrs Thatcher made her decision: Britain would fight. She was to be opposed by much of her Cabinet and only supported by the far right of her Party. The Labour Opposition in the following weeks spoke with forked tongues, preferring to dwell on the alleged iniquities of the Argentinian regime than the case for and against going to war. But all the way, Operation *Corporate* was Mrs Thatcher's war, because only she believed in it as the proper expression of British foreign policy. The old Argentinian cruiser *General Belgrano*, sighted sixty miles from the Royal Navy's blockade around the Falklands, was sunk on Mrs Thatcher's direct order, with the loss of 368 lives; the Royal Navy's 'Rules of Engagement' would not have permitted this act of aggression on the high seas.

The British Government's decision to recapture the Islands stunned Galtieri and his colleagues – but induced no mood of compromise. A fatalism indicative of arbitrary rule and the gambler's throw frustrated Argentinian initiatives. Once the troops had occupied the Islands, they sat there. No realistic plan was made to defend themselves against the British task force. No attempt was made to deter or combat the task force as it entered Southern waters. The Argentinian diplomatic approaches sounded feasible at the United Nations because the sovereignty issue appeared negotiable after all. It was not negotiable to the Argentinian regime, to the 'Junta', as Mrs Thatcher repeatedly called it in tones indicative of contempt for the doings of foreigners who had dared to try a fall with her.

There is no doubt that for a brief period in the middle of 1982 many people agreed with their Prime Minister that the 'Great' had been put back into Britain. The emotion is not ignoble, nor is it derided here. But emotions subside; realities remain. Moreover, the emotion was by no means so widespread as the media pretended. The Service of Thanksgiving in St Paul's Cathedral on 26 July, at which the Archbishop of Canterbury spoke of reconciliation, and suffering which was common to bereaved British and Argentinian families, may have reflected the national mood more accurately than Mrs Thatcher realised. Certainly, Dr Runcie's words faithfully echoed Winston Churchill's belief in magnanimity as one of the greatest of national attributes.

If it was right to recover the Falkland Islands by force, it is right to defend people in other places, whatever the colour of their skins. The cost of doing so, as John Biffen said – although not in the sense in which he meant it – will be high. Mrs Thatcher and Mr Biffen, however, thought that the price of victory was relatively low – 255 British servicemen and civilians killed, another 1 per cent on the defence budget to replace lost ships and aircraft. That is one way to look at Britain's role in the world and a more sober, if more cynical, way of doing so than indulgence in illusions about a resurgent empire backed by nuclear weapons. But the cost of real responsibility is always high. On our side of the looking glass we have to ask: are we prepared to pay for it?

GLOSSARY

References are to British organisations etc., except as otherwise indicated

ABM	Anti Ballistic Missile
Abwehr	Directorate of Military Intelligence, German General Staff – to 1945
APOC/AIOC	Anglo-Persian/Iranian Oil Company
ARAMCO	Arabian-American Oil Company
BP	British Petroleum Oil Company (successor to AIOC)
C	Director-General of SIS
CAS	Chief of the Air Staff
CDS	Chief of the Defence Staff
CENTO	Central Treaty Organisation (successor to Baghdad Pact)
CIA	Central Intelligence Agency of the United States
CID	Committee of Imperial Defence
CIG	Central Intelligence Group (predecessor to CIA)
CIGS	Chief of the Imperial General Staff (now Chief of the General Staff)
CMF	Commonwealth Monitoring Force
COS	Chiefs of Staff
CRA	Civil Rights Association (Northern Ireland)
DIA	Defense Intelligence Agency (United States)
DCI	Director of Central Intelligence – Director of CIA
DDP	Deputy Director of Plans (in CIA)
DMI	Director of Military Intelligence
DNI	Director of Naval Intelligence
EDC	European Defence Community
EEC	European Economic Community
EIS	Egyptian Intelligence Service
EX-COMM	Executive Committee of NSC (in 1962 only)
FBI	Federal Bureau of Investigation (United States)
G2	Irish Intelligence Service
GCHQ	Government Communications Headquarters
GRU	Russian Directorate of Military Intelligence
ICBM	Intercontinental Ballistic Missile
IPC	Iraq Petroleum Company

IRA	Irish Republican Army
IRBM	Intermediate Range Ballistic Missile
IRD	Information Research Department (in Foreign Office)
JIB	Joint Intelligence Bureau
JIC	Joint Intelligence Committee
JPS	Joint Planning Staff
KGB	Komitat Gosudarstevennoy Bezopasnosti. Russian Committee for State Security – the Russian Intelligence Service, operating both beyond and within Russia
KOC	Kuwait Oil Company
MI5	British Security Service
MI6	British Intelligence Service, known usually as SIS
MI9	The branch of British military intelligence responsible during the Second World War for prisoner of war escape and evasion
Mossad Bitachon Leumi	Central Institute for Intelligence (Israel)
Mossad Letafkidim Meyouchadim	Intelligence Service (Israel)
MRBM	Medium Range Ballistic Missile
NATO	North Atlantic Treaty Organisation
Neabs	Near East Arab Broadcasting Service – to 1956
NIE	National Intelligence Estimates (as prepared in CIA)
NIS	Nigerian Intelligence Service
NSA	National Security Agency (United States)
NSC	National Security Council (United States)
OAU	Organisation of African Unity
OPC	Office of Policy Co-ordination (in early years of CIA)
OSS	Office of Strategic Services (United States)
PWE	Political Warfare Executive (in Foreign Office during Second World War)
RAF	Royal Air Force
RUC	Royal Ulster Constabulary
SALT	Strategic Arms Limitation Treaties
SAM	Surface to Air Missile
SAS	Special Air Service Regiment
SCUA	Suez Canal Users Association (in 1956)
SIS	Secret Intelligence Service
SOE	Special Operations Executive
U-2	American high altitude reconnaissance aircraft
UDA	Ulster Defence Association
UN	United Nations
UNTSO	United Nations Truce Supervisory Organisation
UVF	Ulster Volunteer Force
UWC	Ulster Workers Council

NOTES

Introduction

1 David Dilks (ed.), *Retreat From Power; Studies in Britain's Foreign Policy of the Twentieth Century*, Macmillan, 1981, vol. 2, p. 9.
2 Edward McCourt, *Remember Butler*, Routledge & Kegan Paul, 1967, p. 203.

Chapter 1 'May Russia's wicked aggression, ambitions, and duplicity be checked!'

1 Royal Archives, Windsor Castle.
2 Sir Charles Webster and Noble Frankland, *The Strategic Air Offensive against Germany, 1939–1945*, HMSO, 1961, vol. 4, p. 80.
3 Peter Fleming, *Bayonets to Lhasa*, Rupert Hart-Davis, 1961, p. 21.
4 For a detailed analysis of the Arab Bureau and related matters, see Elie Kedourie, *In the Anglo-Arab Labyrinth*, Cambridge University Press, 1976. Kedourie ignores, however, the role of the Bureau's War Office counterpart in Cairo, MO4, which was operationally responsible for the 'Arab Revolt'.
5 A.L. Kennedy, *Salisbury 1830–1903, Portrait of a Statesman*, John Murray, 1953, p. 106.
6 John Biddulph, who explored the passes to and from India's Northern Frontier between 1873 and 1880, used this phrase in his diary of Sir Thomas Forsyth's mission to Kashgar in 1873, of which he was a member.
7 Sir Henry Brackenbury, *Some Memories of my Spare Time*, Blackwood, 1909, p. 351.
8 Field Marshal Lord Wolseley's description, as cited in Jay Luvaas, *The Education of an Army; British Military Thought 1815–1940*, Cassell, 1964, p. 182.
9 Brackenbury to Roberts, 29 October 1886, Ogilby Trust.
10 Younghusband Diary, loaned to the author by the late Dame Eileen Younghusband.
11 Ibid.
12 Younghusband deliberately misled Gromchevsky about sources of forage and water for his horses, with the result that he nearly died.

13 F.H. Hinsley (and others), *British Intelligence in the Second World War*, HMSO, 1979, vol. 1, p. 16.
14 Stephen Roskill, *Hankey, Man of Secrets*, Collins, 1970, vol. 1, p. 50. Hankey, a Royal Marine, was seconded to the CID in 1902; became Secretary in 1912; Secretary to the War Cabinet (1916) and to the Cabinet until shortly before being appointed a Cabinet Minister in the Second World War.
15 Jukka Nevakivi, *Britain, France, and the Arab Middle East*, Athlone Press, 1969, p. 25. 'Improvisation' was not responsible for dividing the Arab spoils between Britain and France, but for ensuring a paramount British role throughout the area during and after the war. The territorial spoils were divided by the representatives of the British and French Governments, Sir Mark Sykes and Monsieur Georges Picot. For conflict between London and Delhi concerning Hussein and Ibn Saud, and for evidence of the *latter*'s willingness in his early days to support British interests, see H.V.F. Winstone, *The Illicit Adventure; the story of political and military intelligence in the Middle East from 1898 to 1926*, Jonathan Cape, 1982.
16 T.E. Lawrence, *Seven Pillars of Wisdom*, Jonathan Cape, 1940 edition, pp. 21–4.
17 Herbert Diaries, loaned to the author by the Hon. Mrs Herbert. For bribery as a whole see the one indispensable *Arab* source: Suleiman Mousa, *T.E. Lawrence*, Oxford University Press, 1966.
18 The Directive to Holman, *Rules and Notes for Guidance*, is in the Papers of Sir Terence Keyes, India Office Library. Keyes was a member of Holman's staff. Both were seconded from the Indian Army.
19 Ibid.
20 The Diary of Captain H. Boustead, South African Scottish, shown to the author privately. Additional source material is provided by the diaries of Lieutenant-Colonel Bailey and Major Blacker, who served in Turkestan and Kashgaria.
21 A partial account of the Baku affair is by C.H. Ellis, *St Antony's Papers, Number Six*, Chatto & Windus, 1959. Ellis was a former SIS officer. He served in Transcaspia during the period in question.
22 Lawrence, op. cit., p. 23.
23 L.P. Morris, 'British Government Missions to Turkestan, 1918–19', *Journal of Contemporary History*, April 1977, p. 375.
24 For additional background on the inter-war period and the intelligence factor in particular see David Dilks (ed.), *Retreat from Power*, Macmillan, 1981, vol. 1, pp. 139–69; and Christopher Andrew, 'The British Secret Service and Anglo-Soviet Relations in the 1920s', *Historical Journal*, vol. xx, no. 3, 1975, pp. 673–700.
25 Ronald Lewin, *Ultra goes to War*, Hutchinson, 1978, p. 36.
26 Hugh Trevor-Roper, *The Philby Affair; Espionage, Treason and Secret Services*, William Kimber, 1968, p. 420.

Chapter 2 Blowing up trains in the Resistance

1 Robert Manne, 'The Foreign Office and the Failure of Anglo-Soviet *Rapprochement*', *Journal of Contemporary History*, 1981, p. 741.
2 Andrew Boyle, *The Climate of Treason; Five who spied for Russia*, Hutchinson, 1979, p. 132.
3 D for 'attacking potential enemies by means other than the operations of military forces', MI(R) Paper of 5 June 1939, R for Research – the latter a favourite euphemism for intelligence or special operations. A contemporary example: Oman Research Bureau, whose objective and methods owe much to SIS.
4 *Foreign Relations of the United States*, 1945, vol. viii, pp. 6–7.
5 Harold Macmillan, *The Blast of War*, Macmillan, 1967, p. 154.
6 For background from primary sources see Graham Ross, 'Foreign Office Attitudes to the Soviet Union, 1941–45', *Journal of Contemporary History*, October 1981, pp. 521–40. The views of the Chiefs of Staff are given in detail.
7 Virtually all SOE files are either publicly unavailable or have been destroyed, thus following SIS and MI5 practice. Most published accounts of SOE, including the quasi-official *SOE In France* (M.R.D. Foot, HMSO, 1966), are partisan, based on the premise that the public will uncritically accept a version of history which projects SOE as a 'liberation' organisation. A notable exception is David Stafford, *Britain and European Resistance, 1940–1945, A Survey of the Special Operations Executive*, Macmillan/St Antony's College, 1980. This is a revisionist account – from an establishment source. Amidst much that is crucially important in Stafford – fortified by his skill in finding SOE material in Cabinet and other Papers – is evidence of reluctant Chiefs of Staff admission that the overwhelmingly Gaullist resistance movement in France was essential to buttress the Allied invasion of 6 June 1944. But the movement remained opposed by SOE as such, although, from early 1944, *résistants* owed much to the Special Air Service and the three-man 'Jedburgh' groups, parachuted into France from Britain. SOE participated *operationally* in the Anglo-American Jedburghs. J.G. Beevor, *SOE, Recollections and Reflections, 1940–45*, Bodley Head, 1981 should also be noted. This account, by a former SOE Staff Officer, is also characterised by too much inside intelligence to escape the definition of 'revisionist'.
8 Stafford, op. cit., p. 208.
9 Anthony Powell, *To Keep The Ball Rolling, Memoirs*, Volume Three, *Faces In My Time*, Heinemann, 1980, pp. 174–5. Powell had direct experience of this affair. See also Werner Rings, *Life with the Enemy*, Weidenfeld & Nicolson, 1982, p. 258.
10 Brian Crozier, *De Gaulle, The Warrior*, Eyre/Methuen, 1973, p. 237. De Gaulle resigned as *President*; SOE was, officially, disbanded

on 30 June 1946. There are incidental references to de Gaulle and SIS in François Kersaudy, *Churchill and De Gaulle*, Collins, 1981.

11 PWE's Director, Robert Bruce Lockhart (who had been in 1918 the first British 'Agent' to the Bolshevik regime) thought SOE 'a bogus, irresponsible, corrupt show which ought to be disbanded' (Kenneth Young (ed.), *The Diaries of Sir Robert Bruce Lockhart, 1939–1965*, Macmillan, 1981; review in *Times Literary Supplement*, 13 October 1981 – by C.M. Woodehouse, a former member of SOE). SOE, on paper, dispensed with its political warfare section in 1941, transferring responsibilities to PWE. The point is of importance in the context of a wartime – and post-war – Foreign Office which saw some virtue in 'progressive', non-communist governments for European countries. One reason why heads were not knocked together on these issues during the war was due to the impotence of a nominal superintending organisation for clandestine activities, the Security Executive, formed on 28 May 1940.

12 *Dictionary of National Biography*; Ronald Lewin, *Ultra goes to War*, Hutchinson, 1978, p. 67.

13 MI5's original designation was the Imperial Security Intelligence Service. It operated throughout the Empire, concentrating on subversive organisations. At home, close links with the right wing of the Conservative Party between the world wars were reflected in a headquarters where twice as much manpower effort was devoted to the Communist Party of Great Britain than to organisations supporting Hitler.

14 John Ehrman, *History of the Second World War, Grand Strategy*, HMSO, 1956, vol. v, p. 95.

15 Ibid., p. 88.

16 Stafford, op. cit., p. 21. See also for SOE and its rivals Phyllis Auty and Richard Clogg (eds), *British Policy towards Wartime Resistance in Yugoslavia*, University of London, 1976. This collection of unvarnished accounts by former participants in the Yugoslav campaigns reduces the Official Secrets Act to an absurdity.

17 Hugh Trevor-Roper, *The Philby Affair*, William Kimber, 1968, p. 42.

Chapter 3 A consequence of peace: Albania, 1949

1 Strictly speaking, MI5 was, until certain Whitehall changes were made in 1951, answerable directly to the Prime Minister. In practice, Attlee delegated to the Home Secretary.

2 Nigel Nicolson (ed.), *Harold Nicolson, Diaries and Letters, 1945–1962*, Collins, 1963, pp. 115–16.

3 Norman Brook succeeded Bridges.

4 Stafford, *Britain and European Resistance, 1940–1945*, Macmillan/St

Antony's College, 1980, p. 198. The IRD was replaced by the Overseas Information Department in 1976. The BBC tasks remain. Routine embassy, consular, and high commission cover for SIS was only finally established in the 1960s.

5 Nicolson, op. cit., pp. 115–16.

6 Arthur Bryant (ed.), *Triumph in the West, 1943–1946, based on the Diaries and Autobiographical Notes of Field Marshal Lord Alanbrooke*, Collins, 1959, p. 363.

7 Towards the end of the Second World War, Churchill told the King that if both he and Eden died on one of their overseas journeys, Anderson should be summoned as Prime Minister (*Dictionary of National Biography*).

8 David Dilks (ed.), *Retreat from Power*, Macmillan, 1981, vol. 2, p. 131.

9 Margaret Gowing, *Independence and Deterrence; Britain and atomic energy 1945–1952*, vol. 1, p. 116.

10 John Connell, *The Office; A Study of British Foreign Policy and its Makers, 1919–1951*, Allan Wingate, 1958, pp. 307–8.

11 Because of opposition to British policy in Palestine the Iraq Government repudiated the Treaty. The RAF remained none the less, and was not finally withdrawn until 1958.

12 *The Conduct of Anti-Terrorist Operation in Malaya*, the (restricted distribution) operational manual for security forces, chapter two, p. 11. In fact, the MCP was overwhelmingly Malay-born Chinese in membership, and thus a genuine, if partisan, nationalist movement.

13 *Doublequick* and *Halfmoon*, the British and American 1948 plans for the defence of Germany did, however, concede that SOE-type operations would have to be considered in default of formations of infantry and armour. An SOE Memorandum of 22 November 1945, dealing with stay-behind parties in Austria following a Russian invasion, stressed that liaison with SIS should be established in order 'to create an organisation capable of quick and effective expansion in time of war'. *Current* NATO planning gives a role comparable to SOE to the Special Air Service Regiment.

14 C.M. Woodehouse, *The Struggle for Greece*, Hart-Davis/MacGibbon, 1976, pp. 148–9.

15 Before the passing of the McMahon Act in August 1946, Maclean had been Joint Secretary to the Combined Policy Committee, which provided for Anglo-American co-operation on nuclear weapons.

16 Woodehouse, op. cit., p. 236.

17 A.P. Thornton, *The Imperial India and its Enemies; a Study in British Power*, Macmillan, 1963, p. 92.

18 Cyril Connolly, *The Missing Diplomats*, The Queen Anne Press, 1952, pp. 24–5. Brigadier Brilliant is a hybrid: Burgess (and Wingate) grafted on to SOE.

19 Allen Dulles, *Craft Of Intelligence*, Weidenfeld & Nicolson, 1963, p. 50.
20 These directives owed much to George Kennan, who thus kept a foot in both the State Department and CIA camps.
21 *Foreign Relations of the United States*, 1949, p. 313.
22 Coral Bell, *Negotiation from Strength*, Chatto & Windus, 1962, p. 20. The Curzon Line was the frontier established between Russia and Poland by the Supreme Council (of the victorious allies) at the Versailles Conference in December 1919. The Polish Government refused to accept the frontier, and succeeded in extending it eastwards. In 1945 Stalin recovered this territory – and went beyond it. Amery's demand, therefore, was similar to Foster Dulles's when he called for a 'roll-back' of communism in eastern Europe.
23 Thomas Powers, *The Man who kept the Secrets; Richard Helms and the CIA*, Weidenfeld & Nicolson, 1980, p. 32.
24 Ibid., p. 30.
25 Franklin A. Lindsay, 'Unconventional War', *Foreign Affairs*, vol. 40 (1961–2), p. 268.
26 *Foreign Relations of the United States*, 1949, p. 321.

Chapter 4 The last temptation: Suez, 1956: Part I

1 Anthony Eden, *Full Circle*, Cassell, 1960, p. 3.
2 Lord Moran, *Winston Churchill, the Struggle for Survival, 1940–1965*, Constable, 1966, p. 643. Moran, as Churchill's doctor, saw – and heard – more than most of his patient's Cabinets.
3 A detailed account of Roosevelt's attitudes and policy towards the British Empire is in W.R. Louis, *Imperialism at Bay; United States and the Decolonisation of the British Empire, 1941–1945*, Oxford University Press, 1978.
4 See p. 55 and note 7 for an indication of Anderson's importance.
5 *Sunday Herald*, 8 February 1920.
6 The Diary of James Scrymegour-Wedderburn for 21 September 1928, referred to in Martin Gilbert, *Winston Churchill*, Heinemann, 1979, vol. v, Companion vol. 1, p. 1342.
7 A.P. Thornton, *The Imperial Idea and its Enemies*, Macmillan, 1963, p. 57.
8 Properly, Urabi or Orabi Pasha.
9 The Anglo-Persian Oil Company became the Anglo-Iranian Oil Company in 1935.
10 'In 1955, 14,666 ships had passed through it [the Canal], one-third of them British.' (Selwyn Lloyd, *Suez, 1956, A Personal Account*, Jonathan Cape, 1978, p. 83.)
11 Kenneth Rose, *The Later Cecils*, Weidenfeld & Nicolson, 1975, p. 205.
12 Cabinet Memorandum of 30 December 1924, cited in Martin

Gilbert, *Winston Churchill*, Companion vol. v, part 1, Heinemann, 1979, p. 317.

13 Lawrence in a letter to Colonel A.P. Wavell (the future Field Marshal) 21 May 1923, David Garnett (ed.), *Selected Letters of T.E. Lawrence*, The Reprint Society, 1941, p. 189.

14 Trefor Evans (ed.), *The Killearn Diaries, 1934–1946; Lord Killearn (Sir Miles Lampson) High Commissioner and Ambassador to Egypt*, Sidgwick & Jackson, 1972, p. 318. Revealingly, Evans heads his Biographical Note 'The Actors'.

15 John Wyndham, *Wyndham and Children First*, Macmillan, 1968, p. 79. Wyndham was Macmillan's Private Secretary at the time.

16 Mossad Bitachon Leumi (the Central Institute for Intelligence and Special State Services) is the co-ordinating body in Israel for both security and intelligence operations. The SIS liaison with Israeli intelligence as such became so close – indeed was for many years a key element in Britain's entire Middle East policy – that it virtually included the Israeli security services also.

17 The CIA's own troubles in the early 1950s, when Senator Joseph McCarthy was active in his anti-communist witch hunt, made Dulles all the readier to criticise SIS.

18 D.A. Farnie, *East and West of Suez; The Suez Canal in History, 1854–1956*, Clarendon Press, Oxford, 1969, p. 677. This is the one genuinely indispensable account of the true economic loss to Britain – and the gain by America – caused by 'Abadan', and Suez. All other factors apart, these blows to Britain encouraged other countries, particularly Japan, to increase their overall economic involvement with, and in, the Middle East.

19 Lloyd, op. cit., pp. 6 and 78.

20 The unknown hand further noted that detailed agreements between the British Government and APOC 'would not necessarily appear in any published document or statement'.

21 For gold and rupees see Elizabeth Monroe, *Britain's Moment in the Middle East*, Chatto & Windus, 1963 edition, p. 105.

22 David Carlton, *Anthony Eden*, Allen Lane, 1981, p. 307.

23 Leonard M. Fanning, *Foreign Oil and the Free World*, McGraw-Hill, 1954, p. 218.

24 M.A. Gwyer, *History of the Second World War; Grand Strategy*, part 2, vol. 1, HMSO, 1964, p. 126.

25 Appreciation by the Foreign Office, India Office, and Chiefs of Staff in preparation for the Washington 1944 Anglo-American oil talks, included in the Foreign Office monthly Middle East summary for March. Churchill was not alone in voicing fears about American intentions and methods. The talks ended not so much in open disagreement as in tacit determination to pursue separate policies, above all regarding concession terms and royalty payments.

26 A paraphrase of the appreciation is in Phillip Darby, *British Defence*

Policy East of Suez 1947–1968, Oxford University Press, 1973, p. 26.

27 Monroe, op. cit., p. 173.

28 Alan W. Ford, *The Anglo-Iranian Oil Dispute, 1951–52*, Berkeley, 1951, p. 123.

29 Cabinet Papers for 1951, summarised in the *Guardian* and *Daily Telegraph* for 2 January 1981, show that American opposition to military operations was sustained and vocal.

30 Gaddis Smith, *The American Secretaries of State and their Diplomacy, Dean Acheson*, Cooper Square Publishers, New York, 1972, p. 452.

31 Kermit Roosevelt, *Countercoup*, McGraw-Hill, 1979. British Petroleum (as the successor company to AIOC) objected strongly to Roosevelt's claim that British staff co-operated with him in restoring the Shah. The SIS role stemmed from a *Foreign Office* Directive of 27 October 1945 which summarised the prospective tasks of the Special Operations branch in 'Persia, Iraq, and the Levant States'. Hitherto the only published account of *Boot* (*Ajax* in its CIA version) has been in Christopher Woodehouse's *Something Ventured* (Granada, 1982). Woodehouse was not only 'attached' to the British Embassy in Tehran, but also exceptionally well placed to see the wider picture. But his statement (p. 111) that Herbert Morrison was the virtual instigator of *Boot* requires qualification. Morrison knew, and approved, of moves against Mossadeq, but his attitude was largely governed by the Chiefs of Staffs' doubts about an operation to redeem the situation at Abadan, and Truman's hostility to its being mounted. Woodehouse rightly stresses that *Boot* was kept in being by Churchill's support. Eden showed no particular enthusiasm for an operation which reflected so much of his outlook. But, by the early 1950s, Eden was an ailing man, and it would take Nasser and 'Suez' to rouse him.

32 For Eden's comment see Nigel Nicolson (ed.), *Harold Nicolson, Diaries and Letters, 1945–1962*, Collins, 1963, p. 258.

33 Monroe, op. cit., p. 184.

Chapter 4 The last temptation: Suez, 1956: Part II

1 Coral Bell, *Negotiation from Strength*, Chatto & Windus, 1962, p. 87.

2 Selwyn Lloyd, *Suez 1956*, Jonathan Cape, 1978, p. 32.

3 Ibid., p. 36.

4 Caffery was Ambassador to France in 1945 – an indication of his standing once Roosevelt 'recognised' de Gaulle. Caffery's appointment to Cairo in 1953 was also an indication of the importance Dulles attached to Egypt. Caffery's views on Britain were widely shared then – and later – by America's diplomatic representatives in the Middle East. In March 1953 Selwyn Lloyd reported from

Khartoum: 'Sweeney, the American liaison officer [Sudan was not at the time an independent State] . . . was outspokenly anti-British. His favourite theme . . . was that Britain had done nothing for the Sudan, and we were finished anyhow.' Lloyd, op. cit., p. 13.

5 Richard Goold-Adams, *John Foster Dulles*, Weidenfeld & Nicolson, 1962, pp. 13–14.

6 Nigel Nicolson (ed.), Harold Nicolson, *Diaries and Letters, 1945–1962*, Collins, 1963, p. 305.

7 Lytton to Queen Victoria, 3 May 1876, Royal Archives, Windsor.

8 A conflict of interest between the American, British, Anglo-Dutch, and French shareholders in IPC about increasing or restricting production prevented agreement on a common policy towards the Iraq Government. The American shareholders wanted to restrict production, because of State Department insistence on the political importance of Saudi Arabia.

9 Dulles died from cancer on 24 May 1959.

10 Martin Gilbert, *The Appeasers*, Weidenfeld & Nicolson, 1963, p. 346.

11 Despite – or because of – the destruction of Cabinet papers on Suez, an 'official despatch' was published in the *London Gazette* 10 September 1957. It is from this despatch that Eden's diplomatic pretext, disguised as an operational directive, is taken.

12 Lloyd, op. cit., p. 59.

13 Erskine B. Childers, *The Road to Suez; A Study of Western–Arab Relations*, MacGibbon & Kee, 1962, p. 130.

14 Nicolson, op. cit., p. 305.

15 Anthony Eden, *Full Circle*, Cassell, 1960, p. 355.

16 Elizabeth Monroe, *Britain's Moment in the Middle East*, Chatto & Windus, 1963 edition, p. 113.

17 Humphrey Trevelyan, *The Middle East in Revolution*, Macmillan, 1970, p. 77. Ammunition for the Centurions had been re-supplied after the conclusion of the Canal Base Agreement – *ten* rounds per tank for the main armament.

18 Roy Fullick and Geoffrey Powell, *Suez, The Double War*, Hamish Hamilton, 1979.

19 Field Marshal Montgomery, speaking in a House of Lords debate on 28 March 1962 (Hansard, HL Deb., vol. 238, cols 1002–3) said that these were Eden's words to him when they met on 20 September 1956. Montgomery, in 1956, NATO's Deputy Supreme Commander, made it clear that destruction was neither a political nor a strategic objective which stood the slightest chance of being attained.

20 Neither the American Chargé, Andrew Foster, nor the French Ambassador, Jean Chauvel, played any part in the proceedings. They subsequently told their governments of the hazardous nature of Eden's plans, and his assumption of American support for them.

21 Fullick and Powell, op. cit., p. 14.
22 Eden lost his nerve on the telephone – on an open line.
23 Dwight D. Eisenhower, *The White House Years: Waging Peace, 1956–60*, Doubleday, 1965, Appendices B, C, D.
24 Fullick and Powell, op. cit., p. 58.
25 *The Times* obituary, 29 November 1980.
26 Trevelyan, op. cit., p. 109.
27 Most published accounts, and several private versions of the 23 and 24 October meetings attempt to argue that Anglo-French-Israeli collusion was only decided upon then. *Ergo*, there was no previous collusion involving Britain. Apart from the story told here, there is the crucial fact that it would have been impossible, in intelligence, planning, and operational terms, for the Royal Air Force to have bombed Egyptian military targets a mere week after collusive action had been initiated. Acquisition of intelligence about the targets, based on the requirement to establish the priorities, would have taken rather more than a week. Ostensibly, the RAF was committed to bombing operations in support of *Musketeer's* ground operations, directed at the Canal; by the terms of collusion with Israel, the targets were in Sinai, and intelligence about them had been provided by the Israelis; in fact, Eden intended to use the RAF against the Egyptian people – and did so. By the time of the 23 and 24 October Paris meetings the French and Israelis had begun to realise this, but gave Dean, present without Lloyd on the second day, the benefit of the doubt. Dean, who did not know all the details, but had a clear conscience where his orders were concerned', made a more convincing case than the deeply troubled Lloyd would have done.
28 Lady Gwendolen Cecil, *Life of Robert Marquis of Salisbury*, Hodder & Stoughton, 1921, vol. 2, p. 341.
29 Royal Archives, Windsor Castle.
30 Anthony Sampson, *Macmillan, a Study in Ambiguity*, Allen Lane, 1967, caption to photograph of Macmillan in Trafalgar Square following text.
31 Ibid., p. 222.
32 Nicolson, op. cit., p. 319.
33 *New Statesman*, 10 November 1956, p. 576.

Chapter 5 Our men in Kuwait: Arabian oil, 1961

1 Harold Evans, *Downing Street Diary*, Hodder & Stoughton, 1981, p. 22.
2 John Wyndham, *Wyndham and Children First*, Macmillan, 1968, p. 194. Wyndham again joined Macmillan's staff in 1957. A rich, loyal man, he could observe dispassionately.

3 Anthony Sampson, *Macmillan, a Study in Ambiguity*, Allen Lane, 1967, p. 127.
4 Ibid., p. 132.
5 Harold Evans, op. cit., pp. 151–2.
6 J.B. Kelly, *Eastern Arabian Frontiers*, Faber and Faber, 1964.
7 There is irony in the fact that the Treaty was negotiated for Britain by Sir Gilbert Clayton, whose Arab Bureau had so solidly backed the Hashemites. By the late 1920s Clayton realised that times had changed in Arabia but was unable to conclude a treaty which gave Britain any positive advantages in dealing with Ibn Saud and his successors.
8 Air Chief Marshal Sir David Lee, *Flight from the Middle East*, HMSO, 1981, p. 173. Lee was Air Officer Commanding Middle East in 1961.
9 *The Times*, 14 November 1958.
10 Sampson, op. cit., pp. 130–1. Nasser's terms for re-opening the Canal were that Egypt should receive all dues from shipping, and should not pay for the cost of raising the blockships.
11 Phillip Darby, *British Defence Policy East of Suez, 1947–1963*, Royal Institute of International Affairs/Oxford University Press, 1973, p. 144.
12 Harold Macmillan, *At the End of the Day*, Macmillan, 1973, p. 263.
13 Anthony Eden, *Full Circle*, Cassell, 1960, p. 574.
14 Oles Smolansky, *The Soviet Union and the Arab East under Khrushchev*, Bucknell University Press, 1974, p. 104 (quoting an official Russian text).
15 Pierre Rondot, *The Changing Patterns of the Middle East*, Chatto & Windus, 1961, p. 14.
16 Ibid.
17 See p. 23.
18 Harold Macmillan, *Pointing the Way*, Macmillan, 1972, p. 354.
19 For reference to Cabinet failures see Lee, op. cit., p. 173.
20 Subsequently to be found in Malcolm Mackintosh, *Strategy and Tactics of Soviet Foreign Policy*, Oxford University Press, 1962, p. 232.
21 Smolansky, op. cit., p. 167.
22 Ibid.
23 The Turkish Government lifted the ban on 30 June.
24 Macmillan, *Pointing the Way*, p. 387.

Chapter 6 Most secret councils: Moscow-London-Washington, 1962

1 William Kaufmann, *The McNamara Strategy*, Harper & Row, 1964, p. 26.
2 Adam B. Ulam, *Expansion and Co-existence; the History of Soviet*

Foreign Policy from 1917 to 1967, Secker & Warburg, 1968, p. 583.
3 Ibid., p. 656.
4 Ibid., p. 667.
5 Ibid., p. 621.
6 Ibid., pp. 638–9.
7 Lawrence Freedman, *U.S. Intelligence and the Soviet Strategic Threat*, Macmillan, 1977, pp. 71–2.
8 Ulam, op. cit., p. 632.
9 Ibid., pp. 649–50.
10 Thomas Powers, *The Man who kept the Secrets, Richard Helms and the CIA*, Weidenfeld & Nicolson, 1980, p. 283.
11 Ulam, op. cit., p. 652.
12 Ibid.
13 Ibid., p. 656.
14 Rebecca West, *The Meaning of Treason*, Penguin Books edition, 1965, pp. 350–1.
15 The story told here is not concerned with Hollis, but it may be recorded that every time his name cropped up incidentally during discussion, either a fervent defence of his innocence was made, or doubts were expressed that one so idiosyncratic in his methods could be regarded as secure.
16 Penkowsky did eventually meet 'C'. Others thought him 'brave, a vital source, the best we ever had, but pretty mad'.
17 *The Pentagon Papers*, Routledge & Kegan Paul, 1971, p. 100.
18 Kaufmann, op. cit., pp. 116–17.
19 David Detzer, *The Brink; The Cuban Missile Crisis of 1962*, Dent, 1980, p. 239.
20 Ibid., p. 66. (Summary only.)
21 Warren I. Cohen, *Dean Rusk*, Cooper Square Publishers, 1980, p. 150.
22 Detzer, op. cit., p. 159.
23 Ibid., p. 113.
24 Ibid., p. 61.
25 The composition of ExComm is described by Robert Kennedy (*13 Days; The Cuban Missile Crisis*, Macmillan, 1968, pp. 34–5): 'The same group that met that first morning in the Cabinet Room met almost continuously through the next twelve days and almost daily for some six weeks thereafter. Others in the group, which was later to be called the "Ex-Comm" (the Executive Committee of the National Security Council), included Secretary of State Dean Rusk; Secretary of Defense Robert McNamara; Director of the Central Intelligence Agency John McCone; Secretary of the Treasury Douglas Dillon; President Kennedy's adviser on national-security affairs, McGeorge Bundy; Presidential Counsel Theodore C. Sorensen; Under Secretary of State George Ball; Deputy Under Secretary of State U. Alexis Johnson; General Maxwell Taylor, Chairman of

the Joint Chiefs of Staff; Edward Martin, Assistant Secretary of State for Latin America; originally, Charles Bohlen, who, after the first day, left to become Ambassador to France and was succeeded by Llewellyn Thompson as the adviser on Russian affairs; Roswell Gilpatric, Deputy Secretary of Defense; Paul Nitze, Assistant Secretary of Defense; and intermittently at various meetings, Vice-President Lyndon B. Johnson; Adlai Stevenson, Ambassador to the United Nations; Kenneth O'Donnell, Special Assistant to the President; and Donald Wilson, who was Deputy Director of the United States Information Agency. This was the group that met, talked, argued, and fought together during that crucial period of time. From this group came the recommendations from which President Kennedy was ultimately to select his course of action.'

26 Kennedy, op. cit., pp. 39–40.
27 Elie Abel, *The Missiles of October*, MacGibbon & Kee, 1966, pp. 143–4.
28 Kennedy, op. cit., p. 84.
29 Ibid., p. 86.
30 Detzer, op. cit., p. 234.
31 Kennedy, op. cit., p. 87.
32 Cohen, op. cit., p. 157.
33 Kennedy, op. cit., p. 92.
34 Abel, op. cit., p. 172.
35 Detzer, op. cit., p. 156. The Jupiters, in fact, had as little capability as the Russian missiles about which Khrushchev boasted.
36 Detzer, op. cit., p. 243.
37 Abel, op. cit., p. 180.
38 Kennedy, op. cit., pp. 107–8.
39 Ibid., p. 108.

Chapter 7 A confidential war: Nigerian oil, 1967

1 A.P. Thornton, *For the File on Empire*, Macmillan, 1968, p. 235.
2 The 'Devonshire Declaration' as it came to be known, was issued on 24 July 1923. An adequate summary is in the *Annual Register* for that year.
3 Sir Alec Douglas Home was formerly Lord Home, Foreign Secretary in Macmillan Cabinets.
4 B. Chakravorty (ed.), *The Congo Operation, 1960–63*, Indian Defence Ministry Historical Section, 1976, p. 9.
5 What actually took place at Nassau must be seen partly in relation to the Skybolt missile. Skybolt was an air-launched missile designed in the late 1950s but conceived by its user, the United States Air Force, as a means of reducing the manned bomber's vulnerability, not of improving accuracy in terms of hitting Russian targets. The American bomber lobby's spokesmen in Congress

believed in Skybolt for commercial reasons; Le May wanted it because he saw the manned bomber with Skybolt slung beneath it as a more potent expression of power than missiles hidden below America's western deserts or the world's oceans. McNamara opposed Skybolt for technical reasons – 'it didn't work, bits fell off' – but even more forcefully on strategic grounds: it was not a true retaliatory weapon. Comparable fears had been expressed before McNamara went to the Pentagon, but there is no doubt that the decision in the last years of Eisenhower's Presidency to develop the Polaris submarine system and to station the boats in NATO's European waters enabled Macmillan to strike a bargain. In March 1960 he made one with Eisenhower, whereby Polaris submarines could be stationed in the Holy Loch on Scotland's west coast, in return for which the RAF would get Skybolt. If Britain had acquired Skybolt, genuine, if limited strategic nuclear independence would have been prolonged, even though the system, its faults apart, was predominantly American. But Eisenhower had good reason to believe that Macmillan would never flaunt Skybolt, as Eden might have done. McNamara cancelled Skybolt in December 1962, and went to the Nassau meeting later in the month confident that as the ostensible reason for Britain's acquiring the system was based on its operational credibility, its cancellation would strip Britain of even the pretence of nuclear independence. But McNamara failed to appreciate that Kennedy regarded the Eisenhower deal with Macmillan as binding – up to a point. Moreover, by December 1962 Holy Loch had been operational for eighteen months. Macmillan had something of an ace to deal. Macmillan succeeded in convincing Kennedy that he had a 'moral' obligation to provide Britain with an alternative to Skybolt whatever the terms in cost, type of weapon, and effective limitation on use. Macmillan has always refused to say whether he would have dealt the ace: no alternative, no Holy Loch. These points are of substance in the light of current arguments about Britain's 'independent' nuclear weapons and the American Trident missile system.

6 *Some* aspects of this issue are dealt with in the *Report on the Supply of Petroleum Products to Rhodesia*, the result of an inquiry instituted by Dr David Owen, as Foreign Secretary, in 1977, and published by HMSO in 1978. The Report was mildly critical of several major and other international oil companies for providing a rebel regime with oil, but declined to pursue the issues, not least because some witnesses 'could be injured by disclosure of their identity' (p. iii).

7 *West Africa*, 22 July 1967. This newspaper, then owned by the London *Daily Mirror* Group, was in almost automatic receipt of confidential information throughout the Nigerian Civil War.

8 Despite the British Government's opposition to the UN involvement in the Congo, two of the more effective formations which

served there between 1960 and 1964, the Nigerian and Ghanaian brigades, were largely British officered. The Nigerian Brigade was, throughout, British commanded.

9 Malcolm MacDonald, son of Ramsay, had been a junior minister in his father's pre-war, pseudo Coalition Government; and a Cabinet Minister under Stanley Baldwin and Neville Chamberlain thereafter. All MacDonald's posts dealt with Colonial or 'Dominion' affairs. During the Second World War MacDonald was High Commissioner in Canada; between 1946 and 1948 Governor-General of Malaya and Singapore; between 1955 and 1960 High Commissioner in India; thereafter Governor, Governor-General and High Commissioner in Kenya. Son of Britain's first 'Socialist' Prime Minister, forty years of honourable imperial service. The point is of some historical significance.

10 Hunt's account is *On the Spot*, Peter Davies, 1975. Thomas had been Minister of State for exactly one month when war broke out. His previous post was at the Welsh Office. James was an experienced Commonwealth official. It was his advice which counted.

Chapter 8 A bitter kingdom: Ireland, 1972

1 Poem by Dominic Behan, quoted from Peter Costello, *The Heart Grown Brutal; the Irish Revolution in Literature from Parnell to the Death of Yeats, 1891–1939*, Gill & Macmillan/Littlefield, 1977, p. 296.

2 F.S.L. Lyons, *Ireland since the Famine*, Collins (Fontana), 1981 impression, p. 31.

3 Ibid., p. 301.

4 Costello, p. 165. The play is *Shadow of a Gunman*, first performed at the Abbey Theatre, Dublin on 23 April 1923 and dealing with Civil War events of two years earlier.

5 *John Bull's Other Island*, Act IV.

6 Broadly speaking, legislation passed at Westminster applied to Northern Ireland during the period of internal self-government. All the Protestant and Roman Catholic Churches in Northern Ireland opposed the Act, but it was applied to the extent that secondary school education (beyond the age of fourteen) became a little more widely available.

7 T.P. Coogan, *The IRA*, Fontana, 1980, pp. xii–xiii.

8 Patrick Riddell, *Fire over Ulster*, Hamish Hamilton, 1970, p. 195.

9 James Callaghan, *A House Divided*, Collins, 1973.

10 Douglas Hurd, *An End to Promises*, Collins, 1979, p. 7. Hurd was a private secretary of Heath, subsequently an MP.

11 Simon Winchester, *In Holy Terror*, Faber & Faber, 1974, p. 147.

12 From 6 February to 23 April 1972 the London *Sunday Times* gave concentrated attention to Bloody Sunday, its antecedents, details and aftermath. The 23 April articles were headlined 'The Decision

to Put Civilians at Risk', and it was argued that not only did the decision emanate from the Cabinet but also reflected an order of 8 October 1971 by Major-General Robert Ford (Commander Land Forces Northern Ireland) to Brigadier McLellan, the Commander of 8 Brigade in Londonderry: 'Your task must be so far as possible to re-establish the rule of law in the Bogside and the Creggan.'

13 Callaghan, op. cit., p. 61.
14 Hurd, op. cit., p. 102.
15 Lyons, op. cit., p. 381.
16 Robert Fisk, *The Point of No Return*, André Deutsch, 1975, p. 53. Fisk's account is the only one publicly available which gives a detailed analysis of the cause, course, and consequences of the strike.

Postscript: The Falkland Islands

1 The two most senior members of the Franks Committee, the Chairman himself and Lord Watkinson, have already been encountered in these pages. Sir Oliver Franks (as he then was) said in 1954, 'We assume that our future will be one of a piece with our past and that we shall continue as a great power. What is noteworthy is the way we take this for granted.' Harold Watkinson, Minister of Defence in 1961 and 1962, was vehement in his belief that nuclear 'independence' for Britain was not only feasible, but could produce a strategy of actually fighting a limited nuclear war in Europe with weapons which would replace substantial conventional forces.
2 Speaking at a Conservative Party rally in Cheltenham on 2 July 1982.
3 For a detailed analysis of the economy of the Falkland Islands see the report of the investigation by Lord Shackleton and others, and presented to the Foreign Secretary (Dr David Owen) in July 1976. For contracts of employment with the Falkland Islands Company, see the *Guardian* of 22 July 1982.
4 The *Observer* of 11 July 1982 reported: 'When Mrs Thatcher was asked by Mr James Callaghan seven weeks before the Argentine invasion whether she was aware that the decision to withdraw HMS *Endurance* from the South Atlantic was "an error that could have serious consequence", she replied: "the Right Honourable gentleman will appreciate that there are many competing claims on the defence budget . . . My Right Honourable Friend (Mr Nott) therefore felt that other claims on the defence budget should have greater priority." '

INDEX

1 With a few unavoidable or obvious exceptions, individuals' titles and ranks are given as held at the time of the events described.

2 For abbreviations used, see Glossary, pp. 345–6.